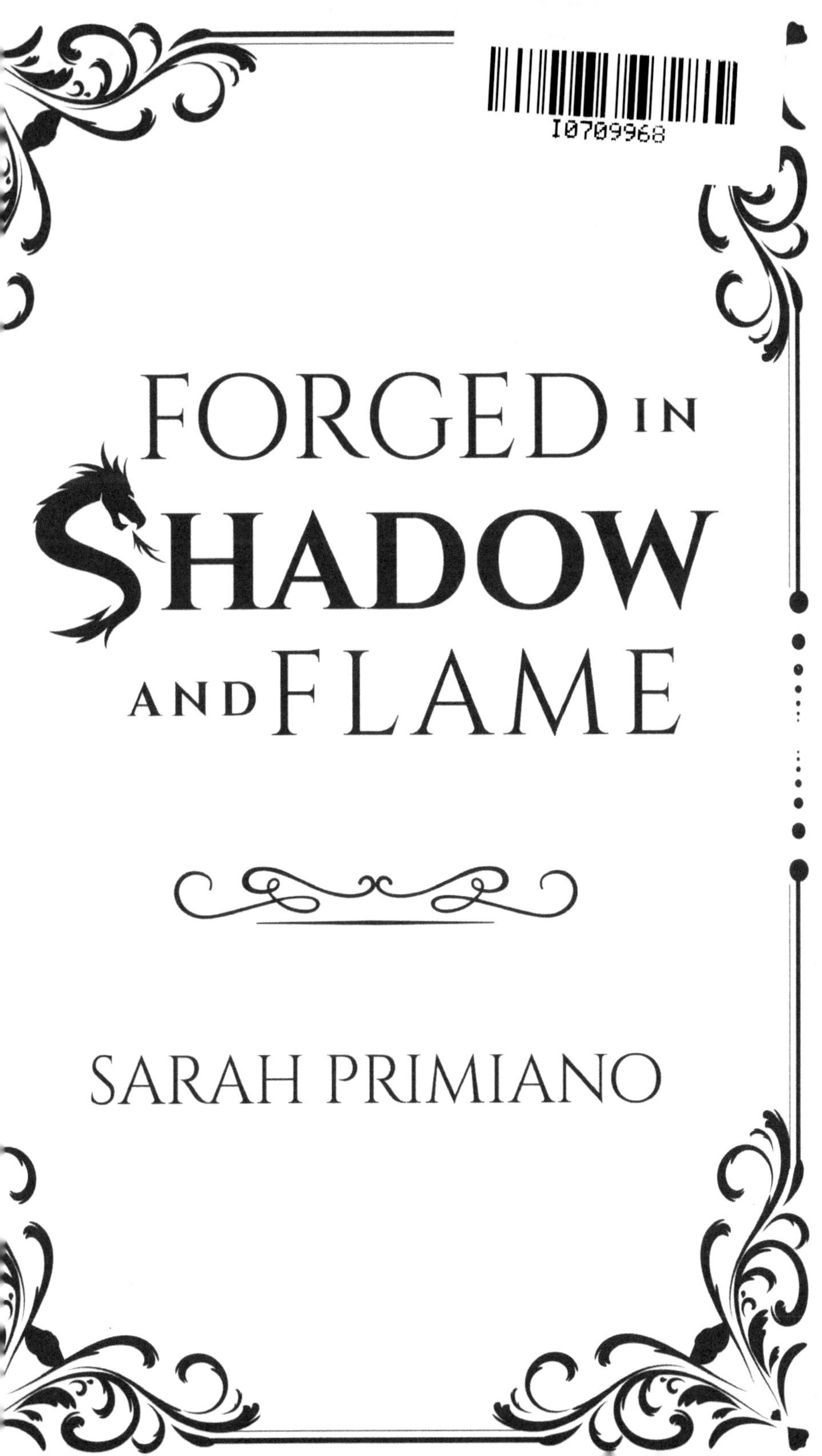

FORGED IN SHADOW AND FLAME

SARAH PRIMIANO

For the dreamers, the fighters, the ones who refuse to bow,
may you always remember that the flame within cannot be taken from
you.

AETHERIA
Mount Solfira
Ironforge
Pyrael
Windhaven

N
W E
S
HOUSE LYTHARIEN
VAELARAN
HOUSE
THAROWEN

PRONUNCIATION GUIDE

Ren (*Ren*)
Elira (*Eh-LEE-rah*)
Kaelin (*KAY-lin*)
Talen (*TAY-len*)
Lucan (*LOO-ken*)
Zakhar (*ZAH-kar*)
Eve (*Eev*)
Maelion (*MAY-lee-on*)
Lyra (*LEE-rah*)
Sylven (*SIL-ven*)
Elric (*ELL-rick*)

R en Harper knew she'd end up in chains one way or another. Just not like *this*.

Ren never imagined her death would be so loud, so public, or surrounded by sneering fae soldiers. It wasn't death itself that she feared most, but becoming just another face on the butchering block when the axe swung down.

The wagon lurched forward, its wooden wheels groaning against the rust-hardened ruts. The iron shackles bit into Ren's wrists with every jolt, rattling with each bounce like the messy clatter of bones. Around her, other prisoners slumped in silence, resigned to the journey's inevitable end. Ren squared her shoulders, shifting against the coarse wood at her back.

If she were going to die, she'd do it with her chin held high.

A groan sounded to her left, belonging to a thin, blonde-haired man.

"Told you to quiet your drinking," barked an obnoxiously loud voice from across the wagon. A heavyset man with a scraggly beard fixed the blonde man with a hard stare.

"Can't cross the Veil dry, can I?" the blonde man retorted. His face's skin held a green tint. Ren hoped he wouldn't lose what little was left in his stomach. She drew back a finger's length.

Ren had accepted she was going to die but not covered in vomit.

Ren's gaze drifted away. The convoy crawled through a forested mountain pass. Despite the dense canopy of branches overhead, heat clung to her skin. It was the harsh lull between summer and autumn, when the air still burned before yielding to autumn's first breath. At least the shade offered a small mercy. Without it, the sun would have scorched them raw. Made of iron bars and splintering wood, the prison cart would have baked them alive. Of course the fae hadn't bothered with a roof; why waste coin and resources to spare prisoners a little suffering before they reached the butchering block?

Everywhere Ren's gaze fell, fae soldiers lined the path in suffocating numbers, their presence making escape not just dangerous but impossible. She and the other prisoners knew it too well. Only yesterday, a scraggly thief had somehow broken out of his chains and made the attempt, hurling himself into the brush with a desperate cry.

He hadn't made it three strides before an arrow shot clean through his chest, and he dropped face-first into the dirt.

The fae soldiers hadn't even bothered retrieving his body. He was still there now, rotting in the shadows of the trees, a grim warning to the rest of them that this was the end of the road.

The fae soldiers wore black and deep purple armor, with clasps fastened to their cloaks. Their helms were adorned with silver crests.

Ren's eyes traced the designs on the fae soldiers' armor. House symbols, likely belonging to House Vaerlan. Or was it House Tharowen? She supposed it was more likely House Vaelaran considering how far House Tharowen lay to the eastern part of Lytharien. The sigils and colors of the different high fae houses blurred together in her mind. Every curve of ink and stroke of silver was a nauseating reminder that she stood deep in fae territory now, where each banner whispered of ancient bloodlines and power older than any mortal crown.

She might have once cared who they were, which house they belonged to — back when names could mean safety or danger and alliances could save or severe a life.

But none of it mattered now.

Back home in the western posts, the world had felt smaller, harsher. The wind there cut sharper, colder, carrying dust instead of abundance. Fields were unable to yield crops. Most people turned to trade, craft, or wandering labor. Life there was measured by survival rather than comfort.

Though the western settlements were made up mostly of humans and a scattering of other creatures hardy enough to endure that kind of life, they still owed their taxes to the crown of Vaelaran, or whichever fae house claimed that stretch of land. The fae called it payment for *protection* and *provision of land,* yet the crown rarely sent soldiers that far west. Attacks from the woods or from bandits desperate enough to kill were common. Out there, people learned to fight for their own because no one else would.

Ren had rarely seen a fae in those days, save for the ones who passed through to collect dues or settle business on behalf of House Vaelaran. The villages may have belonged to the crown in name, but the fae lords rarely lingered long enough to prove it.

The fae soldiers' horses alone were towering beasts standing sixteen to eighteen hands high, with broad shoulders, massive haunches, and proud, arched necks. Their heavy hooves struck the earth like hammers, restless beneath the weight of armored fae riders. Vaelaren horses were prized not only for their size, but for their endurance and strength. Given the long and brutal journey, it was little wonder the fae soldiers rode such beasts.

Ren had seen what those horses could do. Years ago, Ren drew a lucky hand against a man in a tavern who hated losing, especially to a woman. He followed Ren out behind the tavern, drunk on pride and ale. He'd sneered that if she was going to act like a *haughty bitch,* he'd treat her like the *worthless one she was.* He barely brought back his meaty fist before she struck him once, sending him stumbling into the wall. He lasted through two more of Ren's punches before deciding he'd rather try his luck on horseback. The beast had other ideas. It bucked him off in a single motion, then brought its hooves down and crushed his skull like an overripe melon.

Even now, the memory left a bitter taste in Ren's mouth.

The fae riders sat tall and arrogant in their saddles, as if they expected the very earth to bow beneath them. One glanced toward the prisoners with thinly veiled disdain, his mouth curving into a scowl as he nudged his white steed forward.

Ahead, a black-and-silver carriage rolled steadily through the trees. Not regal, not adorned with heraldry, no gilded trim to suggest nobility.

Ren heard the dark-haired man shackled across from her spit to the side. "You see that?" he rasped, jerking his chin toward the carriage. "That's no noble's ride. No silk cushions, no polished wood. Just black iron and steel bolts. You know why?"

Ren's gaze swept over the prisoners, raking across faces pale and hollowed by hunger. Three days they'd been on the road — three days of blistering heat and meager rations. A mouthful of water here, a few stale rolls of bread there. The fae soldiers made a show of their abundance, tearing into dried meat and hard cheese within arm's reach of the prisoners, as if the sound of chewing might break them faster than the chains.

Ren knew it was purposeful; their cruelty always was.

No one dared answer the dark-haired man's question. Not out of secrecy but simply because none of them had the strength left to care. Some had sunk into themselves, lips moving in prayer, clinging to gods who'd long since abandoned these roads. Others wept into their shackled hands, their sobs muffled.

Beside her, the blonde man gave a low grunt, his broad shoulders shrugging as if to say, *what answer would change anything now?*

The dark-haired man said, "Because they're so evil, the fae won't even chain 'em in this piece of shit cart with the rest of us. They say if you so much as look into their eyes, you'll see your own death waiting for you. I'll wager even iron bars can't hold what's in there. That cart's probably lined with runes, reinforced to keep whatever is inside from crawling out."

A nervous hush fell over the cart.

The silence was thick and oppressive until the blonde man sighed. "Saints save us. You like spinning tales, do you? *'See your death in their eyes'*—what utter shit." He leaned back against the wood with a grunt, eyes narrowing at the dark-haired man. "If you ask me, you're just making it up so you can listen to your own voice."

Ren's gaze lingered on the black-and-silver carriage. She didn't believe in whispers. It made no difference who was who. Fae business was fae business.

They were all headed toward the butcher's block anyway.

Ren's path had carried her into the southern reaches of Lytharien, a wild and storied expanse divided between two powerful fae houses. To the north ruled House Vaelaran, a storied and enigmatic fae lineage famed for its opulent courts, artistic brilliance, and lavish celebrations. Far to the south lay the realm of House Tharowen, a proud and unyielding house whose power was hewn from the land itself, a rugged expanse of jagged mountains veined with rare minerals, where roaring forges burned day and night to arm their warriors and sustain their wealth.

Ren had made her way south, to Windhaven, where the sprawling river branches bled into the sea. There, countless trade ships crowded Windhaven's busy waterways, their sails billowing as they carried goods to every corner of Aetheria. But among the merchant vessels lurked darker, sleeker, and faster ships. These were unmarked, used for the illicit smuggling of goods and even humans to the coastal islands.

Ren had gotten so close to freedom she could almost taste it, the sharp tang of salt on her tongue, the wind carrying with it the distant cries of gulls. The horizon shimmered with the faintest band of blue, the sea so near she could see its glimmering expanse.

Her plan was simple — trade what little she had for passage to a quiet coastal village.

For the past two years, Ren had wandered the border towns and villages that clung to the edges of House Vaelaran, shifting through places where no one cared to remember a name. She kept to the shadows, always ready to vanish at the first sign of trouble. Most nights found her in the raucous sprawl of taverns thick with smoke and spilled ale, where dice clattered and fortunes turned in an instant. Luck, fickle though it was, seemed to favor her hand just enough to keep her purse from running dry.

But what earned her the most coin, and the most scars, were the fights.

Underground arenas hidden beneath old ruins or behind taverns with boarded windows. Fights where no one asked your name, only if you'd survive the night. She fought not for glory, but for the weight of a coin purse.

When she finally had enough to barter for passage to the coast, she thought she was finally getting the hell away from this cursed land and as far from the fae as she could get.

But she never made it that far.

Now, as the carriage jolted along the forested path, bitterness coiled in Ren's chest. Each passing tree felt like another nail in the coffin of her failed voyage. And when she saw the jagged silhouette of Mount Solfira rising against the horizon, its smoke curling into the sky like a mocking banner, her stomach sank.

She knew that peak too damn well.

She was back where she had started.

Back in House Vaelaran territory.

The wagon jolted over a rut in the road. The blonde man beside Ren shot her a sideways glance. "What'd you do?" he grunted, jerking his chin toward her shackles. "Murder? Arson? Sleep with the wrong noble?"

Ren didn't answer at first. Her wrists ached, raw beneath the iron cuffs, and the stink of blood and piss was thick in the air. The temperate heat seemed to thicken every foul scent. Sweat slicked her back and trickled down her spine, dampening her hair as she consciously forced herself to breathe through her mouth instead of her nose.

"Well?" the blonde man pressed. "Or are you just one of those quiet, tragic types?"

Ren answered, "I broke a fae's nose."

That earned a low whistle. "Over what? A duel? An overdue debt?"

"A loaf of bread," she muttered. When she noticed his raised eyebrow, she added, "Some skinny brat was about to lose his hand for swiping it. Didn't think; I just swung."

"Over *bread*?"

"He looked like he hadn't eaten in days," she retorted, voice flat though a faint edge crept in as if she needed him to understand, needed to justify it somehow, especially considering the consequences it had for her. "Wasn't thinking about noble causes or clean endings. Just didn't want to see a kid's hand cut off over something that stale."

If she'd just kept walking, kept her head down, she'd have lived to see tomorrow without chains around her wrists. She was a fool for getting involved where she shouldn't have.

And now she'd lose her head for it.

The man chuckled. "So, stupidity, then."

"Doesn't matter now, does it?"

He jerked his chin toward his own cuffs. "I pissed in a fae lord's wine barrel." Across from him, the dark-haired heavy man rolled his eyes.

The blonde man grinned wider. "Didn't know it was a ceremonial vintage for a sacred moon festival. I thought it was just a fancy barrel they left out in the open. So, I pissed in it. Servant saw me, but not before everyone already had their fill."

"You poisoned an entire fae celebration with piss," Ren echoed, as if testing the absurdity aloud.

He puffed his chest. "Didn't poison 'em. Just humbled 'em."

The dark-haired man smirked, showing off a chipped tooth. "Got tossed in here for climbing a fae statue *naked*. It was a full moon, and I drank one too many bottles of blackberry mead. I thought the statue of their God looked pissy, so I climbed it – bollocks out, arms wide, and declared myself the 'new guardian of the realm.'"

"And you *lived*?" Ren asked, half incredulous, half amused.

"They would've just flogged me, but then I puked on the fae's shoes. That sealed the deal."

Ren snorted. "That pissy statue was Varyn, the fae God of protection, strength, and order. One of the most revered deities in all of Aetheria. Half of the fae would rather bleed out than disrespect him."

The man gave a shrug. "That explains the pitchforks from the lesser fae."

"You desecrated a holy symbol — with your balls out." Ren shook her head, although she found herself fighting a smile. "Stupid move, there."

"Maybe. But not stupid enough to think the fae need a real reason to lock up a human." The amusement drained from his features. "They're looking for excuses half the time. You sneeze too loud near a royal, you're a *public threat*. Piss the wrong way? *Treason*. Gods help you if you look like you might be brave."

One of the fae riders separated from the escort. His horse snorted as he reined it to a walk beside the wagon, and his eyes, icy and slitted like a serpent's, locked on the dark-haired man.

"Another word from your filthy mouth, and I'll cut out your tongue and string it on a chain to wear at the next tribunal, *mortal*," the fae growled.

The man held up his shackled hands in mock surrender, "Gods forbid a *mortal* speak the truth."

The fae's lips curled into a cruel smile. "Truth?" he echoed. "Truth is whatever we *say* it is."

Ren's jaw tightened as she met the fae soldier's gaze, memorizing every detail of his sharp, angular face, the pale scar tracing his cheekbone, the cruel glint in his eyes. She wanted to never forget the kind of being who could say such words to humans shackled to a wagon on the way to the butcher's block.

"Slaughtering humans like cattle, pretending it's for some greater cause," Ren leaned forward, her voice lowering. "Tell me, do your gods smile on you for butchering innocents?"

The fae's hand brushed the hilt at his side, eyes narrowing.

A predator scenting prey.

Ren went still, every muscle taut, knowing she'd let her tongue run faster than her sense. She braced herself, realizing her death might come sooner than she thought.

R en knew she was no match for him. Not after days without food, nights without sleep, and wrists rubbed bloody from iron.

This wouldn't be a fight.

It would be a show of power for the rest of them to learn to keep their heads down, their mouths shut, and to *obey*.

But, the fae soldier only scoffed, exhaling a sharp huff as he kicked his horse into motion again, galloping ahead.

The dark-haired man exhaled and leaned back, muttering, "And people wonder why I pissed in their wine."

Ren let the moment of eerie quiet settle around her, broken only by the creak of wheels, the jangle of chains, the soft whimper of a prisoner lost to despair. The air smelled more like sweat, stale blood, and something metallic, something final.

They were near.

"What's your name?" Ren asked and leveled a stare at the heavyset man. "If we're all headed to die in the same pit, I'd rather not call you stupid in my final hours."

"Fair enough. It's Corrin Fenwick. Corrin With Two R's, Puker of Enchanters and Defiler of Statues."

"Noted." Ren's gaze drifted to the blonde-haired man. "And you?"

"Joss."

Ren gave a small nod. "I'm Ren."

Corrin raised a brow. "Ren what?"

She shrugged. "Doesn't matter. No one's going to write it down."

Her gaze drifted back to Joss, whose jesting about one last drink had seemed foolish at first, but perhaps he wasn't so foolish after all.

Ren swallowed, her mouth dry as dust. What she wouldn't give for a last sip of wine — red and heavy, sweet on her tongue, warming her belly just enough to dull the edges of what was coming. Perhaps she wouldn't feel the axe slicing through her neck. She let herself imagine the taste of wine against her lips, a fleeting, indulgent fantasy to cling to while the world as she knew it would come to an end.

"What's one thing you'd want, just once more, before you go?" Corrin's question interrupted Ren's thoughts.

Joss looked down at his hands. His voice was barely audible. "My ma's stew. The kind with dumplings and that cheap yellow root she'd insist was 'a healer's gift.'" He paused. "I hated it, until I didn't have it anymore."

Corrin's expression softened as he gave a slow nod. "I'd want to sleep in a real bed. With sheets. Maybe a soft-bottomed girl named Mara, or hell, any name'll do. Long as she laughs too loud and doesn't mind scars."

Ren shot him a side glance. "You're ridiculous."

"I'm fixing to *die*, Ren. Let me have one last fantasy."

They both looked at her. Ren paused, gaze flicking to the trees beyond the bars. Then she admitted quietly, "I'd like to sail the sea. Not painted on some inn wall, not some story someone tells me. I want to feel the wind, hear the waves. Just once."

The wagon rolled on, and for a heartbeat, none of them spoke.

Corrin cleared his throat. "If we somehow make it out of this alive, we find a bed, a stew pot with dumplings, and a coastline."

Ren smirked faintly. "Deal."

Beside her, a girl no older than fifteen shivered, arms wrapped tight around her frail frame. Matted hair fell in tangled clumps, sunken cheeks pale. Ren wanted to reach for her, to offer comfort, but her own wrists were chained to the post. The fae soldiers hadn't bothered to shackle the girl, some small mercy perhaps. Amidst the sounds of despair, Ren heard the murmur of the girl's voice murmuring words of prayer.

"Figures I survive three border skirmishes, one bandit raid, and two angry wives just to die in a snow-covered piss cart," Corrin grumbled.

"Three wives, actually," Joss pointed out. "You're forgetting Lady Ysra Thornwick."

Corrin scoffed. "She doesn't count. She left me for a bard with softer hands and fewer fleas."

"If this is what's rattling around in your skulls before death, maybe the block's doing the realm a favor," a woman retorted.

The woman was long-limbed and wiry, all elbows and angles, with tangled raven hair that fell around her sharp cheekbones. Her clothes were threadbare and stained, and a thin scar tugged at the corner of her mouth, like the world had tried to silence her and failed. She looked like she hadn't eaten a full meal in weeks, but there was a strange elegance to her still, an old beauty buried beneath grime and defiance, like a wilting flower that dared to bloom through frost.

Corrin raised an eyebrow at the woman's unwavering stare. "Sharp tongue on this one. She'd have made a fine fourth wife."

"And you'd still die alone."

As the men broke off into laughter at the woman's quick retort, the young girl beside Ren rocked gently. Her lips moved with quiet reverence.

"Ash to air, wing to flame,
guard the lost, forget no name.
Though bound and broken we remain...
let the last flame wake again."

Ren barely heard the girl at first. But then, the last line struck Ren like a spark to dry tinder:

"May flame find kin, and stone remember."

Ren's head turned sharply.

The girl's lips were still moving, eyes squeezed shut, as though she hadn't even noticed she'd spoken the words aloud.

Ren's pulse quickened. The chains at her wrists suddenly felt heavier, tighter. Heat prickled up her spine, not from fear, but recognition. The words coiled inside her like smoke searching for fire. She leaned toward the girl, and just when she opened her mouth to speak-

Arrows whistled through the trees.

Ren ducked, hands reaching up to shield her neck, but the iron from the chains around her wrist bit into her skin.

Then chaos erupted.

3

Iron clashed with magic, the air thick with screams and the roar of panicked horses.

Ren yanked at the chains, pulling so hard that the edges bit into her skin, drawing blood.

And then Ren heard heavy, pounding strides that made the ground quiver. Each step was followed by a low, guttural hiss of breath. The foul stench of rot and sour decay hit Ren next, like curdled dairy left in the sun. Ren knew that smell; everyone who'd survived the border raids did.

Ogres.

Forest-dwelling brutes with bone-crushing clubs and maces, and a taste for chaos. They didn't fight for gold or land; they fought for the thrill of it. Ogres hunted anything that crossed their grounds – humans most of all. They were said to hang human skulls from trees to mark their trails home or territories.

A scream tore through the air as an ogre slashed through the bars in the front of the wagon, sending a frail woman scrambling back.

But she wasn't fast enough.

The ogre's claw hooked her neck and sliced through flesh and bone with brutal ease. Blood splattered the iron bars.

Up ahead, Ren caught sight of fae guards shouting orders, trying to herd the prisoners forward. But it was no use. One of the ogres barreled through the ranks and ripped a fae clean off his horse with a sickening *crunch*.

The guards fled, abandoning their orders and leaving the shackled prisoners to face the creatures alone.

This wasn't a brawl.

It was a *slaughter*.

"Don't kill too many of them!" one ogre called. "Some fetch a good price."

A few chuckles answered. Another gleeful voice added, "Humans make good pets if you train 'em young."

Ogres keeping humans as pets wasn't just some cruel joke. It happened. *Still* happened.

They'd drag the living back to their camps and keep them in cages until they got bored, or until the novelty wore off and hunger or sick curiosity took over. Some were tortured. Some were eaten. Some withered away from neglect.

There was a bark of laughter. "Got me one back home who pours wine and whimpers pretty when I beat her."

Ren looked up as a female ogre with rotting teeth and a hooked spear yanked open the wagon door. She towered above them, an ogre twice a man's size, her gray skin slick with sweat and gore. In one hand, she gripped a massive cleaver of blackened iron, chipped at the edges. The blade was thick, crude, but sharp enough to split bone. It dripped with blood, bits of flesh clinging to the iron.

The ogre's eyes raked over the chained prisoners, appraising livestock. She pointed the tip of her cleaver at the small girl beside Ren. "This one's a bit scrawny, but I like 'em young. Easier to break in," she sneered.

The girl shrieked, trying to scramble away, but she had nowhere to go.

The girl looked barely on the cusp of adulthood, her limbs still coltish, her face untouched by the years, yet she carried bruises already blooming beneath the dirt on her skin. For a split second, Ren saw herself before she picked up her first blade in the fighting rings.

When the female ogre reached for the girl, filthy fingers stretching, Ren surged forward with a feral growl, baring her teeth. A crack echoed as the manacles scorched around her wrists, iron warping under heat.

"Touch her, and I'll carve your name into every bone I break." Ren growled. The temperature around her spiked.

The ogre's eyes widened, her smirk dissolving into a flicker of something darker. *Fear.* The ogre stumbled back, gaze locked on something just beyond Ren's shoulders.

"Or what, human? You gonna cry?" Two other ogres lumbered up behind the female ogre, weapons in hand — one with a jagged club spiked with rusted iron, the other dragging a hooked chain still wet with blood. Their eyes gleamed, pupils wide with the thrill of the fight.

From the corner of her eye, Ren caught sudden movement – one of the ogres had unshackled a frail, old man and shoved him forward with a laugh, telling him to run as fast as he could. The old man tried to flee. Another ogre struck him down mid-sprint, the chain snapping forward with a sickening *crack*. It wrapped around the man's leg, yanked him off his feet, and dragged him back across the forest floor. The first ogre brought his club down on the man's skull before he could scream. Bone and blood exploded across the earth, spraying the nearby stones with crimson.

The ogres cackled.

Ren felt the young girl clinging to her from behind. Ren thought of every stolen moment that girl fought to keep herself alive. If Ren yielded, they might let her live. Or they might not. Perhaps one of their blades or clubs would slice through her throat or smash in her skull in the chaos, and that would be the end of her story.

But if they *took* her instead, it might be months, or even years before death finally found her.

Better a clean cut of steel at the butcher's block than the slow rot of captivity in the hands of monsters who would savor every second of her suffering. The flame in Ren's palms flared, scorching away doubt.

Ren knew that the ogres were eager to see her beg, plead, to grovel for her life.

But Ren Harper didn't bow to monsters.

If she was going down, she'd set the world on fire first. She rose, ready to burn the world down if it meant breaking herself free.

The iron shackles glowed red-hot, their grip loosening, cracking. With a shuddering wrench, the chains shattered like brittle twigs. Flames erupted from her palms. Heat shimmered in waves around her as she drew the inferno close, shaping it, feeding it with every heartbeat of rage and defiance.

Then, with a cry that rattled the air, that rattled the *world*, she hurled the fire forward.

And the world didn't just burn; it *bowed* before her.

Moments later, when the flames flickered and died down, the ogres who had taunted her were now charred husks scattered across the scorched earth.

Ren stood frozen, chest heaving. The air shimmered where her flames had been. She stared at her hands as if they belonged to someone else. This was the first time she'd ever unleashed her fire like *that*.

For years, she'd kept it buried. She'd singe the edges of playing cards at taverns whenever her temper flared, sweeping the ashes into her pockets before anyone noticed. Once, she'd even set her own braid smoldering when a drunkard tried to tug her close, pretending afterward that the candle had tipped too close. She could recall countless moments when the fire had risen, hungry and insistent, and each time she'd forced it back into the dark where it belonged.

Each time, the same erratic thrum had pounded in her ears, a pulse that did not seem quite like hers — hungry, coaxing.

And this time, she hadn't fought it. She'd yielded to its call.

Now, staring at the ruin around her, her heart pounded with some-thing between awe and terror. No human should wield fire like this. The fae, maybe. But not her. Some humans tried delving into magic, but their power came only through carefully written spells that demanded years of study to master and even longer to control. Ren had never met anyone who could actually *do* it.

Ren didn't know much about magic, only what she'd seen once in the market square in one of the western outposts — a fae tax collector who froze a man solid when he couldn't pay. She'd watched frost crawl over his skin until he shattered like fragile glass. She'd thought such power belonged only to the fae.

And yet, the scorched earth around her spoke otherwise.

Steel flashed from the right, pressing against Ren's neck before she could breathe.

"What the hell *are* you?" a low voice demanded in her ear.

"**Y**ou have five seconds before I gut you," the voice hissed.

Ren twisted like a flame caught in a gale, seizing her attacker's wrist and driving them to the forest floor in a single, fluid motion. Leaves scattered, the earth groaned, and Ren met wide, familiar emerald eyes beneath her.

The dark-haired woman from the carriage.

"You can sure as hell try, but I don't owe you a damn thing," Ren growled.

The woman shoved Ren back, both of them scrambling upright as the smoke curled around them.

"You turned this place into a damn inferno," the woman coughed, voice cracking as she covered her mouth with her sleeve.

Ren cursed under her breath, grabbing the woman's wrist and yanking her through the haze. When Ren caught the small silhouette, she reached down for the young girl crouched nearby. The girl latched onto Ren's hand without a sound, eyes screwed shut, as though shutting out the world might somehow undo the horror around them.

"I saved your ass, that's what I did," Ren muttered. "And now I'm getting us the hell out of this smoke before it guts our lungs."

Ren's chest burned as she pushed through the smoke-choked air, one arm around the woman's waist, the other gripping the young girl's trembling hand.

The ash was thicker here. Red embers floated like fluttering fireflies. The once-lush trees were blackened skeletons, the road barely visible through the carnage. She turned the corner of a half-collapsed pine, eyes scanning through the haze.

And froze.

Joss lay sprawled across the ground. His shirt was soaked through with blood, eyes open and glazed, a slash across his throat.

Corrin slumped against a boulder beside him. He wavered, blood threading between his fingers where they clutched his head. His face was pale, but he smiled when he saw Ren. "There you are," he rasped.

Ren rushed and dropped to her knees beside him. "Corrin, don't you dare. Don't you *fucking* dare."

"Don't yell," he protested, trying and failing to chuckle. He winced. "My ears are still ringing from the shit you pulled earlier. Stopped those bastards right in their tracks, though. *I* took one of 'em down before he bashed in my skull."

Ren's eyes swept over him with the practiced assessment of someone who had seen too many wounds to count. Blood matted Corrin's hair where his head was struck, but the real danger lay lower.

His stomach bore a deep puncture wound that had torn him open. A stab of a blade, angled cruelly enough that the damage went beyond flesh. Blood spilled in steady streams. Ren didn't need to feel for a pulse to know he had only moments left.

Still, Ren tore a strip from her cloak. She pressed it firmly against the gash, even as Corrin's trembling hand pushed at hers.

"Hold still," she hissed, leaning over him. "If I can stop the bleeding —"

But the look in his eyes silenced her, eyes that spoke of a hollow, knowing resignation. He knew as well as she did that no amount of pressure would keep his life from spilling through her fingers.

Still, she pressed harder, refusing to let go.

"It's no use," Corrin whispered. "You and I both know that."

"We had a deal. The stew, the bed, the sea. Remember?"

Corrin's eyes were half-closed now. "You'll still see it," he murmured. "The sea. When you do, remember me, yeah? Don't remember the chains. Just remember my dashing smile and good humor."

Ren heaved a quiet sigh of resignation and lowered herself beside him, taking his trembling hands in hers. Her presence and a steady touch in the face of the inevitable was all she could offer now. "I will."

His fingers twitched against hers. "And if you find a bed…" he rasped, breath hitching, "make sure it's soft. None of that scratchy straw." Corrin's expression changed, pain giving way to a fragile kind of peace. "And if you find someone, a lover or whatever poor soul's stupid enough to fall for you…" He grinned faintly, voice fading. "Make sure they treat you right. *Like you're worth a whole damn kingdom.*"

And then, with that last flicker of humor in his eyes, Corrin With Two R's, Puker of Enchanters and Defiler of Statues, exhaled.

And was gone.

For a beat, Ren just stared, her hands still gripping his, as if she could will him back with the sheer stubbornness of her grip. But the silence that followed was heavy and final.

For all his bluster, he'd been unashamedly loud, a thorn in everyone's side. Yet somehow he'd carved himself into their strange little band, leaving a mark that would linger long after the echo of his voice faded. Ren hoped that beyond the veil, Corrin found peace.

Ren closed her eyes, drawing in a shuddering breath, before prying her bloody hands away. The world, cruel as ever, hadn't paused to mourn him. But she did.

"The carriage," the young girl rasped, bringing Ren swiftly back to the moment.

Ren followed her gaze. The horses were gone, either bolted or burned. The carriage sat like a wounded beast in the mud, wheels sunken deep, its iron bars scorched black.

And then, it moved.

Not the shifting of settling wood or the creak of a broken wheel. No, this was a deliberate, slow, groaning shudder that rattled the bars in their sockets.

Something had been locked in that cage. Something the fae themselves hadn't trusted to ride with the rest of them.

Ren tensed, expecting a nightmare to step out from the blackened carriage.

From the doorway emerged a tall figure, brushing soot from his tunic. His presence rippled through the air — cold, precise, *ancient*. Midnight hair fell in soft, tousled waves around a sharply cut face. His ears tapered into unmistakable points, and his nose, slightly hooked with the unmistakable edge of aristocracy, marked him as someone born into power.

Fae.

His eyes scanned them, lingering a beat too long on Ren, as if cataloging each sin they'd committed to survive.

"**C**are to explain who set the forest on fire?" the fae male inquired in a silky smooth voice, hand resting on the hilt at his hip.

"What does that matter now?" the dark-haired woman next to Ren found her voice first. "At least those bastard ogres were put down before they had their way with us."

"Ogres?" he murmured, as if tasting the word. His dark hair tied loosely at the nape, a few rebellious strands breaking free across his slender brow. Broad-shouldered and tall, he carried himself more as a warrior than a courtier.

His emerald gaze settled on Ren, and Ren felt like she was being judged or weighed against some invisible measure only he understood.

Though the fae male wore plain clothes in shades of charcoal and navy, he wasn't a low-rank fae soldier. The gold ring glinting on his hand gave him away. A plain gold band, save for the sapphire gleaming at its center. Ren knew that stone alone could buy a ship, a home, maybe a man's life. His voice held the clipped and refined accent of the high fae who had strode through human villages to collect their dues.

An emblem gleamed on his chest: a crescent moon cradling a thorned rose, silver on midnight blue. House Vaelaran.

And Ren knew with a sinking feeling that this was no ordinary fae.

Why someone like him sat in this wagon, she didn't know. But instinct had her scanning him for the bulge of hidden weapons. Was he another threat she'd have to contend with, or the kind of ally who could cut her throat before the night ended?

The male fae in question turned his gaze to the blackened clearing, where smoke still curled from the scorched ground and the ogres' remains. "Impressive. Not many can take down a hunting pack. Brutish bastards and not easily felled."

"*Impressive*?" Ren echoed, eyes narrowing. "Funny, we didn't see your brave soldiers saying that when they left us in chains like bait."

Ren shoved the fury clawing at her chest, forced down the scream rising in her throat. Her hands trembled as she gestured toward the broken foliage where the fae soldiers had fled, the torn leaves and crushed branches still whispering of their cowardice. She buried every wild thought, every roar of rage, and wrenched her focus onto the words spilling out of her.

"The others *ran*," Ren spat. "The moment the ogres burst through the trees, the so-called valiant soldiers of *House Vaelaran* left us." Her jaw locked so tightly it ached, but the words kept coming. "And now the ogres are dead, but so are half the prisoners – torn apart while the soldiers tucked tail." She arched her head to the side, as though daring him to give her an answer worth hearing. "And yet, here you are. Still standing. What's the matter? Couldn't run fast enough, or did you stay just to gawk at the aftermath?"

The male fae's gaze fell to the scorched ground and the bodies scattered across the earth. Ren could have sworn she saw surprise flicker across his face.

"I..." he began, the word catching. "I stayed to cover their evacuation of the prisoners." But it was clear now, even to him, that evacuation had been little more than panic. Then his eyes flicked toward the twisted remnants of the shackles, still clamped around blackened limbs. "Nearly half of them were still chained," he murmured, more to himself than to her. "The priority would be to release them all first."

"Well, they didn't," Ren said flatly. .

"It wasn't enough," he whispered.

"No," Ren muttered, her gaze lingering on the limp, lifeless bodies of the other prisoners. Silence stretched as her eyes stayed fixed on them. "It wasn't."

Ren's expression shifted, the raw edges of weariness giving way to something sharper. Her composure solidified like steel drawn from the forge. "Are you planning to put the rest of us back in chains now, or are you waiting until the blood dries?"

Ren braced herself, arms tense, feet half-shifted to bolt or burn, whichever he pushed her toward first. If he so much as twitched in the direction of binding her, she would raze this whole damn forest to ash, consequences be damned.

Silence followed her question, thick as the smoke still rising from the battlefield.

They stared.

Predator and prey, though who was which, neither of them could be sure.

Then, the male fae drew his steel, a polished curved blade.

Ren's lip curled. Her gaze snagged on a fae sprawled in the dirt nearby, his hand still clenched around his sword hilt. She strode over and pulled hard at the fae's limp wrist. Once. Twice. The stiff fingers wouldn't release, so she snarled and kicked until the blade jarred free with a metallic *clatter*.

She didn't give a damn how heavy it was or how it felt foreign in her grasp. "Mine now," she muttered.

All that mattered was that she had steel. The male fae hadn't spoken a word, only flicked his gaze toward her.

And then he advanced.

Their blades met in a crack of steel. The vibration rang up Ren's arm, but she shoved back. He pressed once, twice, then swirled. Ren countered, gritting her teeth as she locked steel against his again.

He lunged, and she blocked, teeth rattling from the force. His emerald eyes gleamed. There was only a click of his tongue when her guard slipped.

Another when she struck too wide, leaving her ribs open.

A third when her footwork faltered on a patch of scorched earth.

Each sound was a judgment, a mark on whatever ledger he was keeping.

Ren's frustration flared. She bared her teeth, swinging harder, but he twisted smoothly, parrying effortlessly. He was testing her reflexes, her resolve, her limits. Steel rang again and again, until the entire world narrowed to the clash of their blades, the heat of his scrutiny, and the slow realization curdling in her gut.

He wasn't just fighting her.

He was deciding what she was *worth*.

Ren swung with raw fury, but he turned aside every strike with infuriating ease, his curved blade singing as it carved through the air.

Then too quick for her tired arm to counter, he twisted, his weapon slamming against hers. The shock knocked her back. She stumbled, boots scraping across blood-slick earth, until the ground gave out beneath her balance, and she went down hard on her ass. The breath whooshed out of her lungs.

When she looked up, the curved steel glinted above her — pointed straight at her chest. The fae male's stance was unshaken, every line of him honed and deliberate, emerald eyes burning down into hers.

"Yield," he commanded.

Ren's chest heaved, air scraping ragged down her throat. She clenched her jaw, every instinct snarling to spit in his face. But her arms trembled from the weight of the fight.

Her lips parted. With one curt nod, she forced herself to bow to the moment. "I yield."

Ren's attention flickered to the edges of her sight, catching the movement of the others beyond the circle of their clash. The younger girl's eyes hadn't left Ren for a second, her lips moving in what might've been prayer.

The dark-haired woman leaned against a tree, one brow cocked, a crooked smirk tugging at her mouth as though this whole bloody dance had been nothing more than a tavern brawl. Ren caught the way the woman's eyes glittered, sharp and assessing, following every strike, every falter, as though she were weighing Ren as well.

Ren's amber eyes returned to the male fae. Slowly, he drew a breath and straightened, rolling his shoulders back like dawning an old cloak.

"Well," he chuckled, brushing ash from the sleeve of his coat, "I could have you shackled again, but I suspect you'd take that personally, and I'm rather fond of diplomacy." He turned to her, a smile ghosting across his lips. "You just turned a hunting ground into a bonfire, and you know how to wield a sword. You're dangerous – the kind of dangerous House Vaelaran needs."

There it was, the way his tone pivoted, already conniving, as if the dead could be swept aside with clever words and courtly charm. Of course he'd dress it up like a compliment – dangle a proposition like some gilded chain that she'd blindly reach for.

This was precisely why she could never trust the fae.

"I have other problems that require that kind of enthusiasm," the male fae continued.

"Is this your version of a proposition? Because your offer of service could use work," Ren snapped.

"You're quick on your feet and loyal enough to stay and fight when running would have been easier."

"I was trying not to die. Don't confuse that for loyalty."

He stepped over a charred ogre corpse, eyes trained on her. "No, you're not the loyal type. You're the *burn-it-down-and-walk-away* type. Which is exactly why the realm needs you."

Ren laughed bitterly. "The last time someone needed *me,* I wound up here – on my way to the butcher's block."

His gaze lingered on her, calm but assessing. "I'm offering something else. A choice."

"There's always a price with your kind."

As he had deflected her blade before, he deflected her words just as easily. "There are monsters to slay. I could offer you protection, coin – whatever it is, you name it. You can come to court and serve a crucial role in protecting the kingdom. Fight if you choose, leave if you don't."

Ren glanced over at the younger girl watching their every exchange in bated silence. "She goes home first," Ren stated. "Then *maybe* I'll consider your offer. And by maybe, I mean don't count on it."

"Deal."

"And don't think for a second I trust you."

His eyes glinted in amusement. "If you did, I'd be worried." Then he tilted his head, watching her with that same unnerving curiosity. "What's your name?"

Ren hesitated, weighing the wisdom of giving it to him. "Ren Harper." Her chin lifted. "And yours?"

He paused. The air itself seemed to shift as though the forest already recognized who he was. When he finally spoke, the name landed like steel on stone. "Prince Talen of Vaelaran — at your service, or your mercy. Hard to tell which, really. Try not to swoon, it's unbecoming."

6

Trekking through the forest was no small feat.

As the land began to rise, the hills gave way to jagged slopes. The wind sharpened, its icy teeth biting at Ren's skin as though it meant to flay it from her bones. Each gust carried the acrid sting of ash, the taste of soot settling on her tongue. The air grew thinner. Ren didn't need anyone to tell her where they were. One look at the dark, smoke-wreathed peak looming above was enough.

They were climbing the outskirts of Mount Solfira.

Leaves that had crunched under their feet now turned into rock. The four of them moved in a strained silence. The dark-haired woman, Elira, led the way. She hadn't spoken much since the attack other than sharing her name.

Sela trudged just behind Elira, her footsteps light and delicate. Ren brought up the rear, wary of the fae prince walking a few steps ahead. Sela had said her family's farm was across this pass. Ren had overheard one of the fae soldiers sneer about how the human girl had stolen something of value. Valuable enough to earn a death sentence.

Then again, the fae rarely needed a reason to imprison a human.

Each time a fae lord visited a human settlement, the air in every village turned taut with fear. Their arrival was never simple, never harmless. They'd ride in, claiming to collect taxes for the crown, but they rarely left with just coins in their purses. The wagons that rolled out behind them were heavier, laden with humans bound in chains. Sometimes it was the ones who couldn't pay their dues, sometimes those accused of petty crimes.

They were taken deep into the woods, where even sunlight feared to linger, straight into ogre territory. From there, the prisoners were split into two lines. The lucky ones were marched to the work camps. The others were sent to execution.

Ren had always wondered why the fae thought that it was a good idea doing this in ogre territory. Maybe it was convenient. Maybe cruelty. But more likely, it was strategy. Ogres were territorial to the bone, content so long as their borders weren't crossed, savage only when provoked. They didn't care for land or power, just the sanctity of their domain. The fae knew it. Sending humans there meant no pursuit, no witnesses. The ogres would never stray beyond their borders, and they rarely touched fae royalty.

A perfect disposal ground.

The memory of Ren's own sentencing felt like it happened just yesterday, even though it happened just days ago.

The woman in front of Ren broke before they even called her name. When the verdict came for the woman in front of Ren announcing *work camp*, she sobbed into her bound hands, whispering a prayer of thanks as though the gods themselves had intervened. Ren readied herself as the guards dragged the woman aside. She didn't know what the punishment was for punching a fae, but she doubted it was execution. Saints, it wasn't like she'd killed the bastard.

"And you? What's your name?" the thin, wiry fae called to Ren. He met her gaze over his ledger and a quill, poised to write her name when spoken.

Beside him, the lumbering fae commander watched her with open disgust, like she'd already decided Ren's worth and her sentence in the same glance. Ren didn't look away. She met the fae commander's stare head-on, refusing to give her the satisfaction of seeing her flinch.

Ren had only sneered. "Why? Planning to write me a love letter?"

"We keep records of our prisoners."

The female commander beside him scoffed. "She was charged for assaulting a fae noble, and mark me, she'll be a repeat offender."

The male clicked his tongue and began to write. "Working camps, then."

Ren's shoulders slackened. Work camps. Hard labor, pain, hunger, but not death. Not yet. The smallest breath of relief slipped past her lips before the female's voice cut through it like a blade.

"No." The woman's teeth showed in a slow, cruel smile when Ren tilted her head. "To the block she goes."

Ren thought she'd misheard. "What?" The word tore from her throat, half disbelief, half fury. Chains bit into her skin as she jerked against them, the metal clinking in protest.

She hadn't *killed* anyone. Saints, she'd barely bloodied the bastard's nose. And yet this fae was smiling, as if sending her to die was nothing more than a game of amusement.

A hush had fallen. The male hesitated, brow lifting. "Even by our laws, that is a punishment far beyond her crime," he murmured hesitantly to the commander.

"She'll do it again," the commander insisted, letting her gaze pin Ren like a specimen. "Take her to the block. It'll save us time and do the realm a favor. Now get her name for us so we can log the next prisoner."

As Ren opened her mouth to fire off a retort, hands had seized her. Before she could wrench free, a shoulder drove into her ribs and she staggered, knees buckling. A hard palm cracked against her jaw; the world tilted into a burst of light and sound. When she tried to push up, a booted toe shoved her back down, pain flaring along the side of her face. Fingers dug into her hair; another blow sent a hot sting through her ribs and a thin star of dizziness flared at the edge of her vision.

Two fae soldiers set upon her, boots and fists driving her to the ground until she could barely breathe. Every blow stole another scrap of air, another word, until all she could do was gasp and glare up at them through the haze. Each hit was a promise she'd been warned of: *obey, or be erased.*

One of the fae crouched until his face was level with hers. His hands seized her cheeks and tilted her head until her eyes were forced open to meet his. Up close, his smile didn't reach his eyes; it was all unwavering patience and promise of cruelty.

"Tell me your name," he said. "Speak it. Or, you die."

The threat was as clean as a blade. Ren tasted copper and the aftershock of pain. For a second the world narrowed to his breath.

Finally, with a sound half swallowed and half spat, Ren forced her name through clenched teeth. He studied her, thumb hooked under her chin, as if weighing the sound of the syllable. Then, he let go. The fae commander met Ren's gaze. Ren spat toward her boots, still thrashing against the hands that held her down. The woman didn't flinch. Didn't so much as blink.

"Next," she called coolly, already turning away, as if Ren were nothing more than another name to scratch from a ledger.

The guards dragged Ren upright, but the burn in her chest wasn't from the blows anymore; it was from the way that single word hollowed her out.

Back in the present, Prince Talen moved ahead of Ren with maddening steadiness, his cloak sweeping behind him like a shadow stitched in silk. His footsteps pressed into the earth with purpose, each one as measured as his voice had been when he made that damn proposition.

Of course the fae would hide their heir in an unmarked prisoner's cart. Not a gilded carriage, not a royal escort decked in banners—just iron bars and wood, *the perfect disguise*. It was a smart move.

No one would suspect a prince among the condemned.

Her stomach turned, a bitter taste rising in her mouth. All those soldiers she'd thought were overkill, the endless patrols shadowing their journey. It wasn't for keeping an eye on the prisoners.

It was because the prince rode among them.

And *of course* it was the damn prince.

Because why not make this disaster more complicated than it already was?

Now that the fae prince was in their company, she couldn't just vanish into the trees at the first opportunity. No, now she had to watch him carefully because she had no idea what his true motive was.

And the stories didn't help.

She'd heard them whispered in taverns across half the realm, always shifting depending on the drink or the teller. That he'd been banished by his own parents, practically stripped of his birthright for a forbidden love affair with a nobleman's daughter or a foreign prince. Others swore he'd dueled a general of Vaelaran's armies and refused to yield, even when his blade ran red.

And then there was the most ridiculous tale of them all – the goat debacle. That the prince had been caught sneaking into a vineyard late at night, not for wine, but to liberate a herd of prized goats. The goats escaped, ran throughout the markets, and even rampaged through the royal gardens. They devoured the queen's roses and trampled a visiting ambassador's ceremonial cloak. By morning, the prince was gone from court, and the story had become legend.

Out of all the outlandish rumors, this one had to be the most absurd. As if the heir to House Vaelaran would waste his night breaking into vineyards to set goats free. Entire herds of them, no less. She pictured him, flinging open a pen of goats while bleating chaos poured out like a tide.

No. Impossible. The image was so ridiculous she almost laughed the first time she heard it.

Then again, she thought grimly, *this was Vaelaran court politics. Stranger things had happened.*

She had no way of knowing which tale, if any, was true.

But one thing was clear: now, she was shackled to him.

Her jaw clenched as she followed the steady line of his back through the darkened pass. She'd thought her greatest problem was surviving the butcher's block. Now she was stuck keeping pace with a certain male fae who might be every bit as dangerous as the monsters waiting in the trees.

And, gods help her.

She was fucked.

They pressed on, the forest's silence broken only by the crunch of boots over roots and stones. Each step sent a dull throb through Ren's heels, sharp reminders of the endless marching since dawn. Just as her patience frayed, the faint rush of water reached her ears, growing louder until they broke through the trees onto the bank of a river.

Ren dropped to her knees at once, plunging her hands into the cold current. The icy bite stole her breath, but she didn't care. She scrubbed at the dried stains until the last of Corrin's blood slipped away downstream. For a moment, she just stared at the ripples, letting them carry what she couldn't. When she glanced up, she realized she wasn't the only one.

Sela crouched a few paces downriver, sleeves rolled to her elbows as she splashed water over her thin arms to wash the dirt and blood away. Beside Ren, Elira dipped her forearms in, the current dragging trails of crimson from her skin before vanishing into the flow.

Elira's dark eyes lifted, steady and searching. "You all right?" she asked, her voice low but carrying over the river's murmur.

Ren blinked, throat dry. "Yeah," she muttered

Elira tilted her head, like she didn't quite believe her, but didn't push.

Ren turned her focus back to the water. She watched the ripples warp her reflection, the current pulling her face into something unrecognizable. Her thoughts tangled with the stream.

There was no way in hell she was going with Talen to the capital of House Vaelaran, known as Pyraelia.

She had never visited Pyraelia, but she'd heard enough from visitors to know of its luxury. She knew about its inhabitants' love for the arts and fine foods like wine and cheeses that Ren couldn't pronounce the names of. Masquerade balls were famous in the palace's halls, and the royal family was known to be not only strikingly beautiful but also a force to be reckoned with when crossed.

Ren wasn't built for court games.

But the girl with the shaking hands and wide, haunted eyes, trudging quietly ahead of her...

Ren would make damn sure Sela got home safe.

After rinsing the blood and grime away, they resumed their climb.

Mount Solfira loomed larger with every step, its slopes tilting steeper, forcing their bodies to lean forward as though bowing to the stone itself.

Loose gravel skittered beneath their boots, whispering down the incline with each misplaced footfall.

The air thinned the higher they went, turning every breath into a shallow, burning drag that left Ren's lungs raw. Her chest rose and fell too quickly, sweat dampening the collar of her tunic despite the cool bite of the wind. Soon, their pace faltered – steps dragging, their steps grew slower from the exertion.

Prince Talen turned to glance over his shoulder at Ren when she paused by a tree to catch her breath.

Ren met his gaze with a flat stare. "Something on my face?"

"Say the word if you need us to ease the pace."

Ren waved him off. "I'm fine. Let's keep moving."

They had been climbing for only a few minutes when Ren felt the earth shifting treacherously beneath her boots. What had been solid, blackened ground moments ago now felt slick and unstable.

Her foot skidded, nearly sending her to her knees. Heat pulsed up through the soles of her boots, a steady thrum that made her stomach twist with unease. Before she could warn the others, the ground let out a low, guttural growl.

A violent hiss split the air.

Ren barely had time to scream before the world exploded in fire and ash.

T he world exploded in steam.

Gas scorched Ren's lungs as she coughed, vision blurring. Somewhere came a shrill scream. *Sela.*

"Move!" Talen barked from up ahead. "*Now!*"

A fissure to their right exploded. Shards of rock rained down around them.

Ren bolted, but each step sank, as though the ground were softening to molten sludge. More steam rose, obscuring her vision. Sweat slicked her brow, stung her eyes.

"Shit!" Ren spat as her heel struck something jagged. Pain stabbed through her foot with every step, but she didn't slow. Gritting her teeth, Ren fixed her gaze on Sela and Elira fleeing through the smoke and Talen's dark silhouette just behind them.

The mountain groaned closer this time. Ren's gaze snagged on a towering obsidian pillar that jutted from the slope above the pass. It leaned precariously over the pass, and with each groan of the mountain, the pillar started to tilt with an eerie slowness. The shadow it cast stretched over Ren, swallowing her in darkness.

Another vent blew. Steam blasted across the path, scalding Ren's skin, her eyes. She squeezed her eyes shut and stumbled forward blindly.

Fuck, fuck, fuck!

The ground heaved, nearly knocking Ren off her feet. Each step felt like a gamble. Would the earth hold or swallow her whole?

Then came the final groan – this one deeper, louder. The kind of sound that meant something was giving way.

Silence.

Ren turned her head just in time to see the pillar teetering free, its immense shadow rushing toward her, devouring the ground between them. For a breath, awe froze her in place at its sheer size.

It's inevitability.

Ren's heart slammed against her ribs. *Move. Move.*

She tried. Gods, she tried, legs pumping, lungs tearing for air, but she knew she couldn't outrun it. The pillar loomed above her, close enough now that she could see the molten veins glowing faintly along its cracked surface.

And then, a strong arm hooked tight around her waist from behind and flung her forward with brutal force.

The world spun – heat, smoke, stone, and then she crashed to the ground, tumbling across jagged rock until a rough hand seized her wrist, anchoring her.

A voice hissed in her ear. "Get on your feet!" *Talen.*

His grip lingered for just a heartbeat before he shoved her toward the others, his body angled protectively between her and the falling pillar as it crashed behind them with an earth-shaking roar.

Shards of molten rock scattered like sparks. Heat licked at Ren's back as she scrambled to her feet.

"Go!" Talen barked again, already moving, his hand briefly pressing against her shoulder before he sprinted ahead.

They ran. The vents hissed and roared around them, belching steam that burned her lungs raw. Every instinct screamed *faster, faster*, even as her legs trembled beneath her.

Another tremor rippled through the ground, but then the path widened, sloping down into a cooler stretch of earth where the rock gave way to ash-darkened soil.

And then, trees.

They burst through a thicket of charred pines, the forest alive with the scent of scorched sap. The sounds of Mount Solfira faded to a distant grumble.

Ren stumbled to a stop, bracing a hand on her knee as she gulped down air, lungs burning, throat raw from smoke.

Sela collapsed onto a fallen log, her chest heaving as she buried her face in her hands.

Elira paced, her eyes wild, muttering curses under her breath.

Ren eventually straightened, brushing her damp hair back from her face. Her heartbeat still thundered like a war drum, the adrenaline refusing to ebb.

A shadow loomed at her side.

"Are you hurt?" Talen asked quietly. His eyes swept over her, searching for injuries.

For a moment, Ren could only stare at him.

Why had he thrown himself between her and certain death?

Ren opened her mouth, then closed it again, unable to form the words. "I'm fine," she managed at last, the words sharper than she intended.

Talen only gave a curt nod before turning his gaze back toward Mount Solfira, watching its smoke curl lazily into the sky. Ren followed his gaze, the question lingering.

Why did he save me?

They journeyed all day, stopping only when the sun began to set. Silence clung to them, each step and breath measured. No one dared waste energy on words.

At last, they found a small clearing. They collapsed in uneasy silence.

Ren sat with her back against a tree, knees drawn up, her body aching from the climb and the near-death they'd narrowly escaped. For a few blessed minutes, no one moved, each of them lost to their own thoughts.

It was Talen who finally broke the stillness. "We can't stay here long," he said, scanning the woods as if he could already see what hid beyond the trees. "Once night falls, these forests won't be safe. Too many creatures prowl after dark." His gaze flicked briefly to Ren, before settling on the others. "Rest while you can, then we move. We need to be far from here before the dark settles in."

The words carried authority, but his once-pristine cloak was torn and muddied. The dark waves of his hair had come loose in sweat-damp strands clinging to his temples. A shallow cut traced the line of his jaw, smeared with dried crimson. Even his emerald eyes were shadowed by exhaustion. Yet somehow, standing there with his broad shoulders squared and his blade still steady at his side, he looked every inch the warrior prince.

Ren tightened her arms around her knees, staring at him from beneath damp strands of hair. He was right.

The thought of what might be watching from the shadows was enough to make her stand.

They trudged onward, the forest stretching ahead. Ren lowered her gaze to her boots, watching them rise and fall in a steady rhythm. *One... two... three...* She counted silently, forcing her mind to focus on the numbers instead of the ache in her legs or the gnawing uncertainty twisting in her gut.

When she reached ten, she started over. Again and again. Each set of ten became its own small victory, a way to carve the endless trek into something she could control – one step closer to Sela's home, and farther from Mount Solfira looming behind them.

Then the trees opened to a clearing.

Once farmland, the land now lay bare and lifeless. No livestock roamed. No crops grew in the field. Just barren dirt and the outline of a small home.

Sela ran.

Elira cursed and broke into a run. Ren followed without question.

The building leaned crooked, a structure that felt more like a memory of home than a home itself. The front door hung slightly ajar. Ren stepped into the threshold.

The hearth bore only blackened coal. No warmth lingered. The air inside was dry and brittle, like even the walls had forgotten how to breathe. Ren slowed, boots echoing against the worn floorboards.

And then she saw a woman sitting hunched in a rocking chair, staring blankly at the wall as though she could see through it. Her eyes were glassy and distant. Her skin was the color of ash. She looked like she had been carved from dust and held together by sheer memory.

Or what remained of it.

The signs were unmistakable – the brittle bones, the hollow gaze, the slow, rattling breath that scraped through the woman's chest like wind rustling through dead leaves.

They called it the Witherblight, a name that sounded almost poetic until you saw what it did to people.

It began as a fever. Nothing too alarming. But then the skin turned pallid with sickly gray veins. Muscles seized, magic unraveled. Everything began to rot from the inside out.

The Witherblight had already claimed hundreds of lives in Lytharien. Whole villages went silent, windows boarded, bodies buried in pits the ground refused to keep. Some said it came from the ships from Windhaven, carried in by wind. Others whispered it was the gods punishing the realm. But the truth didn't matter when the coughing started and the eyes dimmed.

There was only one cure. The Verdant Elixir, brewed from rare fae-grown herbs and forged by magic, closely guarded by the royal court and priced like it was spun from stardust and gold.

And for a human with no name and no coin, it might as well have been a myth.

Ren and Elira exchanged a glance. Ren saw the flicker of emotions in Elira's eyes, a mixture of recognition and hesitation.

Elira reached for her scarf and tied it across her nose and mouth. Ren mirrored the gesture, tugging her cloak higher, jaw tight. Every instinct screamed to leave, to run before the sickness took root in their lungs. Nobody knew what spread the Witherblight. Some theorized it spread in the air; others whispered that it spread through touch contact.

But neither of them moved.

They had seen worse. *Done* worse.

Talen didn't flinch or look away. He didn't lift a hand to cover his face, and he didn't take a step back from the stench of death.

Of course he stayed.

What did he have to fear, with access to the elixir no farther than a command? While others had done far worse to get their hands on a vial.

Ren had heard stories of how one man carved out his own kidney to sell for a vial. How a woman once approached a soldier at the border post with trembling fingers and a ring in her palm. "It's all I have," she'd whispered. The soldier had only stared before closing the gate in her face.

Ren saw it for herself – a little boy in Briarstead waiting outside the apothecary doors from dawn to dusk, clutching a handful of wildflowers. When the fae merchants emerged, he'd offered them up with both hands, voice trembling. "For my sister. She's really sick. Just one bottle, please." The flowers slipped from his grasp when they stepped over him.

The fae merchants hadn't even paused their conversation to *look* at the boy.

Ren clenched her teeth and turned her focus back to Sela.

"Mama..." Sela whispered. "I've come home."

For a few moments, the woman didn't stir. Then, her eyes met Sela's.

"Who are you?" the woman rasped. Then her tone turned sharp, rising into a hoarse shriek, "Leave at once! *Leave at once, I say*!"

Sela just sank to her knees, gripping her mother's hands, as if holding tight might anchor the woman back to her.

Ren had seen a lot in her life. But this?

This was cruelty.

Because the Witherblight didn't just kill the body. It unraveled the *mind*.

First came the trembling, subtle at first, like a chill that wouldn't leave the bones. Then the fever, burning high enough to strip reason from the mind. And then, the forgetting.

Not just names whispered in passing, but the ones spoken at altars, sworn in love. Faces blurred, even the ones held closest. You could glance at your reflection in a bowl of water and not recognize the stranger staring back. Some would clutch their children, tracing familiar cheekbones, only to recoil because the little face before them was only a stranger's.

And eventually, even *yourself* unraveled. Memories shed until nothing remained but the emptiness where a person had been.

It was like watching someone wither away in pieces. And for a girl like Sela, losing her mother while she was still breathing was a wound Ren wouldn't wish on her worst enemy.

Ren swallowed hard, blinking against the tightness in her chest. No one should have to go through that. Especially not a girl who was so young.

"It's me, Mama," Sela whispered gently. "*Sela*. I couldn't get the medicine, but I'll go again tomorrow. I'll bring it back. I promise."

That was when it clicked for Ren.

The theft the fae guards joked about. Sela hadn't been stealing for herself; she'd risked everything for a vial of the Verdant Elixir.

The woman rose. Her knees wobbled beneath the weight of her frame, finger shaking as she pointed accusingly. "I don't know you. I don't want you here. I want to be at peace. *I just want peace...*" Her words dissolved into a choked sob. Then her legs buckled.

Sela caught her before she hit the floor. But the moment her hands touched her mother's skin, the woman's flesh gave beneath the touch, peeling. Her body was collapsing inward, being eaten away from within.

Sela's mother's breathing had slowed to shallow gasps, her eyes no longer tracking movement and fixed on something beyond this world. Elira found a thin blanket and gently laid it over her frail form. Sela guided her to a cot overlooking the field outside, where no doubt cows or horses once roamed. Sela smoothed the blanket over her mother's legs, tucking it in like she had done countless times in better days.

Sela lowered herself to the floor beside the cot, folding her knees beneath her, and laced her fingers together. "May the Veil be kind," she whispered. "May the stars lead your way to rest. May your memories greet you on the other side."

Ren stood in the corner, arms crossed over her chest. Her gaze shifted to the prince.

Talen stood as still as a shadow, eyes locked on the woman. There was something about the tension in his jaw, the quiet furrow of his brow; it was an observation warping into calculation.

Ren felt the air shifting. She sucked in a breath.

Magic.

It bled into the room like a living thing. It wasn't flame or wind, not earth or sky. It was something older. *Wilder.* Talen's expression remained unreadable, but his hands were clenched behind his back.

Then, as if pulled by an invisible thread, the old woman's eyes flicked open.

And locked straight onto his.

Is he about to hurt her?

Ren lurched forward, ready to throw herself between them. But Talen only lifted a hand, palm out, a silent command to *wait*. His gaze never wavered from the woman's, every muscle gone still, as if some unseen force held the air taut between them.

In the next breath, the woman's hand reached blindly and found her daughter's hand. A final breath rattled from her lips. A gasp that fluttered, then stilled.

Sela choked on a sob but held her mother's hand tightly, tears spilling down her cheeks. She kissed the woman's knuckles and bowed her head over them. And then, as if pulled from the depths of her grief, she lifted her chin.

"I will *end* this," she declared. "I don't know how yet. But I will. I'll help stop this sickness. I'll make them pay for hoarding the cure. For letting you die like this."

Her small frame quivered with fury now, not just grief. Her fists curled around the blanket, her tear-streaked face lifted to them all with a fire that didn't belong to a child. "One day," she vowed vehemently, "*no one* else will be left to suffer like she did."

Silence echoed in the space she left behind.

And no one, not even Talen, dared speak against her.

R en dreamed of a sky on fire.

Winged shadows circled overhead, too large to be birds. They shrieked in unison, not in fear, but in *rage*. Their wings caught the light with scales that shimmered like molten gold.

Below, a city of stone and starlight crumbled. Fae towers twisted and fell. Screams echoed. In the heart of it all, a woman stood barefoot atop a pyre, hair like embers, arms outstretched. Flames danced around her, but they did not touch her.

She *commanded* them.

Flames rose behind her like wings, molten and furious. Her arms lifted, as if bringing judgment upon the sky itself.

Ren stood on the edge of a cliff, with a great chasm separating them, her bare feet skimming cracked stone. The air blistered with heat. Above, the creatures circled, impossibly vast, scaled wings beating, their eyes gleaming like simmering stars.

One of the massive winged creatures swooped low, the irises of its eyes gleaming brightly like the sun.

And then, the woman turned.

The woman's eyes, gilded with age and rimmed in smoke, snared Ren like a hook..

A voice rose in Ren's skull.

"You are the spark that remembers."

The woman's mouth parted to speak. But the words weren't spoken; each syllable burned into Ren's bones.

"Fire chooses the worthy."

The flames surged. Ren's skin split with heat, the world convulsing in a roar of gold and red. Her mouth opened in a scream that caught fire in her throat. She was burning, *truly* burning. The ground blazed to life beneath her feet, and the woman raised her hand.

Ren reached back, half in plea, half in desperation.

The moment their fingers nearly touched, Ren woke up choking, drenched in sweat, with the musky scent of smoke on her tongue.

And somewhere deep in the darkness, a whisper echoed:

"Wake, Flamebearer."

A snore rumbled beside Ren, and she blinked away the dark haze of sleep to find Elira muttering in her dreams. "...no, you can't train chickens to march......if anyone touches my honey cakes, I'll throttle them..."

They lay curled in their makeshift cots beneath the sweeping canopy of a massive willow tree. The cool morning air clung to Ren's skin, yet her body burned with the flush of the strange dream she couldn't shake. No fire crackled beside them; the threat of ogres lurking through the forest had stolen even that small comfort. Instead, they huddled into thin, fur blankets that Sela lent them for the rest of their journey.

But a shadow stretched long across the camp. A figure stood over Ren, arms crossed, cloak rustling in the early morning wind.

Talen.

He watched her with the stillness of a hawk deciding when to strike.

"What a sight to wake up to," Ren muttered, her voice hoarse. Her amber eyes met his with a stubborn flicker of dignity.

A corner of his mouth lifted. "I'm beginning to wonder if anyone ever taught you manners. I am, after all, a prince."

Ren began gathering her things. "A prince for the *fae*. Do I look fae to you?"

He arched his brow. "No, you look like a brutish, stray vagabond someone dragged in from the woods. But I'm feeling generous today."

Ren straightened to her full height. "And I'm feeling like continuing on my merry way and never running into another fae again, but unfortunately for both of us, I'm still chained to this delightful mess we've got."

He gave a soft huff of laughter, the corner of his mouth twitching. "Careful. That attitude might get you into more trouble than you're worth."

"Wouldn't be the first time. Speaking of trouble – what the hell did you do back there to Sela's mother? I felt your magic, so don't deny it."

"My magic…" He paused, as if testing the words. "It lets me see into people's minds when their shields are down. I can reach in, rearrange what's there, erase memories – even create new ones if I choose."

"So, you were in her head."

Talen nodded once. "She was already slipping. I let her see her most precious memories just once more, before she crossed the Veil." His voice softened. "A small mercy. We all knew she was fixing to die."

"That's… *gods*, that's *crazy*," Ren managed. "I need a glass of wine. Or rum. Or both."

Ren shook her head as if to clear it, and stalked toward the trees. Because what else was she supposed to do with that kind of revelation? Ren marched off into the brush, pushing away tree branches, to relieve herself. She lingered a moment, glancing over her shoulder to see if Talen would try to peek, but he was already gathering the blankets, unbothered, as if she hadn't just snapped at him minutes ago.

Normally, a fae – *especially* one with royal blood – would've beaten her senseless for mouthing off like that.

And now Ren knew why.

Ren exhaled slowly, a chill running down her spine as she pulled up her pants. If his magic could slip into someone's mind, twist thoughts, rewrite memories – did he even need to lift a hand to break her? He could reach into her mind and *remake* her without ever laying a hand on her.

She was going to have to be very careful around him.

Once Ren made her way back, a groggy grumble came from Elira's blankets. Elira stirred, rubbing her eyes and swiping her messy bangs from her brow.

Ren asked Elira, "Are you going to Pyraelia?"

"That's where I was headed, until I met a band of fae guards with more ego than brains." Elira heaved a sigh and got to her feet. "I was supposed to start blacksmith training this morning. My master from home sent a recommendation. This was one hell of a delay."

Prince Talen gestured toward the horizon. "Then you're not too late. We'll reach Pyraelia's gates within the hour."

Ren's thoughts flashed to the broken look in Sela's eyes when they left the farmhouse, and her heart squeezed. Even with so little, the younger girl offered them the best she had for their journey, and Ren ran her fingers over the thin fur blankets.

No one moved quickly, their limbs stiff from cold and sleep. Ren folded the furs and caught Talen hesitating, seeming in deep thought.

He spoke with casual calm, but his words cut the morning quiet like a blade, "Your crimes are pardoned."

Ren eyed him warily. "Just like that?"

He shrugged. "You saved my life. That earns you something."

Elira asked, "Do you even have that kind of authority?"

"Does it matter?" Then, as if it were an afterthought, Talen added, "Something's come undone in the outer territories, creatures not seen in centuries or only told in books." He glanced back at Ren. "The realm needs someone who's not afraid of monsters."

Ren should've walked the other way, into the trees, into the silence, and vanished. She could disappear again. She'd done it before – ran, survived, hid from the world that took more than it ever gave.

But something twisted in her chest. A pull, like thread tugging on the edge of an unraveling tapestry.

Talen went on. "These creatures aren't prowling the borders for sport. They're hunting people. Families." His jaw tightened. "*Children.*"

He let the word hang there. "They don't just go for soldiers or seasoned fighters; they go after the weak. They dig out the places people feel safest."

Ren crossed her arms. "Why not ask one of your trained fae soldiers? Surely the crown has no shortage of blades eager to please you."

"Because the fae have trained their whole lives to follow orders," Talen answered. "I can tell you have survived by breaking them."

Her brow furrowed. Although she couldn't deny her suspicion, she was caught off guard by the sincerity lacing his words. Something else lurked in her mind, too – alarm bells. Was this another game or another manipulation from a royal fae who thought himself clever?

But his gaze didn't waver. "I don't need another soldier who doesn't know how to fight when the rules are gone. I'm looking for someone who can do the right thing when hell breaks loose, like it did during the ogre attack. My soldiers scattered. If not for you..." He exhaled sharply through his nose. "More would've died."

Ren scoffed. "You don't know a thing about me," she snapped. "Don't pretend like you do just because you've watched me fight."

"If it's coin you want, it's coin you'll have. Enough to vanish to the edge of the realm, to buy your own castle if that's what suits you. House Vaerlan is salvaging whatever we have to stop these creatures, and if hiring a half-feral mortal with fire in her veins is what it takes, then I'll pay the price."

Elira let off a whistle from where she was leaning against a tree. "Tempting," she drawled, voice lilting with mischief, then shook her head. "It's a shame I forge weapons, I don't swing them."

Ren's gaze narrowed at Talen. "Oh, that's generous. A castle, coin, and all the gratitude of a court that's spent years hunting down my kind. Truly, what mortal girl could resist playing hero for the same bastards who'd burn her at the stake any chance they could?"

Talen's expression sobered. Whatever amusement had lingered on his lips was gone.

"You're right."

"Damn right I am," Ren retorted.

Talen went on, "The court has blood on its hands. People like you have paid the price for generations of cruelty and corruption. I'm not asking you to save the fae – I'm asking you to help fight something worse. If that means tearing apart the old ways to do it, then so be it. You don't owe us your loyalty, Ren."

Ren held his stare a beat longer, searching for the lie, the catch, the trick she was sure would be there.

But Talen didn't flinch.

"You'll have it. Everything I promised. That's not a bribe. It's a vow." Talen lifted his hand, palm open, as if swearing before a court. His voice carried conviction. "House Vaelaran always keeps its promises."

The words landed like steel in the silence between them.

For a flicker of a moment, Ren let herself imagine it.

Not war. Not smoke. But *sky*. A ship rocking beneath her feet, the wind salty-sweet and tangled in her hair. New lands, maybe a quiet life by the sea – far from courts and the bullshit of the fae.

Sure, she had enough coin now to leave Lytharien. But what then? She'd have to start over at a new town, earn more coin, and find somewhere to stay. It would take a while to save enough to find somewhere permanent.

On the other hand, if Ren played her cards right, she could finally settle down and start something of her own – *a flat or a cottage* – a place where she wasn't constantly looking over her shoulder.

The thought lodged deep in her chest, sharp enough to feel *real*.

Ren glanced over her shoulder, jaw tight. "If I say yes, I'm not following you, I'm not bowing, I'm not swearing some royal oath, I sure as hell won't be anyone's puppet, and you won't ever do those mind tricks on me. If you do, I'll leave." Ren thought for a moment, then added, "*With* my payment."

Talen's mouth curved into a grin that was equal parts amused and impressed. "Smart girl. Drawing the rules out before the deal's even struck." He tilted his head, thumb brushing his lower lip, studying her like she was both a challenge and a puzzle he intended to solve. "Fine. If I break any of those, our bargain's forfeit." He straightened, resolve settling in his shoulders. "At court, you'll have my protection. You'll be an honored guest. And if by some cruel twist, you die facing those monsters, I'll make sure a talented bard writes an epic ballad about your bravery. Tragic ending, soaring chorus – all the works."

Ren closed the space between them, offering her hand to seal the deal. "I'll come. But not for you, and especially not for this kingdom. For the coin, and," her voice softened, "for the ones who'll be defenseless when those creatures strike."

After he gripped her hand with a firm a shake, she added, "I'm not afraid of monsters."

As she shoved past him, clipping his shoulder to deliver her point, she swore she caught the smallest flicker of relief in his eyes.

"I didn't think you were," Talen drawled.

Together, all three of them walked. Elira yawned. Ren's stomach twisted on itself, too hollow to growl. When was the last time she ate

– yesterday morning? She vaguely recalled eating a stale loaf of bread yesterday morning that was hard enough to chip a tooth.

Talen fell in step beside Ren. "You fight like someone trained."

Ren didn't look at him. "Maybe I've been in a few brawls."

"A few brawls don't teach that kind of fire. Even for our kind, using that level of magic can take years to master."

Ren's expression didn't waver, but her tone was sweet enough to sting. "You don't know squat about me, and what does it matter if I use magic so long as I can slay your monsters?"

"Just curious where your fire comes from. It's... rare for a human."

"Mm." Ren gave a dismissive wave, taking longer strides to saunter ahead of him. "I'm starving, so unless you want to find out how cranky I can get, let's save the questions until we reach Pyraelia and I get a bite to eat. Then, *maybe* we can talk."

Talen muttered under his breath, "Saints forbid the monsters face you on an empty stomach."

Ren chuckled low. "Guess that makes me the real danger out here, doesn't it?"

She didn't know what Talen had seen.

While Talen was freeing the prisoners from their chains in the wagon ahead, he'd felt the heat rising like a living, breathing thing. In an instant, he'd vanished back into his own wagon, its wards repelling magic with ruthless precision.

There, Talen watched the human woman turn the forest into a living inferno.

He had seen it all from behind the smoldering wreckage of the carriage, eyes slitted against the searing light, breath held as fire swept like a tidal wave.

And he'd seen the wings.

Not crafted of feathers, nor conjured in illusion, but raw, radiant fire – arching from her back with terrifying majesty. With each of her movements, the flames had curled and pulsed, echoing her rage.

And in that single heartbeat, when she'd turned, face rimmed in flame, eyes glowing with wrath, they looked like judgment made into flesh.

Talen caught the fear on the ogress's face before she'd been turned to cinder. A creature of brutality, bred for slaughter, and yet she'd *frozen* when she, too, noticed the wings.

And now the forest feared her, too. He noticed how the trees no longer creaked when she walked beneath their branches, how birds quieted – how even the insects avoided her steps as if they sensed something amiss.

Ren hadn't seemed to notice. But Talen did.

She walked like someone used to surviving. There was recklessness in her, too. The kind born not from ignorance, but from someone who knew what power lived beneath her skin and hadn't yet learned what it could cost.

Talen watched her sidelong during their conversations, her silence too deliberate, her deflections too smooth. She was clearly hiding something, but hunger gnawed at her all the same. He knew what that kind of hunger did to a person. The prisoners meant for execution were supposed to be fed sparingly, a final comfort before the end. But he'd seen how the fae soldiers perverted the mercy, dangling food within reach, laughing as the condemned could only watch with their moldy, stale bread and crumbles of whatever resembled cheese.

He'd already decided that would end the moment he returned to Pyraelia.

One thing he knew for certain. Ren was a weapon.

Among the fae, magic was almost second nature, a birthright that revealed itself when they were still younglings, wild and untempered. But humans weren't meant to wield magic. At best, they spent their brief lives studying spells and tracing runes, learning fragments of power borrowed from older tongues. Most never managed more than sparks or whispers.

Yet Ren commanded fire. The flames didn't just obey her; they *knew* her. Perhaps recognizing something ancient in her bones.

He watched her now, laughing at something the blacksmith woman had said, her breath fogging in the cold morning air. Ren smiled easily, unguarded. But Talen had seen the way her eyes sharpened and how her stance shifted when sensing a movement from the corner of her eye, quickly assessing whether it was dangerous or harmless.

Yes, surely the game had already begun.

And Ren had just stepped onto the board.

By the time the walls of Pyraelia came into view, the journey had drained every last ounce of strength from Ren. Just days ago, she'd been certain she'd never see another town again. Yet here she was, breathing, walking, *alive*.

The thought felt unreal.

Soot clung to her skin in a thin, grimy layer, and sweat had long since plastered her hair to her temples and the back of her neck. Each step felt heavier than the last, her boots coated in dust.

Ren wasn't sure if it was her near-hysterical stupor or sheer disbelief, but the sight of Pyraelia gate's took her breath away. Carved from dark obsidian, the gates were flanked by steel-winged sentinels that watched Ren's every step. Beyond them, Pyraelia unfolded in layers of marble and cypress. Spires rose against the midmorning sky, their tips shimmering with mosaic glass.

Pyraelia had little land to spare, so it had grown upward instead. Buildings stacked on buildings, their spires and balconies entwined. For someone used to the squat villages of the western region, the scale was dizzying.

They wound through streets where opulence danced hand in hand with vice; velvet-curtained windows spilled lively music onto slick cobbles, and laughter rolled out of open doorways. One doorway caught

Ren's eye – marked by a tarnished brass plaque reading *Shades of Love*, Ren wasn't sure if it was an inn, a tavern, or a shop that promised indulgences best left to imagination.

As they passed the open doorway, Ren caught a glimpse of a female fae meticulously choosing between two colors of silks and an ever eager merchant giving her suggestions. "You've got the kind of figure that deserves to be celebrated, not hidden. *This* one would flatter a voluptuous shape. It clings in all the right places and drapes in all the wrong ones, darling."

Ren hadn't realized she had paused to stare until two pairs of eyes fell on her. Ren's cheeks went hot.

Before Ren could muster a response, the merchant chuckled softly and crooned. "Ah, I see. The bashful sort. Don't worry, dear – curiosity isn't a sin here. Come now, try one. We have every color, and the best silk in Pyraelia." The merchant's eyes assessed Ren's figure from top to bottom, lingering on Ren's hips. "A body like yours deserves something daring, perhaps ember silk. It tends to slip off *very* easily."

Ren nearly choked. "I-I think I'll pass," she muttered. She ducked away and hurried to catch up to Talen and Elira.

Around the corner was a tavern. A fae male lounged in the doorway, simmering lazy grace and mischief, his shirt half-unbuttoned to reveal the gleam of skin. His gaze fell on Talen, and his mouth curved in a wicked smile. He shot Talen a wink as if saying *looking for trouble or hoping it finds you?*

Talen's jaw stiffened, and a quick flare of color crossed his cheekbones before he strode away.

They rounded the next corner and came upon a vendor tucked against a stone wall. Wooden tables lined the courtyard where fae drank glasses of wine and ate, the air rich with the scent of roasted nuts and spiced bread. Behind the merchant's table, Ren's mouth watered when her eyes drank in the food laid out in neat rows – honeyed dates and figs nestled among plump grapes and bowls of walnuts dusted with spice and salt. Lastly, loaves of bread were piled alongside porcelain dishes of olive oil.

Talen paused, exchanging a few coins with the vendor before turning back to them. "Go ahead and eat," he said, handing Ren and Elira each a small plate piled with bread, grapes, walnuts, and a few dates. "It's not much, but it'll keep your legs under you."

They found a table tucked beneath a shade of creeping vines. Ren immediately tore off a piece of bread, dipped it into the oil, and groaned. She reached for the grapes next, devouring them one after another until the juice ran down her thumb. Across, Elira did the same, beginning with the walnuts and dates.

Talen returned a moment later, setting down a glass of water. Ren barely managed a breathless, "Thanks," before reaching for it.

"Easy," he said with a faint smile, watching her and Elira eat like starved wolves. "Eat too fast, and you'll both regret it later."

Elira swallowed a mouthful of bread, scowling as she reached for another grape. "You try traveling for days as a prisoner and not shovel everything in sight," she muttered.

They devoured every crumb and scrap, licking the last of the oil from their fingers as if afraid it might go to waste. The vendor's plates were empty before long, the only evidence of their feast a few stray walnut shells and sticky fingertips.

Too soon, all the food was gone. Ren leaned back in her chair, stretching her legs beneath the table.

Ren sighed. "You know," she drawled, eyeing a nearby vendor pouring deep red wine into crystal glasses, "I think a glass of *that* would really seal the meal."

"No," Talen said.

"No?" Ren repeated.

"We're going to the palace," he said simply. "After we show Elira to the forge, of course."

Ren asked, "We're going to the palace to do what, exactly?"

"To present ourselves to the king and queen."

Ren froze mid-stretch, the last of her contentment evaporating. "You're joking."

"Afraid not."

Her stomach gave a low, treacherous churn. "Here's a thought," she muttered, pressing a hand to her middle. "Shouldn't we change first?"

Only then did she glance around and immediately regret it. The fae crowd drifting through the streets looked as though they'd stepped out of a painting: gowns that shimmered, tailored coats gleaming with polished buttons, every strand of hair and fold of fabric immaculate. Ren looked down at her dust-streaked leathers, travel-worn boots, and grime.

Talen adjusted the clasp on his cloak. "It's best not to keep my family waiting. They're not known for their patience. Once we've presented ourselves, you'll have a chance to clean up. I promise."

"Wonderful. Maybe I'll only smell half-dead by the time we get there."

Talen's mouth twitched. "Progress."

They continued deeper into Pyraelia. Ren felt as though she'd crossed through a portal and into another world.

Roses bloomed along the walls and archways. Runic patterns whispered from the cypress, a language Ren couldn't read but instinctively distrusted. Ren was so intent on studying the looming buildings that she didn't notice the horde of rowdy fae barreling down the street until the sound of their raucous laughter broke through her thoughts. They swept past in a flurry of wings, cloaks, and sloshing goblets, and Ren had to sidestep to avoid being bowled over.

She gawked as they passed beneath grand archways built for gods, not mortals. But the awe twisted quickly into something darker as she turned over her shoulder.

Mount Solfira loomed in the distance, its smoke curling skyward like a dark crown over Pyraelia. The sight of it made Ren's jaw tighten. Ren narrowed her eyes, sending the mountain a withering glare – daring it to try and claim her again.

They wove through the bustling square beyond, sidestepping merchants balancing trays of sugared confections and fae dressed in embroidered silks who barely spared them a glance. Few seemed to recognize Talen; he passed among them like just another well-dressed stranger, his presence unnoticed beneath the capital's constant hum of leisure.

Ren's gaze flicked over the faces of the crowd, noting flushed cheeks, bright eyes, laughter spilling freely. It struck her then how far removed Pyraelia felt from the villages they'd passed in the western and southern regions of Lytharien. There were no signs of famine or decay. Perhaps the Witherblight hadn't yet reached this far north.

They stepped into another courtyard where roses spiraled along marble archways, vines curled with lazy elegance, and the air was thick with the scent of melting chocolate and sugar-dusted fruit. Ren nearly stumbled; the beauty was dizzying, decadent, so unlike the hellish climb they had endured to reach the capital.

A female fae sat beside a water fountain just off the center, naked, save for a thin chain draped across her hips and a string of flowers in her hair. She plucked at a silver harp with long, graceful fingers. The melody she played was somehow both soft and sinful.

Her eyes met Ren's mid-note. Her lips curled into a smile.

Ren flushed instantly and looked away, cursing her own reaction. "Is that... normal?" Ren muttered to Elira.

Elira laughed at her side. "Welcome to Pyraelia," she said. "Where beauty is currency and modesty is more myth than law. The city's always been like this, strange and oddly seductive." She nodded toward the harp musician. "They're beautiful here. Every last one of them. But don't let that fool you."

"Why?"

Elira's voice dropped low. "I think she's a siren, and if she asked you to burn the world for her, you'd probably thank her for the chance."

Ren muttered a curse and kept walking, trying not to look again.

She failed.

The harpist continued strumming the harp. The curve of her shoulder, the elegant line of her collarbone, the slope of her waist where the jeweled chain dipped low against her hips – it was art and sin and temptation all at once.

Their eyes met again.

The musician simply held Ren's gaze like it was a secret they shared, a thread stretched tight across the courtyard between them.

Ren inhaled sharply—

And walked straight into Talen's chest.

"Careful, you'll cause a scandal."

Talen stood there, brow arched in amusement, arms crossed like he'd been watching her for longer than he'd like to admit.

Ren scowled. "You could've warned me you were lurking."

"I was enjoying the view," he drawled.

"Are you always this smug, or is it a princely requirement?"

"Only since my exile."

Ren tilted her head, a smirk tugging at her lips. "Speaking of which, what did you do to get banished?"

"I'm sure you've heard plenty of versions already. Most of them exaggerated. Some wildly inventive, although I applaud people's creativity."

Ren arched a brow. "So enlighten me. What's the real story, then?"

Talen shrugged with exaggerated nonchalance. "It involved a royal carriage, a minor explosion, and a somewhat unfortunate misunderstanding with a trade delegation from the Southern Isles."

Ren nearly choked. "Saints, don't tell me – the goat debacle was true?"

That caught him. His expression sharpened, tone suddenly earnest. "The herd had been bred and sold illegally by a court minister. He was pocketing the profits under the guise of 'tribute.' My liberation of the goats was meant to expose his corruption. Of course, the court twisted it to make me look reckless and impulsive instead of him being corrupt. He's since been promoted to Steward." His mouth pressed flat. "They exaggerated the whole thing."

Ren squeezed her lips together, trying not to laugh. "Exaggerated?"

"I only *singed* the carriage," Talen corrected firmly, lowering his voice like he was confessing a sacred truth. "The goats caused the real damage." His gaze flicked to hers. "Did you know goats will try to eat *anything*? Truly, the most disturbing thing I learned that night..." he leaned just slightly closer, lowering his tone, "is how far they'll go to consume things they shouldn't. I'll never look at a cloak the same way again."

"You're telling me the heir of House Vaelaran was nearly outmaneuvered by goats."

"Not nearly," he corrected smoothly, straightening, shoulders rolling back into command once more. "Completely. Let's just say I'm not allowed anywhere near their vineyards anymore." He gestured ahead, as if brushing the topic away. "Now, enough about goats."

Ren shook her head, the edges of her mouth twitching despite herself. "Fae politics sound exhausting."

"They are," he agreed, stepping beside her as they ventured deeper into the city. "Which is why I prefer fire-starting mortals with terrible attitudes and very questionable taste in where to look during a diplomatic walk."

Ren glared.

For a moment, Talen's smirk faded, his gaze drifting over the familiar streets and marble spires rising ahead. "Feels strange," he admitted quietly. "Coming home after so long."

"Strange? You've been gone... what, nine months?"

His mouth curved faintly, but it wasn't the usual sharp-edged smile. "Closer to a year," he said, his tone unreadable.

"And where exactly have you been?" she pressed, watching him sidelong.

"That," Talen replied smoothly, eyes forward once more, "is a story for another day."

As they passed through a lively market of eager vendors trying to sell their items and wares, Ren recalled the whispers she'd heard about House Vaelaran. Rumors claimed they consorted with dreamwalkers and moon spirits, that they bartered with keepers of forbidden lore. Some swore their blood was tainted with something far older than fae, and others told wild tales of their ancestors dancing with ancient magic beneath eclipsed moons.

Talen glanced at her, the faintest glimmer of amusement returning to his expression. "A word of advice, since you'll be meeting my family soon. They're... a little unhinged. Especially my sister. But they're also fiercely loyal and protective, in their own twisted way. If you're honest with them, they may actually like you."

"Comforting."

"You'll survive," he assured with a faint, knowing smile.

The last rays of sunlight vanished behind her as Ren stepped through the towering archway of the palace.

Inside, the air was heavy with the scent of incense, burning myrrh, and something like charred cedar. Shadows stretched across the marble floors, flickering with the dance of distant torchlight.

Ren inhaled slowly, her instincts prickling. She may as well have been walking into sacred grounds.

Or cursed.

Ren's gaze flicked from the courtiers to the high windows, where colored glass caught the sunlight and fractured it into streams of crimson, jade, and gold. One mosaic in particular drew her eye – a sprawling rose garden rendered in painstaking detail, every petal glimmering as though dew clung to it. In the heart of the garden stood a nymph, bare as the day she was born, her body twined with roses that curved tastefully across her hips and breasts, half-concealment, half-display. Her expression was one of languid joy, head tilted back, arms outstretched as though inviting the sun to claim her.

Ren wished that Elira were here beside her. She would have had some irreverent remark about the nymph's pose or the artisans who thought this was what passed for holy beauty. But she wasn't here. Ren recalled the way Elira had clasped her forearm at the forge, soot still clinging to her cheek, bidding her luck before heading off to make her formal introductions.

All of it, beautiful distractions for a palace that would as soon gut you as greet you, Ren mused as she shuffled behind Talen down the hallway.

Ren's feet slowed as they approached the throne room, heart pounding. This place was forged from blood and politics, from the bones of the kingdom's past. The palace itself gleamed like a serpent's skin, admirable in the way a predator was beautiful – precise, honed, *deadly.*

Talen walked ahead with the confidence of someone who had survived its bite before. He shoved the towering oak doors wide, hinges groaning as they swung inward.

Ren followed, but the instant her boots crossed the threshold, she faltered.

The throne room unfurled before her, vast and radiant. Light from high windows spilled over marble floors polished to a mirror sheen, so unforgivingly clean that the mud on her boots felt like a stain on the realm itself. Rows of fae nobles sat along tiered benches flanking the center aisle, and one by one, every head turned. Ren felt the heat rise to her face, suddenly hyper-aware of her traveling leathers – creased, smudged, still faintly smelling of smoke and blood.

Her gaze tipped upward, and she swiftly forgot to breathe.

The ceiling was a world unto itself. Every inch was alive with color, with movement – muscled arms stretching toward the sky, flowing robes, gilded instruments, wings unfolding into flight. There were stories upon stories layered there telling of creation, triumph, sorrow, glory, all woven together in a symphony of brushstrokes.

Ren had heard that the royal artisans of Vaelaran had once devoted decades to painting the ceiling alone, a declaration that beauty conquered over all. She'd thought it was rumor, exaggeration, the kind of thing bards loved to feed wide-eyed villagers by the fire through songs and lyrical ballads.

Yet here it was.

For a heartbeat, Ren forgot the weight of the court, the sting of eyes on her back, even Talen leading her inside. Her entire body stilled, the thrum of her heart lost in the echo of a singular thought: that even in a world so conniving and evil, the fae still demanded art to remind themselves of their divinity.

She clenched her jaw, forcing her gaze back to the here and now. But the paintings lingered in her mind, a reminder of just how far from home she truly was.

On the dais, King Maelion Vaelaran sat on his throne. He was a towering male fae with a presence carved from obsidian itself. His hair streaked silver with age. His eyes were a piercing blue. His angular features were hardened by decades of war and diplomacy, his jaw set with a quiet, commanding strength. A crown wrought from midnight and starlight circled his brow.

Queen Lyra Vaelaran was adorned in jewels that pooled along the swell of her bodice, her earrings glinting as she moved. She watched Talen approach with the look of someone regarding a cracked heirloom. She was a haunting beauty with sun-kissed blonde hair that fell in elegant curls, her eyes a deep amber-gold.

Ren often forgot which fae Houses were known for which branches of magic — there were too many, all tangled in numerous bloodlines — but when her gaze settled on Queen Lyra, the memory surfaced.

House Miraval. A name whispered with both admiration and fear. Their blood was bound to the mind, to illusion and deception, to dreams that bled into waking thought. Some said they could weave false realities, and others claimed the strongest of them could reach into a mind and even turn it against itself.

Ren glanced toward Talen, a flicker of unease tightening her chest. He'd inherited pieces of that power; she'd witnessed it with Sela's dying mother, albeit a mercy. If he could slip between thoughts, rearrange and remake them, then what could Queen Lyra do?

Before Ren could recall the Vaelaran side of magic from King Maelion's ancestry, the third throne caught Ren's attention.

Princess Kaelin sat with one leg draped elegantly over the other, chin resting on her knuckles. Her stature was that of a poised grace of a dancer and the unwavering spine of a warrior; she was a great mixture of the king and queen themselves. Her hair was a rare, arresting blend of pale gold and ashen brown, like sunlight filtering through smoke.

Her eyes were hues of violet, tilted at an angle just a shade too predatory for comfort, depicting her ancient fae heritage. Her skin was pale and smooth, as if she had been carved from alabaster stone. A proud jaw, her father's sharp cheekbones, and her mother's poised elegance made her both breathtaking and unnerving – the kind of beauty that *commanded*, not begged.

Her gown was a deep violet, and silver thread wove through the fabric in thorned patterns. The cut was regal, the bodice sculpted close to her frame, the sleeves flowing into sheer, weightless silk. A crown of obsidian spires sat on her brow, tall and jagged, like rocky mountains reaching for the stars themselves.

There was a stillness to her, a calculated poise that spoke of someone used to being obeyed without question. Ren's stomach coiled tight, her fingers flexing at her sides as if her body sensed a threat her mind hadn't yet named.

Talen knelt before the thrones. Ren hesitated before kneeling behind him, bowing her head. "I have returned," Talen murmured.

There was silence, and then came Queen Lyra's voice. "Clearly."

King Maelion barely inclined his head. "We expected you sooner."

"There were... complications."

King Maelion waved a ring-heavy hand. "Have you come to torch our trade routes again? Or to apologize for defiling a vineyard with livestock and explosives?"

Talen bristled. "I only meant to sabotage *one* barrel."

Maelion arched a single brow.

Talen sighed. "And I've since learned that goats are... not easily contained."

Somewhere behind them, someone coughed to hide a laugh.

But then Talen's tone shifted, more genuine. "I was reckless," he admitted, "and I let my frustration with the court cloud my judgment. Upon returning, I realize now that I weakened us when we couldn't afford it. I take full responsibility for my actions."

There was a beat of silence.

Then Maelion leaned back, folding his hands. "Miracles *do* happen."

Princess Kaelin was the next to move. She descended the steps of the dais slowly.

Her violet eyes fixed solely on Ren.

"You bring us a visitor, brother," Kaelin purred, her gaze sweeping over Ren's wrists, where noticeable welts had formed from shackles when Ren had been carted off for execution. "Do all your companions now come freshly stationed from the butchering block, or is this one special?"

Ren held the princess's gaze, lifting her chin just slightly. Not a bow, not even a nod. Just a quiet, deliberate acknowledgment. And then, she stated softly, "My name is Ren Harper."

The words weren't loud. They didn't need to be. They slipped through the air with the weight of someone used to being dismissed and determined not to be. For a moment, it was as though Ren had drawn a line in the air between them – a challenge.

Kaelin's lips curved into a smile, tilting her head down at her. "Ren," she repeated, as if sampling the word. "A pity. I was hoping for a name far more interesting."

Talen cut in. "We were attacked by a horde of ogres. Ren helped in battle. She saved lives."

Kaelin circled around Ren like a wolf scenting the edge of a hunt. Ren's blood ran cold when the princess disappeared from her right side, the fae's voice coming from directly behind her. "What crime did you commit in our lands, mortal?" she inquired, each syllable dripping with contempt.

"Hardly a crime. I saved a boy from starving," Ren answered.

"Go on," the princess purred. "Enlighten us."

Ren's jaw clenched. "The boy was skin and bone; he could barely stand. He stole a loaf of bread. Your soldiers wanted to take his life for it."

Before the princess could respond, a baritone voice interjected. "Then the guard was out of line."

All eyes turned to the throne.

King Maelion sat forward slightly, his gaze darkened with displeasure. "We do not maim younglings for hunger. Thievery or not. Not under my rule."

The silence that followed was brittle with surprise. Ren's heart pounded because for all the fae games and their cruelty, this moment felt like the ground shifted beneath her feet.

"Lady Ren has agreed to lend her sword to the kingdom's defense," Talen added, his tone even but resolute. "Her skill will be invaluable against the creatures threatening our lands."

Kaelin drifted back into view from Ren's left. Kaelin's gaze burned into her. It was the kind of stare that stripped flesh from bone, assessing every inch. Ren felt like a bug pinned beneath glass. The realization made her jaw tighten. Saints, it pissed her off. So, Ren looked up enough to see Kaelin standing above her.

"A mortal with a sword? How unconventional," Kaelin mused. "I do hope she proves as capable as you say, dear brother. We wouldn't want to waste time and coin on theatrics."

"I've seen her fight," Talen confirmed evenly, but the weight of those words settled over the room like a drawn blade. "She's more than fit to hunt."

A low murmur rippled through the courtiers. Movement from the throne caught Ren's eye. Queen Lyra's lips curved into a sardonic smile. "How quaint," she drawled silkily, swirling the goblet of wine in her hand, yet Lyra's fingers drummed against her goblet, betraying the spark of interest she couldn't quite smother. "Should we call for the court painter now, or wait until she's covered in blood for dramatic effect?"

Her words dripped with mockery, but she let her gaze settle on Ren, her eyes cool, appraising. The smile lingered as she gave a faint nod. "If she fails, it's your reputation, my son."

"Very well, then," Kaelin purred, the faintest smirk gracing her lips. "Our own *little ember*." Then, her eyes narrowed with malice. "Let's see if you last longer than the other mortals who thought they could play at court games. I doubt it."

Her gaze drifted again over Ren, lingering on Ren's ragged red hair, her muddy boots, torn clothing, and dirty cheeks. It was an appraisal and a dismissal in one – the kind of look that said Ren was nothing but a fleeting amusement.

Kaelin turned and ascended the throne once more, like the whole world should kneel beneath her feet.

As the fae princess lowered herself back into her throne, Ren kept her gaze on the floor. But it took every ounce of restraint not to say something out of turn. Instead, she maintained a neutral facade while seething inwardly, *what an absolute royal pain in my ass.*

12

Birdsong drifted through the open window, stirring Ren from sleep. She blinked against the morning light and remembered where she was. She sat up, recalling how she'd stumbled in after the baths last night, barely clean before collapsing into a deep sleep.

The room itself was plain by the standards of Pyraelia. Walls of pale stone, a single wardrobe carved from dark, unadorned wood, and a writing desk that bore only a tarnished candleholder and a half-empty inkpot.

The bed beneath her was an unfamiliar luxury. Thick with layered quilts, the bed was large enough for her to stretch out comfortably. For once in a very long time, she wasn't waking up from a dirt floor, with cold earth pressing into her skin, or in a cheap tavern, drifting in and out of sleep to the laughter of drunkards and the muffled sounds of lovers through thin walls. Here, Ren was wrapped in warmth, her cheek having laid against a pillow that smelled of sun-warmed linen.

Ren let out a slow, reluctant sigh, savoring the sensation as if it were a secret indulgence.

Not bad for a room meant for servants or common fae, she thought wryly, her gaze drifting to the simple silver pitcher and washbasin in the corner, and the low stool set near the window where faint tendrils of ivy crept along the sill.

A soft knock interrupted the quiet, and she fell back into the blankets with a sigh. The gruff voice of a guard at the door meant one thing and one thing only: time to dress for training.

Yesterday, as soon as they stepped out of the throne room, Talen pulled Ren aside and said, "You're quick with a blade, but skill without discipline is a sure way to die."

She'd accused him of being insufferably smug, but he hadn't risen to the bait. Instead, he'd leaned against the doorway, arms crossed, that infuriatingly calm smirk tugging at his mouth.

"Train," he pressed. "Hate me now for saying it, but you'll thank me later."

Ren slipped from the bed reluctantly. She avoided the full-length mirror for as long as she could, but necessity drew her before it.

Her eyes swept over her frame – a thin silhouette carved by hunger and hardship. Her hips jutted sharply, shadows deepened beneath her amber eyes, and her hair hung in tangled, scraggly strands. Her fingers brushed absently over the shrinking curve of her breast, marveling at how even that had withered away. She quickly banished the thought.

The way she looked was the last thing that mattered.

"Well, you're a vision," a voice drawled. "Assuming the vision came from a tavern floor after too much mead."

"Oh, for fuck's sake," Ren hissed, dragging a hand down her face. "Can't I wake up once without someone sneaking up on me?"

The tall wardrobe in the corner creaked, its carved rosewood face splitting into a smile that shimmered with faintly enchanted light. Its handles shifted like eyes narrowing in amusement.

"Oh good, she speaks," the wardrobe murmured breezily. "With very foul language. Your mother would be ashamed."

Ren stammered, "Y-you're *alive*?"

"Enchanted," the wardrobe corrected. "Alive would imply I have to breathe through the stench coming off your boots. My name's Mirella. I manage wardrobes and the occasional existential crisis."

Ren stared in disbelief, then rubbed at her eyes with both hands, as if to check if she was dreaming. "Of course my dresser talks. Why wouldn't it?"

"Now that that is settled, shall we find you something to wear for the day?"

Ren snapped back into action, pulling her nightgown over her head and letting it drop by her feet. She paused, turning away from Mirella. *Can she see?* "I've got it covered. But thank you."

"After seeing your outfit of choice yesterday, you're in desperate need for assistance."

Ren gritted her teeth as she yanked down her pants. "If I'd known I was being judged for my attire, I'd have put on scented oil."

Mirella's door creaked open invitingly. "Too late for that, darling. But lucky for you, I make miracles happen."

Ren tugged on the closest tunic Mirella begrudgingly offered, plain black, simple, but freshly pressed. After, she strapped her boots with quick fingers.

"I'm only going to train," Ren muttered. With a practiced motion, she wove her hair into tight braids, pulling every stray strand from her face. "There's no need to get fancy."

Mirella gave a huff, drawers clacking in disapproval. "Training or not, you could at least pretend you weren't raised by wolves."

"I'm not here to impress anyone."

"Clearly," Mirella replied dryly. "But must you make it so obvious?"

Ren made for the door. "Thanks for the confidence boost."

"Oh, anytime," Mirella called after her sweetly. "Try not to get beaten senseless."

Ren descended the grand staircase, a chill sweeping through her, the palace quiet but for distant footsteps and the soft murmur of handmaidens preparing tea or breakfast.

Outside, the training grounds sprawled beneath a lavender sky, the sun halfway rising over the horizon. The space was immaculate, every flagstone swept clean, the sand of the sparring pits freshly raked into smooth lines. Yet even here, where sweat and steel reigned, beauty had not been forgotten. Marble statues lined the edges depicting warriors captured in eternal motion, their blades poised mid-strike, their faces carved with unyielding resolve. Some were chipped with age, moss creeping into their creases, yet they stood as silent witnesses to every clash of blade and bruising blow that filled this space.

Ren's gaze caught on Mount Solfira looming over Pyraelia, ever present.

Who in all the realms thought it wise to build a capital in the shadow of that beast? she thought bitterly, glaring up at the mountain's jagged peak.

The grounds opened into a leveled expanse of packed earth bordered by tall stone walls and watchtowers, with weapon racks lining the perimeter and target dummies scattered. Fae soldiers stood at attention, their stances sharp, disciplined, almost unnervingly synchronized.

Ren joined the line, settling beside a male fae close to her height with cropped brown hair and steady brown eyes that flicked toward her in silent appraisal. His gaze dropped, and Ren could've sworn she caught the faintest roll of his eyes before he snapped his attention forward again.

She focused her gaze on the figure approaching the front of the line. The commander. Broad-shouldered, silver-cloaked, and radiating an authority that made the air itself still.

He stood tall and lean. Rough and battle-scarred, yet elegant in a way that only the fae could be. His hair was silver-streaked and pulled into a tight knot, and eyes the color of forged steel. A scar curved beneath one eye like a half-moon.

The fae commander paused where Ren stood and watched her with cool detachment, arms folded across his chest.

Ren met his gaze head-on, lifting her chin.

"Five laps. Then, combat forms."

The fae responded immediately. Ren followed, and as she broke into a jog, her feet struck the packed earth in a steady rhythm, heart pounding, lungs clawing for air within minutes. Her muscles burned from the weight of yesterday's bruises, but she didn't slow.

Though she'd never admit it aloud, Talen was right. She needed every drop of sweat, every breath that stung like fire. She needed her body to obey because she needed every fragment of will she possessed to hunt those creatures.

With the other faes' footsteps pounding around her, Ren surged forward, muscles coiled and ready, the world narrowing to the rhythm of her strides.

Beside her, the brown-haired fae male kept pace, too close. Their shoulders nearly brushed with every turn, the space between them charged with unspoken challenge. She pushed ahead, narrowing her eyes. A heartbeat later, he passed her again, silent and steady, as if taunting her with his effortless speed. They traded the lead back and forth, neither willing to relent.

A blur of motion came to her right. A blonde fae male breezed past, far less graceful. But intentionally so. He clipped her shoulder with a nudge that sent her stumbling, barely catching her footing.

The bastard snickered.

Ren swore under her breath and shot him a venomous glare, only for the blonde to glance back and wink, a cocky smirk on his lips.

Oh, she was going to enjoy wiping that smirk clean off his pretty face.

Her breath came ragged, muscles burning with effort, but she pushed onward. Just as her legs threatened to give out, the run ended. She collapsed against a sturdy tree trunk, gasping for breath.

As she regained her breathing and braced herself for the next round, the brunette male fae across the yard shot her a scowl.

"Humans always start strong, full of noise and pride," he drawled, straightening up. "Let's see if you're still standing by sundown, or if you'll be crawling back to whatever mud hole they dragged you out of."

"Is this the part where I'm supposed to be intimidated, or are you just trying to convince yourself?" Ren retorted, leaning against the tree.

He laughed bitterly. "You really think you belong here? You're a mistake waiting to happen."

Ren didn't give him the satisfaction of acknowledging his words. Instead, Ren whistled under her breath and bent to stretch her legs, imagining the bastard's fingers cracking beneath her boot.

From the corner of her eye, two figures entered her line of vision, along the winding path leading from the Royal Gardens. Kaelin, and beside her, another fae female whose mouth was set in the kind of sneer that looked practiced from years of disdain.

Ren forced her jaw tight and looked away, burying herself in the steady rise and fall of her chest.

Kaelin let Esme's chatter drone around her like a persistent gnat as she tipped back the last of her wine.

Elderflower Blanc. One of her favorites. Smooth as silk, kissed with white peach and wild honey, leaving a whisper of spice curling on her tongue. It was the sort of wine that tasted like sunlight bottled in glass.

Esme hadn't stopped talking since they'd left the terrace. Kaelin knew Esme since they were both younglings, back when Esme's idea of amusement was mocking anyone uglier or poorer than herself. Now, she'd traded childish cruelty for polished vanity.

Kaelin regarded her over the rim of her glass, noting her wide, wine-glazed eyes and the gown the color of apricot that left little to the imagination. It clung tight over her hips, scandalously low at the bodice, every inch a declaration that subtlety was for other nobles. A flowered fae noble, as ripe and perfumed as the vineyards they loved to visit.

Marriage was the only war Esme ever intended to win.

"Brightbane," Esme breathed, a dreamy smile curving her lips, her gaze lingering on Lucan Brightbane. The fae heir hailed from the eastern reaches of Lytharien, where the soil breathed richness and the grapes grew fat beneath the warmth of the autumn sun. His family's vineyards alone could fill half the royal cellars.

Kaelin followed Esme's line of sight, more out of habit than interest to watch Lucan shoulder past a smaller figure on the track. The figure stumbled but didn't fall.

Red hair caught the light like a flame.

Kaelin's head tilted, a flicker of recognition sparking through her. The human criminal Talen had seen fit to rescue from the butchering block, though Kaelin could hardly fathom why. Kaelin's lip curled ever so slightly at the memory. The girl had stood in the throne room reeking of sweat and grime, a smudge of dirt streaked like war paint across her cheek. Kaelin had endured every word of the interrogation only by reminding herself she could return to her throne afterward, where the stench of human filth didn't cling to the air.

Esme wrinkled her nose. "What's her name again?"

"Ren Harper," Kaelin answered smoothly, bringing the rim of her glass back to her lips. She took another measured sip, watching the human steady herself, then surge forward with a burst of resolve.

Ren ran alongside the fae soldiers, refusing to yield even as her steps faltered. Kaelin counted three more laps. Ren came in last, chest heaving, cheeks flushed. Kaelin thought she might bend over and vomit all over the training grass.

Esme sighed. "Why did your brother bring her again?"

Kaelin's gaze lingered on the human, noting the defiance in her stance, the spark that refused to dim even as the fae soldiers openly watched her, laughing and trading remarks about how weak she was, making it abundantly clear she didn't belong here.

"That is what I intend to find out. My dear brother sometimes has questionable judgment," Kaelin responded.

Esme laughed. "Sometimes? Have you forgotten the goat debacle?"

Kaelin's smile vanished, her expression darkening. She turned away before Esme could pursue the subject. "Come," she said, her tone clipped. "Let's finish our walk."

Below them, the fae soldiers paired off for sparring, voices raised in challenge. Kaelin's eyes flicked back to the mortal girl standing amidst them, wondering if she was even aware of the looks from the other fae or simply too stubborn to care.

The morning sun had begun its slow climb, gilding the gardens in gold. Esme's voice trilled beside Kaelin, lilting and constant, like a bird that did not understand the beauty of silence.

"Lord Therian might be at the Harvest Gala this year," Esme droned, fanning herself despite the mild air. "And did you see how Commander Ivan looked at me? Honestly, I think he means to court me. Though of course, he's not quite as handsome as Lucan – "

Kaelin made a polite hum of acknowledgment, the sort she'd perfected after years of court banquets and hollow conversation. Her gaze drifted toward the vineyards beyond the palace walls, the neat rows of autumn leaves blazing crimson and gold. Esme's words became a melody she didn't have to listen to.

Just had to tolerate.

" – and if not Virel, then perhaps one of the Brightbane cousins," Esme prattled on. "They've a new estate in the eastern hills, and I heard – *oh*."

The sound escaped Esme like a gasp, and Kaelin followed her gaze to the sparring grounds below.

Ren Harper stood across from one of Lucan's companions, a tall, broad-shouldered fae male with dark hair pulled from his angular features into a topknot. The circle of onlookers gave them room, murmuring in anticipation. The fae lifted his practice blade lazily.

The first clash was swift. Ren's form wasn't elegant, but it was fierce. She struck with precision, ducked when she should have been flattened, and when the fae male summoned a flicker of water from the air, she barely managed to twist away before it struck her shoulder.

Kaelin's lips tightened. Using magic when sparing hand to hang combat was against the rules and generally looked down upon.

"Is he – " Esme began, but Kaelin silenced her with a quiet flick of her hand.

The spar wore on. The fae used his element sparingly, masking it behind sweeps of motion — a splash to blind, a ripple of water to unbalance. Yet every time Ren stumbled, she forced herself upright again.

When he knocked her to one knee, she rose.

When he sent a wave of water slapping across her chest, she staggered but swung again.

It was reckless. It was madness.

It was... relentless.

Kaelin found herself leaning forward. The mortal should have yielded long ago. The match could have ended with just a simple phrase. *Why keep fighting when defeat was inevitable?*

Esme clucked her tongue. "Doesn't she know when to quit?"

Kaelin didn't answer. Her nails pressed into her palm, the cool bite of her rings grounding her as she watched Ren fall again, hard this time. The crowd murmured, a few laughs rippling through them.

Ren pushed up on trembling arms. Her hand slipped, caught, and still she dragged herself upright. The fae male frowned now, irritation cutting through his arrogance. He lunged forward, blade flashing, but Ren met him mid-strike. It wasn't graceful; it wasn't even clean. But it landed against his blade.

For a heartbeat, silence reigned.

Then Ren swayed, her knees buckling. The male caught her out of reflex, muttering something that didn't reach Kaelin's ears before dropping her to the ground.

"Enough," one of the instructors barked. "She yields."

But Ren hadn't spoken. She hadn't said a word.

Her head lolled to the side, eyes half-closed, her lips pale.

Kaelin exhaled slowly as a healer hurried to the mortal's side, hands glowing faintly with restorative magic. Around them, the soldiers began to disperse, some snickering, others shaking their heads.

Esme sighed. "Well, that's one way to embarrass herself."

Kaelin's eyes lingered on the mortal girl, as if some unseen thread held her fast, watching the rise and fall of her chest, the faint tremor in her fingers.

She should have stayed down. She should have yielded.

And yet, something about that sheer, stubborn defiance lodged itself in Kaelin's chest and refused to let go.

Kaelin bristled. "Come," she said to Esme. "We've seen enough."

"Clearly," Esme muttered. "Still, it was nice watching them spar. I do appreciate a good pair of biceps."

As they walked deeper into the gardens, Kaelin found herself glancing back. Just once.

Ren still lay on the sparring grounds, the healer's magic glinting over her skin like dew in sunlight.

The world tilted for Ren. She swayed once, then darkness claimed her.

The darkness barely had time to claim her before she came to. She blinked up at an elderly fae woman, gray hair loose around a face etched with age, and steady gray eyes.

"Easy now," the fae healer murmured. Her hands glowed with soft, green light as she pressed them to Ren's temples, checking her pulse. Over her shoulder, she stated, "She's overexerted, nothing more. Foolish girl."

Ren pushed on her elbows to sit up but paused when the healer shook her head. She uncorked a small vial and poured it into a cup of water. Slices of red fruit drifted in the mix, likely cleverly hiding the bitter tang of whatever draught she'd slipped in.

"Here," the healer coaxed, lifting Ren's head with a surprising gentleness. "Drink this. *Slowly.*"

Ren's lashes fluttered. A groan escaped her, before she obeyed, lips parting as the healer tipped the cup to them. Some of the water spilled down Ren's chin.

"It'll dull the pain," the healer said, smoothing Ren's hair back from her damp forehead. "By the gods, you're lucky you didn't crack your skull," she muttered, slipping an arm behind Ren's shoulders to help her sit upright. "What possessed you to keep fighting when you could barely stand?"

"I was fine," Ren rasped, though the words came out more like a wheeze than conviction.

"Fine?" the healer snorted. She uncorked another vial from her satchel and held it beneath Ren's nose. "Breathe that in. Slowly. That's frostmint; it'll help steady your lungs."

Ren obeyed, grimacing as the sharp scent invaded her nose. "Did I at least – "

"Win? No, but you won a lesson in idiocy."

"He played dirty. He used his magic on me."

The healer pressed another small cup of water into Ren's hands, this one faintly pink. "Drink. All of it." When Ren hesitated, the fae snapped, "That wasn't a suggestion."

Ren bristled, convinced this fae woman could lead an army into battle with that voice alone. She downed the drink before the healer could start issuing any other orders.

"My son was just as stubborn once," the healer muttered, half to herself. "So don't think you're my first."

Ren downed it, wincing as the tartness hit her tongue. The healer watched, arms crossed, until the cup was empty. Then she straightened.

"You're done for the morning. Go stretch over there by the trees while the others finish. And don't so much as *think* about doing another spar until I say so."

Ren gaped, incredulous. "*What*? No, I can keep – "

A sharp smack landed on the back of Ren's head. Ren yelped, eyes widening as the healer muttered something low and quick in a tongue Ren didn't understand, something that sounded equal parts exasperation and curse.

"Off with you, stubborn fool," the healer snapped, flicking her hand toward the edge of the field. "Before I bind you to the ground myself. And don't think I won't."

Begrudgingly, Ren found a towering tree at the edge of the grounds and leaned against it, the rough bark biting into her palms as she began her stretches. Each movement pulled at sore muscles and split her breath into quiet, uneven gasps. Still, she refused to give the watching fae even the satisfaction of seeing her rest.

A few minutes later, once Ren had worked through her stretches and shaken the stiffness from her limbs, movement flickered at the edge of her vision. From her peripheral, she caught sight of Kaelin approaching across the training yard, each step deliberate, unhurried. Ren's stomach tightened as the princess drew closer and closer.

By the time Kaelin's voice cut through the morning hush, Ren's teeth were already gritted. "Good morning, little ember. Come stroll with me."

The group fell away, a ripple of courtiers parting like silk curtains drawn back, leaving only the fae princess standing in the early light.

As Ren stepped forward, a blonde fae male sneered. "Careful, human. Wouldn't want you tripping over your own clumsy feet."

The glare Ren sent him over her shoulder could've frozen fire itself. He just grinned, smug and unbothered.

Ren's jaw tightened, her teeth grinding together. *It's too damn early for her games*, she thought. Still, her feet moved almost of their own accord, drawing her closer to the princess, the defiant set of her shoulders the only protest she could muster.

Kaelin led Ren down a winding path and through an arched doorway that led into the royal gardens.

Ren had never seen grass so green, she thought it was fabricated somehow. Flowerbeds spilled over with vibrant bursts of color. Ren, who had long grown accustomed to the barren fields in the west, had to admit there was something radiant about this place, as though the earth itself breathed with a different kind of life.

Statues of the Gods stood along the path, marble faces worn smooth by centuries of devotion. A few fae knelt before them, their lips moving in hushed prayers, fingers pressing offerings of flower petals or coins into shallow stone bowls. Not far beyond, other fae lounged at tables shaded by curling trellises, sipping tea, their laughter drifting light as the breeze.

Ren's steps slowed despite herself. Could Mount Solfira be the source of this unnatural vibrancy?

Ren's mind wandered back to tavern whispers and old tales of the lore of Solfira. Some said mountains that spewed ash and molten rock were portals between the Veil and the mortal world, where gods could tread when they wished to remind mortals of their dominion. When the gods grew pleased, the mountain slumbered, blessing the land with fertile soil and radiant life. But when angered, the mountain bled molten fire, spewing lava to scourge all it touched.

Kaelin's voice pulled Ren back. "Are you thinking of fleeing the palace walls already?"

Ren arched a brow. "Would you blame me?"

"Between the sickness in the border towns and the monsters, everyone's tense."

"That's why I'm here, apparently. Talen seems to think I'm suited to aid in hunting the creatures."

"Prince Talen," Kaelin was quick to correct.

Ren'slips curling into a wry smirk. "Oh, forgive me. *Prince* Talen."

"A noble task, certainly," Princess Kaelin quipped, easily ignoring Ren's sarcasm. "Admirable, even. I suppose we all must play our part in protecting the realm."

Kaelin's gaze swept over Ren in a single, dismissive pass, lingering no longer than one might glance at a cracked goblet or a dull blade. The faint curl of her lip made it clear.

She found Ren *vastly* boring.

Before Ren could craft a biting retort, the soft patter of feet came sweeping past. Two young fae girls darted along the garden path. Their gowns were simple but light, fluttering as they ran, and flower crowns of violet and gold perched in their hair. One nearly barreled straight into Ren before the other grabbed her hand, tugging her into a twirl as they disappeared between the rose-hedged arches.

Their giggles lingered like faint bells in the breeze.

Kaelin's gaze had not strayed once from Ren. The faintest tilt of her head, a predator's study, as though she were cataloguing every rough edge that set Ren apart from the polished elegance surrounding them.

"And where do you hail from, Ren of…?" Kaelin's voice trailed off, lilting and expectant, her tone the very picture of polite inquiry, save for the faint smirk tugging at her lips. As if she already knew the answer wouldn't be impressive.

"Ironforge."

"Ironforge. Once the crown's jewel for production, before its mines choked on themselves. They say the explosion buried half the town, whole families entombed in fire and stone. Generations gone in a single day." Her tone was casual, as though reciting history, yet the words landed sharp as flint.

Ren forced a shrug. "Didn't stay there long."

But the memories came anyway — how the air always stank of sulfur, acrid and thick, the scent of burning coal stitched into her lungs. The town never breathed clean.

"My father used to be a miner," Ren said. "One day the tunnel caved in and crushed his leg. He couldn't work after that. Guess he was lucky. Some of the men with him never came out at all."

The sound that left her was half-grumble, half-bitter chuckle, a small shield against memories that still stung. Kaelin regarded her in silence.

"Ironforge was a world apart from here," Ren admitted flatly. "Nothing like your polished palace halls. Now, it's a ghost town. Some of the houses still stand. Cabinets are still full of bread and wine that no one's there to eat. Looks like the families just... stepped out one day and never came back."

"And your family?"

Ren's throat tightened, but she forced herself to meet the princess's unyielding violet gaze. "I used to have a sister. They're all gone now. It's just me."

Kaelin inclined her head slightly, a cool acknowledgment, before moving on with the same measured grace.

Somewhere deeper in the training field, the sound of training steel echoed faintly.

Kaelin moved like silk over steel, each step measured, each word carefully chosen. Ren could see it now, the way her hands fluttered just enough to seem delicate, the tilt of her head suggesting curiosity while her eyes stayed narrowed in assessment.

Ren took a moment to drink in Princess Kaelin's appearance. Her gown was a masterpiece of lavender silk, the fabric catching the morning light like liquid moonlight. Delicate embroidery traced roses and thorns along the sleeves and hem, and her golden curls were arranged in flawless waves, pinned back with a gleaming combs.

"How tragic," Kaelin murmured after a few moments of bated silence, though Ren could almost hear the calculation beneath the words. "Family is everything, wouldn't you agree?"

Ren had heard that line before from tavern lords and from conniving merchants. It was never about family.

It was about leverage.

"Family is everything," Ren echoed softly. "But sometimes, the family you choose also makes a difference."

She watched the subtle flicker in Kaelin's eyes, a brief pause in her polished mask, as if she wasn't used to someone matching her step for step. Ren's gaze drifted, not toward Kaelin's face, but to her hands, the delicate rings glinting in the sunlight.

"Some say blood is thicker than loyalty. And you, Princess?" Ren asked, voice deceptively light. "Do you believe that?"

For a moment, the only sound was the whisper of leaves stirring in the breeze. They rounded the corner of a marble fountain, water spilling in soft cascades that caught the afternoon light.

Kaelin's lips curled into a very unpleasant scowl that marred her otherwise delicate features. "I believe loyalty is a rare and precious thing. But blood is inescapable."

For a moment, neither of them spoke, the silence weighted with things unspoken. A nightingale trilled from a high branch.

"Training like a soldier, or a pit fighter?" Kaelin's abrupt voice curled with mockery as her eyes flicked to Ren's tightly braided hair, a style common among the pit fighters, worn for both practicality and pride. "Though I am certain the arena is far less forgiving than these soft palace grounds. It's always the mortals, isn't it? So eager to bleed for sport, to claw and bite over scraps like feral animals. Tell me, do you all pride yourselves on being so marvelously uncivilized, or is it simply bred into you?"

The words dripped like honey laced with poison, meant to sting. Ren's breath hissed between her teeth, but she held her ground, her eyes narrowing as she stepped forward, the tightness in her chest unfurling into something molten and sharp.

"I fight because sometimes, when the world gives you nothing, the only thing left to do is fight," Ren asserted, her voice steady and firm.

Kaelin's smile faltered for a moment, just enough for Ren to catch. But then the mask smoothed back into place, and Kaelin's lips curved again. "Fighter pits have their uses, but some battles require more subtle blades. You fight like a gladiator. All flame and fury, as if you think the world will bow to brute force alone." She let the words linger, her tone light, almost amused, but her eyes gleamed. "I suppose that's the difference between a fighter and a strategist."

Ren met Kaelin's gaze without flinching. "Or maybe it's the difference between someone who's been in the ring, and someone who's only ever watched from the stands." The weight behind Ren's words was unmistakable — another subtle pushback.

Another challenge.

And for a heartbeat, Ren thought she saw it in the subtle tightening of Kaelin's clasped hands. Not amusement, but the faintest hint of something sharper. *Recognition.*

But that recognition turned sour, as if the fae princess remembered who she was talking to, and she abruptly turned, as if cutting off both the conversation and Ren's subtle challenge.

"Then perhaps you should've stayed in the ring where you belong – covered in dirt instead of pretending you're worth my time."

"It's a good thing my worth isn't something *you* get to decide."

"No? The world doesn't seem to agree with you."

Ren's jaw tightened. She felt the heat rise in her chest, a low burn of irritation she couldn't quite swallow. *How in the hell was this creature related to Talen?*

"You talk about worth," Ren spat. "Go live your perfect, pampered life, Princess. Let others fight and die to keep your throne polished. I hope it's sparkly clean – "

The world flipped before she could finish. Kaelin moved so fast Ren hadn't even seen her – just a blur of motion, before her back slammed into the dirt, breath torn from her lungs.

The princess crouched low, pinning Ren with a forearm braced across her collarbone, their faces *inches* apart, so close Ren could smell the faint sweetness of wine on her breath.

"Careful what you wish for, *mortal*," Kaelin murmured, her breath brushing Ren's cheek. "Keep mouthing off like that, and someone might make sure you choke on that dirt you love so much."

Ren snarled, trying to get up, but Kaelin's strength surprised her. "Oh, I'm shaking. Tell me again how polished your throne is while others do the scrubbing. You probably even have handmaidens who wipe your own *ass*."

"You think I'm bluffing?" Kaelin retorted. "Do you know how easy it would be to end you here and now? A flick of my wrist, and you're gone before you even understand what struck you. Humans are brittle things; pathetic, really, compared to what we are. It's foolish to mouth off as if you stood on the same step as me." Kaelin leaned down to murmur into Ren's ear, "You're not my equal, Ren. Not by a long measure." As she spoke, Kaelin's fingers brushed a loose strand of hair from Ren's forehead with almost tender precision.

Ren jerked away. "*Fucking hell,* don't touch me."

Kaelin only smiled. Then she rose in one smooth motion, the air seeming to shift with her departure, leaving Ren sprawled in the dirt and burning with fury.

Thump. Thump. Thump.
The sound came steady, rhythmic, like a heartbeat echoing through the brittle bones of the house.

The boy stirred, lashes fluttering in the pale hush before dawn. Hunger gnawed at his insides, a dull, familiar ache. He hadn't eaten since midday yesterday. Stale bread and crumbling cheese, barely enough to fill a palm. For dinner, only broth. Water, really, with the memory of vegetables.

Thump. Thump. Thump.

His stomach gave a hollow growl in reply.

He kicked off the threadbare cloth tangled around his feet, no thicker than gauze, hardly worthy of the name 'blanket' and sat up. Beyond the warped windowpane, a rooster's call broke the silence, distant and strange, like a sound from another life.

Then—

A cry.

From downstairs.

Not loud. Not shrill. But sharp enough to cut through the fog of sleep.

He was already moving, shoving his cap over his unruly curls, heart thundering to a tune too fast, too wild. The narrow stairs creaked beneath his bare feet as he flew down, nearly stumbling on the final step.

And then the world stopped.

His mother, crumpled on the floor, weeping with her face in her hands.

His father, pale and hollow-eyed, standing frozen.

And his sister...

She stood by the wall—no, pressed to it. Her head thudded against the wood. Again. And again.

Thump. Thump. Thump.

Blood streaked her temple, soaking through her nightdress in slow, red rivulets. Her skin had turned a ghastly gray. Dead-leaf gray.

The boy didn't need to ask.

The illness.

It had found them.

A guttural sob tore from his mother's throat. "How could the gods forsake us like this?"

Darkness fell.

A board of wood slammed across the window from the outside.

Then another.

And another.

BANG.

BANG.

BANG.

"No!" his father roared, voice ragged with something the boy had never heard before.

Real fear. "My boy's not sick. Please, he's not—"

From beyond the wall came a cold voice: "The Veil is sealed. None shall pass."

Steel on wood. Hammers striking home. Each blow a nail in their coffin. The boy trembled. "Pa... they're not really going to leave us here, are they?"

He waited for a smile, a soft hand on his head, a gentle lie. Something. *Anything.*

But his father only looked away.

"I'm sorry, my son," he whispered, and turned to pull his sister from the wall. She shrieked, inhuman and feral, and slashed at him with clawed fingers. He caught her wrist just before her nails could score his cheek.

His mother had gone quiet.

And then she began murmuring something beneath her breath, something the boy only half remembered, yet the words stirred deep in his chest, like a sleeping ember.

"Ash to air, wing to flame,
Guard the lost, forget no name.
Though bound and broken we remain...
Let the last flame wake again."

He remembered now. His mother used to say these words when they passed the scorched ruins of their neighbors' homes. When the smoke still clung to the wind and the ash scattered like black snow.

His lips moved without thinking, joining hers.

"May flame find kin, and stone remember..."

Again they whispered it, a litany against the horror creeping in. His mother pulled him into her arms, kissed the crown of his curls, and pressed his face to her chest.

"Ash to air, wing to flame..."

The heat came first, radiating from the floorboards. Then the smoke, thick and choking.

The house groaned.

The fire had come for them.

"Guard the lost, forget no name..."

It moved faster than anything he could have imagined. Like it knew. Like it wanted them.

Like it had always been waiting.

"Though bound and broken we remain..."

Flames danced across the ceiling, hungry and bright. The boards groaned. His sister shrieked. His father held her tighter.

And his mother just rocked him, whispering the final line into his hair as the world turned to cinder.

"Let the last flame wake again."

And in the end, there was no pain.

Only heat.

Only light.

Only the quiet, terrible beauty of the fire that claimed them all.

B y the time Talen reached the council chamber, the treasurer's voice was already echoing down the corridor.

The double doors slammed open hard against the wall. Talen winced. He hadn't meant to put *that* much force behind it.

"Your Highness," Sir Reginald, one of Talen's tutors as a boy who recently became councilor, exclaimed, half-rose from his chair. The older man's sigh was long-suffering, but there was a flicker of fondness in his weary eyes. Glad to see the prince heir returned home at last. "By the gods, must you always enter as though storming a battlefield?"

Talen's mouth curved. "Old habits, Sir Reginald." He cleared his throat, addressing the others in the room. "Apologies, I was detained by Lady Merren insisting her cat requires a personal guard. Apparently, 'budget cuts' mean the palace can no longer afford feline security."

A ripple of stifled laughter moved around the table that was quickly silenced when the king's glare cut through it.

The chamber itself felt cavernous this afternoon, the torches throwing uneasy shadows across an expanse of polished oak. Nobles, generals, and advisors ringed the table like vultures around a carcass. At the head sat Kaelin, poised and composed beside King Maelion.

"So good of you to join us," the king said flatly. "Lord Thaddeus was just beginning the treasury report."

Talen inclined his head, stepping around the table until he came to sit next to Kaelin's chair. She didn't so much as glance at him, her focus sharp on the treasurer who cleared his throat.

"Continue," Kaelin prompted.

Lord Thaddeus bent over his parchment, the quill trembling faintly between his fingers. "A deficit of twelve thousand crowns this quarter, due to the continued suppression of the human uprisings in the western villages. The reagents for the Verdant Elixir remain volatile in price." He paused, dabbing sweat from his brow. "However, Your Graces, prison expenditures have declined notably since the restructuring. Reduced rations, consolidated guards resulting in an overall efficiency. Fewer mouths, fewer coins, as they say."

Talen's head snapped up. "Efficiency?".

Lord Thaddeus' quill stilled. Talen felt his father's gaze bore into his.

Talen straightened. "If you call efficiency starving prisoners with moldy bread and beating them bloody in their chains, then yes, your numbers are thriving." He tossed a parchment onto the table that he produced from his coat pocket. "I rode with the last convoy to Pyraelia. I saw what this *restructuring* looks like. I also saw humans condemned to death for stealing something as insignificant as a loaf of bread."

A murmur rippled through the council.

Talen continued. "We were given dominion over humans to serve them as subjects of this realm. This is not justice, and it is not what the gods would want of us."

Talen's eyes cut toward the king, then Kaelin. "I have names," he said quietly, gesturing to the sealed parchment laying on the table. "Of the guards who took it upon themselves to twist the crown's law into cruelty. They should be brought to question and be held accountable for their misuse of power."

Kaelin's gaze lingered on him long enough for the others to shift in their seats. "There is merit in what Prince Talen proposes," she said. "Rebuilding the prison system would not only reflect better on the crown's reputation among the lower provinces, but it could also improve productivity. This may add some cost at the start – more fresh food, cleaner water, medical oversight, but the long-term benefits would far outweigh the expense. Healthier prisoners live longer. They work longer. The mines and forges would benefit from that alone."

She leaned back slightly, eyes sweeping the council. "If the western mines resume full capacity, our silver production increases – more coin, more trade, more raw material for both jewelry and the royal armory. The treasury stands to gain in the long run."

Kaelin's tone shifted. "And while we're on the matter of expenses, executions drain more from the treasury than most care to admit. The distance to the execution blocks, the transport, the soldiers required to oversee each journey — even the rations needed to keep the prisoners alive until the day they're killed — all of it adds up." She folded her hands neatly on the table. "It would be far more cost-effective to reduce the number of prisoners sent to execution altogether and reassign them to labor camps. Let them serve their sentence productively. Fewer deaths, fewer wasted resources — greater return for the crown."

A few councilors exchanged uneasy glances, but Kaelin's expression didn't waver. Talen watched her in silence. Kaelin's persuasion was a weapon she wielded better than any blade. Appealing to their purses had always been her strength; mercy wrapped in profit was the only language this council would ever heed.

And she knew it.

"Either way, it must go to a vote," Kaelin said. "Per council protocol, a majority must agree before any reform can be enacted."

Her eyes swept the chamber – ten in total.

Talen's jaw flexed as he drew in a breath. "Then, let's have it."

He looked to each of them in turn, from lords draped in fur, generals with silvered armor, clerks with ink-stained fingers. Men and women who'd never smelled a prison corridor, who spoke of human lives in ledgers and coin counts.

"Those who would reconsider the reconstruction," Talen said, his voice even but tight with restraint.

For a moment, no one moved. Then, Kaelin raised her hand. Her chin lifted, eyes still locked on him. King Maelion's hand followed, though his expression was unreadable, a flicker of calculation behind his calm mask.

Sir Reginald lifted his trembling hand. His mouth curved into a faint, proud smile — one that belonged in the memory of a classroom. Talen's chest tightened. He could almost hear Reginald's voice as it had been years ago, warm and steady as he corrected a boy too quick to temper and too slow to think.

"Strength without mercy is merely tyranny, my prince. A good ruler knows when to raise the sword and when to stay the hand."

Three hands raised.

Seven stayed still.

The numbers spoke for themselves.

"So noted," Kaelin said coolly, lowering her hand. "The majority has spoken. The current structure remains."

There was the scrape of a quill, the shifting of ledgers – someone coughed.

And the meeting moved on to the next subject.

But Talen barely heard the next line of discussion. The words blurred into static—grain tariffs, bridge repairs, trade routes. His pulse drummed in his ears, his mind circling back to the convoy, to the hollow faces behind the iron bars. Whispering prayers to the gods, mothers rocking their children who wept out of hunger.

"I'll handle it myself," Talen said.

Every head turned.

"I will personally oversee the reconstruction of the western prisons. Whatever costs it takes to do it properly, I'll pay out of my own funds."

Lord Thaddeus blinked. "Your Highness, surely that's unnecessary –
"

"If this council won't act, I will." Talen said, his gaze sweeping the room once more before landing on Kaelin.

A dangerous silence followed. The king's expression darkened in warning.

Still, Talen didn't look away.

And when the treasurer finally stammered back into his notes, the torchlight caught on the prince's hand, still clenched, knuckles white.

As if he were holding the weight of the entire realm in his palm.

16

R en's boots echoed through the halls of the palace.
She could still hear Kaelin's infuriating voice rattling around her skull like a wasp in a bottle.

She needed *out*. Not more training, not more lectures from the fae guard commander, Ivan, or silent glares from fae who regarded her like she was dirt tracked across their polished floors.

Ren wasn't surprised. That barely concealed contempt came as naturally to them as breathing. But it was annoying all the same.

She let the weight of their stares roll off her shoulders, though the effort cost her more than she'd admit. Gods, Ren wished she could be far from this suffocating place, somewhere on a ship, with salt spray in her hair, heading for some nameless coastal village where nobody knew her name and nobody cared enough to look twice.

But that was a dream. She had to remind herself to take this day by day, to choke down the bitterness and endure. This was temporary. It *had* to be. Still, when would she hunt her first creature? Talen hadn't said a word about it. She hoped it would be sooner rather than later; maybe she could pry the details out of Talen before long.

A grim reminder, too, of why she trusted no one because trust was just another word for giving someone a blade and daring them not to use it when your back was turned the other way.

Ren paused as she came to the stables. The soft whicker of restless horses came between wooden walls, and the golden light of sunset spilled in through the wide barn doors, casting everything in a warm, honeyed glow. A bronze-haired wood elf mucked out one of the stalls, raking fresh dung into a bucket. Like most of his kind, he carried the lean build of one shaped by forests and long days beneath the boughs.

The wood elves were a fae bound to nature, their homes hidden within living trees or caves. Renowned as archers, hunters, and druids, they thrived on agility, stealth, and harmony with the land. It was a sharp contrast to the high elves of Vaelaran. Where wood elves bent to the rhythm of untamed forests, high elves flourished in rigid order – structured courts, sophisticated traditions, and a court law to keep its subjects in obedience.

Two fae races born of the same root, but shaped into entirely different worlds.

Relief stirred in Ren's chest when her gaze landed on a familiar figure. Elira leaned against a wooden beam, her long crimson coat half-unbuttoned, a flask dangling from her gloved fingers. She sipped lazily from it, her eyes fixed on the fading sun like she hadn't a care in the godsdamned world.

Ren didn't know Elira well, not really. But in a place where every glance felt like a warning and every smile a trap, Elira was the closest thing she had to solid ground. Maybe it was the sarcasm, or the way she never looked surprised when Ren spoke her mind.

"Didn't realize I needed a familiar face until I saw yours."

Elira turned, and recognition lit her features. She raised a brow at the sour look on Ren's face. "Let me guess. You met the royal family?"

"Said three words and managed to piss me off with all of them. I need a drink. Or some chocolate."

Elira gave a weak laugh. "If it makes you feel better, I'm sure I've managed to annoy at least half those at the forge without even trying."

"Join the club. Membership includes cheap wine."

A slow grin spread across Elira's face. "Lucky for you, I know just the places. Vaelaran has a *chocolate* district."

"You're kidding."

"Fae don't kid about chocolate." Elira tucked her flask away. "Let me show you what indulgence tastes like in this ridiculous city."

Elira and Ren made their way back through Pyraelia.

Lanterns swung from iron hooks above the streets, their amber glow painting pools of gold over cobblestone slick with fallen leaves. Laughter drifted from every corner, mixed with merchants calling their last sales, minstrels tuning their lutes beside crackling bonfires. Pyraelia was alive in celebration, the autumn harvest nearing its peak; garlands of crimson and orange leaves twined around doorframes, and bundles of grain stood proudly beside every stoop as offerings for the season's bounty.

Children darted through the crowd with sticky hands clutching toffee apples, and somewhere a woman's voice rose in song, carried by the crisp autumn wind.

It was dark by the time Elira and Ren reached the heart of Pyraelia, and the town still hummed with life. Ren stepped through the carved onyx doorway of The Bitter Kiss, and it was like crossing from warmth into temptation.

The air was warm and perfumed with spiced cocoa, roses, and something darker. Candlelight flickered along the walls. Music curled through the room, a mournful violin that sounded like heartbreak dipped in sugar.

Elira shrugged off her coat, her eyes scanning the tables of gossiping nobles and lounging fae.

A massive two-tiered chocolate fountain shimmered at the center of the room, dark and white streams intertwining. Guests dipped fruits and edible jewel-dusted confections into the flowing decadence.

A fae male stood upon a small velvet-draped stage, framed by crimson curtains. His bow danced across the violin with fluid grace, coaxing out a sound that unfurled like shadow at dusk. Hair the color of sunlight on snow spilled over his shoulders in loose waves, and his violet eyes glinted beneath lashes too perfect to be fair.

"Careful," Elira murmured. "You'll fall in love twice in this place. First with the chocolate. Then with the woman who serves it."

That was when Sorrena Vire appeared.

She glided across the floor without sound, as if the shadows themselves parted for her. Her skin was dark and lustrous, a canvas for the cascade of silver curls that spilled down her back, each coil shimmering. She wore a gown of sheer black silk and a veil of the same color, covering her eyes but not her lips.

"Two new souls," Sorrena purred. "What will it be tonight, darlings. Pleasure, memory, or madness?"

Elira leaned one elbow against the velvet-lined table, lips curling into a grin that Ren recognized as trouble dressed in charm. "Why not all three? We'll take the best sampler you have. Three truffles, each laced with your finest magic, and wine to match."

"A brave choice. Or a foolish one. But those are often the best kinds."

Ren raised a brow at Elira as Sorrena glided away. "You've done this before?"

"Once," Elira shrugged. "I lost a bet and nearly married a river spirit. But I woke up in my own bed, so it worked out in the end."

Ren snorted. "That still sounds better than dealing with Kaelin. Gods, she is infuriating. It's like she was born to get under my skin. Always smirking, always knowing exactly what to say to make me want to throw her off a balcony. And of course, she's got the perfect hair, perfect dresses, perfect way of making me feel like a fool every time I open my mouth."

Elira chuckled softly, shaking her head. "At least she notices you. My master tore into me for meddling with one of his forges, and I've been smithing my whole life. But being a woman in a man's world means I get to prove myself three times over before anyone takes me seriously."

"Sounds like we both need a drink."

"Or two," Elira agreed with a rueful smile.

Ren let out a groan, dragging a hand down her face. "How is it only day one, and she's already crawled so far under my skin I can't stop thinking about her?"

Elira tilted her head, a sly smile tugging at her lips. "I hear the princess heir is a sight to behold."

Ren froze for a fraction of a second, frowning as if she could physically swat the thought away. She huffed, crossing her arms. "I mean, sure, the princess would be pretty if you're into that sort of thing. Blondes aren't really my type. And that scowl she gets when she's pissed off? It's like she's eaten something sour. She's really not that much to look at."

Elira's brow arched, amusement sparking in her eyes. "You're getting defensive."

Ren shot her a sharp look. "I'm not defensive."

"Uh-huh," Elira said with a grin. "Relax, I'm only joking."

Ren muttered something under her breath and looked away, but the warmth creeping up her neck betrayed her far more than she'd like.

Before Ren could reply, a female dryad server glided forward. She stood tall and willowy, her moss-green skin kissed with golden undertones. Long tendrils of ivy and willow leaves cascaded over her shoulders, some twisting gently around her arms, others blooming with tiny pale blossoms that hummed with magic.

Ren had only seen one dryad before. A surly male who once chased her out of a glen for stealing fruit and singing off-key when terribly drunk on ale from a nearby tavern. But this one was beautiful in a way that made Ren feel like her voice was too loud and her boots too muddy to be in the same room.

The dryad offered the obsidian tray lined with velvet. Three truffles glistened like jewels, each paired with a crystal glass filled with shimmering wine.

The server gave a small bow and murmured, "Please enjoy."

As the female dryad wandered away, Elira sliced one of the sugared truffles cleanly in half. "Haven't seen a dryad before?"

Ren grumbled under her breath, "I have. Just... not like *her.*"

Elira shot her a knowing look as she reached for her first glass. "Eat slow, sip slower. Fae wine doesn't always play nice with mortal blood."

Ren hesitated, her fingers brushing the glass. Ren raised a brow. "And the truffles?"

"Choose carefully. They don't just taste sweet; they may show you something. Past, future, truth... sometimes all three."

The first truffle melted on Ren's tongue like sin wrapped in cocoa. Dark, rich, and spiced with something that warmed her from the inside out. Her breath hitched as a tingling sensation spread through her chest, her thighs, her throat.

Her fingers curled around the glass of wine. The wine had a heady sweetness — the smell of ripe cranberries and wild elderberries. Ren sipped.

And the world loosened.

For a moment, she felt boundless. Like she could kiss a stranger in the middle of the street or scale the palace walls just to feel the stars kiss her skin.

She exhaled sharply. "What is *in* this?"

Elira smirked. "Desire. The *expensive* kind."

The second truffle came in the shape of a curled blossom, elegant and soft at its edges.

Elira gave a low, amused hum. "I recognize that one. It's from Florneira. They say it reveals your greatest love." She popped hers into her mouth without ceremony.

Ren hesitated, then bit.

Her vision tunneled.

There was a flicker of a female silhouette, the image shifting to reveal what looked like a tea room aglow with sunlight flickering through jaded glass, its windows dripping with rain, the world outside muffled. Steam curled between porcelain cups, but it was the female's breath Ren tasted, hot, uneven, *too close*.

Their bodies tangled on a bench, the female's fingers threading through Ren's hair, tugging as if grounding herself. Ren felt herself climb further into her lap, knees bracketing the female's thighs, their mouths hovering but trembling on the edge of something vast.

A storm of restraint and unashamed wanting.

The female voice whispered something Ren couldn't make out, then their lips met.

And the vision shattered like glass.

Ren cursed under her breath, the image warping as she blinked back into the present. What in the seven hells was that supposed to mean? *A kiss?* As if she had time for that nonsense. It had been years since she'd been intimate with someone. A barmaiden with dry wit and a smile that could halt an entire tavern mid-rowdy song. Their fling had burned fast, brief, and bright, but sometimes, Ren still caught herself missing the warmth of it.

Ren almost laughed at the absurdity of her, tangled up in visions of romance.

Ridiculous.

"Gods," Ren muttered, shoving the empty truffle wrapper away like it had betrayed her.

"Not who you expected? Or worse?"

"That was more like a *nightmare.*"

"Then maybe it was one of those 'deepest fear' ones. Who knows?" Elira winked and sipped her second glass. "I may have gotten them confused."

Ren didn't respond. Her heart was still racing, and not entirely from the sugar.

Elira's laughter faded as she toyed with the corner of a folded napkin, twisting the fabric absently between her fingers. The candlelight flickered across her face, casting flickers of shadow beneath her eyes.

Ren asked, "What did yours show?"

Elira shrugged, too quickly. "Nothing. I've tried that one before," Elira traced the rim of her glass with her finger. "Same thing. Just a void." She looked at Ren and smiled, but it didn't quite reach her eyes. "Guess the truffle knows what I already do. Not everyone gets a love story."

Ren leaned back in her chair. "Maybe not. But I've found those tend to end with someone getting stabbed or backstabbed anyway. Who needs love?"

Elira plucked the last truffle from the plate, turning it between her fingers before slicing it neatly in half. "Well said. Shall we gamble again?"

Ren raised a brow. "After the last one? You first."

Elira smirked and popped her half into her mouth, chewing thoughtfully. A beat passed, then her russet eyes widened. "Oh," she said, except it wasn't her voice.

It was *Ren's* voice.

Ren froze, staring for a heartbeat before a smile ghosted across her lips. On impulse, she popped the truffle into her mouth, the shell giving way with a soft crack, rich chocolate melting over her tongue. "You're kidding me," she said slowly, only to hear Elira's lower, huskier voice come from her own mouth.

For a moment, they blinked at each other in stunned silence. The laughter and music around them seemed to melt into the soft hum of candlelight and clinking glasses.

Elira picked up her glass and took a slow sip of her wine. "Gods, you sound like you're one bad day from murdering someone. Do I always come across this intensely?"

Ren groaned, dropping her head into her hands. "Saints save me. I sound like *that*? No wonder no one likes me."

Elira smirked across the table. "Don't worry. It's growing on me. Must be the enchantments."

"Enchantments?"

"Oh, Ren," Elira drawled, her grin widening, "you didn't think these were *ordinary* confections, did you? Everything here is infused by enchanters. They don't use incantations — too crude for something this delicate. They work with emotion."

Elira gestured toward the counter and Ren followed her gaze, where robed confectioners moved with almost ritualistic precision, stirring caldrons of molten chocolate. "Every step of the process holds a feeling. A touch of joy in the stirring, a whisper of longing in the tempering. The chocolate absorbs it — warmth, intention, memory. Then it gives it to you."

"Gives it how?"

"Depends on the confection. The first truffle we had tonight brought us bodily pleasure. The second showed us a glimpse of love that's to come." She gave a wry smile. "And the last one must've been infused with *mirth*. The chocolatier who made it probably stirred in a little too much joy and mischief — emotions can tangle if they're not balanced just right."

Ren hesitated, eyed the empty plate sitting between them. "You're telling me someone poured feelings into this."

"It's all a suggestion, really. Enchanters are masters at swaying perception. They can make you believe the world's shifted under your feet, when all they've done is *coax* your body into feeling it."

"So it's not real magic?"

"Oh, it's magic," Elira said, swirling her wine. "Just not the prophetic, stars-whispering kind. Enchanters aren't seers; they're artists. They work in illusion, in sensation. The right blend of emotion and craft, and suddenly your heart thinks it's falling in love."

"That's mildly horrifying."

"Mildly?" Elira smirked, leaning back. "If you think chocolate is powerful, just wait until you see what they do when they get their hands on scented oils. One drop of the right enchantment, and a whiff of jasmine can make you forget your own name for an hour. There's a reason half the nobles of Pyraelia spend their fortunes on perfumes. They're not after the smell. They're chasing the *feeling*."

Ren didn't answer. She'd gone quiet, her expression thoughtful. She took a long sip of her wine as if the taste might anchor her. But then she paused. *Is this enchanted, too?*

Elira studied her over the rim of her own glass. "Why do you know so little about magic?"

"Why do *you* know so much?"

"Because where I come from," Elira said, swirling her wine, "ignorance gets you killed. I've seen enchantments used for more than sweets and scented oils," she added, her tone turning dark. "Some mages weave them into weapons."

Ren set her glass down with a soft *clink*, the humor draining from her face. "Weapons?" she echoed, though her voice came out tighter than she meant.

"Oh, yes. I've seen blades that sap the strength right out of you — drain your endurance and fortitude until you can barely lift your arm. Swords that steal magic with a single cut. Even arrows laced with enchantments that slow your steps the moment they strike."

"This sounds like a very creative way to kill someone."

"Come to think of it, enchantment is a kind of magic that is subtler, quieter," Elira said, her voice a low purr now. "It doesn't roar like fire magic or flare like light. It seeps in. You never even notice you've been affected until it's too late."

The words hung between them, soft as the flicker of candlelight, and Ren couldn't help but wonder what else Elira had seen and how she'd survived it.

Then Elira stood abruptly, draining the last of her wine and straightening her jacket. She slipped a few gleaming coins onto the table, enough to cover their meal and a generous tip.

"Let's go give the bards something worth singing about."

K aelin exhaled a slow breath as her handmaiden's fingers threaded through her hair, massaging her scalp.

She had spent the past hour being pinned, laced, and polished for her Name Day celebration, and the only things she looked forward to now were the wine she would drown herself in and these blessed few minutes of silence.

Sera, the new handmaiden, moved with the kind of grace that came from surviving unnoticed. Her russet hair was cropped close to her jaw, a deliberate cut that softened the shape of her slightly pointed ears – marks of her half-fae blood. Too human for the fae, too fae for the humans. Kaelin wondered briefly what it must be like to live always between worlds.

"Which scented oil would Her Highness prefer?"

Kaelin opened her eyes, half-lidded, and arched a brow. "Surprise me."

Sera inclined her head without another word. Blessedly quiet again, she poured warm water over Kaelin's long hair, her fingers gentle as she worked soap through the strands. Kaelin tapped her nails against her knee, eyes flickering across the room when the door opened.

Kaelin's mother's reflection appeared in the gilded mirror first. Queen Lyra's curls were pinned in place, ready to be let down and brushed out, and the kohl lining her eyes and the crimson on her lips were already flawless. She wore her evening robe, the silk sash wound tightly around her thin hips.

"Another year," Lyra murmured, sweeping into the room. "And look at you." She trailed her fingers along Kaelin's shoulder. "Taking after me, thankfully. Your father likes to think himself the clever one, but it's *my* beauty and wit that's endured."

Kaelin's lips curved. "A beauty that terrifies half the court."

"As it should." Lyra took the seat beside her. Kaelin noticed not a goblet of wine in sight, just her mother's steady hands folding in her lap. "It's your Name Day again. That means I owe you another story."

It had become something of a tradition between them. After every Name Day, Lyra would share a story from Kaelin's birth or the long months before it, as though piecing together a mosaic. Last year, she had spoken of how restless Kaelin had been in her womb, always kicking and turning until Lyra rode horseback; only then, lulled by the steady rhythm, had Kaelin grown still.

"I labored for three days with you," Lyra began. "Three days, and your brother sat by your father's side the entire time. He tried teaching Talen chess, but your brother was far too young. So he read to him instead, telling fairy tales of beautiful princesses and mystical beasts slayed by brave knights."

Her voice faltered. The candlelight caught the faint shimmer of tears that did not fall.

"After the second day, the healers grew worried. They told me to turn this way, then that way. I remember the pain like it happened yesterday. I begged the gods for strength. I was ready to let them cut me open, to take you and let me go into the veil if it meant you would live."

Sera's motions slowed, as if she too were listening to a sacred thing. She wrapped Kaelin's hair in a warm towel and eased her upright.

Lyra's gaze never wavered. "When you finally came into this world," she whispered, "your fist was clenched. I'll never forget it. You screamed – so fierce, so *alive*. And I wept with you. *You* were my victory that day."

Lyra reached across the space between them and took Kaelin's hand. "You and your brother are my soul's two halves. Whatever storms come, remember this – you were *born* fighting. You defied every odd before you even took your first breath." Her gaze softened, voice lowering as if confessing a sacred truth. "Whether it was the gods who answered my prayers or your own will that refused to yield, I'll never know. But you fought, my daughter. Even then. *Never* forget that."

Kaelin pressed her lips together, the ache in her throat sharp and sudden. She turned her mother's hand in her own, holding tight.

"I won't," she murmured. "You have my word."

Lyra studied her for a long, quiet moment, her thumb tracing idle circles over Kaelin's knuckles. Then, as if she'd merely been waiting for the right pause to strike, she said, "Tell me, my heart — who will you choose for your first dance tonight?"

Kaelin's hand stilled beneath her mother's.

"I have yet to decide," Kaelin answered at last.

"Oh, but this is important, my love. The first dance sets the tone for how they'll see you – for how they'll see *us*."

Kaelin's jaw tightened.

Her mother tilted her head as if weighing Kaelin's tenseness like a gemstone in her palm. "There's the new mortal in the realm. The one Talen brought in last week."

Kaelin's head snapped up. "*That* girl? She's a rat. Did you not see the way she looked at me in the throne room — with such *insolence*? Every time I speak to her, she mouths off. She's a fool whose mouth runs faster than her small brain. She shouldn't even be allowed at the celebration. In fact," Kaelin lifted her chin. "*I* forbid her attendance. It's my Name Day, after all. I don't see why she needs to be there and not rolling in the mud where she belongs."

Lyra's laughter broke the tension. "Perhaps," she allowed, eyes gleaming with mischief. "But it would look good for the crown to be seen offering such generosity. The court would whisper about your grace instead of your temper for once."

"Maybe I prefer my temper. At least it's honest."

Lyra rose, her silks whispering. She cupped Kaelin's chin, her voice lowering. "Honesty has never ruled kingdoms, my darling. Appearances have." She brushed her thumb along Kaelin's jaw, studying her with a mother's fondness and a queen's scrutiny. "But in the end, it is your choice. My words are merely a suggestion." Her lips curved, the faintest ghost of a smile. "You were born to rule, Kaelin. I only mean to remind you of the game we play."

And with that, she pressed a kiss to Kaelin's forehead – the briefest brush of warmth before retreating into the echoing hush of the corridor, leaving Kaelin staring at her reflection and the clenched fist resting in her lap.

Morning sunlight spilled through the half-open windows of the room where Ren slept.

She stirred with a groan, her muscles protesting as she rolled onto her back, staring at the ceiling. Her head throbbed with the ache of too much wine, and the faint taste of sweetness still lingered on her tongue.

Bits and pieces of last night came rushing back in a haze. Ren recalled her and Elira winding up at some tavern as their last stop for the night. Elira grinning wickedly as she slammed back another glass, Ren declaring herself "Queen of the Blade" before hurling her dagger at a tavern dartboard, the two of them clambering onto tables to "prove their skills." There had been cheers, laughter, and at some point, Elira shouting "Bow to your champion!" just before missing the board entirely.

"You're awfully chipper for someone who was out so late last night," Mirella's amused voice chimed.

Ren turned her head toward the corner of the room where Mirella's carved oak doors had swung open, the wardrobe's polished surface glinting.

"Gods, I forgot you existed for a second."

Mirella's doors creaked in mock offense. "Tragic, really. My heart is shattered."

Ren pushed herself up. "Please. You don't *have* a heart."

"True," Mirella purred, "but if I did, it would still be far more generous than yours. Now up you get. You can't lie in bed all day."

Ren dragged herself to her feet, gathering her clothes and padding toward the stairwell that spiraled down beneath the tower. Her head still throbbed, her throat dry as parchment. She paused at a nearby basin carved from pale stone, scooping cool water into her hands and drinking deeply. The relief was instant, the chill sliding down her throat and waking her more than Mirella's words ever could. As she reached the bottom of the stairwell, the air grew humid and fragrant with herbs as she neared the enchanted spring baths, a series of natural pools fed by underground streams.

They were communal, but Ren was the first there.

Steam curled over the water's surface, faint runes etched into the stone walls glowing.

Ren slid into the nearest basin with a sigh, the heat seeping into her sore muscles. The mineral-rich water left her skin tingling, a sensation both soothing and invigorating. For a while, she simply let herself float, mind wandering as the faint burble of water and the distant hum of enchantment filled the chamber.

She stirred when she heard the soft padding of footsteps and saw another fae enter the bath. Ren gathered her clothes and hurried back to her room, water dripping down her arms as she scrambled to dry off.

"Tick, tock," Mirella's voice called as soon as Ren swung open the door. "At this rate, you'll be late enough to make a memorable entrance. But, I don't recall Commander Ivan appreciating memorable entrances."

Ren cursed under her breath at the thought of the ruthless commander and tugged on her clothes in a frantic rush, muttering a hurried thanks to Mirella as she shoved on her boots and bolted for the door.

Ren yanked open the door and nearly collided with a young courier standing poised with an envelope in hand.

"Message for you," the courier quipped curtly, holding it out as if eager to be anywhere else.

Ren blinked at the sealed letter, the royal crest pressed into the wax. Her stomach sank as she broke it open and scanned the neat, precise handwriting.

> *Ren Harper,*
> *You are hereby invited to attend my Name Day gathering this evening. If you're wondering, yes, attendance is expected. Proper attire is required. Try not to start any duels with your temper, at least not before dessert.*
> *—Royal Princess Kaelin of House Vaelaran*

Ren stared at the letter for a long moment, her jaw tightening. "Of course it's from her," she muttered.

Mirella's voice drifted out from inside the room, rich with amusement. "Oh, this will be interesting."

Ren shot a glare over her shoulder. "Do you ever stop talking?"

"Not when you make it this easy," Mirella purred.

Ren groaned, shoving the letter into her pocket before leaving.

Training had been brutal.

Ren's jaw still ached where someone's elbow had caught her cleanly, though she was lucky it hadn't blossomed into a bruise. The sting lingered as a reminder of another day spent on her back in the dirt, fighting to keep up with the fae.

That evening, Ren stepped with weary legs into a world of silk and moonlight.

The air shimmered with laughter and the clink of crystal. Apparently, the kingdom was celebrating Princess Kaelin's Name Day with an extravagance fit for a goddess.

The palace's banquet hall glittered like a hoarded dragon's trove. Silver-trimmed columns soared upward, while enchanted chandeliers floated overhead. The music swelled and fluttered like birdsong in spring, violins weaving under the chatter of fae nobility.

As Ren stood there beneath the velvet drapes and jeweled light, something in her curled with quiet fury.

A thousand silver goblets, ornate forks, and sugared petals on cakes set in intricate designs, while outside these glittering walls, children starved on muddy floors, families drank rainwater and begged for mercy from healers who had no medicine left to give.

Ren watched in bated silence as a noblewoman laughed, dabbing sweet wine from her painted lips with a napkin threaded in silver.

Ren's thoughts whirled. What kind of kingdom drowned itself in luxury while the rest of the realm suffocated in rot and ruin?

The sickness was spreading. She'd seen it, smelled it, lived it. Yet here, the only thing spreading was perfume and gossip.

Kaelin presided like a goddess of starlight, lounging on her raised throne at the head of the hall. A glass of wine balanced lazily between her fingers, her other hand resting on the polished arm of her seat. Every so often, her voice lilted in a soft, silvery laugh that made Ren's skin crawl.

Ren's gaze caught on the glittering arc of Kaelin's smile, the effortless grace in the way she held the room's attention. Sometimes, Ren never knew if the real enemy was the sickness creeping through the realm or the fae themselves.

As if on cue, Ren caught sight of King Maelion standing near the throne's base, tall and draped in a deep blue cloak embroidered with silver designs. He sipped from a heavy goblet but didn't partake in the laughter or the dancing.

His gaze was steady, assessing, and cold as he surveyed the room. When his eyes met Ren's for a fleeting moment, she felt as though her thoughts were laid bare, like he had already weighed her, found her wanting, and coolly dismissed her.

Queen Lyra, seated not far from her husband, was draped in gauzy silks of moonlight and shadow, her pale hair pinned up with gleaming combs. But what struck Ren was the flush painting her high cheekbones, the soft gleam of sweat at her temples. Her laughter, too, was a shade too loud, the musical quality tinged with something giddy and unrestrained. She twirled her goblet between her fingers, the jeweled stem catching the candlelight as she leaned back, her voice lilting through the hall.

Drunk on wine or drunk on her own power, Ren wasn't sure which.

The queen's gaze drifted lazily over the gathered nobles, her lips curling in a flirtatious smile as she exchanged murmured words with a silver-haired fae seated nearby. For a fleeting moment, her gaze slid over Ren. Then her attention shifted again, back to her wine, her laughter spilling through the air.

"I wasn't aware vermin received invitations to royal affairs."

The smug words slithered in from Ren's left. Her jaw tensed even before she turned.

There he stood, the blonde fae male from training, swathed in layers of sapphire and silver. His golden hair was swept back to reveal a face carved in aristocratic angles, the kind that might've been considered beautiful if not for the sneer twisting his mouth and the gleam of superiority flashing in his glacial blue eyes.

He looked like the kind of man who'd toast your name at a feast, then plant a dagger in your back before dessert.

Ren arched a brow. "Do your feathers always ruffle this easily, or is it just me?"

The fae male let out an airy, mocking laugh, the sound as polished and hollow as crystal glass.

"You won't last long in training," he sneered, stepping closer. "Fae courts aren't meant for humans who think a few lucky swings in the pits make them worthy." His eyes flicked over her plain tunic with disdain, lips curling. "This realm eats girls like you alive."

Ren met his eyes with a slow smirk. "Then the realm better sharpen its teeth."

Before the fae male could respond, another voice cut through the charged air.

"Lucan," Talen said. "Good to see you again, mate." He turned to Ren with the faintest smile tugging at the corner of his mouth. "Ren, meet Lucan Brightbane. One of our more decorated soldiers."

Lucan's jaw went taut, annoyance clearly written on his face, before he schooled his features into false pleasantries. "Glad to see you back at court," he managed to Talen, though his tone lacked warmth. "It's been too quiet without you."

Talen tilted his head with an amused gleam in his forest-green eyes. "Careful, Lucan. Say something sincere and people might think you've grown soft." He added with a light chuckle, "Though if you're really aching for noise, we can always spar sometime. See if all that pomp and polish still holds up under pressure."

Lucan's lips thinned, but he bowed stiffly and stalked off into the crowd, leaving only the scent of burnished amber oil laced with white pepper and myrrh, along with bruised pride in his wake.

Ren raised a brow. "Friend of yours?"

Talen gave a short laugh. "Lucan Brightbane's father holds a seat on the High Council and has more coin than half the realm. The Brightbane estate spans half of the eastern coast."

Ren frowned, eyes following Lucan's retreating figure. "Is that why he looks down on people like me?"

Talen turned to her fully now, his expression softening into something more reflective. "Honestly? I don't know. Maybe it's because humans live shorter lives. Maybe because we hear more, feel more, see further in the dark." He shrugged, the gesture unguarded. "But that's not a justifiable reason. The truth is, it's just always been that way. Prejudice passed down like tradition."

Ren crossed her arms, jaw tight. "Sounds like a tradition worth breaking."

Talen smiled. "Then I suppose it's a good thing you're here." They lapsed into a few moments of silence until Talen mused softly, "My family, on the other hand, likes the finer things."

"It appears they do."

Talen's gaze slid toward her. "If you're really lucky," he said, voice low, "you'll be chosen for the first dance."

Ren arched a brow. "Is that so?"

"At nightfall," he explained, "the royal family dances with chosen citizens, those who've proven loyalty or valor."

Ren gave a faint scoff. "How intriguing."

Still, her eyes drifted back to the throne. Princess Kaelin was draped in violet silk and threaded amethyst, her gown clinging to every enviable curve.

Ren, in contrast, stood in a plain emerald-green tunic, its sleeves slightly rumpled, dark pants tucked into scuffed boots. She had wiped mud off them hours ago, but it clung stubbornly to the seams like a second skin. The moment she stepped into the ballroom, she realized that she was woefully underdressed. The weight of a hundred burning fae eyes followed her like judgment incarnate, making her skin prickle beneath the wrinkled fabric.

Beside her, Talen murmured under his breath with the hint of a smirk, "Ever been to a ball before?"

"Only the kind where someone breaks a chair over your head after you mouth off in a tavern."

Talen chuckled. "Charming."

She resisted the urge to tug at her sleeves. "I fit in just fine."

"You know," he said, voice low so only she could hear, "Fae can be uptight about tradition. Clothes, etiquette, posture. But honestly?" His lips twitched. "You walk into a ballroom in boots like that and still hold your ground. That says more than any jewelry or dresses ever could."

Ren blinked at him, caught off guard by the sincerity.

He shrugged. "Still, I'm sure my sister could lend you a dress or two. She's got more embroidered gowns than any sane person should, and she owes me a favor."

"You want me parading around in court silks and glitter like a fae noble?"

Talen laughed. "Just saying the option's there. Might be amusing to watch."

Then applause erupted, seizing their attention.

A hunched figure was brought before the throne, small, nimble, with pointed ears and bells braided into fine, sea-glass hair. A fae court jester.

"An offering, gifted from one who withholds their name," the herald intoned.

Kaelin tilted her head. "Do something amusing, jester."

The fae bowed low, flourishing his hands in dramatic flair. He juggled three crystal goblets, each one catching the golden chandelier light. The crowd clapped.

Ren watched with growing unease as the fae jester stumbled and bumped into a noble watching from the edge of the dais, her eyes tracking the wobble of the tallest goblet as it spun a little too wide. But he regained his footing, receiving another round of applause.

Gods, those glasses probably cost more than a living wage in Ironforge. One slip, one shattered curve of crystal, and she wasn't sure if the court would laugh harder, or if the poor fool would be flogged behind the rose hedges by nightfall.

Kaelin leaned back against her throne, swirling the wine in her glass as though bored. "Enough with your charades."

The jester hesitated, his eyes darting around the room. "Your Grace?"

"Let's see you mimic something more entertaining."

A sharp, collective breath swept through the court.

The jester hesitated, before nodding and rising. With a deep, sweeping bow, he began to move, arms limp and flailing as though pulled by unseen strings.

He danced in jagged, puppet-like motions across the marble floor, his steps exaggerated and his knees jerking as though he were a marionette caught in a twisted ballet. His hands fluttered, mimicking the graceful gestures of courtiers, only to collapse suddenly into grotesque, rag-doll slumps.

A few courtiers chuckled, uncertain whether to laugh or watch in silence as the jester's dance mocked their every move, the dips of their heads, the sweep of their arms. Each gesture was amplified into a grotesque caricature of civility, the kind of silent submission that underpinned court life.

The jester's limbs flailed higher. He bowed, he curtsied, he collapsed, rising again and again like a puppet on fraying strings. The silent beat of his performance pressed against her ears, louder than any music could have been.

"Her magic," Talen told Ren, his tone grim. "She can control a person's bones, muscles, and limbs. Make them move however she pleases."

Kaelin watched with a faint, amused smile, her posture relaxed as though she were merely admiring a well-executed performance.

Ren's breath caught as her eyes flicked to the king. He stood at the base of the dais, his posture rigid, the muscles in his jaw tightening as his gaze narrowed on his daughter.

But when Ren's gaze shifted to the queen, she found a different reaction. The queen reclined in her chair, her goblet of wine tilting precariously in her hand. The flush on her cheeks deepened, her smile loose and sultry as she raised her glass in a salute to the performance.

"Well," the queen murmured, words slurring just enough to betray her indulgence. "At least *someone's* providing entertainment tonight."

The contrast between them sent a shiver through Ren's skin.

This family was as twisted as the hall they ruled.

This wasn't just cruelty, it was something colder, sharper. Like Kaelin didn't see the jester as a person at all, but as a piece in a game she'd already won.

And the worst part? The court laughed along with her.

This is what power looked like here. Polished, painted, and dressed in silk, but it was no different than the fighting pits.

And then, Talen moved forward, his dark cloak whispering over the marble as he closed the distance between himself and the throne.

"That's enough," he said softly.

Kaelin's smile faded, her brows arching just slightly. "Oh? You object to my entertainment, brother?"

Talen's gaze was on the jester. His voice dropped lower, edged with steel. "I object to cruelty disguised as amusement."

Kaelin held Talen's gaze for a long, simmering moment, her fingers poised midair as if she could still pull the jester's strings. Something unspoken passed between them, old wounds, perhaps, or a challenge neither wanted to voice in front of the court.

Then, with a delicate, almost dismissive tilt of her head, Kaelin purred, "Oh, brother. I suppose you're right. He was becoming a bore anyway."

She slowly stood, her voice sharp enough to cut through the noise like a blade.

"Drop them."

"Is something wrong, My Lady?" the jester asked.

Kaelin's eyes gleamed. "I commanded you to drop them."

The silence that followed was suffocating. The court went still.

"The moment you brushed against Lord Darien's cloak, you stole his signet ring. And I'd very much like to see if you're as good at catching your own teeth as you are with glass."

Gasps rippled through the hall. Lord Darien looked down, eyes wide, his hand already clutching where the ring should've been.

The jester's composure cracked.

He dropped the goblets with a clatter of shattering crystal and tried to run, the bells on his boots chiming as shouts erupted around him. He surged forward, cutting through the crowd.

Someone screamed. The jester lunged toward the dais, steel flashing in his hand. He barreled into the nearest guard, shoulder-first, sending him sprawling aside, and then he was surging up the steps two at a time toward Queen Lyra, whose eyes went wide as the jester's dagger caught the light.

"Guards!" King Maelion roared, his voice breaking across the chaos.

And then –

The jester froze mid-stride, his blade poised. He stood a few feet away from Queen Lyra. His eyes were impossibly wide, as if some unseen hand had reached into the moment and wrenched it still.

Heads turned. Ren looked back at Kaelin. Kaelin's hand was raised, and the jester hovered there, caught between movement – a trembling puppet without strings.

Kaelin approached him slowly, with the grace of a lioness stalking her prey.

"You insulted the crown in its own court. You dared to wear the mask of jest while you plotted treason against your sovereign." She raised her chin, and the ring floated from the jester's sleeve and to Lord Darien's palm.

Then Kaelin said to the guards, "Take him to the cells. Let him juggle knives until he begs for mercy and tells us who sent him."

As the guards dragged him away, the court resumed breathing again.

Ren was speechless, unable to tear her eyes from the fae princess.

Kaelin hadn't raised her voice once, and somehow, that was more terrifying than if she had.

The music shifted, decadent as honey. A hush settled over the ballroom like a held breath, the nobles parting in instinctive reverence as Kaelin stepped into the center of the marble floor. The glow of the enchanted chandeliers caught in the jewels laced through her curls.

"This," whispered a woman beside Ren, breathless with awe, "is the first dance."

But the way Kaelin prowled through the crowd was not ceremonial.

Her gaze swept the gathering like wildfire, sparing no one, searching for something, or someone. Courtiers subtly positioned themselves in her path, hopeful, eager. She ignored them all.

Until her eyes found Ren.

A heartbeat passed. Then another.

And then Kaelin moved straight for Ren.

E very instinct screamed at Ren to move, to vanish into the nearest shadow, to suddenly remember an urgent reason to be anywhere else. Maybe she'd left a window open, or her boots needed polishing, or perhaps Mirella needed company.

But Ren's body betrayed her, held fast by the weight of too many eyes and the suffocating pull of Kaelin's presence.

Kaelin stopped before Ren. Ren clenched her jaw. Gods, Kaelin lingered close enough that it felt like a provocation – close in a way that made Ren want to shove the fae princess back.

Ren's mind whirled. She considered pretending to faint. Or vomit. Or spontaneously combust. Anything to escape the way Kaelin pressed closer, leaving Ren no choice but to lift her gaze and crash straight into those violet eyes, far too close to deny, searing through whatever half-formed excuse might've passed for a graceful retreat.

So, Ren stayed. Because leaving now would mean running.

And Ren didn't run from anyone.

At least, not where they could see her do it.

"You," Kaelin murmured, voice low enough only Ren could hear.

Kaelin reached forward, and brushed a gloved finger along Ren's collarbone where it peaked above the neckline of her tunic. A mere ghost of a touch, but it certainly swept the air from Ren's lungs.

"Your outfit is bold," Kaelin drawled. "Though I anticipated you wouldn't have much to wear. Being mortal, after all. Your first ball?" Her tone dripped with honeyed mockery. "I do hope someone warned you it wasn't a *tavern brawl*."

Kaelin's violet gaze lingered a beat too long, flicking down Ren's form. Ren arched a brow. "And here I thought overdressing was a fae sport. You must be in the lead."

Kaelin's smile turned razor sharp, but she responded by extending her hand, palm up. Ren hesitated, but the predatory look in Kaelin's expression dared her to refuse.

Kaelin's lips curled, just enough to bare a hint of teeth. "It's only fitting I dance with the one entrusted with the noble task of hunting monsters for the realm. A proper send-off, wouldn't you agree?"

Ren's teeth clenched, her jaw tight from the effort of swallowing the retort rising hot in her throat. The urge to yank her hand back flared, to defy, to shove the fae princess back. Nevertheless, Ren placed her hand in Kaelin's.

Fine, I'll play your stupid game.

Gasps stirred as Kaelin led Ren forward, their footsteps the only sound on the marble.

The music resumed.

Kaelin's movements were smooth, precise, her body flowing through the steps with the ease and grace of a trained dancer. Though Ren supposed that shouldn't come as a surprise, considering Kaelin's royal status. Kaelin probably received dancing lessons as soon as she learned to walk. Ren, unaccustomed to the refined dance, followed by instinct, but with each step, she felt Kaelin's subtle need to control. The fae princess's touch lingered just a breath too long on Ren's waist, her fingers tightening slightly, guiding Ren's steps with a quiet insistence.

But Ren wasn't without fire. She shifted her weight, subtly challenging Kaelin's lead, forcing her to adapt. The fae princess's gaze flicked to hers.

You're not as easy to bend as you look, Kaelin's eyes seemed to say.

Neither are you, Ren thought fiercely, matching Kaelin step for step, her pulse racing with a growing defiance.

They spun, a whirl of lavender silk and scarlet braids, the air between them charged with a silent battle neither dared voice aloud.

Then, with a graceful twirl, Kaelin spun under Ren's arm. As she turned back into Ren's space, Ren caught a glimpse of Kaelin's cheeks faintly flushed, her eyes half-dazzled from the wine, her lips parted slightly as if the dance had drawn more from her than she'd intended.

For a heartbeat too long, they were close, *too* close. Ren's breath caught, her pulse thudding wildly as she felt Kaelin's scent, jasmine and frost, curl around her like a lure.

Heat flared in Ren's cheeks, and she pulled away, breaking the spell with a jerk of her arm.

Kaelin let her, her smile widening into something equal parts mockery and delight. "Careful," she purred softly. "Blush too brightly, and you might catch fire." Kaelin's smile deepened as they spun again. "Though I suppose that would match your dancing. Wild, unrefined... but certainly spirited."

"Funny," Ren retorted flatly, maintaining Kaelin's gaze. "Seems like *you're* the one struggling to keep up."

Kaelin leaned in just enough for her breath to brush Ren's cheek. "Oh, darling," she whispered, "I could dance blindfolded and *still* lead better than you. But by all means, keep pretending you're not out of your depth."

Ren's jaw tightened, but she kept her face neutral, her steps measured as they moved across the polished floor. *Arrogant, insufferable*, she caught herself thinking, her lips pressing into a hard line. *She's nothing but a spoiled fae with too many knives and far too much power.*

Kaelin's gaze flickered down to catch Ren's eyes lingering. "Stare too long, and the court might think you're hoping to be more than just my latest amusement. Not that I would want you, of course. It's nothing personal. You're just not my type. I find myself more drawn to women with more refinement."

Ren's gaze locked on Kaelin's, like a blade drawn and leveled at its mark. Ren eyed Kaelin like she would an opponent in the fighting pits. "Don't worry. You're not my type either."

Kaelin's returning scowl gave Ren a sweet satisfaction with her comeback, knowing it landed its mark. Then, Kaelin dipped Ren low enough that Ren's hair nearly brushed the floor.

Kaelin hovered close, her breath ghosting over Ren's cheek, violet eyes catching the light like shards of amethyst. Ren's stomach curled, every muscle locked in place as she stared up at the fae princess. The music around them continued, but Ren could hear only the frantic pounding of her own heart.

Before she could even gather her bearings, Kaelin pulled her upright in one smooth motion. The suddenness of it sent Ren stumbling a half step, surprised by the effortless strength and quickness behind the move. Kaelin didn't release her hand. If anything, her grip tightened, her smirk widening as though she knew exactly how easily she'd unsettled Ren.

"You know, I have more dresses than I could ever wear. Perhaps I'll let you borrow something that wouldn't make the nobility flinch when you pass."

"There's always a price with your kind. I'd rather shove my body in a tunic than owe you a hemline."

"Who said you'd owe me anything?" Kaelin asked sweetly.

"I'm not stupid. Your kind never gives without carving the debt into stone first."

Kaelin let out a soft laugh. "You're learning."

Ren should have put distance between herself and the fae princess whose eyes could set whole kingdoms to ruin. But her feet stayed rooted, heart hammering like she'd just stepped into the ring.

Only this fight didn't require fists.

Kaelin's fingers lifted again and toyed with a loose thread at the neckline of Ren's tunic. Her gloves had come off at some point, and her bare touch was far too cold against the exposed skin of Ren's neck.

Ren reared back and caught Kaelin's wrist. Her skin was the kind of softness that came from scented oils, from never knowing the bite of rope burns or the sting of iron cuffs. Ren's own hands, calloused and chiseled by years of hardship, felt coarse in comparison.

"And one more thing," Kaelin murmured, her voice like a blade's edge against Ren's skin. "You say you're here with the noble goal of defending the realm." Her gaze swept over Ren, sharp and assessing. "But I don't believe you."

They continued the dance, Kaelin's voice even, resolute. "I've seen the way your eyes wander the palace halls. Not like someone protecting it, but like someone memorizing its weaknesses. Its exits. Makes me wonder what you're *really* after."

"Maybe I just like knowing where the exits are in case I ever need to make a dramatic escape from a certain insufferable princess."

"Only a fool wouldn't keep a close eye on strangers who stroll into their court. Especially ones with a knack for setting things on fire."

Ren's lips curved into something closer to a snarl than a smile. "Then maybe you should watch me a little closer, Your Highness, because the last time someone underestimated me, I left nothing but ash behind."

Ren knew that prodding a fae princess was the kind of mistake mortals rarely walked away from unscathed. And yet, something inside her wanted to shove back, to see if Kaelin's poise would crack, if her control would falter.

Kaelin's eyes flashed, something fierce and deeply protective burning behind them. "If you so much as look at my family with ill intent, I will personally have you rotting in the dungeons until you *beg* me to finish the job."

Kaelin whirled, sweeping Ren into another dip with the elegance of a predator, her violet gown sweeping behind her like a storm cloud. Ren's pulse stuttered, fury and something hotter pooling in her chest. *Arrogant witch*, she thought viciously.

But just as the final turn ended, the heavy doors of the ballroom slammed open with a *boom*.

A figure staggered through the arched entryway, half-dragging himself across the polished marble floor. His cloak was shredded, his armor slick with blood, one eye swollen shut – the other wild and glazed with terror.

Conversation died like a candle snuffed. Music screeched to a halt mid-note.

He made it only a few steps in before collapsing to his knees, gasping. "The plague…" he rasped. "It's… it's at the palace gates—"

And then his body seized. A violent jerk, a spasm that arched his spine with a crack. His mouth gaped open in a soundless scream.

His eyes rolled back.

And he dropped.

For one heartbeat, the hall was frozen in silence. Even the chandeliers seemed to still, their crystal lights flickering like they, too, sensed what had come.

Then the screaming began in earnest.

Nobles scrambled in silks and heels, trampling one another for the exits. Chairs overturned, silver clattered across stone, and the scent of scented oil curdled into sweat and fear.

Ren remained rooted. Her gaze stayed fixed on the body now twitching faintly on the floor, as if something beneath the flesh still stirred.

She felt the piercing sense of being watched. Looking over her shoulder, she met Talen's gaze. His eyes matched hers, and they didn't need words to communicate their thoughts.

Because whatever had arrived, it wasn't just a sickness.

It was a *message*.

Kaelin's Name Day had ended in a scream, and now the palace held its breath, as if that might keep the affliction from pressing closer.

Ren strode through the winding corridors. Her chest felt tight, her thoughts a storm she couldn't rein in – recalling the sneer of Kaelin's lips, the slight tilt of her chin, the gleam in her violet eyes that spoke of amusement and superiority all at once. Kaelin's burning look—half challenge, half mockery—etched itself into Ren's mind, mixed with the fae princess's razor-edged taunts, her unbearable talent for getting under Ren's skin, all tangled with the darker weight of reality that came crashing down all too soon.

The Witherblight was *here*.

As Ren turned a corner, a fae female glanced up from her threshold. Their eyes met, and then the woman slipped inside her private quarters, shutting her door with a soft *click*.

Fear had already rooted itself here.

Ren hadn't even meant to find the library. She'd stumbled upon it by chance as she prowled the endless halls, refusing to shutter herself away in her chambers like some pampered noble clinging to false safety. Even with the sickness creeping through the palace, she would not be locked inside. The irony of it all struck her—the fae panicked at the thought of disease brushing their gilded walls, when beyond Pyraelia's borders, humans lived with the Witherblight waiting on their doorsteps every single day.

For a race who considered themselves superior, they sure had a talent for cowardice when danger came too close to their own gates.

By the time Ren reached the library doors, her hands had curled into fists, her jaw tight enough to ache. She needed somewhere quiet, somewhere to think, to shove aside her irritation toward the fae princess long enough to remember why she was here in the first place.

She pushed the doors open and stepped inside.

The library was smaller than she expected for a kingdom that boasted of grandeur.

Its shelves leaned with age, their contents packed tightly into the narrow space, and the scent of old parchment and fading ink clung to the air. Pale light filtered through high, arched windows, casting elongated shadows across the stone floor.

Ren ventured further, weaving between precarious towers of parchment until she stood before an oak desk. Her amber gaze fell upon a carved nameplate that was cracked in half and barely clinging to a teetering stack of leather-bound ledgers. It read *Veylan*, though the figure behind the chaos hardly needed an introduction.

The fae librarian stood tall and thin as a reed, draped in layers of misbuttoned robes dyed in shades no one had business combining. Mirella would have a field day trying to sort him out—she'd probably take one look at the disaster of colors and fabrics and demand he march straight into a fitting. The librarian munched on a biscuit, mid-page-turn of a book that was hanging by its spine, crumbs dusting a nearby codex. His skin shimmered a deep, opalescent violet, and his silver hair fell in ringlets. For all his disarray, though, his face was surprisingly clean-shaven.

And his pale, lilac eyes beheld the sleepless gleam of someone who'd fallen too deep into a book and never quite climbed back out.

The last library Ren had stepped into had every shelf standing in rigid, suffocating order. Pyraelia's library had towering piles of books leaning like revelers at closing time of a tavern. Scrolls fluttered through the air on unseen currents, occasionally swooping low to smack passersby in the head. A roped-off wing shimmered with wards, and something with too many eyes peered out from a crate labeled *"Sorting. Eventually."*

Ren stepped forward, clearing her throat and immediately regretting it as a cloud of dust ambushed her. Coughing into her sleeve, she managed, "Excuse me... where do you keep your older tomes?"

Veylan startled, knocking his round glasses askew. Ink-smudged fingers fumbled to straighten them, and he blinked at Ren as if surfacing from underwater.

"Apologies, I didn't mean to startle you. You don't get many visitors here, do you?"

"Sometimes," Veylan admitted. "But I was... in the middle of something." He gestured vaguely to the open volume before him.

Ren's amber eyes flicked down, catching a glimpse of the lurid illustration across the page, what looked suspiciously like an orc entwined with a merefolk, both males nude and half-submerged in crashing waves.

She arched her brow. "Enjoying yourself?"

Veylan flushed a deep shade of violet, snapping the book half-shut against his chest. "It's not what it looks like," he stammered. Then, with a huff, he pushed his glasses back into place. "Well, I mean, it *is a* sensual narrative, obviously, but it's descriptions are shallow, the pacing uneven, and there are some frankly abysmal word choices." His tone sharpened as he leaned over the book again. "Though, to be fair, the author is highly renowned, so I'm going to see it through. But sometimes, I suppose the name sells more than the craft these days—" He stopped abruptly and cleared his throat.

Ren watched him squirm for a moment before she said, "Fascinating critique. But I was actually wondering where you keep your older tomes." She folded her arms, tilting her head toward the looming shelves around them. "Unless you plan on recommending me more... sensual narratives. Though if I had a preference, it would probably be the kind with detailed illustrations."

The poor fae nearly dropped his book, violet skin flushing darker as he spluttered into his collar. "I couldn't agree more! Illuminated manuscripts of sensual narratives are most intriguing," he blurted, voice pitching higher. "The layering of inks, the gilding techniques—their cultural value far exceeds their, ah, base intent—"

Ren burst out laughing, the sound echoing off the crooked towers of books. She shook her head, grinning at his horrified earnestness. "Saints, I was only pulling your leg, though I do appreciate your enthusiasm on the subject." She tipped her chin toward the shelves. "Now will you show me where you keep your older tomes, or do I need to dig through the chaos myself?"

He beamed. "Ah! A seeker of stories, are we? Come, come. They're in the back."

Ren followed as he swept past, muttering to himself in what might've been two different languages. He glanced over his shoulder as they strode through a crooked aisle. "Looking for historical records? Magical tomes? Or perhaps…" He leaned in conspiratorially, voice lowering to a hushed whisper, "forbidden grimoires?"

Before Ren could answer, he straightened and continued, "We don't believe in censorship here. But do be careful and don't return them with torn pages or bloodstains. That's where I draw the line."

Veylan's boots made soft thumps against the dusty stone as he led her through a narrow corridor flanked by towering shelves. "This wing was once sealed after a minor cataloging revolt," Veylan explained cheerfully, stepping over a toppled stack of books. "The sentient shelving tried to alphabetize the archivist by species."

"That seems excessive."

"Oh, it was."

As Veylan led Ren deeper into the maze of the library, past swaying ladders, humming scrolls, and a shelf that appeared to be snoring rather loudly, they turned a corner into a dim corridor.

And promptly walked into mayhem.

A stack of books flew into the air with a *whoosh*, scattered parchment spinning like leaves in a storm. In the center hovered a portly ghost in a crooked powdered wig, arms flailing as he recited something that may have once been poetry but now resembled a cursed limerick.

"—and lo! She wept 'neath moonlit flame,
Though I, her knight, forgot her name!
'Twas love, or lust, or tragic fate—OH DAMNATION, WHY COULDN'T SHE WAIT?!"

Veylan let out a long sigh. "Sir Pindlewhip, must we do this again?"

The ghost turned mid-rant, his misty face lighting up at the sight of company and training on Ren. "A visitor! Oh, dear parchment, she has the look of a muse! A sharpness in the eye and calluses on her hands. Clearly, an adventurer."

"She is not your muse," Veylan grumbled. "She's here to read, not to be serenaded by your unfinished epic."

Sir Pindlewhip clutched his feathered quill like a sword. "I died mid-sentence while drafting the greatest literary masterpiece the realm has never read!" His voice echoed with righteous indignation.

Ren asked, "So you're haunting the library... because of your unfinished poem?"

The ghost clutched his translucent chest. "Artistic injustice, madam!"

Veylan waved a hand through him, making Pindlewhip sputter. "If you don't quiet down, I swear on the Sacred Index of Everturning Tomes I'll exorcise you with lemon water and blessed vellum."

Sir Pindlewhip sniffed and floated backward into a nearby bookshelf, muttering lines of rhymes under his breath.

Veylan looked to Ren. "He's harmless. Just don't let him edit anything, or you'll end up with fifteen prologues and a tragic love triangle that never resolves." Veylan paused mid-step, glancing at a tattered romance tome floating by. "Ugh, another love triangle," he muttered, snatching it from the air. "Why is it always two brooding males and one 'conflicted' heroine? Honestly, I'd have more respect if she just left them both."

At last, they reached a section nearly swallowed by ivy that had forced its way through cracks in the ancient stone. A gilded archway overhead bore faintly glowing script in fae and other ancient languages, the letters humming low, like a sleeping creature murmuring in its dreams.

Veylan waved a hand, and the vines seemed to hesitate before recoiling with a hiss.

"Here we are," he said, gesturing grandly. "Writings on the old blood. Histories, theories, sightings. And of course, my favorite creatures. Dragons. Some call them a myth, but myths don't leave claw marks in the rafters."

The shelves here were curved and blackened, some singed at the edges, as if the knowledge itself had once ignited. One thick volume on a pedestal bore the mark of a dragon coiled around a blade, its eye inset with a dull ruby. Ren reached out, fingertips grazing the ancient leather, and the cover vibrated under her touch, warm.

"They say the dragons vanished," Veylan murmured behind her. "But the records indicate they were hunted. Betrayed. Or worse. *Bound.*"

"Have any you'd recommend?" Ren asked, letting her fingers trail along the dusty spines. If she was going to be living in Pyraelia, she might as well brush up on its history and customs — better to know what sort of vipers' nest she'd wandered into than go in blind.

Knowledge, after all, was just another kind of weapon.

Veylan winced, scratching the back of his ink-smudged neck. "I'm awful with names, book titles included. But if you're looking for something with teeth..." His eyes gleamed. "Let me see, it's here some-where."

Ren drifted into one of the dim aisles nearby, where the spine of a gold and red bound book had caught her attention. The gold foiling gave off a faint glow that pulled Ren in like a moth to a flame.

"Ah," Veylan exclaimed. "Here it is. The legend of *Vortharax the Godbreaker.*"

"Never heard of it."

With a satisfied sigh as if he was hoping for that response, Veylan collapsed into a crooked old chair beside the nearest stack. The wood groaned in protest but held. "Then you're in for a story," he said, voice dipping into something between reverence and fear. "Go on," he gestured to another chair across from him, "get comfortable, my dear."

Ren lowered herself into the chair, its frame groaning beneath her like an old beast. The cushions were threadbare, stuffing poking through seams worn thin by years of use, but the chair held.

"Long before kings claimed thrones and fae etched their courts into being, the skies belonged to winged beasts. The greatest of them all was Vortharax, a dragon said to have been forged in the belly of a fallen star. Dragons love their treasures, hoarding anything of value. But Vortharax didn't hoard gold. He hoarded *dominion* – conquest." Veylan leaned forward, lowering his voice as if the walls themselves might be listening. "At that time, much like now, the land was carved into territories, each ruled by a great fae house. Every house had its lord, and with them came the responsibility of protection for those who dwelled within their realm. People looked to their lords for shelter, for safety, for strength." His mouth curved into something between awe and dread. "But against Vortharax? No house, no lord, no *realm* could stand against him. The fae courts were the first to fall. No magic could touch him. No sword could cut him. Even time seemed to flinch in his presence. And when he breathed fire, it raged so hot it turned searing blue, an all-consuming inferno that incinerated anything in its path."

Ren's pulse thudded faintly in her throat.

"They say he even slew a god – snapped its spine like a dry twig. A minor deity, left shattered across the northern wastes of Lytharien. That's how he earned the name Godbreaker."

Veylan let that information sink in, then continued.

"For once, mortals and fae and other magic folk didn't turn on each other. They united into one fragile, desperate alliance. Together, they crafted something – a pact, of sorts. No one remembers what exactly, only that it required magic and great sacrifice. And somehow, it worked. Vortharax fell. Only, his body was never found. Some believe he's chained beneath the earth. Others swear he slumbers beneath the sea or even within Mount Solfira itself, dreaming of sunlight. But me?" He paused, a slow, eerie smile spreading across his face. "I think he's waiting."

"And what happens if he wakes?" she asked.

Veylan blinked, as if the thought had never truly occurred to him. "Let's hope we've learned something since the last time the world was nearly swallowed in darkness by that ungodly beast."

He stood. "I'll be up front having lunch. Likely near the window, where the residential feline likes to hiss at me even though he refuses to leave. Bugger, he is."

Then, as he turned to leave, he paused and glanced back. "Books deserve to be read, not buried. If you find one you like, let me know. Just... don't bleed on it. Or burn it. Or tear out pages in some dramatic fit of emotion. Trust me. It's happened before."

And with that, he shuffled off down the crooked corridor, humming an old tune, leaving Ren alone with legends, dust, and the flickering possibility that monsters never really died.

Or stayed buried forever.

She found herself flipping idly through the brittle pages of a forgotten tome when she turned to a page with a sketch of a scrawled warning etched in scrambled ink.

Whispers of an age lost to flame. Of winged beasts whose scales gleamed like molten obsidian, said to turn aside even the sharpest blades and arrows. Their wings blotted out the sun, their breath a searing inferno that stretched the span of towers, and wherever it reached, nothing survived.

Nine towns were named in desperate, trembling script:

Haverdale. Brimholt. Noren's Reach. Vaelrun. Elswith. Daggerpine. Silverthatch. Korrin's Glen. Thornmere.

All reduced to ruin.

She stiffened when she felt a low hum in her chest, like something ancient stirring deep beneath her skin. The hairs on her arms rose.

Then she heard it, not with her ears, but inside her bones. A voice, whispering her name in a tongue she did not recognize but somehow understood.

Flamebearer.

20

The word slithered down Ren's spine. Her feet moved before her mind could catch up, following the pull.

As Ren passed the front of the library, Veylan was already lost again in his book, brow furrowed in the kind of concentration usually reserved for ancient battle records. Given the cover, it was probably just another passionate tangle between the merman and the orc. Veylan didn't so much as twitch at her footsteps, and she decided not to interrupt his reading.

The palace halls were dim, the torches guttering low. Ren's footfalls echoed, the only sound in the silence that now ruled the court. She turned a corner and came upon a stairwell of cold marble, its edges draped in webs thick with dust. The chill deepened the farther she descended, the hum in her chest growing stronger.

The voice had gone quiet now, as if waiting.

At the bottom loomed a wooden door. The door bore no crest, no inscription, no embellishment—only wood so plain it felt wrong amid the cascading marble and silver bones of the palace.

Ren laid a hand on the latch. The hum in her chest fluttered.

The door groaned open.

Darkness stirred beyond. Ren squinted as a figure lurched out of the gloom. The dark-robed figure startled at her presence, a bottle slipping from their grasp to shatter on the stone.

"Are you okay?" Ren called.

The figure pushed upright, limping toward her with a hand at their ankle. "Just a moment!" rasped a hoarse voice.

"Do you need help?"

There was another thud, followed by a muffled curse.

Then, the figure removed their hood, revealing a wild halo of silver-grey hair that sprang upward. He was fae, and shorter than Ren by a head at least, his slight frame half-lost in the folds of his robe. Despite the gray hair spilling around his face, his features were youthful, though sickly pale. Ren's gaze swept over him, taking in the pallor of his skin that seemed luminous in the low light. His eyes were icy blue.

"Don't think we've met. I'm Zakhar. Court Mage, on most days."

Ren figured *a name for a name* and said, "Ren." Ren eyed the crate held in his arms. "Potions?"

Zakhar's grin widened proudly. "Ah, yes! Been down here for three days mixing batches. Didn't even attend the princess's Name Day. See, I prefer my company bottled." He gestured to the spilled remains of one such bottle, his smile faltering just slightly as he muttered, "There goes twelve hours of work down the drain.".

Ren's gaze shifted past him, her eyes adjusting to the darkness behind the wooden door. The table behind Zakhar was covered with rows upon rows of vials and bottles filled with shimmering liquid.

The Verdant Elixir.

Her stomach lurched as the sheer scale of it hit her. She'd never seen so much in one place. There had to be enough here to save entire villages, families who were waiting, dying, praying for even a fraction of what sat on that table as if it were nothing more than wine ready to be uncorked.

"You made all of this?" she breathed, her voice barely more than a whisper.

"Indeed. Got several crates near ready for delivery. Word is the affliction is at the gates – no time to waste."

She didn't have to ask why it was sold for such a staggering price. Deep down, she already knew. The demand was too great, the suffering too vast – this stockpile would never be enough. Each bottle looked less like salvation and more like a cruel reminder that only a select few would live, while countless others would waste away waiting for a cure they could never afford.

In her mind, Ren saw Sela again—remembered the way Sela's mother had withered from the Witherblight, flesh sinking against bone, memory slipping into nothing. She recalled the helplessness of watching it happen, of knowing there was nothing she could give, no vial to save them.

Not everyone could be saved, and the court knew it.

Zakhar noticed the look on Ren's face and murmured, "The Witherblight's outpacing us, far faster than production. Death waits for no cauldron, and I may work with magic, but even I can't perform miracles."

An uneasy silence followed as Ren stepped back. Zakhar shifted awkwardly, gesturing toward the stairs. "Right, then. Best get these ready for transport." Zakhar's jovial mask faltered. He sidestepped her, bumping his knee on the railing in haste.

Ren lingered, her hands curling at her sides. Zakhar was smaller than her, distracted. If she shoved past him, or could take him down, if she could just get her hands on one of those crates, she could bring the vials back to families who were waiting, praying to the Gods for divine intervention. It would be easy.

But if she stole from the stockpile and got caught, she'd be imprisoned again. Kaelin was already suspicious of Ren as it was. Ren would be locked away again and powerless to help anyone.

Unease twisted in Ren's gut as she turned. She forced her legs to move, making her way back up the stairs, each step heavier than the last.

She nearly ran into Talen rounding the corner.

"Well, there you are," he said, steadying her. "I looked for you in your room, but it was empty." His gaze swept the corridor, then returned to her. "Aren't you afraid to be roaming about? The plague's practically at our doorstep."

"This isn't the first time I've stared death in the face. Doesn't frighten me as much. Not anymore, at least." She shrugged, adding, "It takes more than this to scare me."

Talen's smile faded, just slightly. "Then you're either brave or foolish. Or both."

"Depends who you ask." Her gaze flicked over his polished breastplate, gleaming even in the dim light, gauntlets strapped tight, every buckle fastened. "You look ready for a war," she observed. "What about you, prince? Aren't you out past your curfew?"

Talen exhaled, a quiet huff that might've been a laugh if he weren't so obviously trying not to smile. "You could try calling me Talen," he said as he turned toward the corridor. "Especially since we're going to be working together. Titles get exhausting after the hundredth time."

Ren followed. "Fine, *Talen*." she drawled, making it sound almost like an insult. "Happy now?"

"Ecstatic."

They reached a tall, oak door embossed with the crest of House Vaelaran. Talen pushed it open, and the room was spare but warm: shelves stacked with ledgers, maps pinned to the walls, and a great desk strewn with scrolls, sealed documents, and half-drained inkpots.

Talen crossed to the desk and pulled a single parchment free, smoothing it over the desk. "This is your contract."

"Contract?"

"You didn't think I'd let you hurl yourself at monsters without putting something in writing first, did you?"

Ren leaned an elbow on the desk, gaze flicking over the parchment. "Here I was thinking the fae were always trying to take advantage of humans."

"Oh, don't worry. We love taking advantage of humans — we just prefer to have it in writing." He gestured her closer. "Three creatures. That's the agreement. Defeat them, and the full payment is yours." He tapped the bottom line with a gloved finger. "Your room and meals will be provided, as will any armor or repairs you need. I'll have someone assigned to help you armor properly because you'll need more than those patchwork leathers you favor."

Ren leaned in, scanning the elegant script. When she reached the line with her payment, her breath caught. "This can't be right," she murmured. "That's – "

The number staring back at her was more coin than she'd ever dreamed of earning in her life. More than enough to buy passage to the coast twice over, maybe even a small ship of her own if she bargained well.

"More than you've ever seen?" he finished. "You'll earn a partial payment for each creature you fell. I don't make promises I can't keep, Ren."

She picked up the quill resting beside the parchment, twirling it once between her fingers. "And if I don't succeed?" she asked, eyes flicking up to meet his.

Before Talen could answer, another voice sliced through the air.

"If you fail, you owe the crown."

Ren's hand stilled midair.

Kaelin stalked across the threshold with her usual effortless grace. "Contracts go both ways," she added. "If you break the terms, or flee, or fail to deliver, then you'll pay for the losses you've caused. That's how the court works. There are no exceptions."

Ren set the quill down with deliberate care. "And who decides what qualifies as failure?"

Kaelin smiled. "We do."

Talen shot his sister a look that hovered between warning and exasperation. "Kaelin."

"What?" Kaelin lifted a shoulder, feigning innocence. "I'm simply ensuring your new... partner understands the stakes. It's only fair, for both parties."

Ren met her gaze evenly. "Fair," she repeated, voice low. "Right."

Kaelin reached up, idly twirling a strand of pale hair around one finger, her tone deceptively light. "After all, it's not every day a human is promised *that* much gold. I imagine it would take you a lifetime to earn the same, wouldn't it?"

Ren said nothing, jaw tightening.

"Then I'd suggest you take your training very seriously," Kaelin murmured, releasing the strand of hair to let it fall back against her shoulder. "We don't take kindly to wasted effort or squandered coin."

Talen's sigh cut through the tension. "Ignore her," he told Ren, reaching for the parchment and turning it slightly toward Ren. "You're not here to lose. You're here to do the realm a great service."

Ren hesitated, the weight of the moment pressing in. Then she took up the quill again. "Nothing like a good cause to make the possibility of dying feel worthwhile," she muttered, then signed her name.

Kaelin's eyes flicked once to Ren, then to the parchment. "I'd like a word with my brother. Privately."

Ren's gaze darted between them but she pushed away from the desk with a shrug. "Fine. I'll be in the corridor" she muttered, heading for the door.

The latch clicked behind her.

Talen let out a long sigh and sank onto the edge of the desk. "Gods, she's something," he murmured. "I don't know if I want to throttle her or recruit her permanently."

Kaelin crossed her arms, leaning against a nearby column. "You always did have a weakness for the reckless ones. That girl could use a lesson in restraint and in knowing when to keep her mouth shut."

Talen huffed a faint laugh, dragging a hand through his hair. "You're not wrong." His voice grew quieter. "It is so hard to sit through these endless meetings, arguing over ledgers and levies, knowing what's crawling through lands outside of Pyraelia." He looked up at Kaelin, eyes hard with exhaustion. "They talk about numbers while people are *dying*, Kaelin. I've seen it with my own eyes."

Her gaze softened a fraction, though her tone stayed even. "Then we'd better make this quick," she said. "There's one out tonight, isn't there?"

Talen nodded grimly. "A big one."

"So I'll be direct. What the hell were you thinking at the treasury meeting yesterday?"

"What?"

Kaelin's composure cracked, her voice rising. "Announcing you'd personally pay for the prison reform? Are you out of your mind?"

He pushed off the desk. "I did what was right."

"Right?" She laughed once — bitter, incredulous. "You think these nobles care about what's right?" She stepped closer, jabbing a finger at his chest. "You're lucky I was there to steady the room before half of them decided you'd lost your senses."

"Let them whisper," Talen snapped. "Someone had to say it. Someone has to *do* something."

Kaelin shook her head, muttering under her breath, "You're lucky I was there."

He glared at her. "I know how to handle the court."

"No," she said softly, "you know how to fight battles. There's a difference." She turned away, pacing a few steps before facing him again. "These nobles don't give a damn about morals. They care about money and prestige."

"Wonderful. I'd almost forgotten how inspiring home can be."

"That idealism of yours is what got you exiled in the first place. Don't forget Father sent you away because you couldn't think before you acted with the goat – "

Talen cut Kaelin off, "I remember. Believe me, I won't forget anytime soon."

"Well," she said at last, crossing her arms and tilting her head, "for what it's worth, it's good to have you back. The court's been dreadfully dull without someone to make the old men squirm."

Talen looked up at her, a corner of his mouth twitching. "That almost sounded like affection."

"Don't flatter yourself. I'm just relieved I'm no longer the only sibling stuck in this den of thieves."

He huffed, a wry smile ghosting across his face. "Touching as ever. There's nothing like scheming nobles to make a prince feel useful."

The silence that followed was heavy, familiar. Kaelin studied him quietly. Then she asked softly, "Why did you bring her here? You could've hired anyone. Why *her*?"

He hesitated, glancing toward the closed door as if he could still sense Ren's presence beyond it. "Because she's survived what most wouldn't," he said finally. "And because she doesn't flinch. Not from me, not from you, not from this court." He looked back at Kaelin, his voice dropping. "And gods help me, we need someone who still remembers what fear feels like and fights anyway."

Kaelin was quiet for a long moment. Then, she smiled. "You always did have a talent for surrounding yourself with trouble."

Talen smirked. "Takes one to know one."

Kaelin rolled her eyes. "Get going then. I'll handle the rumors you've stirred."

He gave a mock bow. "As always, sister, you're the savior of the realm that we need but don't deserve."

She sauntered toward the door, but at Talen's parting remark, she paused mid-step. With one hand resting on her hip, she glanced back over her shoulder and shot him a wink. "Don't you ever forget it, dear brother."

Ren and Talen rode on horseback for nearly an hour.

Ren was mounted on a white gelding whose ears flicked and tail lashed as though he shared her dislike for the errand. His name was Biscuit, a fitting choice for a horse with an insatiable sweet tooth. It had taken a handful of sugar cubes to pry him from his cozy stall, but Talen had assured Ren he was one of the best mounts for night rides. Talen's mount, by contrast, was a chestnut mare with gentle eyes and a steady gait, her demeanor so sweet it almost looked ridiculous beneath the weight of a warrior prince.

When they paused at the edge of a densely thick forest, Ren stroked the gelding's pale mane in an absent motion. Her stomach growled, a reminder of how little she'd eaten at Kaelin's Name Day celebration. If she had her way, she'd get this over with quickly and be back in her chambers with a bite in hand before sleep.

Ren's stomach growled again, louder this time. Talen's head turned at the sound, his eyes flicking toward her with the faintest twitch of a smirk before his expression settled back into something grim.

"It's time we go on foot," he announced, pulling on the reins to halt his chestnut. He swung down in one smooth motion, tying the mare to a weathered post half-hidden in the underbrush.

Ren glanced at the forest ahead, then back at Biscuit pawing impatiently at the earth. "Why not stay on horseback? We'd cover more ground and may even find the creature sooner."

"A horse's hooves will announce us long before we ever see it." He glanced toward the dark treeline. "And the terrain's too thick. Roots, gullies, brambles – they'll break a leg before they carry us through."

"So *we* stumble through instead?"

"On foot, we control the pace. Horses spook easy, and one panicked scream in the dark could cost us both our lives."

Ren pressed her lips together, conceding with a small nod. Ren dismounted with less grace. She patted Biscuit's neck once before securing him beside Talen's mount, the leather creaking as she tightened the knot.

The forest loomed ahead, swallowing the last remnants of the starry sky.

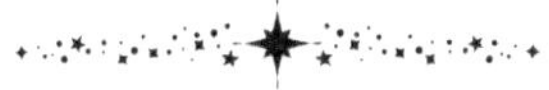

Ren and Talen traveled in silence save for the soft crunch of their boots on leaves.

They followed the curve of the riverside, its dark waters moving sluggishly beside them.

Both of them kept their senses sharp, every creak of a branch and rustle of undergrowth sharpening the tension that threaded between them.

Mist curled between gnarled roots and skeletal branches. Even the wind seemed to cower, the hush too complete, too deliberate.

Ren felt it crawling over her skin, that wrongness.

Beside her, Talen walked with measured steps, his sword loose in his grip, his silver-etched armor catching what little starlight filtered through the clouds. She glanced up to see no moon. Just a sea of darkness above.

"This creature has no name, and I couldn't find any information in the library on it," Talen murmured, his eyes scanning the trees. "Villagers say that it calls to you in the voice of the one you've lost."

"You mean it mimics them?"

Talen shook his head. "It *becomes* them. In memory, in movement... even scent. It's a weapon – our own grief turned against us."

"Do you think my fire may repel it?"

He nodded. "It's worth a shot. We haven't had time to figure out its weaknesses. There was only one other in the kingdom who ever wielded fire like yours, and she's been gone for a century."

"Great odds."

"It hunts on moonless nights."

The shadows beneath the canopy pulsed with a darkness so complete it felt alive, as though the forest itself was waiting to exhale. Ren's gaze narrowed as her eyes swept through the trees, searching for any sign of movement.

She ducked beneath a gnarled branch, fingers grazing the wet wood. "Tell me, Your Highness, why is the fae prince of House Vaelaran trudging through haunted woods instead of staying behind the palace walls? Shouldn't your court be panicking that their future king is hunting these things?"

"That's not how our court works. The king and queen choose their heir at the end of their reign. The crown goes to the one deemed worthy." He flicked a glance at her. "My sister may very well be the next monarch."

Ren nearly tripped. The image of Kaelin seated on a throne slithered into her mind like a *very* bad omen.

Ren asked quietly, "And how do you feel about the crown?"

He didn't answer right away. Finally, he said, "I haven't had the luxury of thinking about it. But if it's what the realm needs, then so be it."

"You really don't care if it's you?"

"I care about the realm," he said, each word deliberate. There was no bravado in his voice, no arrogance. Just a quiet conviction that struck deeper than any polished speech.

Ren had never hunted a creature like this. This was far different from fighting in the pits. There, the roar of the crowd filled her ears, the scent of blood and sweat heavy in the air. She could feel the weight of every eye upon her, the press of bodies screaming her name or cursing it. The chaos had been more of a distraction from her own racing heartbeat from the adrenaline.

But here, there was no audience – no jeering or applause, no opponents she could read like a book. Just the eerie stillness and the knowledge that something ancient and hungry was waiting beyond the trees.

And no roaring crowds to hide her racing heartbeat hammering within her chest. It was so loud, she wondered if Talen's heightened sense of hearing could hear it.

They passed a circle of scorched bark, trees that had blackened from the inside out. Signs that the thing had fed here before.

And then—

A sound.

Ren's name, spoken in a soft and familiar voice.

Her blood turned to ice.

She knew that voice. She would have known it in a crowd of thousands, even after all these years.

Her older sister, Eve.

B etween the trees, Ren caught a flash of emerald green eyes that gleamed in the darkness.

Hello, little sister.

The voice was a low whisper, a memory dragged out from some forgotten place in Ren's soul.

You've come at last.

A silhouette emerged between the trees, flickering in and out of view like candlelight in a storm. Eve's face smiled at her. Same moon-pale skin. Same chestnut curls tumbling over one shoulder.

The creature tilted its head just like Eve once had, one hand reaching playfully toward the tree beside it.

And suddenly, Ren was six again. Barefoot in a summer field, wind tugging at her braids. Laughter echoed through the trees – *Eve's* laugh. Always too loud, too free.

"Come find me, Ren!"

They'd play hide and seek for hours, but Eve always made it easy, leaving behind clues. A trail of snapped twigs. A bright ribbon tied around a low branch. Emerald eyes peeking out from behind a tree trunk that was far too thin to properly hide behind.

"You always find me," Eve used to whisper when Ren caught her.

Ren's vision swam, the memory bleeding back into the present. She stumbled forward. The forest blurred.

"*I finally came for you,*" the voice's whisper turned into a hiss.

Ren's knees buckled. Her weapon slipped from her fingers.

She spun, only to see Eve standing just a few feet away. The sight of her hit Ren like a blow to the chest.

She hadn't realized how much time had eroded the edges of memory, how Eve's face had started to blur in her mind. But seeing her face again, it all came rushing back. The delicate curve of her sister's cheekbones, the pointed nose and chin they both shared. But it was the eyes that undid Ren, their mother's eyes, staring out from a face Ren thought she'd never see again in her lifetime.

Somewhere beyond the haze, Talen was shouting her name, but she didn't hear him. All she saw was Eve.

When Talen suddenly charged, sword drawn, Ren lunged forward instinctively. "No!"

But Talen caught her by the arm, shoving her hard behind a tree. The bark scraped her back as Talen pressed her to it. "Ren, it's not real. Do you hear me? It's *deceiving* you."

She blinked, heart pounding, the world snapping back into focus. Her heart ached at his words, but she couldn't help peering around the tree, longing for one more glimpse of her sister. Even knowing it was a lie.

There she is. Eve moved closer, and her smile curled unnaturally, splitting too wide.

"*You always find me.*"

Just as Ren remembered her before that night. Dark hair in loose curls, wearing a nightgown Eve used to wear when pulling Ren into her bedroom, when shouts and glasses of ale or rum or wine shattering sounded from the kitchen, followed by her mother's cries and father's bellows.

A sob tore through Ren's chest. Tears burned hot trails down her cheeks.

As much as Ren feared her sister for the night that split her world open, Eve still haunted her in quieter ways. The memory of her laughter. Her protective hugs. The warmth of her bed when the house below was a battlefield.

The grief inside her was a sea, but she didn't let it drown her. She forced herself to swim in it, to breathe it in, to let it fill every hollow place inside her. Because the image she fought was the sister she ached for, the sister she remembered.

Not the sister who betrayed them all that night.

"Eve," Ren sobbed through the tears as she came around the tree and into the open, "I never stopped looking for you. But I couldn't find you this time."

Her chest ached with the weight of the words she had never spoken, the ones that had haunted every sleepless night. Because deep down, she had always known the truth.

Her sister hadn't *wanted* to be found.

The creature tilted its head.

"I enjoyed hearing their screams. Your mother first, her throat breaking open under the sharpness of the blade, so fragile humans are, the sound of her pathetically gurgling as she tried to breathe, choking on her own blood. And your father – I enjoyed watching the light drain from his eyes as he clutched at nothing. Did you know that your father begged them to spare him? He even tried to give them your *life, if it meant saving his own. A coward to the end."* It licked its lips. *"When I tear you to shreds, will you beg for your life like your cowardly father did?"*

Ren's jaw locked, teeth grinding. "Here's an idea," she snarled through her teeth. "Why don't you come find out for yourself?"

Its voice seethed with anticipation. *"Very well. I shall enjoy hearing your screams."*

It lunged.

Smoke curled from its limbs, long and skeletal, unraveling like tendrils of ash. Its face melted mid-air, features distorting into a swirling, dark void.

Ren's scream tore from her throat, not of terror, but of fury so raw, it felt as though it had lived in her bones for years, waiting for this moment to be unleashed. The weight of every betrayal, every loss, every night she'd endured gasping from the nightmares.

The creature struck, slamming Ren into the earth, its jaws opening wide to devour her.

But Ren didn't get to her feet and run.

She didn't beg.

She *burned*.

The flames burst from her like a falling star made flesh – a light so pure and furious that the creature recoiled. Her fire struck it head-on, ripping through shadow and devouring the void where its heart should have been.

And the thing screamed as Ren's flames consumed it whole. Its illusion flickered and collapsed, revealing the truth beneath. A twisted, withered corpse, and in its sunken sockets were eyes as black as coal.

Ren stood trembling in the scorched ring of earth, and she whispered the name she hadn't spoken aloud in years.

"Goodbye, Eve."

Her knees buckled, the strength bleeding out of her all at once, and she collapsed. The world around her felt muted, as though the roar of her flames had stolen all sound and left behind only silence.

Talen was at her side in an instant, sword lowered. The creature disintegrated before them, ash caught in the wind.

Talen knelt beside Ren's shaking frame. He didn't speak at first. He simply stayed there, grounding her with his quiet presence while she tried to remember how to breathe.

Finally, his voice broke through. "It fed on your grief. It tried to twist it, to turn it into darkness."

Her eyes burned as tears gathered.

Talen's gaze held hers. "But instead, you turned it into light."

As the heavy silence settled around them, Ren understood with bone-deep certainty that this was only the beginning.

And she needed a better weapon.

23

After the creature had crumbled into the earth, Ren remained on her knees in the clearing, her palms pressed into the damp earth.

Talen's shadow stretched long beside her. Then, he offered his hand and rested it on her shoulder. His touch was warm and steady.

Ren hated that it steadied her. She hadn't meant for Talen to see her like that.

"I'm fine," she managed. "It's over. It's gone." But her knees trembled, and she couldn't quite meet his eyes. And she couldn't help but add, "We kicked its ass, though."

"You mean *you* kicked its ass. I was just trying to keep you from setting the forest on fire. Still, we make a good team."

"I don't know about a good team," Ren muttered, dragging a hand through her tangled hair. "My head's all jumbled, like someone took it apart and put it back wrong."

Talen's expression softened, the teasing gone. "That's what magic does," he said quietly. "Especially illusions. They get inside you and twist what's real until you can't tell the difference."

"Stupid magical bastards. Next time, I'll shove my boot up its ass. We'll see what its illusions can do then."

She turned on her heel before Talen could respond and stalked toward the forest clearing with the storm still thundering in her bones.

She barely remembered the path, barely even registered riding back to the palace, or roaming the corridors of the palace to her room. She only remembered that when the door closed behind her, she collapsed against it.

That thing had hit too deep.

And she couldn't let Talen, or any of the fae, for that matter, see just how close she was to shattering.

Ren lingered in the spring bath far longer than she meant to, and she was thankfully alone.

The water clung to her skin, but no matter how hot she made it, it couldn't burn away the ache inside her chest. She sank deeper until the water crept over her shoulders, lapping at her collarbones, her throat.

She hadn't spoken that name in years.

The realization made her stomach twist. Shame tangled in her throat until she could hardly swallow. She let her head fall back against the edge of the bath, her eyes fluttering shut.

She had taken her first steps not toward their mother or father, but to Eve. Chubby arms outstretched, eyes lit with blind trust, she giggled as she toppled into Eve's waiting arms. Eve used to swear that she'd protect her.

The night that changed everything, Ren had been dreaming the best dream of her life. She dreamt she was in a field of wildflowers, sunlight warm on her skin, painting while Eve read aloud beside her. The air had smelled of honey and earth, and for once, everything felt whole.

Then, she was wrenched from her bed and dragged down the stairs with ropes binding her wrists. Her parents were shoved beside her, bound like cattle. Ren tried to scoot closer to her mother, searching for any sign of comfort. But her mother looked into Ren's eyes, and her eyes were wide with terror. There was a shout, an order given, and rough hands yanked her mother away.

The world fractured into noise – boots, screaming, and the heavy scent of iron thick in the air.

Blood hit Ren's cheek, and she twisted frantically, only to see Eve descending the staircase, her steps unhurried, face eerily calm.

Ren's eyes had bulged in terror, refusing to believe what she saw. Eve wasn't bound. She wasn't fighting.

No, she was *with* them.

The intruders muttered what sounded like prayers or chants, their voices too low to make out words. And in that moment, Ren remembered the certainty that sank into her bones. She would die here.

Eve just looked at Ren as their parents died beside them and the flames took everything they ever knew, meager as they were – their beds, books, clothes.

And then, Eve walked away.

Some nights, Ren still saw her shadowy form flickering over the flames.

Ren missed Eve like a phantom limb, aching in the quiet, in the places no physical touch could reach. And yet, part of Ren hoped she was dead. Because if she were alive, if she were still out there, then she *chose* to kill their parents and leave Ren to suffer their deaths alone.

Ren sighed and opened her eyes. There were days the grief dulled. But tonight, it roared back with a vengeance.

I wish you were here.

The Eve who would kiss Ren's forehead and rub her back when she was so hungry her stomach ached, and the cabinets were empty no matter how hard they searched for something to fill their bellies. The Eve who read her stories, her voice soft and steady as war raged below them, screams and shattering glass and their mother's cries muffled by the turning of pages.

A sob caught in Ren's throat. The grief continued its slow, consuming journey. She felt it creeping into her lungs, her limbs – a slow drowning.

Pull your shit together, a voice seethed in her mind. A whisper she had heard many times over the years, usually when she hit rock bottom.

So Ren shut her eyes, pressing her forehead to her knees, and whispered, "Five things I can see…" Her voice cracked, but she inhaled deeply before she opened her eyes.

"The way the spring's surface ripples with each movement," she began. "The runes carved into the stone walls, glowing. Stray petals floating across the water. My bruised knees beneath the water..." Her gaze fell to her trembling fingers just below the water. "My own hand."

She swallowed hard. "Four things I can touch... the smooth stone edge of the spring. My calloused fingertips. The warm water brushing against my skin. The braid in my hair."

Her breath began steadying. "Three things I can hear... the trickle of the spring as it feeds the pool. The hum of the runes carved into the walls. My own breathing in the chamber."

A tear slipped down her cheek.

"Two things I can smell," she whispered. "The bite of the spring water... and herbs, steeping at the edge of the pool."

Her voice dropped to barely a breath.

"One thing I can taste." Her lips parted. "Salt. From my own damn tears."

The silence after was almost reverent. The kind that lingered like a hand pressed to a wound. And yet, somehow, she was still breathing.

Still here.

Her grip on her knees loosened. Though the ache in her chest remained, it was bearable.

Ren leaned her head back, blinking up at the dark ceiling. "Where did you go, Eve?"

Talen didn't know what hour it was when he finally pushed open his chamber door. He expected blessed, empty silence after the night they'd had.

Instead, Kaelin was perched on the edge of his desk, one long leg crossed over the other, a half-empty glass of wine dangling from her fingers. "You survived."

"Clearly," he muttered, unfastening his cloak and hanging it on the wall peg. "We had one hell of a fight. The thing had strong illusion magic. It makes you see something you miss, maybe someone you've lost, and uses it against you."

"How'd the human do?"

"*Ren* burned it to ash. Hell, the thing turned in on itself. You should've seen its true form; it was hideous."

Her brows rose slightly. "Did she fall under its magic?"

"Yes." He leaned against the wall. "When I charged, she nearly came after me. I think it made her see someone she'd lost and she tried to protect them."

Kaelin scowled. "You know, if you'd hired a trained fae warrior, they might have had the sense and the mental wards to resist an illusion."

"Maybe. But where's the fun in that?"

"Not all things are fun and games," she snapped. "You're putting your life in *her* hands. Do you really trust her to have your back?"

He began unbuttoning his shirt. "I trust that she won't go down without a fight."

"That didn't answer my question."

Talen smirked faintly. "Didn't it?"

Kaelin pushed off the desk, finishing her wine in one long swallow. "She hates our kind, that much is obvious," she said, pacing toward him. "I say we get rid of her now before she becomes a liability – "

"No."

Her head snapped toward him. "But – "

"We made a contract," Talen cut in. "I'm not breaking it."

They stared at each other, the silence between them tense. The low fire in the hearth popped, breaking the stillness.

Kaelin's eyes narrowed. "There's something you're not telling me."

"How do you know?"

She crossed her arms, the faintest smirk ghosting across her lips. "Because I know you better than anyone. Now talk."

Talen exhaled slowly, shoulders loosening in resignation. "The day of the ogre attack—when she first used her fire—something about it was... different."

Kaelin gestured impatiently. "Different how? We've seen elemental wielders before. How is the human's fire any different?"

He hesitated, searching for the words. "The human has a name," he said finally, his tone low. "And Ren's fire didn't seem elemental. It wasn't drawn from the air or the ground. It was like it came from within her, not from the world around her."

"So you're also keeping her close to watch her."

Talen met her gaze, the faintest flicker of conflict behind his eyes. "I'm keeping her close," he said quietly, "because something tells me her magic isn't done with us yet."

Kaelin studied him for a long moment, the firelight flickering across her face. "Careful, brother. Curiosity can burn hotter than any flame."

Talen's mouth quirked in a grim half-smile. "Then let it burn."

The next morning, Ren went to the market.

There weren't throngs of people out, likely due to the Witherblight. Thankful for not having to swerve in between crowds, Ren sauntered with purpose, with one destination in mind.

The Iron Maw was a living beast. The forge roared with heat, and the walls were built of rough-hewn stone and daub, the kind of structure meant to withstand centuries. Smoke curled from the tall brick chimney. The fire hearth, a waist-high structure of dry-laid brick, glowed, its heat searing. Nearly stacked piles of charcoal were kept just beyond the forge's reach, safe from stray sparks. Within the open-faced workshop, Ren caught movement of flashes of steel and sweat, hammer-strikes falling in sharp rhythm, purposeful as a battle drum. The air smelled of iron, heavy with the promise of creation.

Ren paused at the entrance. Blades hung along the inner walls, gleaming axes, curved swords, bone-handled daggers. Some bore runes that glowed faintly, whispering of bloodshed and magic.

"Hey, you." Elira swaggered toward her, iron bars resting over her shoulder, her muscular arms dusted with sweat. Soot streaked across her cheekbones like warpaint, and her forge leathers clung to her like a second skin.

"Miss me?" Ren asked.

Elira dropped the iron with a *clang*, wiped her brow with a gloved hand, and gave Ren a once-over. "What's got you sniffing around the market this early? Looking for something sharp and deadly?"

Ren stepped closer, eyes drifting past her into the glow of the forge. "Just browsing."

Elira snorted. "Bullshit. You need a weapon."

Ren's gaze met Elira's with steady resolve. "You're from House Tharowen, aren't you?"

"What gave me away? The smoldering glare or the divine biceps?"

Ren nodded to the mark inked into Elira's left shoulder, an intricate knot of flame and steel. "The Forgemark. Hard to miss."

That earned a full grin from Elira, fierce and wicked. "Perceptive. I like that." She leaned one shoulder against the stone wall. "We take the mark at thirteen. Call fire our first teacher. If it doesn't burn you, it'll forge you."

Ren gave a low whistle. "That's one hell of a teacher."

"Damn right it is. We forge our first blade during what we call *the Tempering*. We work side by side with a master smith. When it's done, the forge brands your skin."

A voice bellowed from inside the forge. "I don't have long," Elira told Ren. "What are you hunting?"

Ren's expression darkened. "Monsters I don't have a name for. I don't know what it'll take to kill them, but I need steel that won't fail."

Elira's eyes widened. "By the Hollow... that bad, huh?"

"Worse."

For a beat, Elira just studied her. Then she straightened. "Alright, then. I'll make you something that sings fire when it swings and drinks fear when it cuts." Her eyes sparked. "Give me a week."

Ren offered a crooked smile. "Thank you. Use whatever you'd use to protect someone you actually like." She pulled a small coin purse from her belt and held it out, the weight of it soft but promising in her palm. "Here," she offered, giving it a little shake. "Will this cover half to get started?"

Elira accepted the coin purse. "I'll put a blade in your hand that makes monsters rethink their life choices." She turned to return to work, then paused, adding over her shoulder softly, "You don't need to thank me, Ren. Just come back alive."

Ren wove her way through the outer edge of Pyraelia. She passed a crooked bookshop tucked beneath a narrow archway, where a raven sat perched above the door. It tilted its head as she walked by, as if weighing her soul.

Next came a bakery, its windows fogged with heat and scented with cardamom and clove. But no laughter spilled into the street, no footsteps echoed on cobblestone. The market square, where she had her first meal with Talen and Elira the day they arrived in Pyraelia, was smothered under the looming dread of the Witherblight.

Then she saw Zakhar.

He stood before an apothecary, handing over a pouch of coins to the weary-eyed keeper before noticing Ren.

"Getting ready to bunker down," Zakhar called, his voice bright despite the gloom. "Planning a few fresh brews for the warehouse. Useful things. Potions to make you run faster, leap higher... maybe even dance with death and walk away smiling."

Ren lifted a brow, stopping just short of the step. "Any chance you'll tell me what other kinds of potions you keep stashed in there? Or is that one of your many secrets?"

Zakhar just winked, his tall staff in his left hand. It towered over him, crowned with a twisted crystal that pulsed faintly, like it was breathing.

"Where's the fun in telling?" he quipped, a wicked grin flashing. "But truly, shapeshifting? Memory tampering? There's a spell for nearly everything. Even fire, if you're asking."

"Do you work with elemental magic?"

"I know the theory. I've studied the nature of magic. But I'm no battlemage. Still, you're welcome to visit. There might be a tome or two tucked away in my shelves that you may find enlightening."

They began to walk. Zakhar whistled softly under his breath, a low, unsettling melody that didn't quite sound like a song. Then he clicked his tongue and pulled his hood low, muttering as if annoyed with the wind or perhaps with himself. Ren had quickly learned to tread carefully around Zakhar. His moods shifted like storm fronts, sunlight one moment, thunder the next.

"Strange," he murmured. "Now that I think about it... the last time a *flamebearer* walked the realms, the stars themselves seemed to tremble. That was generations ago."

Ren froze mid-step. "What did you just call me?"

Zakhar didn't stop walking. "Hmm?"

"That name. Flamebearer."

She said it like it burned her tongue. The same name she'd heard whispered in her dreams, those visions of a woman wreathed in fire.

Zakhar looked at her for a long moment, as if weighing whether to speak or to flee into silence. But at last, he muttered, "It is an old title. These days, it's only murmured in hushed voices around firesides, buried in legends."

Ren folded her arms. "Continue."

Zakhar's gaze darted. "The Flamebearer is a soul born with dragon fire in her blood and the strength to carry it. The last Flamebearer brought an age to its knees. Some say to save it. Others say to end it."

Ren's mouth had gone dry. "And you think that's me?"

Zakhar tilted his head ever so slightly. "Elemental mages wield fire that already exists. Think of a candle's flame, a burning torch. But your magic creates itself. That kind of magic doesn't come from elemental discipline. It comes from something older."

Zakhar stepped back slightly, as if distance might protect him from whatever storm he'd just stirred.

Then, he continued walking. Ren hurried her pace to keep up with him. His pace didn't falter. He only offered a distracted hum, as if she'd asked about the weather.

He turned a corner before she could press him again.

"I've seen many deaths in my time," he swiftly changed the subject. "Too many to count. But this illness... this Witherblight is different. It doesn't behave like sickness should." Zakhar's gaze slid sideways, the usual gleam in his eye dulled by something darker. "With most plagues, you can trace a pattern. Eventually, scholars can record how they spread, how they are cured. Even the worst of plagues follows rules. This one *unravels* them."

"You think it's magic?"

Zakhar's staff tapped against the stone road. His voice lowered to a whisper, just loud enough for her to hear. "There are no known herbs, no natural remedies that so much as slow it. Every attempt to treat it with traditional healing fails. It drains life... and something else."

He hesitated. "*Magic*. It leaches the very essence from those who have even a spark. And the stronger their gift, the faster it withers them. The only cure? Magic itself." He clicked his tongue, in deep thought. "Tell me, does that sound natural to you?"

He paused. He looked at her then, *truly* looked, and Ren felt the weight of something vast pressing in around them, like the stars themselves were listening.

"No," he said softly. "This illness was crafted with a dark purpose."

Zakhar met her gaze, and for a heartbeat, there was no trace of his previous mischief.

"Curses crave legacy, and this one was made to endure. You don't create something like the Witherblight without knowing exactly who you want to destroy."

He turned from her then, staff tapping the stone again.

"The question isn't what it is, Ren. It's *who*." He walked in the direction of the palace and murmured over his shoulder, "Be wary where your curiosity leads, Flamebearer. The answers rarely come without a price."

24

Ren's breathing sputtered, and sweat soaked the back of her tunic. The morning sun had long since risen, but the air still bit with a chill that clung to her skin. Her arms ached from drills, her thighs burned from endless footwork, and her ribs protested every inhale, but she kept moving. Kept pushing.

"Line up!" Ivan's voice cracked through the air like a whip.

Ren fell into formation. Her eyes flicked down the row of fae warriors and then stilled.

Lucan Brightbane stood across from her, twirling his blade like it was an extension of his ego. His smile was all teeth, and the glint in his eyes sent a familiar churn through her stomach. Dread, yes. But also something else.

Anticipation.

Lucan sauntered forward, blue tunic pristine, his golden hair catching the light like a halo. "I'm going to enjoy tearing you to shreds," he purred.

Ren rolled her shoulders, planting her boots into the packed earth of the sparring ring. Her knuckles cracked one by one as she flexed her fingers around the hilt of her training blade.

Lucan, smug as ever, looked like he thought this fight was already won.

"Careful," Ren called back flatly. "Wouldn't want you to chip one of those perfect teeth when you eat dirt."

His expression flickered a beat before he lunged.

Steel clashed in a violent crescendo. Lucan's attacks were fast, furious, meant to overwhelm. But Ren moved like smoke and fire, ducking, sidestepping, parrying with brutal precision. She let him believe she was tiring, let him gloat with every near miss. Then, when he overreached with a wide slash, she twisted under his arm, slammed her boot into the back of his knee, and brought him crashing down.

Ren pinned the tip of her blade at his throat. "Still enjoying yourself?"

Lucan growled, but didn't move.

She leaned in just slightly. "Next time, don't underestimate the human from the pits. I've fought far worse than you."

Lucan bared his teeth and shoved her off of him, stumbling to his feet. Noting the stares, he said loudly, "Next time, I won't go as easy on you."

Ren fought the urge to roll her eyes as Lucan sauntered off and joined a few other fae.

Ren adjusted her grip on the practice sword as she faced the brown-haired fae from her first day of training.

They circled each other. He was quiet, focused, his brown eyes sharp beneath a furrowed brow. Muscles coiled beneath his tunic as he moved, measured and efficient. Not flashy like Lucan, but dangerous all the same.

Ren struck first, feinting low before pivoting and slashing high. He blocked it, steel singing against steel.

"You always come out swinging?" he asked.

Ren grinned wickedly. "Only when I know I'm being underestimated."

They clashed again. Back and forth they went, grunting, spinning, parrying. The ring filled with the sound of blades and boots scuffing dirt. Ren landed a strike to his ribs; he caught her off guard with a swift kick that knocked her balance. They both panted, sweat dripping.

Neither willing to yield.

But it was his endurance that won out. Just as Ren launched one last impulsive strike, he twisted, locked her wrist, and swept her legs from under her. She hit the ground with a grunt, sword skidding out of reach.

Before she could push herself up, a gloved hand appeared in front of her. She eyed it warily.

"Take it," he muttered.

With a sigh, she clasped it. He pulled her up in one swift motion.

"Name's Elric," he said, releasing her hand. "You fight decently... for someone with your odds."

"Is that supposed to be a compliment?"

A faint smirk tugged at the corner of his mouth. "I suppose it is."

Ren trudged up the stone steps and out of the sparring pit, every muscle in her body aching like it had been wrung out and hung to dry. Her arms felt like lead, her legs wobbled with each step, and her knuckles were still raw from sparring. All she could think about was a bath. A *long* one.

She reached her chamber door and shoved it open, already peeling her sweat-soaked tunic over her head when a knock sounded at her door.

Ren stared at the gown like it might bite her.

It lay draped across the bed like a trap, midnight blue velvet, off-the-shoulder, with embroidered silver designs curling along the bodice.

The handmaiden who delivered it had said nothing, only placed it on the mattress with the careful reverence of someone handling something enchanted. Maybe it was. Maybe if Ren wore it, she'd lose what little sense she had left.

There was a note folded atop the dress that read:

Ren,

Blue doesn't suit me.

But on you? It might just look decent. For a mortal.

—Her Royal Highness Princess Kaelin of House Vaelaran

Ren unfolded the letter again, her eyes skimming over the words for a second time. By the time she reached the end, she let out a laugh, unable to stop herself. *Gods, the sheer arrogance,* she thought wryly.

She crumpled the letter in her fist before tearing it clean in one go, the pieces scattering like petals as they hit the floor. Crossing her arms, she glared at the dress.

"I ought to burn this damn thing and send the ashes straight to Her *Royal* Highness."

Outside the high window, bells tolled in the city, counting down the hour until the Winter Solstice ball. Until Ren would be expected to smile and drink and pretend she didn't want to throttle half the fae court.

Ren exhaled sharply and paced the room. She didn't belong there. Not in Kaelin or Talen's world.

But she *had* to go. Zakhar's words echoed in her mind, about how the Witherblight might not be as natural as everyone believed.

A cold unease settled in her chest. The Witherblight spread so quickly, the elixir's price so impossibly high; none of it felt like co-incidence. And Ren couldn't shake the suspicion gnawing at her gut that whoever was responsible was right here, behind the glittering walls of this very court.

Still. She eyed the gown again like it might sprout fangs. Perhaps Kaelin enchanted it to do just that, and it would take a swipe at Ren when she let her guard down.

"She can go to hell," she eventually muttered, grabbing the fabric like it insulted her ancestors and tossing it aside.

Ren's fingers closed around a green gown tucked in the back of the armoire. Simple, elegant, and modest enough, aside from the sharp dip at the neckline that left a bold sweep of cleavage exposed.

She glanced back at the velvet blue dress sprawled across the bed, opulent and perfect and undeniably Kaelin's style.

Through gritted teeth, she decided, "I'm doing this on *my* terms."

Then she turned her back on it and yanked the green gown from its hanger like drawing a blade from its sheath.

"Green does wonders for redheads," Mirella declared as Ren stepped out from behind the folding screen. "Earthy and moody, perfect for a grounded but bold look."

Ren scowled at her reflection. "I feel like a plucked pheasant."

"You look divine," Mirella corrected.

Ren tugged at the bodice, glaring down as though sheer will might summon her leathers back onto her frame. "I don't know why I'm even going to this cursed thing."

"The Winter Solstice Ball? Only the most opulent event in the kingdom's calendar? It's not just any celebration, darling. The Winter Solstice Ball marks the longest night of the year. It is a night when the Veil between realms is said to thin, when old pacts are renewed and new ones are forged. Deals sealed under the solstice moon are believed to last a lifetime."

Mirella's tone softened, almost conspiratorial. "Which makes it the perfect night for politics dressed as revelry... and perhaps, for truths to come to light where no one expects them." Her voice chirped up. "At any rate, the royal family adores it. Especially Her Royal Highness." A knowing lilt colored her tone. "She has a particular affection for her balls and her dancing."

Ren's lips twitched. "She sure does. I've been here for two months now and can only imagine how much coin she designates to hosting these insufferable balls. If you asked me, they could use that coin for something far more helpful for the realm."

She crossed to the window, arms folded, eyes tracing the curve of the mountains beyond the palace walls. A gust of wind rattled the frosted glass. Down in the garden, torches flickered to life, preparation for the evening's revelry.

"With her footwork," Mirella went on, undeterred, "I daresay Her Highness could make a rather skilled swordfighter."

Ren snorted. "Please. She's probably never so much as lifted a blade."

"Perhaps. But if she ever did... she'd be a force to reckon with."

"Why bother? She has others do her fighting for her."

Mirella didn't answer at first. Only watched as Ren pulled her copper-red hair into a loose half-up twist.

"I've known Her Highness since she was a youngling. She enchanted me herself, you know. Not for vanity. Not for fun. But because she had no one else to speak to. No friends. Not even her guards would meet her eyes back then."

Ren listened quietly. That wasn't the version of the fae princess the court whispered about.

"She barely spoke aloud until she was eight," Mirella continued. "Her magic frightened people. It was too wild. There's more to her than you see. Far more than even she lets on."

And though Ren rolled her eyes, grumbling something about manipulative royals and overly talkative wardrobes, she couldn't shake the image of the fae princess alone as a youngling, giving life to a wardrobe for the chance to speak to someone, to anyone.

Mirella hummed thoughtfully, her fabric-laced voice drifting. "And the prince was always running off to the training yards with scraped-up knees and a sword too heavy for his arms. When he wasn't swinging blades, he was buried nose-deep in texts. He'd train until his hands bled, then sit in the library and read until the candlewax melted. He once tried to write a treaty between two fictional kingdoms in the margins of a swordsmanship manual. Said it was a test of diplomacy and precision."

"That sounds insufferable."

"It was," Mirella agreed. "But he had this maddening sort of patience and wanted to hone his diplomacy skills, even at a young age. Talen always wanted to be the kind of leader his father is."

Ren turned from the mirror, rolling her shoulders. "Sounds like a royal problem."

"And yet, you've been rather entangled in their royal problems of late, haven't you?"

Ren shot her a look. "Don't start."

The wardrobe gave a theatrical sigh. "Fine, fine. Off you go, then. Try not to look like you're walking to your own execution."

Ren didn't respond. Her gaze drifted back to her own reflection. Her hair, brushed and pinned back from her face, her freckles dusted across her cheeks, and her shoulders bare and tense.

She sighed. "Let's get this over with."

As she stepped out into the hallway, the air shifted, carrying with it the scent of snow, spice, and rosewood. The palace pulsed with life. Fae servants flitted from corridor to corridor, laughter and music seeping from grand archways.

The ballroom doors loomed ahead, massive and intricately carved. The guards stationed at the entry gave Ren a skeptical once-over. One of them smirked, as though amused by the sight of a mortal dressed in royal splendor.

Ren clicked her tongue. "Your jaw's hanging open." Ren leaned in, whispering, "Don't worry. I'm still dangerous." she winked. "Just *shinier.*"

He cleared his throat, grumbling, "Just go in," before stepping aside.

The doors opened.

And once again, Ren stepped into a world she had no business entering.

25

The ballroom glittered with winter's splendor.

Velvet banners of deep silver and pale ivory draped from the vaulted ceiling. Glass chandeliers swirled with slow-turning enchantments, scattering prismatic light that danced across the marble floor. Fae nobles drifted across the floor, gowns and cloaks glistening, their movements weaving seamlessly with the lilting music.

Ren felt their stares as she entered, a tantalizing mixture of curiosity and judgment.

Her boots clicked against the polished floor as she descended the grand staircase. She didn't *need* to belong here. She only needed to earn her coin and get as far away from all this bullshit as her legs could carry her.

At the heart of the ballroom, a high fae female rested upon a dais veiled in gossamer silk. Long, slender fingers danced effortlessly across the strings of an ornate harp. Her beauty was so striking, it felt otherworldly – skin like moonlit porcelain, hair a cascade of silver that spilled over her shoulders like liquid starlight. Each note she plucked seemed to breathe magic into the room.

Ren's eyes shifted and inevitably fell on someone whose very sight had a *very* different reaction for Ren.

Kaelin stood like moonlight carved into flesh. She wore crimson silk that clung to every lethal curve of her body, the fabric flowing like liquid fire over hips and waist, daring the eye to linger.

Their eyes met across the ballroom, and for a moment, the world narrowed. Kaelin's mouth curved into a smile that promised nothing but trouble.

Ren exhaled. "Gods save me," she muttered under her breath. Without breaking stride, she snatched a glass of wine off the tray of a passing servant and took a deep swig. She wiped her mouth with the back of her hand and muttered, "Let's get this over with."

Ren lingered near the refreshment table, sipping wines that were too sweet and far too strong as nobles spun past her as if they were stars in orbit, unsurprisingly uninterested in speaking with Ren.

And Kaelin was a constellation all her own.

She moved through couples like the wind before a storm, a force to be reckoned with. She was laughing softly against the shoulders of those who dared step close. A tall male with storm-gray eyes twirled her once, and Kaelin's answering smile was all teeth. Then a female with midnight-dark braids took her hand, pulling her into a faster step. Kaelin didn't miss a beat, her skirts a swirl of crimson.

But in between those steps, those dances, her gaze kept flicking back to Ren. A glance over a partner's shoulder. A fleeting sweep across the room.

Not enough to be obvious.

But enough to piss Ren off.

Ren hated balls. She hated velvet and tight corsets and wine that tasted like spiced cranberries and mulled plums. Realizing she was on her second glass, she figured okay, perhaps she didn't *hate* the wine, but if anyone asked, she'd die before admitting she liked it. Ren reached for another glass of wine when she caught the scent of expensive scented oil and ego.

She didn't need to turn to know it was Lucan Brightbane because his presence slithered into the space beside her like a cold draft. But when she did glance, she was met with his usual display: blues and whites tailored to perfection, a cascade of golden hair swept back from his sculpted features, glowing beneath the enchanted lights overhead.

"Lucky me," Ren muttered under her breath, raising the glass to her lips. "We always seem to find each other. Tell me, Lucan, are we star-crossed lovers, or is the universe just playing a cruel joke? What's next, tragic ballads about our forbidden love?"

Lucan didn't bite. And that threw Ren more than a venom-laced insult would have.

Instead, he asked quietly, "What's your intention here? Climbing the ranks? Plenty of humans have tried. None made it far."

Ren took a slow, deliberate sip of her wine. She kept her gaze locked on his over the rim.

"Your kind doesn't belong here."

Ren barked a humorless laugh and shook her head. "Believe me, I'm well aware. You think I want to be here, playing soldier in a court that sees me as dirt under its boots?" She set the glass down, her voice leveling. "I'm here to help Prince Talen deal with the lovely nightmare creatures clawing their way out of the hells. That's it. I have no ambition to climb any ranks. In fact, I don't give a damn about ranks." When Lucan's mouth twitched in open doubt, she added, "As soon as this is over, I'm gone. So if you're worried about me being a threat to your place at the top, don't be."

His face gave nothing away, but her eyes caught a faint discoloration marring his otherwise flawless cheekbone. Concealed beneath whatever fae powder passed for vanity.

She tilted her head, hiding a smirk. "Rough day at training?"

Lucan scowled. "You could say that."

Ren sipped her wine, secretly savoring the image. He was probably used to winning, used to everyone stepping aside when he entered a room. It was oddly satisfying to know she'd left a mark.

She let out a long breath. "Look. I'm not saying we have to braid each other's hair or whatever it is your kind does to bond. Let's get through training without killing each other. After that, I vanish from your world. You'll never hear my name again."

Lucan studied her. "You give me your word?"

Ren raised her glass and gave a toast. "You bet, and I never back from my word."

As their glasses clinked, Mirella's words about the Winter Solstice tugged at Ren's mind, how this was a night for pacts and promises, for fates to be reshaped beneath the solstice moon. *Maybe tonight doesn't have to be just their bargains. Maybe it can be the start of mine.*

Lucan slipped away into the crowd, and movement flickered at the edge of Ren's vision. Ren turned, instincts flaring. Kaelin glided toward her between songs, her steps lazy and unhurried, like a lioness with no need to chase. A half-circle of nobles trailed in the fae princess's wake.

"Happy Winter Solstice," Kaelin greeted, her gaze sweeping over Ren from head to toe, lingering a moment too long at her hips. "Interesting choice of attire. Did you receive my generous gift?"

"I received it. Just not my color." Ren raised her glass without warmth. "Happy Winter Solstice, Your *Royal* Highness."

"You do clean up nicely. I almost didn't recognize you. Mortals look so very different when they're pretending to be one of us."

A sharp, too-loud laugh echoed behind the fae princess, belonging to one of Kaelin's courtiers, lips curled with mockery.

Color bloomed in Ren's cheeks. "Funny. I was just thinking how easy it must be for you to pretend you're above everyone else."

The laughter cut off sharply.

One of the courtiers stepped forward, eyes flashing as her canines bared. "Watch your tongue, mortal. You'll not speak to Your Highness that way and leave with it intact."

Kaelin's hand came to rest lightly on the courtier's arm, her touch calm but commanding enough to halt the lesser fae mid-step. Her eyes never left Ren's.

"It's fine," Kaelin purred. "She's still learning how to behave. It's endearing, really, how she thinks mouthing off makes her look brave, when all it does is prove how desperately out of her depth she is."

The words landed with such effortless disdain that Ren's breath caught in her throat. For a moment, she could only stare.

But that wasn't all.

Kaelin tilted her head. "Word says you were impressive with that first creature. So impressive, in fact, that word has already reached me of how you froze like a startled doe and nearly lost your head when it caught you in its stupor. Makes me wonder if you're really a worthy investment for the crown... or just another mortal playing at heroics until the game turns too real."

A ripple of laughter rose among the courtiers behind Kaelin, soft at first, then sharper, crueler, until it filled the space around Ren. She swallowed it down, turned on her heel without another word, and stormed toward the balcony.

The cold met her like a slap, wind tugging at her hair, at the silk of her skirts. She pressed her palms to the railing.

"She's got a sharp tongue," came a voice behind her.

Ren didn't have to turn. "Your sister's a piece of work."

Talen stepped beside her. "That's one way to put it."

Ren let out a slow breath, trying to calm the flicker of heat that threatened her palms. "Why did I even come tonight? First dealing with Lucan, then her."

"She invited you because she wanted to see if you'd show."

Ren shot him a look.

"She's testing you. She does that. Especially with people she doesn't know how to feel about."

"Is that what that was? A test?" Ren snorted. "It felt more like a public execution."

"She's... protective," Talen admitted. "Of her family. Of this court. Of the people she trusts. She doesn't give that trust easily, but she'll fight like hell for the ones who earn it."

Ren sighed. "I wonder what she does to the ones who don't earn it."

Talen offered her the flask tucked at his hip. Ren took it, drank, and stared out at the stars.

Inside, the ballroom spun on without her.

Ren stared out at the gardens a moment longer. The world beyond the balcony was still, pristine, perfect.

But the storm inside her had only just begun.

The chill curled around her like a second skin, but it wasn't the cold that made her shiver. It was Kaelin's voice still echoing in her ears, each word laced with mockery and sharpened with dismissal. Words meant to cut, and though Ren would never admit it aloud, they had.

You froze like a doe.

Out of your depth.

Not worth the crown's investment.

Ren felt the weight of the words pressing down on her chest, stealing her breath for one suffocating moment. Her fingers curled into fists at her sides, nails biting into her palms as the laughter from behind them echoed in her ears.

Why was she even here? Was the money worth it?

Her mind dragged her back to the pits, back to the bloodied knuckles, split lips, the copper taste of her own blood as she stumbled home with coin heavy in her pocket but pain deeper in her wounds. She thought of sleepless nights bent over her own lacerations, of the victories that had kept her alive but left her empty and alone at night.

It would be slower, harder, but she could always go back and fight for her own coin. She wouldn't have to deal with Kaelin and her fae court.

And for a heartbeat, the idea almost sounded like freedom.

"Thinking about running?"

Talen's voice broke through her thoughts. His gaze was already on her, as though he could read every word she hadn't said aloud.

"You'd leave all this," he said, gesturing faintly to the glittering palace behind them, "and let someone else decide who you are, what you're worth, before you've had the chance to prove them all wrong?"

"I don't give a damn what they think." The words came sharp, but the faint glisten in her eyes betrayed her resolve.

Talen's gaze softened as he studied her. "Gods help me, Ren… you're already more than worthy. You just haven't realized it yet."

His words landed heavier than she expected, sinking deep, leaving her chest tight and her breath seizing in her throat. The question – *thinking about running?* – lingered, cutting through her doubt like a blade. And though she hated to admit it, she already knew her answer.

Fine.

Ren would be damned if she let these arrogant fae decide what she was capable of and, more importantly, *who* she was.

And so, on this cold winter solstice night, beneath the glittering towers of the palace that mocked her very presence, Ren made a silent vow to herself: *she would show them all.*

Starting tonight.

If Kaelin wanted to make her the evening's entertainment, then Ren would give her a performance that no one in this palace would forget.

One *Kaelin* would never forget.

Ren turned sharply from the balcony, skirts slicing through the air as she stalked back into the ballroom. Out of the corner of her eye, she barely caught the ghost of Talen's approving grin, his flask lifted in a silent salute before the crowd swallowed him from view.

Inside, the music had shifted, something fast, bright. Laughter rose from the crowd, but it dulled the moment Ren crossed the threshold.

Her gaze found Kaelin instantly.

Kaelin stood at the edge of the dance floor, a courtier murmuring something into her ear. But Kaelin's eyes flicked past them and straight to Ren.

Ren didn't slow. She didn't hesitate. She crossed the room like a storm with a purpose. Kaelin straightened ever so slightly.

"Care for a dance, Your Royal Highness?" Ren asked.

Kaelin raised a brow. "Bold of you to assume I would say yes."

Ren extended her hand anyway, lips curling. "Bold of you to pretend you'd say no."

A beat passed. A flicker of challenge sparked in Kaelin's gaze.

Then she took Ren's hand.

The crowd around them thinned as they stepped into the center of the ballroom. Eyes followed their every move, curiosity mingling with amusement.

The music surged.

Ren didn't wait.

She spun Kaelin hard and fast, catching the fae princess off guard. Kaelin let out a startled laugh, but she recovered with grace only the fae possessed, shifting into the lead with a pivot that forced Ren to follow.

They circled each other like flames tasting dry wood.

One step forward, one step back.

Spins. Swerves. Palms pressed too close. Hips brushing in rhythm.

Neither relented.

"Is this how mortals dance?" Kaelin purred, voice low enough for only Ren to hear. "Like they're fighting for their lives?"

Ren smirked. "This is how mortals dance when they've got nothing left to lose."

She gripped Kaelin's waist, dipped her low and fast before pulling her back upright, their faces a breath apart.

"Maybe it's time you learned."

Kaelin's laugh was startled, and for a heartbeat, her polished mask cracked. But then Kaelin spun them again, reclaiming control.

And still, they danced. Spiraling in time to a song too fast, too wild, for anything royal.

By the time the final note hit, both were flushed and breathing hard – hands locked tighter than necessary.

Ren released Kaelin's hand first.

They stood in the eye of the ballroom, the world watching, the silence electric.

"Just so we're clear," Ren murmured to Kaelin, low enough for only the fae princess to hear, "no one makes me feel less than. Not you, and especially not your court." Her gaze flicked meaningfully to Kaelin's crown. "And that pretty thing on your head is more breakable than you think. Don't forget," she added, smirk deepening, "*fire melts steel.*"

26

The sheets clung to Ren's legs, twisting around her ankles like tangled vines.

Ren tossed again, her breath coming too fast, heart hammering too loud. The bed beneath her felt more like quicksand.

And then the darkness swallowed her whole.

Ren stood barefoot on the crumbling edge of a city. Ash snowed from above. Stone towers cracked and fell in molten chunks as shrieks rippled through the air.

Then came the shadows wreathed in fire, wings spanning the skies. One of them banked low over the burning rooftops. Its golden eyes locked with Ren's.

Ren bolted upright in bed. Her hands clenched the blanket like it could anchor her back to this world.

The room was quiet. Across, Mirella's form remained dormant. Even enchanted dresses needed their sleep.

Ren couldn't stay here – not for another second. She seized a torch from the bracket by her bed and yanked on the first set of clothes fit for the world beyond her chambers.

The corridors were cloaked in the kind of quiet that made Ren feel like an intruder in someone else's dream.

She took a turn she didn't recognize, past tapestries of fae wars and revered gods, past doors she didn't dare open. And then, an archway with ivy curling along its pillars.

A greenhouse.

Ren hesitated at the edge, fingers brushing the carved stone frame. Golden light spilled through the tall glass panes, illuminating the wild tangle of flora inside. It was nothing like the polished grandeur of the rest of the palace. This place was living, overgrown and riotous and humming with quiet magic and life.

And there, kneeling among the lilies and foxglove and starflowers, was Kaelin.

She had shed her formal silks for a simple cream blouse, her sleeves rolled to the elbows. Her golden hair was pulled into a loose braid, wisps curling around her face. Dirt clung to her elbows as she gently coaxed new life into the soil.

There was no crown here, no sneer, no sharp words on her tongue.

Only... softness.

The curve of her cheek turned in profile as she leaned down to inspect a cluster of pale violet blooms.

She looked... oddly beautiful.

The thought struck Ren so hard, she blinked, stunned at her own reaction.

Kaelin shifted, head tilting toward the flowers. For a moment, Ren thought Kaelin would notice her.

Ren stepped back, retreating before the fae princess could see what had flickered across her face.

Before Ren could understand it herself.

The Iron Maw glowed like the heart of a dying star.

Sparks danced above the anvil, and Elira stood at the center of it all, her golden-brown arms slick and strong as she slammed her hammer down onto heated steel.

Ren leaned against the doorframe. "Do you ever sleep?"

Elira lifted her head with a lopsided grin, teeth gleaming in the firelight. "Not when the steel sings to me."

Ren stepped inside, heat wrapping around her like a familiar embrace. Elira tossed Ren a flask. Ren took a quick swig. The burn of it was hot and *exactly* what Ren needed.

Elira handed Ren a pair of leather gloves. "You're not just going to stand there looking pretty. Grab the tongs. We're finishing this blade tonight."

"You always force your guests into labor?"

"Only the ones I tolerate." Elira winked at her. "Besides, this is your blade."

They worked in tandem, the hiss of metal and swirl of heat filling the quiet spaces between them. Ren fell into the rhythm. Elira's commands were sharp, her movements fluid, and somehow, they moved as if they'd done this a hundred times.

Elira wiped her brow with the back of her gloved hand, squinting down at the gleaming blade cooling on the anvil. "Well," she muttered, nudging the weapon with the flat of her tongs, "it didn't explode. That's a win."

Ren exhaled, chest tight with the kind of pride she wasn't sure how to name.

Elira shot her a sidelong glance. "Your first forge, and you managed not to embarrass us both. Well done."

Ren laughed. "Coming from you, that almost sounds like praise."

Elira handed Ren the blade, still warm. "She's all yours. Split-blade."

Ren turned the weapon over in her hands, eyes tracing every inch. The firelight caught the blade's mirrored halves.

"Two pieces forged as one," Elira said. "Yet ready to break apart when the moment calls for it." She stepped closer, tapping the hilt with the tip of her finger. "Together, it's a short sword. But split it, and you get twin daggers. Faster, more unpredictable."

It needed a name.

Ren traced the green-wrapped hilt with her thumb.

"Ashrend," she said quietly.

"Ashrend?" Elira repeated.

Ren nodded. "Because anything that stands in my way," She glanced up, her lips curling into a wicked smile, "will know what it means to be turned to ash."

Elira mirrored Ren's smile. "Dramatic. I approve."

They each took another swig from the flask as if to commemorate Ren's completed blade. Elira said quietly, "My sister would like you."

Elira sat on a bench, her back against the stone wall, and a second flask was cradled between her knees. "She's younger than me. Thinks she's taller and smarter than she is. I want to surprise her this spring and forge her something, maybe a scabbard."

Ren sat beside her, letting the stone cool her sweat-slicked back. "She has a good role model."

Elira took another swig from the flask. "And what about you?" she asked. "What the hell is your story?"

Ren didn't answer at first.

The clang of cooling metal filled the silence. Smoke drifted lazily in the warm air between them, and for a second, it smelled like that night – burnt wood and scorched earth, hot iron and singed cloth, the acrid bite of ash thick in her throat.

"My house burned down when I was eight," Ren said at last. "Wood burns fast. The smoke came so thick. Every breath felt like drowning. People think fire is all noise and chaos. But when it's really burning, really taking everything, it *groans*. Like it's in pain. Or maybe like it's enjoying it too much. Beams split with this horrible, cracking sound."

She paused.

"I still hear that groaning every night when I go to sleep." Her fingers curled around the flask in her hand, knuckles white. "There were intruders in the house. They wore crimson cloaks and had white masks. They bound my parents. Tied me up, too. But not my sister." Ren pulled her knees to her chest, leaning her chin on her knuckles. "She didn't even flinch," Ren whispered. "She walked right over my legs like I was a broken chair in the way. I called her name. I thought she didn't hear me over the flames, so I screamed. My parents weren't saints. My sister and I spent most of our lives tiptoeing around their brutality. But no one deserves to die like that – watching the people they raised set the fire."

Her voice turned brittle.

"Eve just nodded to the intruders like it was all agreed upon. They slit my mother's throat. Quick. A mercy, I suppose. But they took their time with my father. Maybe Eve wanted it that way. He was always crueler than our mother was."

Ren's stare had gone distant. She ignored Elira's heavy stare as tears streamed down her face.

"You know the strange thing? Sometimes I wonder if I imagined this. For a moment, I swore Eve looked back at me. Just for a breath. And I thought, I saw a shine in her eyes. Tears of grief, maybe. Or regret. Or perhaps the smoke actually did get to her. Why would she cry when she played a role in our parent's murder?"

A long silence followed, pierced only by the crackling of the forge and the distant howl of wind through stone.

"They wrapped me in a bag," Ren grumbled bitterly. "Threw me like rubbish on the roadside. Left me with smoke in my lungs and fire stitched into my bones. And that's where an elderly couple found me. Half-dead, half-alive."

Elira gently knocked her flask against Ren's. "To the girls we were," Elira said quietly.

Ren raised her flask. "To the women we've become."

And they drank.

Ren fumbled with the hem of her jacket, still reeking of forge smoke and cheap rum. The aftertaste of both lingered on her tongue.

"Stairs," she muttered as she reached the base of the sweeping staircase. "Enemy of the people. Fae probably float up these things. I'm pretty sure they glide like smug little peacocks. Pointy-eared prissy bastards."

The first step met her foot wrong, and she lurched forward with a graceless *oof*, catching herself on the banister. She blinked hard, squinting as if the marble had somehow shifted under her.

"Rude," she informed it, wagging one finger at the step as though it should apologize.

She tried again.

One step.
Two steps.

A triumphant hum slipped from her throat, followed immediately by her toe catching the edge of the next stair. She pinwheeled her arms, whistling through her teeth in sheer panic before careening sideways into the wall.

The impact made a dull *thump.*

"Fine," she announced to no one. "I meant to do that. Testing structural integrity. Gotta hand it to whatever prissy fae built this place."

With renewed determination, Ren pushed off the wall and trudged upward, steps loud, gait crooked, humming a tune of a song she did not remember the words to. Halfway up, she paused to steady herself.

"Gods, if I fall and die here, I'm going to haunt this place."

She took another step, then another, making her way toward her chambers with all the grace of a newborn foal learning how legs worked.

She nearly missed the tall shadow cutting across her path until she collided with something distinctly... regal.

"Oof," Ren grunted, catching herself with a hand against cool velvet. She blinked up, blinking again just to be sure. "Oh, no. Just my luck. The last person I wanted to see right now."

Kaelin stood before her like the embodiment of frost. "You reek."

Ren groaned, dragging a hand down her face. "You're everywhere. Like a damn fly."

"And you're clearly drunk."

"I prefer delightfully unrestrained. Besides, I was forging. For a noble cause. *I* have my own sword now. Do *you* have your own sword?"

"You're lucky no one took advantage of you in this state. Some fae have a taste for foolish, reckless mortals."

Ren tilted her head, grin widening. "Oh? And are you one of those fae, Your *Royal* Highness?"

Kaelin narrowed her eyes. "Don't be ridiculous."

"Right," Ren muttered, swaying.

Kaelin grabbed Ren's elbow, steadying her with a surprisingly gentle grip. "Come. You're going to trip over your own pride next."

"I'm shocked," Ren drawled as they turned down the corridor toward her room. "Why soil your precious reputation for helping me? A mere mortal? Filth, vermin...what else have I been called? Useless?"

Kaelin was quiet for a beat, her gaze fixed forward as she led Ren to her door. Then, she asked, "Why are you staying when it's obvious you're not welcome here?"

Ren let out a bitter laugh. "I'm not a complicated person. The answer is simple. It's because I need the coin. Unlike you, I wasn't born with a title or the luxury of choice. I just want to get far away from here. But I can't do that without money. Everything comes with a price." Ren's lips curled into something that was almost a snarl. "Tell me, Your *Royal* Highness. Have you ever struggled a day in your life?"

"More than you think," Kaelin answered.

Ren huffed out a short laugh, the bitterness softening into something almost playful as they stepped in front of her door. "Gods, you're impossible. You know..." She gave Kaelin a deliberate wink. "I'm beginning to enjoy pushing your buttons. Maybe I'll stay just for that little bit of entertainment. Do we need to sign a contract for that, too?"

Kaelin's gaze slid to her, assessing, but there was the faintest twitch at the corner of her mouth, as if she were holding back a smile. "Let's get you to bed before you say something even more ridiculous."

"Ridiculous? I'm making *perfect* sense."

"Of course you are. Which is exactly why you need sleep, because you clearly have no idea what you're saying."

Ren fumbled with her keys, dropping them once, then again, before finally jabbing the wrong one at the lock. "Saints, I swear the fae cursed these things."

"Mortals don't need curses to be clumsy."

Ren leaned a little too heavily on Kaelin as they entered her room. "You're lucky I'm drunk, or I'd have the perfect comeback for that."

"Mm, I'm counting on it."

"Well, you're still a frigid, royal pain in my ass."

Kaelin's fingers lingered a moment longer before letting go. "And you're still a fool who clearly doesn't know when to stop drinking."

By the time they reached Ren's bed, her steps had slowed, the flush of rum fading into something quieter, more tender. The room flickered with soft light from enchanted sconces, casting gold across the wood paneling.

"You don't have to tuck me in. I'm an independent, grown ass woman," Ren muttered, trying to tug off her boots with far less grace than she'd like.

"And yet," Kaelin said coolly, stepping in front of her, "you can barely walk in a straight line."

After three failed attempts of taking off her boots, Ren gave up with a huff and switched to pulling the tie from her braid instead. "Must be your ego. Throws off my balance every time."

Before Ren could protest, Kaelin sank gracefully to her knees, deft fingers brushing against Ren's ankles as she reached for the boots. "Hold still before you topple over and embarrass yourself further."

Ren jerked her foot back. "Hey! I'm a grown-ass woman," she repeated, pointing vaguely at her own chest. "I can take off my own boots."

"You could scarcely climb the steps. You *talked* to them."

Ren opened her mouth, closed it, then tried again. "That's beside the point."

Kaelin finally lifted her gaze, one pale brow arching. "You held a full conversation with the stairs."

Ren gawked. "Were you *watching* me?"

"Yes," Kaelin said without an ounce of shame. "You were very loud. I'm certain the entire palace heard your drunken humming."

Ren sputtered. "They should be honored to hear my voice."

Kaelin tugged another boot free and set it neatly aside. "It was off-key."

Ren flicked her hair over her shoulder with drunken dignity. "We'll have to agree to disagree."

"No. You will disagree, and I will be correct." Kaelin rose smoothly to her feet, dusting her hands as if the task had soiled them. Pausing at the door, she glanced back over her shoulder, voice dry. "It's polite, you know, to say *thank you*."

Ren's braid slipped free, auburn waves cascading down Ren's back. She didn't miss the way Kaelin's eyes lingered. Ren snorted, sprawling back against the mattress. "Yeah? Then thank you kindly, now piss off. Go do whatever it is you do in your free time. Scheme, spy, alphabetize your grudges – whatever makes your cold heart happy."

Kaelin leaned a shoulder against the doorframe, arms crossed. "I've seen less refined creatures stumble into this room with more charm."

Ren met Kaelin's gaze. "Why are you always testing me?"

"Because mortals always act in their own interest. Your kind would trade trust for advantage if they could."

"And you think I'm like that?"

"I think you're dangerous precisely because I don't know."

"Maybe you should just try to get to know me instead of scheming around me." Her mouth curved in a humorless smile. "I'm pretty awesome once you get to know me."

"You're drunk. You don't know what you're saying."

"And you're deflecting. Did I hit a sore spot?" Ren leaned in, her words low and laced with venom. "Someone must've done something truly terrible to you, to make you this distrusting." She gave a slow shrug before stretching out among the pillows, crossing one leg over the other with deliberate ease. Her gaze raked over Kaelin, cool and unhurried. "Or maybe you were born that way."

"Or maybe," Kaelin said softly, "you know nothing of the brutality of the fae."

Ren gave a humorless laugh, the sound brittle. "Oh, that's where you're wrong. I've got an idea. Two months ago, I was shackled to a wagon on my way to the butcher's block *because* of the fae. So don't tell me I don't know your kind's brutality. I've seen it up close."

Kaelin's mouth tightened. "That was... unfortunate. Things like that happen when order must be kept."

Ren's eyes narrowed, fury flashing hot. "*Order?*" Her voice cut like a blade. "If chains and butcher's blocks are your idea of order, then maybe your kind doesn't deserve to survive at all."

"Careful. Words like that tread close to something worse than insolence. Something that sounds very near treason."

"Isn't treason for subjects? Last I checked, I'm not one of yours."

Kaelin's lips curved, the faintest edge of mockery in her smile. "You've lived in Vaelaran territory long enough. That places you under *our* domain," she bared her teeth, the expression caught between a grin and a snarl, "whether you like it or not."

Ren went to retort, but Kaelin was gone, leaving only the scent of jasmine and frost behind.

Ren glared at the empty doorway. "Yeah, well, your domain can kiss my mortal ass."

The carts rolled in at dawn, just as they did every day, wheels creaking beneath the weight of death.

She'd grown used to the sight. To the slack jaws, the stiff limbs, the vacant eyes. But not the smell.

Gods, not the smell.

No cloth mask, no amount of ash rubbed under her nose could mask the sick-sweet rot. It was a slug that refused to leave, embedding itself into every part of her body, leaving no part untouched. Not her hair, nor her pores, not even her memories.

"Over and out!" the overseer called, voice raw from barking orders all morning. "Just a few more, and we're done for the day."

A lie. They were never done.

She gritted her teeth and picked up her shovel, knuckles whitening. Her hands were blistered, lined with hardened calluses, her muscles aching from the endless toil, but she supposed she should be grateful for the pain. It reminded her she was still alive.

She dragged the next body to the edge of the trench. An old man, bones brittle and yellowed, skin like parchment. With a grunt, she flung him in. He landed with a dull thud against a corpse whose eyes had never shut—wide and glassy, locked forever.

She didn't flinch. She didn't cry.

She hadn't cried since she buried her daughter.

The babe had been barely a year old when the Witherblight took her—one moment giggling, gumming at her fingers, the next burning with a fever no poultice could cool. Gone before she could even speak her first word. Gone like her husband, ripped apart by ogres outside their home when he tried to stop them from taking her.

Now she lived in silence. The four walls of her house echoed with memories she no longer dared to remember. And out here, where the dead waited to be burned, she found purpose. Or maybe penance.

Perhaps she wasn't brave enough to take her own life. But every day she faced this plague, every day she lifted another body, she hoped it would take her, too. That one day she'd stop waking up. That she'd be reunited with her family beyond the Veil.

But not yet.

Today, she lifted a corpse so small her knees nearly buckled.

An infant.

She turned the infant's face, refusing to look at its features. Her throat convulsed as she tossed the tiny body into the pit like it was nothing. Like it hadn't once been loved.

Her soul cracked a little more.

And then she reached for another.

A man. Middle-aged. Stiff with death. Her fingers hovered over his wrist, the skin waxy and cold. For an instant, there was only the biting wind and the stench of rot. Then, movement – the faintest twitch beneath her touch.

She froze. She turned slowly, almost unwillingly, to the worker crouched beside her. His eyes were already fixed on the body, wide and unblinking. A silent question passed between them, raw fear threading the air: *Did you see that, too?* Neither of them breathed; neither wanted to give voice to the impossible.

But when the corpse's hand jerked again, this time stronger, the worker flinched back with a strangled sound. The corpse's fingers snapped tight around her arm, iron-hard.

Its eyes shot open – wide, *aware*. They locked on hers, the dull glaze of death burned away in an instant replaced by an unearthly green. Its jaw clenched, then unhinged, releasing a rasping hiss.

The body lurched upright, jerky, unnatural, like a marionette dragged on frayed strings. Its limbs twitched with an eerie, broken rhythm. Beneath it, another corpse stirred. Then another. A ripple of motion shivered through the trench, the dead no longer still.

"THEY'RE MOVING!" her shriek tore through the air, raw and ragged.

Chaos erupted.

From the corner of her eye, she saw one of the younger boys, barely more than a teenager, swing a torch at a twitching corpse. Another ran in to help, only for the thing to whirl unnaturally fast and tear his face open.

The sound—*that sickening wet rip*—would haunt her forever.

She spun, wielding her shovel like a blade, swinging wildly. She caught one creature across the head, sending its skull flying into the ash, but the body didn't fall. It kept coming. Reaching. Hungry.

Groans echoed around her. Not human. Not anymore. Something else.

Something grabbed her leg. She kicked it off, stumbled back—into another. She was surrounded.

And realization dawned on her.

She didn't want to die.

Not like this. Not here, in a pit of writhing corpses.

She fought. Fought harder than she ever had. Her shovel arced again and again, slick with blood and filth. She clawed for space, for breath, for life.

But there were too many.

She slammed into a tree behind her, back heaving, weapon raised, but her arms were weakening. Her body was giving in.

A hand latched onto her wrist. Another gripped her throat.

She tried to scream. To pray.

But the last thing she saw was a thousand soulless eyes opening, and a wave of the dead rising to consume the living.

28

The throne room was so shiny, it gave Talen a headache being there too long.

Talen stood very respectfully before the ornate silver dais where his parents sat, exuding all the casual regality of people who didn't have to beg for favors. Beside them, Kaelin perched with the sharp poise of a hawk on its perch, one leg draped elegantly over the other, and her chin balanced lightly against her hand.

"Well?" Maelion asked with a sigh, drumming his fingers. "What is it this time? Another half-burned barracks or an impromptu duel with another noble's son?"

Talen flashed a grin, hiding a grimace. "Nothing quite so exciting, Father. I come bearing a simple request. I'd like to bring a guest to dinner tonight."

Lyra leaned forward, raising a perfectly arched brow. "Who?"

"Ren Harper. She's been instrumental in our recent efforts against the creatures plaguing our kingdom."

Kaelin's scoff was so delicate it could have been mistaken for a sneeze. "Instrumental? She arrived reeking of a peasant, challenged me within minutes in front of the court, and looked like she'd rather be gutting someone than curtsying to a royal family." She narrowed her eyes at Talen. "A true diplomatic treasure, indeed."

"Impressive, really," Talen insisted. "She doesn't back down from a challenge."

"The mortal pit-fighter?" Maelion clarified.

"She prefers renegade heroine, I think," Talen quipped.

Lyra's lips thinned. "We do not often dine with mercenaries."

"She's not a mercenary," Talen replied. "She's a crown-backed hunter."

"*You* appointed her," Kaelin pointed out. "Which is not the same."

Talen turned to his sister. "Correct. I did. But you'll be pleased to know she didn't want the job, either. It took some convincing."

Kaelin examined her nails with exaggerated interest, the telltale sign she didn't like the direction of this conversation.

Talen refocused on his parents. "If we're going to send Ren to bleed for the realm, the least we can do is offer her a decent meal and get to know our champion."

Maelion frowned, glancing at Lyra. Lyra looked thoughtful, twirling the red wine in her hand.

Dangerously so.

"Appearance is everything," Lyra murmured. "And we cannot appear ungrateful. It would be tasteless, uncouth."

Kaelin let out a loud sigh. "This is going to be a disaster. She's a *nobody*!"

"Most dinners with us are a disaster," Talen quipped brightly. "But Ren has adequate table manners, I think." He paused, then added as an afterthought, "And she only sets things on fire when absolutely necessary."

Maelion stared at his son, not sharing an ounce of humor in his stone features, then finally gave a slow nod. "Very well. She may attend."

Kaelin added sharply, "But she better dress properly."

Talen clapped his hands once. "Excellent."

Kaelin narrowed her eyes and said flatly. "You already invited her, didn't you?"

Talen's grin was positively sinful. "I might have sent a note. Because who can deny my powers of persuasion?"

Kaelin rolled her eyes. "Dear brother, you're insufferable."

"And yet you keep inviting me to dinner," he said, pivoting on his heel and striding from the chamber before anyone could change their mind.

Behind him, he swore he heard Lyra murmur, "Do make sure she bathes."

And Kaelin's response?

"She'd better not sit next to me."

Talen smirked and held back a laugh. This was going to be fun.

Ren let out a sigh that could've shaken the rafters.

"Are all sentient wardrobes this indecisive?" she snapped, yanking the fifth dress over her shoulders for what felt like the hundredth time, "or is it just you?"

"Enchanted," Mirella intoned with glacial offense, her carved edges gleaming under the lamplight. "Sentient is what they call furniture that's been cursed by accident. I, darling, am a masterpiece of magical design. A legacy, if you will."

Ren rolled her eyes so hard she was mildly impressed they didn't pop out. "Well, this masterpiece is subjecting me to fabric-based torment. I'm two gowns away from losing my sanity to the gods."

"You exaggerate."

"I do no such thing." Ren turned stiffly in front of the mirror, hands on her hips. "Well? Is this one finally good enough for your standards?"

Mirella tilted slightly, the faint creak of wood betraying thought. "If you didn't look like you wanted to stab someone with a salad fork, then yes. That emerald brings out the amber in your eyes."

"I hate how much the bodice is showing," she muttered, tugging it up uncomfortably. "It's so – "

"Don't pull! You have a more modest upper department, true, but in royal circles that's a delicate feature. Understated elegance. And your skin is flawless. Truly. If I had hands, I'd applaud."

Ren let out another groan and dragged a comb through her hair with more force than necessary. Her stomach turned again, a slow churn of dread.

Dinner. With the king and queen.

Why now? Why her?

A trap, surely. Or a test. Something Kaelin had orchestrated just to watch her squirm. Maybe it was revenge for the night before. Ren could not recall much about making her way back to her chamber, but she did remember vaguely running into Kaelin. The memory was a blur of sharp words and Ren's own slurred bravado.

It killed Ren that she couldn't remember exactly what they'd talked about.

Which meant it was probably bad.

"I don't fit in with these people," Ren blurted before she could stop herself. Her voice cracked. "I never will. I've got scars that'll never fade. My skin isn't perfect. My manners definitely aren't. I don't belong in these expensive dresses."

Silence.

Even the flickering candlelight seemed to hold its breath.

Ren sighed again, this one softer. "I appreciate your help, Mirella. You're probably the only one in this place who helps me without expecting something in return." She forced a half-smile. "But let's not pretend I'll ever look the part. I'm sticking with this dress. Let's just... get this over with."

Mirella didn't speak for a long moment.

Then, with the kind of exaggerated patience only furniture could muster, Mirella said, "Try the red one one more time. Just so I can see how it makes your skin glow."

Ren groaned, dragging the dress over her head again. "I hope you get termites."

Mirella's hinges creaked with laughter. "Not in this grain, darling."

With each step Ren took, the knot in her stomach pulled tighter.

She hated this.

She'd rather face a feral beast than walk into a room with a royal dinner table and Kaelin watching her like a hawk poised to tear flesh. *Especially* after last night.

Ren tried to focus on anything else. Maybe after this ordeal, she'd sneak down to the springs for a long soak. Or find Elira and convince her to have another night in the town that didn't involve crowns and court politics.

But just as her nerves threatened to take over, Ren spotted Talen.

He was leaning casually against the wall, one foot crossed over the other, as if he didn't have a care in the world. He dressed in deep sapphire trimmed with silver thread.

"You clean up well," he greeted, pushing off the wall and walking toward her. His eyes lingered on the deep crimson of her gown. "The color suits you. Dangerous and defiant." Before she could retort, he reached for her hand and pressed a warm kiss to her knuckle, a hint of amusement lighting his features.

"Careful, Your Highness. If you keep this up, I might start thinking you're charming."

Talen grinned. "And that would be the end of me, wouldn't it?"

Together, they approached the massive arched doors. A servant opened them with a bow, revealing a long dining hall. The table stretched nearly the length of the chamber, draped with crystal goblets and porcelain gleaming in the candlelight.

At its head sat Maelion. Lyra was beside him. And at the far end of the table, sat Kaelin. Kaelin was draped in a gown of twilight silk. On anyone else, it might have been simply beautiful. On Kaelin, it was armor disguised as allure.

For a moment, Ren remembered the other night. Heat pricked her cheeks even now, a flicker of shame.

As if summoned by the thought, Kaelin's violet eyes slid toward her. There was the faintest curve at the corner of her mouth, a private reminder that she remembered all *too* well.

"Our guest of honor," Maelion said. "Ren Harper, welcome. Please, join us."

Ren swallowed hard and stepped into the lions' den.

Of course, the only available seat was right next to Kaelin whose gaze could flay skin from bone.

Ren's stomach twisted as she approached the table. Servants waited along the edges of the room. Talen pulled out her chair. Ren hesitated a moment before sinking into it, her fingers brushing against the velvet cushion.

"Thanks," she murmured under her breath, then added, "Your Highness, sir, I mean."

A low chuckle rumbled from Talen, but he said nothing.

Ren straightened her posture, trying not to fidget with the tight sleeves of her dress as her gaze flicked up and met the deliberate lift of Kaelin's wine glass beside her.

"Lovely you could join us," Kaelin remarked coolly.

"It is an honor to dine with you tonight," Ren offered quickly.

A beat passed.

Then, mercifully, the doors opened, and more servants filed in. Dishes were set before them – lemon-roasted chicken, golden potatoes dusted with herbs, soft buttered rolls, glazed root vegetables, and meats roasted with sprigs of rosemary and wild pepper. Enough food to feed a dozen families for a week.

The scent should have made Ren's mouth water, but Ren only took a sip of the ruby-red wine before her that was sweet and rich, like pomegranate and plum.

"You are doing House Vaelaran a great service," Maelion said. "We offer this meal as a gesture of our thanks and our good faith."

Ren inclined her head again. "Your Majesty, I'm grateful."

Lyra leaned forward next, her cheeks already tinged with pink from her wine. She raised it languidly, and the server filled it nearly to the brim. "My darling son has shared quite the tale of your exploits. You must tell us. How does a mortal valiantly fight off a horde of ogres?"

Kaelin grumbled, "And light half the forest aflame while doing so."

Ren ignored Kaelin's comment. "It all happened fast. One moment I was chained in a wagon, being hauled to my execution... and the next, the ogres descended. The ogres were everywhere – there were too many of them and not enough of us."

Next to Ren, Kaelin didn't speak, but her grip on her dinner knife tightened as she sliced cleanly through a piece of meat with far more force than necessary.

Ren could feel Kaelin's glare burning into the side of her face like a physical heat, *very* unamused that Ren easily ignored her comment.

Ren continued. "I broke free of the wagon. I don't know how, only that the flames answered. I fought my way through the chaos."

And turned them all into burning crisps, she wanted to finish, recalling how the ogres once stood, eyes alit with the thrill of the hunt, ready to take them prisoner or bash their heads in, and then her fire answered and created an inferno.

Kaelin stated, "Ogres don't usually travel in such numbers."

Talen nodded. "It's also rare that they would brazenly attack a prisoner convoy."

"Could they have been after Talen?" Kaelin wondered.

"Only a handful knew of Talen's return," Maelion mulled.

Ren stiffened. Who would've expected the crown prince to travel with prisoners?

"Unless someone who knew had informed them," Kaelin leaned forward, her voice low but edged with thought. "Either someone tipped the ogres, and those brutal bastards saw a chance at glory for felling the heir to House Vaelaran." Her eyes flicked to her father's. "But ogres don't want to entangle themselves in our politics. Which points to the darker possibility that someone wanted Talen assassinated. They *knew* he was there. Perhaps the ogre attack was a distraction."

Maelion's expression darkened. "Court schemes are blades drawn in shadow. This may be one of them." His eyes cut to Talen, then lingered on Kaelin. "Keep sharp. Always."

The weight of his words pressed down on the room. Kaelin lifted her glass and took a slow sip of wine

From her seat, Lyra gave a delicate laugh, swirling her own glass. "Enough of politics and plots. You'll sour the wine." She tilted her head at Ren. "Tell me, Ren... What of your fire? You wielded it without spell or the element. What are you?"

"I don't know," Ren answered honestly. "I've had it for as long as I can remember, but never like that. When I was younger, it used to slip, but it was nothing dangerous. Just little accidents. It feels stronger now."

Kaelin muttered under her breath, "Not surprising, given how clumsy you are."

Movement caught Ren's eye. Something nudged under the table, aimed for Kaelin. Kaelin visibly stiffened, eyes narrowing as they flicked to Talen sitting across from them. He didn't look at her, didn't move, didn't break his carefully neutral expression. But his boot slid back to his side of the table with far too much innocence.

Ren's brows lifted. *Really?*

Talen glanced her way, just long enough for him to give Ren an unmistakable wink before looking away again as if nothing had happened.

Lyra said, "Magic like that doesn't lie dormant without reason."

Ren stared down at her wine, the liquid suddenly too bright, too red. She wasn't sure if she was being honored here, or dissected like a creature caught in a gilded cage. And she had a sinking feeling the real dinner had only just begun.

Ren drew in a slow breath, forcing her voice to stay level. "Maybe so. But I don't rely on my magic to fight. I know how to use steel and even fists to stand my own. Whatever my magic is doing, whatever reason it has for waking up like this, I won't let it affect my ability to uphold the end of the contract. I'll kill those creatures no matter what it takes."

Kaelin grumbled, "For the price we're paying you, that's the least we'd respect."

A sharp kick landed against Kaelin's ankle under the table. She startled, eyes snapping to Talen again.

He just sat perfectly straight, as though he couldn't possibly be responsible for anything happening below table level. Ren caught the exchange, the corner of her mouth tugging upward despite herself.

"And what of before?" Lyra asked Ren, eyes gleaming behind the rim of her goblet. "You clearly weren't always a beast hunter. Tell me, how does a mortal like you learn to swing a blade with such ferocity?"

The question was innocuous. Curious, even. But Ren recognized the glint in Lyra's eyes. That too-still quality to her posture. Interrogation, not conversation. Just like her daughter.

Ren glanced at Talen, who only gave her a shrug as if to say *your move.*

Her first instinct was to fabricate some cleaner version of the truth. She could say she was trained by a reclusive swordmaster. Or hired muscle for some forgotten noble house.

But then, something in her bristled. *What the hell? May as well be honest.*

So Ren set her wine down and leaned back in her chair. "I learned to fight in the pits. Underground rings. Illegal, mostly. Not the kind of place you walk into unless you're desperate or have nothing left to lose. The first fight I ever won, I was sixteen. I entered the ring with a man twice my size and fists like bricks. I barely had time to think before I was on the ground." Ren's lips quirked. "He knocked me out cold but just for a second. I came to with the taste of blood in my mouth and the roar of the crowd in my ears."

Kaelin made a faint sound, an unimpressed hum, barely concealed beneath her sip of wine.

Ren ignored her again.

"I got back up. Didn't think – just moved. It felt like the longest fight even to this day and took everything in me to stay on my feet, but I won. He was slow, and I was faster."

"And the reward?" Maelion asked.

"A few coins and a lot of bruises," Ren smiled faintly. "The pit master took me out for drinks after, and he said that I had fire that would either burn me alive or make me some coin."

Lyra laughed. "And which did it do, I wonder?"

"I'm still figuring that out."

"Charming," Kaelin murmured under her breath. "A woman of the people. Noble, indeed."

Ren cut her a scathing glance. Her knuckles whitened slightly against her wineglass.

Talen cleared his throat before the tension could snap. "You should've seen her when we fought the creature. That creature tried to twist her, drag her under with grief, fear... the kind of darkness that devours from the inside out. But she didn't run. Didn't even turn away. She stood her ground. Took all of that weight and turned it into fire so bright, so blinding, it carved through that thing like the sun breaking through a storm." He shook his head. "It's been decades since I've seen fire like that. And never wielded by someone so new to it. It was..."

He trailed off, lips quirking into a half-smile. "Terrifying, honestly. And incredible."

Maelion leaned back. For a fae male so famously stoic, there was a rare spark in his eyes now, something thoughtful, assessing. "Well," he said, lifting his glass, "cheers to perseverance and rising when you've been knocked low."

Lyra raised her glass next. "And for reminding us all that power can be found in the unlikeliest of places."

Kaelin exhaled an audible sigh. The eye roll she gave was subtle but sharp enough for Ren to catch it out of the corner of her eye. With a deliberate slowness, Kaelin lifted her glass and clinked it against Ren's with a faint *tink*. "To perseverance," Kaelin murmured flatly. "Or whatever we're calling recklessness these days."

As Kaelin took a small, measured sip, Ren automatically mirrored her, though she couldn't help the flicker of amusement warming her chest. Maybe it was the wine, maybe the fact that she was still upright at this dinner table, but part of her delighted in the way Kaelin seemed to bristle every time she opened her mouth.

Ren hadn't expected this. The king, so regal and cold from afar, was surprisingly gracious. And the queen, though sharp-tongued and imperious, had a way of peeling back a person's secrets. Twisted, yes. But entirely reasonable.

Still. Ren wasn't naive. Graciousness was often the sharpest disguise of all.

Ren drummed her fingers on the table. "You want to hear something actually insane?" she asked, eyes glinting. "Once, in the pits, I got thrown into a match so twisted the crowd *booed* the organizer for suggesting it."

Maelion asked, "Who was your opponent?"

Ren gave a wicked smile. "A shapeshifter. Apparently, he was not as adept in his abilities and kept turning into animals that were increasingly unhelpful. At one point he tried to charge me as a duck. As you can imagine, the chaos was... memorable."

"A duck?" Lyra echoed incredulously. "What other creatures did he turn into?"

"Oh, plenty. First he tried a wolf, which was a big mistake because he tripped over his own paws. He must not have been used to four-legged animals. At one point he became a pigeon and just flew in circles. I think he *forgot* he had wings."

It surprised Ren how strangely natural it was to recall the pits without the usual weight pressing on her chest.

Maelion leaned forward, elbows on the table, an intrigued light softening his regal features. "And you still managed to overcome him?" he asked, sounding almost impressed.

"Saints, Ren," Lyra added, wiping at her eyes, "I haven't heard a story *that* ridiculous in ages."

Even Kaelin's simmering glare seemed to ease. The ice around her expression thawed by a fraction, tension loosening in her shoulders. Ren could have sworn she heard the faintest snort of laughter from next to Ren, but when Ren's gaze flicked toward her, Kaelin immediately seized her wine goblet and took a deliberately long sip, staring very pointedly at anything but Ren's face.

Ren bit back a grin.

Just barely.

R en lounged at her usual corner table in The Iron Bridle, turning her coin purse over in her hands. Her fingers adjusted twice. The purse dipped lower in her palm than she expected, coins shifting with a heavy *clink*.

She wasn't used to it having *this* much inside.

The tavern's interior wasn't pretty. It was filled with splintered tables, uneven flagstone floors, but Ren liked the place. It was gritty, and most importantly the food was cheap. Better yet, the cooks made the best bread rolls in the city, warm enough to steam in your hands and buttery enough to make you want to sell your soul for more. Old, battle-worn saddles hung along the walls, relics from fae warriors long dead or long retired.

Ren dragged a fingertip through the crumbs left on her plate, swiping it through a streak of olive oil before bringing it to her lips and savoring the lingering taste. The bread had still been warm from the oven.

"Hey, you," Elira called as she slid up behind her. "Hope I didn't keep you waiting too long. I got slammed with work orders."

Ren barely heard Elira at first because her attention was fixed on the far corner of the tavern, where a small crowd had gathered around the Iron Bridle's prized attraction: an enchanted wooden horse.

For a few coins of silver, anyone could ride it. If they managed to stay on for a full minute, their bet doubled. If it bucked them off, they lost. Simple as that.

It was Ren's favorite source of entertainment so far.

Tonight, a lanky young fae strutted toward the enchanted horse. His friends whooped and hollered, shoving him forward.

Ren snorted. "Look at him." She jerked her chin toward the spectacle as Elira sat across from her. "He's got five seconds before he eats floorboards."

"Five? You're generous."

"No, I'm bored," Ren muttered, propping her chin on her hand as the cocky fae mounted the enchanted horse with all the confidence of a warrior king.

The horse's eyes flared with a pulse of blue light.

The fae grinned at his friends.

One... two...

The horse lurched upward, bucked sideways, and launched him off like a sack of potatoes. He crashed into the railing with a breathless *oof*.

The crowd roared with laughter.

Ren smirked. "Called it."

"Ren, please. A child could've seen that outcome."

Ren shrugged, then gestured to the empty plate. "Sorry I didn't wait on you. I was starving."

Elira laughed. "Clearly." Her eyes snagged on the coin purse Ren was still palming. "Pay day, huh?"

Ren hummed and shoved the purse back into her cloak. Then she pushed to her feet, patting Elira's shoulder as she passed. "I'm getting us drinks. And tonight?" She leaned in, grin crooked. "Everything's on me."

"Are you sure?"

"Hell yes." Ren sauntered toward the counter. "I'm celebrating."

"Celebrating what?" Elira called.

Ren only whistled. She returned with two glasses of whiskey. When she set them down, Elira gawked. "Starting off strong?"

"Like I said." Ren lifted her glass. "I'm celebrating."

Their drinks clinked and Ren welcomed the familiar burn as it slid down her throat.

Movement near the door caught her eye. A small group of fae males filed into the tavern, Lucan Brightbane among them. They were speaking loudly, shoulders thrown back in that irritating way all highborn males carried themselves.

Ren braced herself for the usual sneer when Lucan's gaze found hers. Instead, his stare brushed hers and then flicked away. Ren's lips twitched.

A quiet victory. She didn't need his approval. But his silence? That was its own kind of triumph.

"Don't keep me waiting," Elira said, nudging her knee under the table. "What are we celebrating?"

Ren leaned in, lowering her voice. "Today, I wasn't last."

"In what?"

"Our morning run. I wasn't the last to finish. First time ever. I was second to last, but today I finished before a fae."

Elira's brows shot up. "Wow. That *is* impressive."

"Hell yeah it is." Ren lifted her whiskey again. "So like I said, everything's on me tonight. No arguments." She winked and took a swig of her drink.

Elira swirled her whiskey, studying Ren with renewed interest. "How many soldiers were in that run? You beat out one fae, sure, but out of how many?"

Ren grimaced, dragging a hand through her hair. "Enough that it still counts," she muttered. Then, waving the topic away, she added, "Besides, there's going to be another ball next week which means the palace will be crawling with more soldiers."

"How many guards does it take to babysit a ballroom?"

"Fewer than you'd think. Even with more coming to oversee the balls, most of the soldiers are stretched thin these days."

Elira tilted her head. "Doing what? I thought palace guard duty was a cushy assignment."

"Half of them are stuck running convoys to the villages. The crown decides whether they need them elsewhere or at the palace. The end of autumn means tax season, and apparently every noble wants their coin hauled in yesterday."

Elira let out a low whistle. "So that's where the manpower went."

"Yep," Ren said, lifting her glass. "And here we are, toasting to the chaos of it all."

Elira hummed thoughtfully. "So, excellent food, stiff drinks, fancy outfits, and only a handful of guards on duty? Sounds like a recipe for disaster."

"Please. Fae love to pretend they're invincible. Sure, they're powerful, but take away their magic and I wonder how tough they'd *really* be."

Elira snorted, but her expression shifted. She traced a finger along the rim of her glass. "Maybe," she murmured. "But power's funny, Ren. Half of it's appearances. So long as they play the game, they get to keep *looking* untouchable. Until someone reminds them otherwise."

Ren stilled, the words settling.

Elira tossed back the rest of her whiskey and stood. "Anyway, you said everything's on you tonight. So let's make sure it hurts your coin purse."

Ren barked a laugh and followed her into the noise and warmth of the tavern.

A week of drills and sparring had left Ren's body aching, but she could feel her muscles growing stronger.

When she caught her reflection in the mirror, she thought she saw more life in her eyes than when she first arrived, as if a spark was returning piece by piece.

Tonight was another lavish ball. Ren didn't even know the purpose for this ball; it seemed Kaelin just enjoyed the opulence. Ren tugged at the dark red satin of her gown, wondering if this was what passed for responsibility among the fae nobility – dressing in frills, drinking endless wine, nibbling cheeses she couldn't pronounce, and dancing until dawn. She had lost count of how many of these gatherings she'd been gently obligated since her arrival. At least five, maybe more.

There were other balls she hadn't even bothered with, nights she'd remained curled in her room amidst satin blankets, either savoring the rare solitude or trading whispers with Mirella, whose scandalous tidbits from around the realm proved far more entertaining. Just last week, Mirella confided that a certain fae councilman's son had dyed his hair silver to look more 'regal,' only for the rain to wash it all down his neck during a public procession. Or, "The Duke of Merrow? Caught with not one mistress, but two. At the same time. And the fools still argued about who he favored most."

The ballroom glittered, just as it always did. Kaelin moved through her guests like a wraith of charm and calculation.

But never once did her eyes seek Ren. Kaelin had been avoiding her for the past week. And that was fine. Good, even.

Ren took a deep swallow of wine that was honey-sweet and far too rich. She was done with the push and pull that came with Kaelin, along with the veiled insults, the games. Maybe Kaelin had realized Ren wasn't a piece on her board worth moving anymore.

There were more in attendance tonight than usual. There were new faces – fae with lean builds and scar-lined grace of those who lived far from the gilded walls of the capital. Their shoulders were squared in a way that didn't speak of dance lessons or politics, but of battlefields and fighting.

She caught snippets of conversation drifting between clinking glasses.

"…from the northern outposts, I heard…"

"Returned last night. The fighting near the outposts has worsened –"

Some nobles gave the newly arrived warriors wide berth, while others fawned with over-sweet compliments.

Ren set down her empty glass and slipped toward the quieter halls, where the smoke hung heavy and the conversations carried teeth. Here, small groups gathered in corners, nursing wine and smoke dried local herbs through clay or wood pipes, voices low and intentions lower. The kind of place where masks slipped and alliances were born.

Or broken.

Ren lingered by the hearth, sinking into one of the worn velvet chairs as the quiet hum of distant conversation faded behind her. For several long minutes, she simply watched the fire, its golden tongues dancing lazily over blackened logs. The flames crackled softly, a sound that once made her flinch with memory. Even now, the brittle crinkle of burning wood sometimes curled her stomach with dread.

She let herself stare, the heat brushing her cheeks like a familiar hand, and for the first time in a long while, she didn't recoil.

She looked up when a shadow crossed her path and froze. She swore even her heart stopped beating for a second.

The male fae from the wagon was unmistakable – the one who'd ridden ahead of her that first day in chains, looking down from his sleek midnight horse like they were something stuck to the bottom of his boot.

Now, he stood before her in full court regalia, adorned in a black doublet stitched with silver thread that gleamed like spider silk, his raven hair slicked back with ruthless precision. Onyx colored eyes gleamed like polished stone, his features carved with the kind of elegance only the cruel ever wore well. And she was shocked at his towering height and frame; he seemed to swallow the entire room with his suffocating presence.

"Well, well," he purred. "The mortal prisoner. I almost didn't recognize you without the chains." He held out his hand, adding, "Sylven Draeth."

Ren's fingers curled slightly around her glass. "And yet I recognized you immediately," she said coolly. "Ren." She reluctantly settled her fingers in his, summoning all the restraint she could not to cringe when he brought her knuckle to his dry, thin lips.

"Prince Talen mentioned your valiant efforts. Ogre-slaying, was it?" He tilted his head, eyes flicking over her form with idle disdain. Her stomach lurched when his eyes roamed her slowly, up and down, as if appraising cattle.

Ren arched a brow. "Someone had to deal with them. You and your soldiers seemed awfully absent during the fight."

"Ah, yes. While you were setting half the forest on fire, some of us had the far more dignified task of keeping the prisoners from panicking. Order must be maintained, even in chaos." He clicked his tongue. "Still. Incinerating most of the forest. A bit dramatic, but effective."

Ren smiled sweetly. "Oh, right. Order. Is that what you call it? Because from where I stood, you and your soldiers were galloping away the moment things got ugly." Ren leaned in slightly. "You fled at the first sign of danger and left chained prisoners to fend for themselves. Where I'm from, we call that cowardice." She didn't wait for his reply. "Next time, I'll try not to ruin your scenic view with all the flames and carnage."

The barb landed. Silence stretched between them, brittle.

Then, Sylven laughed softly. "I didn't realize you were aiming for a theatrical debut. I suppose congratulations are in order. You've clawed your way from shackles to...this." His gaze drifted down the length of Ren's dress, lingering just long enough to sting. "Shall we dance? It would be a shame not to see how well you navigate the floor."

"No," she said flatly. "I'd rather dance with an ogre."

Sylven's smile faltered, but he recovered and stepped in closer, his voice dropping low. "How quaint. The mortal pretends she has teeth. Careful. Pride may keep you upright in a ballroom, but it won't save you on the battlefield or at court. There are games here far older and crueler than you can fathom. And some of us never forget the ones who arrive in chains."

Ren's jaw tightened, but she didn't flinch. He held her gaze for a beat longer, as if waiting for her to shrink under the weight of his words.

She didn't.

With a final sneer, he pivoted on his heel and disappeared into the ballroom, his presence leaving a trail of frost in his wake. She watched as he stalked off.

It wasn't until he disappeared from her view that Ren exhaled slowly.

She'd already survived worse than his contempt, and she wasn't done fighting yet.

The fire in the hearth had simmered down, no longer the roaring blaze that had greeted her. She watched it for a long moment. Then she stepped closer. Ren knelt before the flames. Her fingers hovered in the space just beyond the heat, and still, she leaned in farther.

The flames licked higher as if reaching back, responding. Her breath hitched. Her hand moved on instinct until her fingers brushed the edge of the fire. There was no pain. Only warmth. Familiar and ancient.

Like it *knew* her.

The flames curled around her hand without burning, wrapping her skin in gold, whispering through the blood in her veins.

Ren's eyes widened. The moment she touched the flames, the vision struck.

Smoke choked the world. A silver forest bathed in moonlight warped before her eyes, branches curling like talons. And in the center was a massive beast cloaked in shadow and mist.

Its voice was a deep pull in her chest like a second heartbeat. Words whispered through the fire:

"Flamebearer... come to me."

Ren staggered back, the brazier flaring with sudden heat, then extinguishing into smoke. Her breath came fast. No one else had seen it. No, this was not a message for the court, or for Talen, or even Kaelin.

It was for her.

Her head spun with the weight of it. She could feel her magic stirring. The first creature had crossed her path. This second one *knew* her.

And it was waiting.

She pressed a hand to the wall to steady herself. Somewhere deep in the castle, voices murmured: what sounded like violin music and harps, Kaelin's preoccupation with ballroom dancing, the usual noise of royalty moving in circles.

She didn't have time to wait.

Without another word, Ren turned on her heel and headed toward the direction of her room, fully intending to get the hell out of this dress the moment she reached her door, and with a haunted bog in her mind.

The bog had taken Ren nearly an hour's walk from the castle grounds, its isolation pressing on her as heavily as the mist itself. Out here, there were no watchful guards or lantern lights – only the endless mire, the stench of decay, and the uneasy hush of a place where even the air seemed to mourn.

Her boots sloshed through bone-white stone and soft, sucking mud. Gnarled roots curled from tree trunks, and everywhere, she stared back at her own reflections. They shimmered across the stagnant water, stared back at her from the trees.

Ren paused before one.

In it, she saw a version of herself hunched and burning, her skin charred, eyes gold with madness. It grinned at her with teeth like embers.

"You always knew you were a catalyst. Now look at what you've become."

Ren turned away, only to stumble into another reflection. This one cowered in the water's edge, small, bruised, trembling. The girl's lips moved, voice too soft to hear, but Ren was able to read them.

"You're nothing without fire. Just a scared girl pretending to be brave."

Ren's hand inched toward the hilt of Ashrend. There was a whisper of movement behind her, and she whirled in its direction.

The third version stepped across the stone. It beheld a shadow with her face, a sword held in her grip, and no hesitation in her stance.

Ren lunged.

Steel met steel. Sparks screamed between them. Ren blocked, pivoted, struck. The doppelgänger moved like a memory sharpened into violence. Every strike was precise. Every movement the perfected version of a warrior.

The fight drove Ren back into the spiraling heart of the creature.

And then the creature rose from a black pool. Its body rippled and shifted, a fusion of dark water and jagged shards of reflections, each one catching her face, her form, twisted, broken, laughing. A hundred versions of her screamed from its surface. Some wept. Some snarled.

One mouthed her sister's name.

Ren squinted up at it muttered under her breath, "What an ugly bastard you are."

Ren reached for the fire in her chest.

Nothing.

She realized far too late that this was a trap that she fell into. This thing stripped her of her magic.

The creature surged forward, its limbs forming into arms.

Run, something deep in her whispered. But Ren planted her feet. Her other self, the silent one, rushed her again, blades flashing like twin stars. Ren ducked, rolled, and screamed as she buried her blade through the silent version's chest.

It vanished.

Ren lifted her head. The creature still loomed at the edge of the mire, its body unmoving, yet the weight of countless unseen eyes crawled over Ren's skin.

Ren bared her teeth. "You're next."

And she charged, but another stepped forward. The burning one. Flames poured from its mouth, followed by a howl of rage and power.

"You're a monster waiting to lose control."

"I'm not like you," Ren snarled.

She slashed. The flames vanished.

The meek one rose last.

It whispered:

"You don't deserve to be here."

Ren stared into her own terrified eyes.

And for a moment, her breath stuck in her throat. Her fingers went numb around Ashrend. She hadn't realized how much she resembled Eve until she saw her own eyes. Those same soft, amber colored eyes.

"I know."

And then she went toward the girl –

The image shattered.

The creature let out a guttural roar that rattled the bog itself, its limbs unfurling like wings, blotting out what little light remained.

Ren lifted Ashrend, knuckles white around the hilt. No magic surged to meet her. No fire coiled in her veins.

Only the raw, unyielding force of her will.

Her voice cut through the darkness. "You don't get to tell me who I am."

She charged, fury carrying her steps.

The creature lunged, its limbs striking. Ren ducked one, rolled beneath another, and leapt, blade first, right into the heart of its mirror-slick chest.

Glass exploded.

Water howled.

Faces melted.

Ren drove Ashrend deeper. The creature shrieked with a hundred mouths, a chorus of howls.

"I *choose* who I am!" Ren roared.

And with a final cry, she split the creature in two.

Silence fell over the bog.

And for the first time since entering that cursed bog, Ren saw her true reflection. Tired, bloodied, breathing. But *whole*.

The shattered remnants of the creature shimmered. Bits of mirrored flesh floated on the bog's surface. But then something stirred in the stillness.

A tremor rippled through the water. One shard, larger than the rest, twitched, then glowed faintly with a silvery light. Ren lifted her blade.

From within the fragment, a shape began to stir. A face took form, blurred, fractured, almost human.

"*You believe this is death,*" the voice said, soft and splintered, echoing from nowhere and everywhere. "*But I do not shatter so easily.*"

"What the hell *are* you?"

"*I was someone once. I was given a name. I had a life. I had hands that built, a heart that bled. Until I was made into this – a prison of memory.*"

"Why did you call out to me?"

"*Because you are not like the others. I felt it the moment you fought me, how you refused to yield. Most mortals beg. Most mortals break. But you are a fighter worth sparing. There is power in you. Old power – older than this court, older than the crowns that play at ruling this land. It thrums in your blood, and I have not felt it in ages.*"

The reflection leaned closer, the surface of the water trembling as though drawn toward her. "*Give me one of your most precious memories, mortal. Let me keep it, savor it, make it mine. In return...*" Its eyes glinted, dark and knowing. "*I will give you a truth from your past.*"

"What truth?" Ren whispered.

The creature's lips curved into a faint, terrible smile. "*The truth of what really happened that night.*"

Ren's throat tightened, her pulse drumming in her ears. Every instinct screamed at her to walk away, but the promise of truth dug in deep. Her fists clenched at her sides. "I *know* what happened. I watched them die – murdered in cold blood. And Eve—" Ren's voice cracked, fury bleeding into it. "She walked away without a scratch. Like she *welcomed* the intruders inside. As if she opened the door herself."

Ren shook her head, taking a step back. "So don't dangle lies and riddles in front of me. I already know the truth. She betrayed *us*." She turned on her heel, but as she strode away, the water shivered again, and the creature's voice followed her.

"*Wouldn't you really like to know what happened that night? That maybe... your sister isn't what she seems?*"

Ren froze, her breath hitching, before forcing herself to keep walking because if she looked back, she feared she might not leave at all. Then the creature inhaled, as though savoring something unseen.

"*Mmm. I can taste it. That memory you keep locked away. The moment Eve looked back.*"

Ren's breath stuttered. Against her will, the image surged forward – Eve's silhouette framed in the doorway, head turning just once. Their eyes had met, locking for a single heartbeat that felt like forever, before Eve slipped into the darkness and Ren never saw her again.

"Didn't you see the glistening in her eyes? Was it truly cold blood she carried that night... or something more?"

The words slithered into her, coiling tight around her ribs. Ren clenched her jaw, shaking her head as if the motion alone could scatter them. She told herself not to listen, not to look, that to turn back was to surrender. But her chest tightened, and before she could stop herself, her gaze flicked back.

"Fine," she rasped, barely more than a whisper. "Take it."

She shut her eyes, sifting through her memories. The first thing that surfaced was warm and silly; sitting cross-legged on the tavern floor with Elira, laughing through mouthfuls of chocolate, both of them half-drunk and sticky-fingered.

A low, guttural growl rippled through the creature. *"Not that one. I do not feed on scraps of fleeting joy. Give me the one you treasure most. The one that makes you* you.*"*

Ren flinched. She pushed deeper, beyond the small comforts of the present, into a part of herself she had long buried.

And then she found it.

A dimly lit room. The rattling of her own shallow breaths as fever consumed her. She remembered lying small and frail in bed, the world hazy and distant. Her mother's calloused hands gently wringing a cool cloth, Eve curled at her side, clutching her hand and whispering nonsense words to keep her awake. Their father snoring in the next room, blessfully absent.

It had been the last time Ren could recall anyone truly caring for her.

Her chest ached as the memory unfurled, soft, fleeting, and then it was gone. She felt it pulled from her like a thread unraveling, leaving her suddenly hollow where it had once lived.

The creature let out a long, shuddering sigh. *"How fragile you mortals are... yet how bright you burn when you have someone to make life worth living. It is the cruelest and most beautiful thing about you."* Its flickering eyes met hers. *"Now... let me show you the truth of that night."*

It began to dissolve, splintering into mist, but its final words lingered like smoke in her lungs. *"I was not the first they locked away. And I am not the last. Beware, the fae court is not what it seems, and friends will be the ones to bury blades deepest."*

Then the shard sank into the bog, leaving only silence.

And Ren, standing alone among the fragments, felt the burn of uncertainty flicker beneath her skin. Not a creature. Not a reflection.

A memory.

The mist shifted, revealing a shrine, half-swallowed by fen and time. Built of black stone, it rose like a broken tooth from the earth, wrapped in ancient roots and draped with moss. Symbols Ren didn't recognize shimmered faintly across the stone – some half-carved, others burned as if by fire long faded. The ground beneath her boots was more solid here. Less bog, more grave.

She stepped forward.

And the shrine responded. The mist coiled inward, wrapping her in its embrace.

Then, the world vanished.

R en stood in the snow.
  She knew immediately where she was.

Home.

The faint, acrid scent of coal drifted in the air, smoke carried from the mines that had long been Ironforge's lifeblood.

Their small home sat just across the field from where she stood; she could see candlelight through the slats in the wood and hear her father's deep voice from within. It was shabbier than she remembered, the timber walls weathered and thin, patched in places where the wind slipped through, no matter how her mother tried to stuff the cracks. When the figures in crimson cloaks came calling, they had to bend their heads to step through the door.

From inside, her mother screamed.

Ren flinched from the sound that had invaded her nightmares for years since this night. She wanted to run to them, to scream, to change things, but she was a spectator trapped in her own memory.

It took every shred of will to force her feet forward, to cross the threshold and step into the night that had broken her.

Immediately, her gaze fell on her younger self writhing against the ropes, small wrists rubbed raw. Looking at the girl she once was, Ren was struck by how frail she'd been – bony arms, hollowed cheeks, a face carved thin by hunger and years of going without. Her mother's final gasp rattled the cabin walls as she drowned in her own blood. Even now, Ren couldn't bring herself to watch her mother's life pass, but her younger self couldn't look away.

Movement caught Ren's gaze. Eve stood near the kitchen, her fingers drifting across an object on the counter. Ren's old crimson scarf. Eve touched it softly, as if it were some precious relic instead of a child's worn scrap of cloth.

Ren's pulse thundered in her ears.

The creature's voice slithered through the scene, low and gloating. *"Ah... there it is. Look at her. Not a tear for your mother. Not even a glance at your father's blood. No, but see how she attends to your scarf as though it were the only thing worth her touch? Precious Eve... worshipping scraps while your family bled."*

Ren's nails bit into her palms until she felt the sting of her own skin breaking. Her attention snapped back to her younger self again. She could barely stand to look. That child's face was blotched with tears, her cries raw, too young and so innocent.

So *helpless.*

One of the figures opened a flask and began splashing oil across the walls, the table, the very floorboards soaked with her family's blood. The figure upended the flask over their father's slumped body. Oil dripped down her father's hair, his beard, pooling beneath him.

A ragged cough tore from her father's chest, startling in its frailty. His head jerked, eyes glazed. "Please... just end it," he begged. "Don't leave me to burn. End me now."

The plea hung heavy in the cabin. Even the figures paused, the oil dripping from the flask punctuating the silence like falling tears.

"This house will be cleansed and burned," a male intoned from behind his mask. "And you will burn with it."

Her father surged forward. "No-no, please. Take her instead," he begged, stumbling as he tried to reach them. "Take *her* life. She'll do whatever you want – serve, obey, just spare me." He pointed a shaking hand at Ren's younger self. "She's nothing – she's no one. Do anything you wish." His breathing hitched. "Just... let me live."

Ren's younger self didn't even look at him. Her eyes were locked instead on the dark, spreading pool beneath her mother, on the way it crept across the floorboards toward her bare feet. She stared at it as if the world had narrowed to nothing but that red stain, as if the screams and bargaining around her were happening behind a closed door.

But Ren looked at her father now and realized for the first time what her life had been worth to him. Ren snorted and said aloud to nobody in particular, "What a man. Nothing says paternal love like selling your kid to save your own shitty life."

One of the figures towards the back shifted their weight and grumbled, "Saints, let's just end it already."

Ren's younger self screamed as the fire unleashed. It was as if *she* heeded his words before anyone else. And Ren saw wings unfurling from her younger self's back, vast and terrible, each feather a living flame. They arched wide, blue and searing, painting the cabin walls with light that swallowed everything in its touch.

Flames erupted from her hands, from her chest – it surged toward the figures like a storm given form. One blink and they were gone.

Through the flames inside the house, a figure stepped out.

Her sister.

Untouched.

Eve's dark hair was unbound, her eyes wild. Her gaze swept over Ren's collapsed younger self, and the fire curled around her as if obeying an unspoken command. Two other figures stepped in through the front door and swept Ren's younger self into a bag. The tallest figure tossed the bag over their shoulder like a weighty flour sack.

"It is done," Eve murmured.

Then she turned and walked, soundless as a wraith, toward where Ren watched. Steps away, Eve came to a stop. Then her eyes met Ren's directly.

Ren's breath stopped in her throat.

"You are the flame that remembers."

As many times before, Ren felt a thum that was not just hers. Her hands shook.

Eve turned and left into the darkness.

The vision splintered away.

Ren stumbled backward, falling to her knees in the shrine's center. She clutched the hilt of Ashrend tighter, her knuckles white.

All this time, she thought her power had devoured her life. But it had been *protecting* her.

And the hunger in Ren's magic? The way it curled like a beast behind her ribs? It wasn't madness. It was a *legacy*.

She rose to her feet with trembling legs. Not whole. But no longer fractured.

A daughter of fire.

The bog recognized it, too because the shadows pulled back, as if bowing before something ancient that had finally woken. Ren closed her eyes. She did not try to silence the power inside her. She listened.

And in the silence, the fire purred.

33

"You are radiant tonight. I almost forgot how striking you can be, Your Highness."

Kaelin heard Sylven's voice before she allowed herself to look at him. Her fingers tightened around the stem of her wine glass. She had watched him circling the ballroom all evening like a vulture seeking an unguarded scrap, and she had made a precise art of weaving around him.

Until now.

Sylven, commander of prison transport and border control. The same Sylven whose heavy-handed cruelty had been mentioned in Talen's last report. Whose incompetence, or defiance, had delayed his return to Pyraelia by nearly twice the time the crown allotted. Maelion had already prepared the formal reprimand.

But tonight, Kaelin had been instructed to be civil.

So, she lifted her gaze to him. His eyes were already tracing her from the hem of her gown upward, lingering with interest at the line of her bodice before dragging reluctantly back to her face.

Kaelin arched a single brow. "You are prompt in your observations."

It was a verbal door shut cleanly in his face.

But Sylven stepped forward anyway, sensing a crack. "Only fitting I notice what the entire court already sees," he murmured. "You've stolen the room tonight, My Lady. I couldn't look away if I wanted to."

Kaelin took a deliberate sip of her wine, letting the pause sit heavy between them. "Then do try harder."

But Sylven only chuckled as though she were flirting and not issuing a warning. Sylven extended a hand toward her, palm up. "May I have this dance, Your Highness?"

The music swelled around them and for a breath, Kaelin simply stood there, wine glass cooling her fingers. Then, her gaze drew upward. Across the ballroom, raised above the crush of nobles and courtiers, Lyra stood at the dais.

Their eyes met. Lyra gave Kaelin a single, solemn nod.

Kaelin felt the familiar tightening in her chest. Her expression smoothed into a mask of effortless grace.

She set her wine aside.

Then, with the elegance expected of the princess heir of House Vaelaran, Kaelin placed her hand into Sylven's outstretched palm. His smile brightened with misplaced confidence.

Kaelin's fingers lay cool and light in his grasp, offering nothing more than what politics required.

Sylven guided her into the turning ring of dancers, his palm settling at her waist with the confidence of a man who'd mistaken tolerance for interest. Kaelin followed the steps flawlessly because a princess always did.

"Tell me, Princess," Sylven began as they spun beneath a chandelier, "have you many suitors for your hand?"

"A few," Kaelin answered with the same energy one uses to acknowledge a housefly. "None worth noting."

Sylven leaned in closer, breath brushing her ear. "Then allow me to offer my name to that list. I would like to court you, My Lady."

Kaelin's spine stiffened. Her lips parted, a pointed refusal danced on the edge of her tongue.

But she never got to speak it.

"Dear sister."

Both she and Sylven turned as Talen stepped into their path, boots planted, posture sharp with authority. His expression was polite enough for court, but the muscle ticking in his jaw betrayed him.

"Sylven," Talen said coolly, "I will need to steal my dear sister."

Irritation pricked Sylven's features. "Now? I'm in the middle of – "

"Yes," Talen replied, tone brooking no argument. "Now."

Kaelin felt Sylven's hand falter at her waist before he reluctantly released her, slipping away with a stiffness that suggested he believed himself wronged.

Kaelin lifted her chin. "Your interest is noted, but misplaced. You're not what I'm looking for." Talen nudged her side, warning her to stop there, but Kaelin continued. "When I choose a suitor, it will be a woman. So, courting me would be a waste of both of our precious time."

Sylven's jaw twitched. His gaze darted toward Talen, something calculating sparking behind his eyes. "Well, desire can often be confused. Perhaps you simply think you prefer women. You might discover you want someone like me."

Kaelin's answering smile was luminous and utterly lethal. "Oh, Sylven," she said sweetly, smoothly slipping her arm through Talen's. "I assure you, I know exactly what I want." She paused. "And it will never be you."

Before Sylven could sputter another word, Kaelin tugged Talen away, her heels clicking like punctuation marks of finality.

Kaelin didn't stop dragging Talen until they slipped behind a column near the far edge of the ballroom, far enough that the music muffled their steps yet close enough that Sylven's wounded pride still burned in the air.

Kaelin dropped Talen's sleeve and muttered, "That was pitiful. I could smell the desperation from across the room."

Talen snorted under his breath. "Mother and Father might find his eagerness charming. You know they'll expect you to consider suitors soon. In fact, I think Mother keeps a list – "

Kaelin's head snapped toward him, but the irritation on her face evaporated instantly. "Why do you look like that?" she demanded.

"Like what?" Talen tried to school his expression.

"Like someone on the brink of panic. What's wrong?"

Talen hesitated a beat too long.

Kaelin stepped closer, voice dropping. "Tell me."

He raked a hand through his hair. "Ren is gone."

"Gone... meaning she's left the ballroom to get air, or gone meaning –"

"She's not in the ballroom," Talen said quickly. "I checked twice. Then I went to her room. Empty. Training yard? Empty. Library, stables – nothing." He swallowed hard, voice cracking just enough to betray the panic he'd tried to hide. "Kaelin, she's just... gone. But all her things are still in her room."

A long silence stretched between them.

Then Kaelin's expression flattened into a deadpan. "And this is exactly why I never trusted her." Kaelin folded her arms. "You give a human a ball gown and a contract, and the moment you look away, she vanishes. Remind me again why we're surprised?"

"She wouldn't just *run*," Talen insisted.

"Wouldn't she?"

Talen began to pace short strides at first, then longer ones as his thoughts spiraled faster than his boots could keep up with. "No, Ren wouldn't just run. She's many things, but a coward isn't one of them." He dragged a hand through his hair again. "Unless... something came up."

He stopped, staring at a point on the wall as though it might answer him.

"She's impulsive," he went on. "Gods, she throws herself headfirst into danger without thinking. Maybe she got wind of another creature. Maybe she thought she could take it alone." His jaw clenched. "But she wouldn't leave without me. She knows that's not how this works. She knows – "

He cut himself off, resuming his pacing with renewed agitation.

Kaelin leaned a shoulder against the marble column, watching him with a face carved from icy calm. Her gaze tracked him back and forth, back and forth, like following a tethered storm.

Finally, when he passed her for the fifth time, she spoke softly, "Talen."

He froze.

"In the contract, there was no clause stating she had to hunt *with* you."

Talen's throat bobbed. "That's... not what she would do."

"Ren answers to coin and whatever reckless instinct drives her. Not to you."

"That's not fair," Talen protested.

"It's realistic," Kaelin countered, pushing off the column with a graceful ease. "You assume loyalty where none was promised. And you forget Ren is not one of us. Her world doesn't revolve around the crown. Or you." Kaelin stepped closer, lowering her voice. "If she heard whispers of a creature and if she thought it would earn her coin faster, she might very well have gone alone."

"No," Talen whispered.

Kaelin brushed past him.

"Where are you going?" Talen asked.

Kaelin lifted a hand in a lazy, dismissive wave. "To get more wine. And a good book."

He stared at her, appalled. "Kaelin – "

She paused just long enough to glance back over her shoulder, expression cool as winter frost. "Oh, relax. Something tells me this is going to be a very long night, and I refuse to endure it sober *or* bored."

The Hall of Embers was quiet save for the crackling hearth.

The vast chamber, built for feasts and war councils, now felt cavernous and hollow, its benches empty. At the far end, Kaelin was seated on a velvet bench near the fire, wine forgotten in her grasp, posture still, like she'd been waiting longer than she cared to admit. Talen lingered a step away, leaning against the carved table with a casualness that didn't reach his eyes.

Ren stopped just past the threshold.

It was Talen who spoke first. "You're alive."

Ren said, "Last I checked."

"Where were you?" Kaelin demanded.

Ren clenched her jaw, gaze flickering between them. "I didn't have time to explain."

"Explain now," Talen urged.

Ren inhaled once, steadying herself. The memory of it still made her skin prickle. "I had a vision of the second creature during the ball. I saw where it was hiding, and I had to go. If I waited, it would've been gone."

Talen's brows drew together. "So, you just ran after it?"

Kaelin's stare sharpened. "And you didn't think to tell anyone?"

"What did you expect me to do? Tap you on the shoulder while you were dancing with half the court and say, 'Excuse me, Your *Royal* Highness, I'm off to hunt a monster that called to me?"

Talen's tone softened this time. "You could've told me."

"I didn't have time. It felt... urgent. Like if I didn't go right then, something terrible would happen." She met Talen's gaze fully. "I *had* to go to it."

Kaelin straightened slowly, eyes narrowing as they raked over her. "So, you went in alone." She gave a pause before adding, "Foolish."

Ren gave a weak shrug. "Maybe. But it needed to be done."

Talen asked, "What happened?"

"We fought. It didn't die, but it fed me a memory," she answered at last. "The truth of what happened the night everything went to hell."

"And?" Kaelin pressed.

"My sister, Eve. She betrayed my family and left me to die." Her lips curled bitterly. "And the worst part? I don't even know if I blame her. We were just a broken family pretending to be whole." Ren's voice turned brittle. "Fifteen years ago, my parents were murdered, my house was burned down, and I was left for dead in a body bag and tossed somewhere on the road. My sister was behind everything that night. I don't know how, and I still don't know why." Her voice turned fierce, bitter as she gritted, "I was the one who set the blaze that killed some of the bastards. But there were too many."

Ren's voice was hoarse as she stared past the flickering sconces along the stone wall, her arms crossed tightly over her chest like she could contain the weight of her words. "She wanted it to be her," Ren said quietly.

"Wanted what?" Talen asked.

"The night our house went up in flames... that was some kind of ritual. I'm not sure what, but I remember some of them murmuring what sounded like prayers or chants. Surely, my sister planned it. Perhaps she thought if she lost enough, the fire would awaken in her."

She paused. Talen filled the silence quietly, "Flameborne." He earned a sharp glance from Kaelin.

Ren nodded. "Flameborne lineage runs in blood, but it can stay dormant until something ignites the spark."

Talen murmured, "I've read that the Flameborne are awakened when pushed to the brink. Their magic lies dormant until a moment of intense emotional upheaval, most commonly a near-death experience, or the soul-shattering loss of someone they hold dear. In your case, your loss of innocence. For Flameborne, grief and fury act as catalysts. When they are broken, the fire rises to remake them. It is the soul's final act of defiance, igniting when all else has been stripped away."

Kaelin's gaze flicked toward Ren, then back to Talen. Her lips curled into a small sneer. "How poetic. Forge a mortal through suffering and call it destiny." Kaelin tilted her head at Ren. "I'm curious about what you'll become once the fire settles."

"Perhaps that's what Eve thought," Ren wondered aloud. "She thought she could call it to her. But it wasn't her the flames chose."

She recalled the roaring in her ears as the flames closed around them, scorching her parents' lifeless bodies. And though her own clothes seared under the heat of the flames, the heat did not harm her.

Ren raised her chin. "It chose me."

"I've noticed your magic doesn't come from harnessing the fire around you." Talen said. "Even with the old bloodlines, elemental fire wielders don't create fire. They manipulate what already exists. They pull from the world around them. But you..." He tilted his head at her as if seeing her for the first time. "You conjure it from nothing."

Ren remained quiet, Zakhar's words from earlier lingering. Talen made the second person to conclude the observation about her magic.

Kaelin's gaze lingered on Ren. "Then you're Flameborne," she said simply.

The word fell across them like a death sentence.

Ren understood why. She knew about the legends. Flameborne were a rare bloodline believed to descend from dragons themselves, beings who could summon and breathe fire from within. She didn't know as much about their magic abilities but knew they were given a reputation for a reason amongst magic folk.

"You poor, furious thing," Kaelin drawled. "You think you're still the same girl from that burning house, but you're not. You were *forged* in that fire."

Ren's throat worked. "I'm not – "

"A threat?" Kaelin smirked. "Oh, but you are. That's why I am particularly coming to understand you."

Talen's expression darkened in disagreement. "You're not a threat, Ren."

"I don't want to be a threat," Ren whispered.

"Then let us help you. You came to us with this information, which shows we can all trust each other and be allies in this cause," Talen explained.

"Careful, dear brother," Kaelin purred, taking a sip of her wine. "Say 'trust' and 'allies' in the same breath again, and I might think you've gone soft. Or worse. *Optimistic.*"

"As much as I enjoy being the mortal tangled in fae politics and prophecy..." Ren looked between them pointedly, "The realm might stand a better chance if we stop quarreling and scheming and work together." She shrugged, voice edged with irony. "Strange times, when trusting fae sounds like the reasonable choice."

Kaelin's eyes glinted. "Strange times indeed." Then she added, "Never a dull moment here in our kingdom, wouldn't you agree?"

At that, Ren couldn't help but breathe a laugh.

The moment shattered as the doors slammed open behind her.

Zakhar entered like a storm. His face was drawn, pale beneath the streaks of ash and sweat.

Everyone stilled.

Zakhar didn't speak at first. He stepped forward, his heavy boots echoing on the stone.

Talen spoke first. "What happened?"

Zakhar exhaled slowly. "The western trenches. The field pyres. They were meant to contain the infection, stop the spread."

"Didn't they?" Ren asked.

Zakhar shook his head. "The bodies we've burned – they're *rising*."

Talen visibly stiffened. Kaelin's wine glass cracked in her grip.

Zakhar's voice was grim. "And they're hunting. They're organized. Some even speak names."

The firelight guttered in the hearth.

And Ren knew with bone-deep certainty: something had awakened. Something that would not rest until the living were dead.

34

No matter how Ren tossed and turned, sleep refused to come. Every time she shut her eyes, she saw them.

Dragons.

She kicked off the covers, sitting up so fast her head swam. It was all too much.

Talen and Kaelin had accepted the truth with all the gravity of a weather report. *Flameborne.* As if that title explained anything.

She pressed the heels of her hands to her eyes and tried to reach back through the fog of a childhood she'd long buried. Surely, if she had this power, this *lineage*, there would've been signs.

But there was nothing. Just an ordinary, human existence leading up to the night Eve betrayed them all and then something inside Ren had... snapped.

A creak split the darkness.

"Tough day?" Mirella's voice drifted from the corner, heavy with sleep.

Ren sighed, dragging her legs over the edge of the bed. "You could say that."

The wardrobe's carved wood groaned as it adjusted itself in the corner. "I'm told I'm an excellent listener. Also, I don't judge."

Ren shot it a sideways glare. "You judged me for wearing brown and gray together yesterday."

"I said you could do better. That's not the same."

Ren tugged her robe over a plain tunic, fingers moving stiffly as she twisted her hair into a quick braid. "Apparently, I'm Flame-borne."

"Is that... contagious?"

"It means I have the blood of dragons. So unless you've got fireproof lacquer, you might want to keep your distance."

"Ooh." Mirella's corners pinched in what could only be described as a wooden grimace. "No offense, but I'm not a fan of dragons. Fire and smoke are terrible for my varnish."

"Yeah. That makes two of us." She crossed to the door, casting a final glance over her shoulder. "I can't just sit here stewing in questions. I need answers. And the only place I'm likely to find any is that chaotic excuse of a library."

"Ah, yes. The Great Pile of Knowledge. Veylan's a genius, though. He knows where everything is, even if it seems he doesn't."

"I've noticed," Ren muttered. Ren opened the door, saying over her shoulder. "Good night, Mirella."

"Good night, Ren." Then, almost teasing but with a thread of genuine care, Mirella added, "Don't stay up too late with those books. You've got training in the morning."

Mirella was already snoring peacefully when Ren closed the door.

As Ren stepped inside the library, Veylan's voice called from behind the front desk. "Fresh biscuits tonight." He lounged with his feet up and a plate beside him. "My husband's trying a new recipe. Do let me know if you think the cinnamon is too much."

Ren grunted her thanks and snatched a couple of biscuits without slowing. "I'll be in the back," she called, already moving.

"More dragon lore?" he asked, voice dropping a notch.

She gave him a furtive glance over her shoulder. "Something like that."

The shelves swallowed her whole. Scrolls rustled in a phantom breeze. She ducked under a parchment that swept past her face and muttered an apology when she nearly stepped on a dwarf dabbing his eyes with a handkerchief, enraptured by whatever he was reading.

Finally, the vines pulled back for her, the enchanted archway recognizing her presence with a soft shiver. She exhaled in relief as she stepped inside the restricted stacks.

And that's when she saw a figure sat in the shadows of the far corner, half-shrouded in dim light.

Ren's fire flared in instinct because she *knew* that silhouette.

"Oh, *saints screw me sideways*, not tonight..." Ren groaned.

35

Kaelin was perched in a high-backed chair like she owned the place, one leg draped over the armrest and a half-empty glass of deep red wine balanced between two fingers.

Kaelin tilted her head. "Do you ever pause to actually think before you speak, or is this – " she gestured at Ren " – your natural pace of processing? You are *so* vulgar. I've met sailors with cleaner tongues."

Ren considered turning around and leaving and coming back tomorrow. But pride was a venomous thing, and she'd already swallowed too much of it today.

"Well, I guess somebody has to raise the bar," Ren plopped into a nearby chair. "I just didn't know this section came with royal accompaniment."

Kaelin raised her glass, eyes gleaming over the rim. "Only for the truly blessed."

"Then I'm in the right place."

They both thumbed through the old tomes piled on the table.

"You skipped dinner," Kaelin drawled without looking up. Her voice was calm, but threaded with that clipped tone Ren had come to recognize as concern disguised as irritation.

"I wasn't hungry."

"You're contracted to fight for this realm. Paid with coin, clothing, housing. We're not just feeding you out of kindness. If you collapse in battle because you're not eating properly – "

"I've survived worse than skipping a meal. I don't need you monitoring my plate," Ren shot back, slamming her book closed. "Didn't realize feeding me meant you owned me. Go back to drinking your wine and playing princess. I didn't come here to be lectured."

"You're right," Kaelin murmured coolly. "You didn't. You came here because your world tilted sideways last night, and you don't know which way is up. So you're snapping at the one person who is actually trying to do something about it."

The words struck deeper than Ren expected. Heat bloomed behind her eyes, hot and unwelcome. She looked away, pretending to study the spines of nearby books, but the fire had already risen in her throat.

For a split second, just one traitorous heartbeat, she almost thought that Kaelin regarded her not as the realm's precious asset but as a person.

But the wineglass still sat half-full beside Kaelin's elbow, and her voice had held too much steel, too much duty, to be anything close to tenderness. Ren knew better. Kaelin didn't care about her. She cared about the realm's investment.

That's all she was to them.

An asset left unfed and unrested was a liability. What more would she expect?

"I'm not the enemy here."

"You may not be my enemy," Ren retorted. "But you're not a friend, either."

She turned back to the table, reached for another biscuit with hands that trembled just slightly, and took a bite. It practically melted in her mouth.

Kaelin sighed. It slipped past her lips like steam from a cracked kettle, and for the first time that night, her carefully cultivated calm fractured. Kaelin set her wineglass down with a soft *clink* and leaned against the back of her chair, folding her arms. "Why are humans so dramatic about friendship? You all cling to the idea, as if every interaction must fall neatly into a box – friend, enemy, stranger, lover." Her mouth twisted. "I've lived over a hundred years, and if I wasted my energy trying to define every connection, I'd have lost my mind long ago. Maybe I'm not your friend. Maybe I never will be. But does that mean I don't care whether you survive?" She held Ren's gaze. "This isn't about friendship. It's about what has to be done for the safety of the realm. And what has to be done involves both of us, whether we like it or not."

Ren hated how much sense Kaelin made. But instead of staying quiet, like she probably should have, Ren's mouth ran ahead of her better judgment. "You're right, but I'm so tired of the masks." Ren sighed, pushing a hand through her hair as the words kept tumbling out. "I don't hide things from people. What you see is what you get. I am who I am. And maybe that's too much for some, but I'm not going to pretend to be something I'm not just to make someone else comfortable or to get something I want out of someone. What I say is what I mean. I don't understand how you all do that, day in and day out. It's exhausting."

Kaelin didn't say anything. The silence stretched.

Ren's eyes widened slightly as realization struck her.

Shit.

Her face flushed, heat rising all the way to her ears. Ren stared resolutely at the wall, suddenly fascinated by the cracks in the stone.

Then—

A soft sound broke the air.

Kaelin *laughed*.

Ren turned toward her, blinking in disbelief.

"I've been performing since I was old enough to braid my own hair. There's not a soul at court who doesn't wear a mask so long they forget the shape of their real face underneath. The truth is, I envy you. You walk into a room, fire blazing, and you don't dim it for anyone."

Ren shuffled in her chair, unsure how to respond.

Kaelin's eyes flicked back to the scrolls before them. "You should rant to me more often. Your thoughts are rather interesting." She paused, then added, "For a mortal."

Ren's brain struggled to catch up. Her mouth, however, had no such delay. "Has the wine gotten to you?"

The corners of Kaelin's lips twitched into a ghost of a smile. "Possibly. But don't let it go to your head. I'll deny everything come morning."

Ren huffed a laugh, the tension in her chest loosening just a little. "Good to know the realm's future rests in the hands of a tipsy noble."

"*And* a stubborn, sword-swinging fire hazard with a flair for dramatics."

Ren grinned, despite herself. "So, did you find anything worth mentioning?"

Kaelin's gaze flicked up from the book in her lap, the hint of wry amusement vanishing from her face. "Do you remember anything specific about the people who invaded your home?"

Ren's spine went rigid.

A familiar heat crawled up her neck, the kind born of pain that still hadn't scabbed over. "You mean the night my parents were murdered?" she snapped before she could stop herself. The words came too fast, too bitter. Her jaw clenched tight, but Kaelin didn't flinch. She merely raised one perfectly shaped brow, as if braced for the lash of Ren's temper.

Ashamed of her outburst, Ren bit into another biscuit. "They wore red cloaks. Their faces were hidden behind bone-white masks." Her voice faltered, her fingers curling into her sleeve. "They chanted something. It sounded like... a prayer."

Ren stared at the table, her mind peeling back the years like old wallpaper. That night had a sharpness to it—jagged edges of memory too painful to touch, yet impossible to forget.

Her heart began to race. "Wait."

Ren pushed to her feet, pacing.

"When I was headed to the butcher's block," she said, half to Kaelin, half to herself, "Sela said something – a prayer. I remember the words. They hit me like a blow at the time, but I couldn't place why." Her eyes narrowed, thoughts spinning. "How did it go? *Ash to air, wing to flame—*"

Kaelin's smooth voice finished the verse:

"Guard the lost, forget no name.
Though bound and broken we remain...
Let the last flame wake again."

Ren's breath caught in her throat. "Yes," she whispered, then louder, "Yes! That's it. That's what they said. How do you know that?"

Kaelin lifted the heavy leather-bound tome in her lap, the worn cover stamped with a sigil Ren didn't recognize. "I've been reading," Kaelin answered simply, eyes gleaming. "Drinking, of course, as well. But more importantly, reading."

Ren studied the sigil on the tome. It depicted a coiled dragon, but its body was made of what looked like burning cinders rather than scales. At the center of the circle was a single, vertical eye, and Ren felt like it was watching her.

Noting the tightness in Ren's jaw, Kaelin gestured toward the page between them. "This is the sigil of the Embersworn. They are a cult that believes the dragons were never meant to vanish from this world, that their extinction was a betrayal against the natural order. They preach that without dragons to rule over us, mortals and fae alike have grown weak, arrogant. The Embersworn seek to awaken the last slumbering flame... to resurrect Vortharax."

Ren's breath hitched. "Veylan mentioned him."

"Where the Flameborne vow was meant to contain the dragons' legacy and keep Vortharax from devouring the world, the Embersworn have twisted it into something darker. Their chant is now a ritual. Their devotion... blood sacrifice."

She flipped through the tome with practiced fingers, pausing on a stained page covered in smudged ink. Ren opened her mouth—half a joke ready, half a plea for alcohol—but before she could speak, Kaelin held out a fresh glass of wine, halfway full.

"Thanks," Ren whispered, accepting it like a lifeline.

"I can read most of this book," Kaelin said, her brow furrowed. "Until I reach this. Admittedly, I'm not well-versed in reading Draconic."

She rotated the tome toward Ren. The page was messier than the rest, as though scrawled in haste or madness. Some of the text bled into illegible black scratches. In the margins, symbols resembling claw marks curled around Draconic phrases.

"Their high priests are called Ashbinders," Kaelin said, tapping a passage. "They speak fluent Draconic, and some even say they've heard Vortharax's voice in their dreams."

"And what exactly does a dragon say in a dream?"

Kaelin's gaze darkened. "That the fire must rise again. That the unworthy must burn. They believe the dragons are divine punishers, returned to burn away corruption and usher in a trial by fire. Only the 'worthy' will survive."

Ren took a long, grateful drink of the wine and stared into the page like it might open up and offer her answers, or at least a way out.

Then the silence was shattered by a voice so loud it rattled the shelves and sent several books tumbling from above.

"—AND LO! She wept 'neath moonlit flame,
Though I, her knight, forgot her name!
'Twas love, or lust, or tragic fate—
OH DAMNATION, WHY COULDN'T SHE WAIT?!"

Ren groaned audibly before she spun toward the sound, eyes narrowing to slits as a translucent form drifted straight through the wall of shelves.

"Sir Pindlewhip," Ren muttered, as the ghostly apparition floated into view, quill in one hand, a thick, ink-stained manuscript in the other, his spectral cloak billowing with ghostly flair.

"Ladies," he greeted dramatically, flourishing the quill like a rapier. "A pleasure. I was merely refining my epic ballad when I felt a tremor of darkness cross the archive wards – terribly inconvenient, I assure you. Broke my rhyme scheme."

"We're discussing the Embersworn."

"Ah." Pindlewhip's theatrical energy dimmed a fraction. "Those cretins." He hovered closer, his joviality dampened by something darker. "I had the misfortune of encountering them once. Long after my... well, current state."

Ren arched a brow. "You mean after you died?"

"Indeed. I was minding my own ghostly business, wandering the old ruins of Blackmere Keep, when I stumbled upon them. They were hooded and chanting what sounded like incantations. They were also surrounded by bones and fire." His translucent eyes met Ren's. "They were trying to summon something. There was so much blood, as well. And did I mention all the bones?"

Kaelin's expression sharpened. "What did they summon?"

The ghost shivered, a strange thing to see. "I don't know if they succeeded. But something answered. I couldn't understand the language, but I fled. Even in death, I wanted no part of what they were bringing through."

Ren's blood froze in her veins.

Sir Pindlewhip set the manuscript down atop the tome Kaelin had shown her. "You two may find this all riveting. But take this advice from a ghost with more regrets than glories: If the Embersworn are stirring again, pray they haven't found a Flameborne heart still living."

Ren exchanged a look with Kaelin, and for once, neither had a retort.

Because deep down, they both knew.

A heart was living.

Hers.

R en stretched, each movement loosening the knots in her sore muscles.

Birds trilled overhead in the cypress trees, their songs high and bright against the hush of solitude. She flowed through the stretches with practiced grace, her body remembering even when her mind wandered back to the night before.

"Maybe I'm not your friend. Maybe I never will be. But does that mean I don't care whether you survive?"

Kaelin's voice had been a low murmur in the space between them, a sense of what seemed like honesty laced in her tone. And that was what confounded Ren most. Kaelin didn't extend warmth lightly. Every word from her mouth was calculated, deliberate.

So why waste it on Ren?

Ren knew how the world worked. She wasn't the kind of woman invited to courtly luncheons or afternoon strolls through royal gardens. She wasn't the daughter of a house with a name embroidered in history.

She was a weapon someone else had sharpened out of desperation. She had no use for crowns, no desire for thrones. All she had ever wanted was a life that belonged to her, unshaped by duty or legacy. A life where bloodlines didn't dictate worth – where her name was enough.

Gripping a training sword from the rack, she shifted into sparring form, every movement crisp and purposeful. The burn in her muscles grounded her, gave her control. But the heat in her gut only grew, flaring each time Kaelin's words resurfaced in her mind.

"...I am particularly coming to understand you."

Ren swung the blade in a wide arc, the air parting with a whistle. Her strikes came faster now, clean, efficient, ruthless. She welcomed the sting in her palms, the ache in her shoulders. Pain was easier to manage than whatever the hell Kaelin was doing to her.

Because what irritated her more than Kaelin's sharp tongue or unreadable glances was the maddening possibility behind them.

The possibility that Kaelin *wasn't* playing some political game.

That maybe, for reasons Ren couldn't begin to fathom, Kaelin actually meant it.

And wasn't that the most dangerous thing of all?

Her movements were sharper now, her breath quickening as her body pushed harder, faster, chasing distraction.

Then—

Clap... clap... clap.

Talen descended the stone steps like he had all the time in the world.

"To what do I owe this pleasure?" Ren asked.

Talen clicked his tongue, strolling toward the weapons rack. "Can't a prince enjoy a quiet morning without being interrogated?" He selected a sword and twirled it once. He grinned. "Care for a spar?"

Amber eyes slid to his, holding his gaze. "Only if you're ready to lose."

Steel clashed against steel as they met in the center of the ring, blades singing with each impact.

"You've been practicing," he managed, dodging a feint that nearly took his ear off.

"I don't need practice to beat you," she teased sweetly.

He laughed. "Remind me never to get on your bad side."

"I thought I *was* your bad side."

"Oh, no," he panted, blocking a vicious strike. "You're far more dangerous than that."

They circled each other, eyes locked. His grin turned wicked. "Is this how you flirt? Because it's working."

She rolled her eyes. "You'd flirt with a blade if it was pointed at your throat."

"*Especially* then."

Ren used his momentary surprise to twist, pivot, and sweep his legs out from under him. He went down hard, flat on his back with a grunt, sword skidding across the stone.

Ren straddled him, breath coming in soft pants, their lips barely inches apart. She could feel the heat of him, the tautness of muscle beneath her knees, the unguarded grin stretching across his face.

"You keep surprising me," he murmured.

Before Ren could fire back, a smooth voice cut through the air.

"She has a talent for that."

Both their heads turned. Kaelin stood at the edge of the ring.

Ren rose, brushing dust from her trousers. Talen sat up with a groan, shaking his head. "Come to supervise, sister?"

Kaelin descended the steps. "Oh, I do enjoy watching you lose, dear brother. But mostly I was curious to see if your ego could survive another bruising." She glanced down at him. "She had you on your back in under three minutes."

Talen raised a brow. "Jealous?"

Kaelin's smile curled into a sneer. "Not in the slightest."

Ren's stomach did something traitorous. Her tongue fumbled for a retort, but all she managed was a scoff and a quick turn to retrieve her blade, anything to avoid the heat creeping up her neck.

Kaelin stepped closer. "If you're going to leave a man breathless, at least make sure he's worth the effort."

Ren turned to Talen with a grin and shrugged. "Let's just say you're not my type."

He pressed a hand to his chest in mock injury. "Saints, you wound me. Do you know how rare it is for someone to resist," he gestured to his body, "all of *this*?"

Ren patted his shoulder. "Don't take it personally. You're lovely. If *only* you were a woman."

Talen raised his hands in mock defeat. "Noted."

Kaelin's voice followed Ren like a trailing ribbon as she turned to leave. "We should spar sometime. It was so easy to knock you to the ground your first day here, I almost felt guilty."

"Oh, right," Ren retorted. "That time you blindsided me mid conversation? Truly inspiring combat prowess, Your Royal Highness." Ren added sweetly, "Next time, try sparring someone who's actually ready. Might make for a fair fight."

"If you need to be ready to keep up with me, we have bigger problems than fairness."

Kaelin stroke out of the ring with all the poise of a queen, her shadow stretching long in her wake.

Talen whistled low.

Ren sheathed her blade, eyes still locked on Kaelin's retreating figure. "She thinks she can rattle me," Ren grumbled. "Let her try."

Talen's lips curved into the barest grin as they locked eyes. "Keep staring like that and people will start writing ballads."

Ren scoffed. "Relax. If anyone writes a ballad, it'll be about how I throttled you in your sleep."

As soon as Kaelin reached the quiet alcove off the east corridor, she poured herself a glass of wine and took a long sip, letting the sweetness drench her tongue.

Ren was just sparring, and she was just a mortal with a sharp tongue and a hellish bloodline that they knew nothing about, which should make her someone not to be trusted.

But nothing could drown the image still burned behind Kaelin's eyes.

Ren, flushed and breathless, straddling Talen like a goddess of war. The wild light in her eyes. The smirk. She looked like fire wrapped in mortal skin – something ancient and untamed, barely contained beneath the surface. Ren's tangled auburn hair, the sweat-slick curve of her jaw, the cut of her shoulders under leather. Solid, stubborn, brash. Not the graceful elegance Kaelin usually preferred in a lover.

Not her type *at all*.

And yet, some treacherous part of her mulled what it might feel like to have Ren standing over her like that. The image struck something deep in Kaelin's chest, something sudden and unwanted.

A spark she had no intention of feeding.

She wasn't some court fool, tripping over herself for an attractive face. She'd trained her entire life to guard her power, her throne, her family. To want was a weakness. To need, even worse. That path led to ruin.

And yet... here she was unable to shake Ren's image from her head. It was *infuriating*.

Because Ren didn't try to charm Kaelin. She didn't fawn, didn't beg for favor like so many others. She *challenged* Kaelin, even mocked her at times. Ren met her blow for blow, word for word. And Kaelin, who had always held power like a blade, found herself disarmed.

Unsettled.

Yet inevitably drawn.

It shouldn't have mattered. But it did.

"If only you were a woman."

At least she wasn't blind to women. A dangerous comfort.

A dangerous hope.

Kaelin closed her eyes for a moment to compose herself. She buried these thoughts deep, where things like that belonged. She was heir to a court with a traitor in its wake, and Ren was a mortal girl with dragonfire in her blood and a past full of ghosts.

There was a quiet shuffle of boots on stone that broke the stillness.

Kaelin didn't turn at first. She didn't need to. "Subtlety was never your strength."

Talen stepped into the alcove behind her. "Didn't realize brooding was your new pastime, sister."

"What do you want?"

"I could ask you the same. You've been standing here so long I thought you might have turned to stone."

"I needed a moment."

Talen studied her. "You're not usually so easily rattled."

"I'm not rattled."

"I wanted to talk before we both pretend none of that just happened in the training ring. You are drawn to her. She's something else. Fire and edge and all that. But you might want to tread carefully."

Kaelin raised a brow. "You seem to find her trustworthy. You've fought with her."

"She's strong. Fierce. I admire her. But that was before we discovered she is Flameborne."

"She saved your life nearly a month ago."

"I'm not ungrateful." He leaned against the opposite wall. "But she's not just some angry human with a sword now. She's a Flameborne, which means that there's not much we know about her bloodline. None of us, including Mother and Father, have ever met a Flameborne. We only know what we can read from texts and legends." Talen's eyes met hers. "I've seen her power firsthand. I certainly wouldn't want to be on the other end. We'd be foolish not to watch her closely."

Kaelin turned back to the window, but this time, her reflection stared back with narrowed eyes.

Talen pushed off the wall. "It's no coincidence she shows up on our doorstep in the midst of this deadly plague and when the dead rise."

A tense silence stretched between them. Kaelin moved to pour another glass of wine.

"Something else is moving behind all this, Kaelin. And whether she knows it or not, Ren didn't just stumble into this war. She was *placed*."

Kaelin's expression hardened. "There's certainly something brewing. While you're out gutting monsters, I've been smiling through every cursed ball, every royal feast, pretending I enjoy dressing up and dancing." Her fingers curled tightly around the stem of her glass. "I watch every guest, listen to every whisper. The ogre ambush was no coincidence. Someone knew you'd be there." She finally looked at Talen. "So, yes. We both play our roles. While you are beyond our borders and fighting those creatures, I throw the balls, I wear the dresses. But while they toast to politics, I'm hunting down a traitor amidst our court."

Talen looked past her, toward the horizon bleeding fire across the sky. "That's what I'm intending to find out as well."

Kaelin swirled the wine in her glass, her tone casual but laced with thought. "Ren is impulsive, unpredictable. Half the time, I can't decide if I want to throttle her or applaud her." She shot Talen a sidelong glance. "But there's good in her. Stubborn, blindingly noble good – the kind that's both annoying and a little ridiculous. Whatever else she is, Ren's not our enemy."

"I know she's got the heart for this fight. But if she lets that fire consume her, there may be nothing left to distinguish her from the very forces we're fighting."

The next morning, Ren groaned into the pillows.

Her limbs felt heavy, her lower back pulsed with a dull, persistent ache, and nausea curled low in her stomach like a coiled serpent. Her time of the month had arrived.

She counted silently in her head. Five seconds. Ten. Fifteen. On twenty, she forced herself upright. Getting dressed felt like a battle in itself, every tug of fabric a war.

"It's times like these I'm thankful I'm not human," Mirella chimed from the corner, her carved features animated with sympathy as Ren staggered to her feet.

Ren grunted in reply.

"The infirmary has tonics for pain. The princess used to drain the entire supply when she was younger. Poor thing had it worse than most."

Ren paused mid-step. "The fae have cycles, too?"

"Why wouldn't they?"

Ren thought for a moment. "Fair point."

Ren pulled the door closed behind her with a soft *click*, her boots whispering against the stone floor as she made her way down the quiet corridor. Morning light filtered through the stained glass windows, painting the walls in fractured gold and rose hues. The sky outside was barely touched by sunrise, still kissed with lavender, Mount Solfira beyond a shadowed silhouette.

The infirmary sat tucked into a quiet corner of the keep and was almost holy in its stillness. Curtains stirred with the early breeze, sunlight dappled across linen-covered beds, and shelves of glass bottles glinted like gems.

Ren stepped inside, rubbing the tension from her temples.

And froze.

Lucan sat on the edge of a cot with his back exposed, muscles taut as he attempted to stitch up a wound that looked like it had been torn open viciously. His hand trembled slightly, the needle pausing mid-thread.

There was no healer in sight.

Ren stepped inside. Lucan turned at the sound, and their eyes met.

Ren took one look at the wound and knew it wasn't from training. She'd seen enough to know the difference. It was too deliberate. Too angry. The wound wasn't clean like a soldier's cut, quick from a blade. No, this was ragged, cruel, the kind of tearing left by something swung in anger rather than battle. The skin was split in uneven gashes, as though he'd been struck with a belt buckle or the edge of a whip, the force brutal enough to break flesh instead of merely bruising it.

Dark, mottled bruises bloomed along the edges, older layers of pain marking him even as fresh blood welled beneath Lucan's fingers. It was evidence carved into his skin of someone's wrath.

This was *personal*.

The sight dragged Ren somewhere else, back to a night when Eve had hunched in the dim light of their cabin, a gash across her brow where their father's bottle had broken. Ren remembered the way Eve's hands shook as she stitched her own skin closed, teeth clenched against the pain. Ren had been only a child, voice trembling as she read aloud from one of their worn books, hoping the story would be enough to keep the pain at bay.

Ren shut the door behind her. "Do you want help, or are you planning to bleed all over the floor?"

Lucan didn't respond. But he didn't look away, either.

And he didn't stop her when she approached.

Ren rinsed her hands at the basin and grabbed the needle and thread. As she knelt behind him and threaded the needle, she murmured,

"Whatever story they fed you about why you deserved this, it's a lie. Pain shouldn't be a test you have to pass to be worth something." She lowered her voice, "Especially not to family."

When she tied off the final stitch, he whispered, "Don't pity me."

"I don't. But I've worn bruises that weren't from battle, too, Lucan."

Lucan flinched instantly, like she'd struck him. "Don't say my name."

"Why? Because hearing it from someone like me makes it feel real?"

He looked away, shoulders still drawn with tension.

Ren sat back on her heels, letting her hands fall to her lap. "You look at me and see every insult your people have whispered behind your back. That you were outmatched, outranked... by a human." She shrugged nonchalantly. "They'll judge you for it. Even if they don't say it to your face, they'll think it. You weren't strong enough. *You* weren't enough."

Through gritted teeth, Lucan seethed, ""Gods above, will you stop already?"

She pressed on. "But it shouldn't be that way. I know what it's like to never be accepted, no matter what you do. To always be the outsider. The other." She held his gaze. "You think you're the only one people talk about behind their hands? I bleed for this kingdom, and I still don't belong. I won't ever belong."

"Leave me be."

And in that worn, weary look, Ren saw the truth.

He didn't hate her.

He hated what she proved. That someone like her could win and that someone like him could fall short.

Ren stood, setting the bloodied thread and needle aside on the tray. "You keep bleeding in silence like it's a penance for not being who they want you to be. But you don't owe anyone their version of you." She rummaged through a cupboard, and then another one until she found a bottle of pain tonic. She paused to check the label before shutting the cupboard. "You want strength? Start by owning the one thing they can't take – who the hell you *really* are."

Ren uncorked the pain tonic and drank straight from the bottle, wiping her mouth with the back of her hand before grabbing the needle again. She shot him a raised eyebrow. "So, do you want actual company, or should I leave you to wallow in your tragic *woe is me* routine? By the way you were holding this needle, I can tell you've never stitched a damn thing in your life."

Lucan shrugged in defeat.

"Thought so." She sat beside him, rolling up her sleeves. "Brace yourself. This is about to hurt like fuck. Bite down on something if you need to. Preferably not me. And try not to scream too loud – someone will think I'm murdering you."

Lucan mustered a smile. "You're full of demands, you know that?"

"Damn right. Someone has to keep this disaster moving."

Ren lay in bed. The walls felt too close, her thoughts too loud.

She'd spent years like this, nights where her mind wouldn't stop whirling, no matter how exhausted her body was.

So she dressed quietly, pulling her tunic over her head and tugging on her boots. She hesitated when it came to the last piece. *Ashrend.* The blade rested where she'd left it near the windowpane. She strapped the sword to her hip.

Then she stepped out into the night.

She made her way silently to the forge, hoping Elira might still be awake. But the windows were dark, the fires cold.

Ren drifted toward the training grounds, then stopped short at the threshold. Her bruises throbbed in protest.

She wandered through the castle's moonlit courtyard. The hedges here were sculpted into elegant, sweeping shapes depicting fae warriors frozen in dance, roses the size of her head unfurling in green leaf. Her boots carried her along the same winding path she had walked on her very first day in Pyraelia, when Kaelin had strolled beside her.

Back then, the air had been alive with autumn's warmth, the gardens still humming with bees and color. Now frost rimmed the leaves, and her breath fogged in the cold night. Ren marveled at how two months had slipped away since her arrival. Winter had come into its full reign.

Tiny sprites fluttered past, their soft golden glow illuminating the path in flitting patterns. Ren caught fragments of their hushed conversation in a language she didn't recognize, musical and ethereal.

The courtyard opened into a wide, circular clearing, where ancient statues loomed in the darkness. She paused beneath the gaze of one, its face fractured but still regal, a fae god with wings of stone stretched wide as if to shield the world.

And then she rounded the final hedge.

Ren stopped short.

There, standing like a monument himself beneath the largest statue in the circle, was Sylven Draeth.

The moonlight caught the silver edge of his pauldrons, casting his sharp features in a ghostly glow. He didn't turn to look at her, but she could feel his awareness shift the moment she arrived, like a predator clocking a ripple in the underbrush.

"Well," Ren said, folding her arms and eyeing him with wary curiosity. "Either you're communing with the gods, or you're brooding dramatically for attention. Which is it?"

"Must it be one or the other?" Sylven replied. "Perhaps I find divine inspiration in my own company."

"Must be nice, having that much self-love. Do you pray to yourself before bed, too?"

He turned then, just enough for her to see the faint curl of amusement at the corner of his mouth. "Only when I've done something truly magnificent, which, unfortunately for my sleep cycle, is often."

Ren rolled her eyes. "And here I thought the gods' statues had the biggest heads in the courtyard."

Sylven's gaze slid to her. "What brings you out at this hour?"

"Thought I'd check on all the nobles who run like hell the moment something dangerous stirs in their view. Congratulations, you're at the top of the list."

His features darkened at her insult. And for a moment, even she was shocked she said such a thing to a renowned soldier of the fae court. But every time she looked upon his sharply chiseled face, snake-like eyes, and that conniving sneer, she saw Joss and Corrin in her mind.

And she remembered what Sylven and his soldiers did.

Or *didn't* do.

Sylven returned his attention back to the statue. "How much do you know about our gods?"

"I know enough. This one is Varyn. One of the oldest gods of the fae pantheon, said to have been born from the first oath ever spoken in the realm, an unbreakable vow made between the primal forces of earth and sky to preserve harmony. The god of protection. Strength. Oaths." She paused. "Seems very unlike yourself, considering you seem to break all three."

He looked at her again, more sharply this time. "I'd sooner risk my men for something that mattered. Not for humans already marked for execution. You burned a forest to rescue *criminals* bound for the butcher's block."

Ren stepped closer, her voice a low snarl. "And yet you stand here, under the statue of a god who swore to protect. Tell me, does Varyn's creed not apply to humans as well as your kind? Varyn is who stands between others and ruin. It is said that every time a shield is lifted in defense of another, Varyn's spirit bears part of the weight. You're just another coward who only protects what's convenient or what you deem worthy of living."

A tense beat passed. The wind stilled.

Ren's fists clenched at her sides, heat coiling in her chest like a struck match.

"If words don't get through that thick skull of yours, maybe a blade will." She took a step forward, her voice trembling with restrained rage. "Draw your weapon, Sylven. Or are you only brave when your enemies can't fight back?"

Sylven didn't move. His expression shifted with something colder. He looked past her, to the looming statue of Varyn behind them. When he spoke, his voice had lost its bite. "This is sacred ground."

The words hit like stone.

Ren hesitated, her breath seizing in her throat. Sylven's gaze stayed fixed on the statue, on the god of strength, oaths, and honor.

"I don't draw my blade beneath the gaze of the Guardian. Not in anger. Not for pride. Not even for you."

"Corrin," she spat, voice cracking. "And Joss. Gods, he was barely entering adulthood. They were both on that wagon. And you left them to be slaughtered by those ogres."

Sylven didn't look at her.

"I hope you remember their names, Sylven." She took a step closer, her voice low and shaking with fury. "And when the time comes for your gods to weigh what kind of fae you really are, I hope they give you exactly what you deserve."

She walked away, the gravel crunching under her boots in sharp bursts, like the earth itself was flinching with every step. Her shoulders were tight, jaw clenched, fists balled at her sides as if keeping her fire from leaping out and torching something.

Behind her, the statue of Varyn stood tall, unmoving.

And Sylven Draeth remained at its feet.

Corrin. Joss.

Ren stumbled over a loose stone, barely catching herself before she hit the ground. She swore violently into the wind. Her rage was bleeding into her steps now, wild and uneven, like her body couldn't contain it anymore.

The arrogance of the fae. The way they stood so tall while stomping others into the dirt, cloaking cruelty in tradition and pride. She'd met vile creatures with sharper teeth, but none who smiled while they drove the blade in like the fae did.

Her breath came in sharp bursts as she rounded a corner of the courtyard, head down, still muttering curses under her breath.

Before her loomed a statue she hadn't noticed before. It stood twisted, between eight and ten feet tall, hunched slightly as if the weight of its own form was too much to bear. The figure looked wrong, as if reality had tried to shape it and failed.

Its body was made from a jarring mixture of materials – black obsidian, cracked glass, corroded bronze, and bone-white marble, as if several gods had fought over what it should look like and no one had won.

Three faces spiraled around its head like a crown:

One, smiling.

One, screaming.

One was completely smooth where eyes, nose, and mouth should've been.

Six arms jutted out in every direction. One reached for her. Another grasped at nothing. One bled obsidian ink from its palm. One pointed toward the stars. One was folded in an almost reverent prayer. The last was broken, twisted at the elbow like it had been snapped mid-movement.

And in the center of its chest was a gaping split where ribs should've been, hovered a glowing orb, pulsing with swirling void. A heart made of stars and ink, moving as if alive, beating in an impossible rhythm. At the statue's base, serpents, moths, and shattered mirrors curled together in a chaotic mosaic that made Ren's skin crawl to look at too long.

Then came the whispers.

Low. Murmuring. Slithering. Fluttering.

Dozens of voices humming in a broken choir, rising from beneath her feet, from the statue, from inside her own skull. She couldn't understand them at first, as they were just fragments, sibilant and overlapping. Words half-formed, too fast, too slow, too wrong.

Her hands flew to her ears, but the sound wasn't coming from outside.

It was *in* her. The voices merged, sharpening into one.

"Tear off your skin and wear your truth. Let the bones of the world rattle in your wake."

Ren flinched, stumbling back a step.

The statue hadn't moved.

Ren's throat was dry. Her heart thundered from the sick, gnawing realization that some part of her understood.

She knew the God of Chaos when she saw him. The Many-Faced One. The Shattered Truth. Also known in some whispered circles as the God Who Unmade Himself. But nobody knew his true name.

This deity was not born like the other gods; he was *unmade*.

Legend claimed he had once been a god of foresight, balance. But he'd stared too deeply into the fabric of reality – into the threads that bound divinity, fate, and belief. And when he saw what truly held it all together, he split into mania and madness and *laughed*.

And in that laugh, he shattered.

His name was broken. His face, split. His essence unraveled into a storm of contradiction and ruin, a god no longer of balance, but of everything underneath it.

Now, he was the whisper behind madness, the crack in the mirror, the doubt that never leaves. His chaos was a tearing away of the beautiful lies to expose the raw, writhing truth that is attempted to be buried. According to legend, of course.

His influence didn't always come with blood or fire. Sometimes it came in quiet solitude. In questions. In the slow, creeping undoing of the soul's comfort.

He bred rebellion. Madness. Brilliance. Collapse. Those who followed him didn't always want to set the world free.

Some merely wanted to watch the world burn.

Ren stepped closer to the statue again. The orb inside its split chest pulsed with slow, rhythmic light, like a heart beating not for life, but for unraveling.

And in that moment, Ren didn't just see the God of Chaos. She *felt* him.

She took one final look at the statue, at the bleeding hand, the screaming face, the broken arm, and whispered to the chilled air, "I see you."

The whispers didn't return.

But the silence that followed felt like a breath held in the dark.

Waiting.

38

The morning sun slanted through the high windows of the dining hall, but the usual clamor of others' presence was blessedly absent.

Ren was grateful for the silence. She stifled a yawn and trudged across the empty space, her limbs still heavy with sleep, or what little she'd managed to get of it.

She'd tossed and turned for hours, mind replaying every word from her exchange with Sylven the other night, crafting a thousand responses she wished she'd said. But none had come when she needed them most. Instead, she'd buried her face in the pillow, only to realize in a hollow sort of irony that she had kept one of Corrin and Joss' promises after all.

She had found herself a soft bed to lie in.

Ren selected a thick slice of bread and a bowl of porridge that steamed in her hands. She settled into a seat at the far end of the table, dragging the spoon through the grainy mush. The first bite was comforting. She tore a chunk of bread free, chewing mechanically.

Then came the rustle of fabric.

Ren glanced up just as Kaelin glided into the seat across from her, every inch the picture of composed elegance. The lilac velvet of her dress clung to her frame, the fabric catching soft glints of silver embroidery with each movement. Her golden hair tumbled in carefully sculpted curls, cascading over her shoulders. With deliberate poise, Kaelin set down a porcelain cup before her, steam curling in the air between them.

Kaelin's gaze flicked to Ren's food. "You're eating. That's good."

Ren grunted, lifting her spoon.

Kaelin studied Ren with cool precision. "And you seem pale. Trouble sleeping?" Kaelin reached for the small pitcher of cream, tilting it with the kind of precision that made the gesture feel ceremonial, ivory ribbons swirling into the dark tea until it softened to a warm amber.

"Yes. I ran into Sylven in the courtyard the other night."

At that, Kaelin's brows arched, just enough to show interest. "Ah."

"Ah?" Ren repeated, scoffing. "You mean 'ugh.' He's insufferable. Every word out of his mouth makes me want to set something on fire."

Kaelin's lips twitched, almost imperceptibly. "He is intense."

"That's a pretty way of putting it."

"Sylven's seen more bloodshed than most of us care to count, more than even he'll admit aloud."

Ren stirred her porridge absentmindedly. "Still doesn't give him the right to play judge, jury, and executioner."

Kaelin leaned back, folding her hands in her lap as if the subject were closed.

Ren reached for another piece of bread. "Why do the fae hate humans so much? When did you all just wake up one day and decide we're beneath you?"

Kaelin didn't answer at first. Her spine straightened, the muscle in her jaw flexing as she set down her teacup with deliberate care. "It's how it's always been," she answered finally, voice clipped.

"That's not an answer. That's a deflection wrapped in centuries of prejudice."

Kaelin's fingers twitched in her lap.

Ren leaned forward, eyes narrowed. "Do *you* hate me?"

"I don't always understand you. You're reckless, obnoxiously loud, most often underdressed for when the occasion calls for it —"

Ren thinned her lips. "Should I give you parchment so you can finish the rest of that list, or is this the abridged version?"

"But," Kaelin continued, "I've never seen anyone rise from so little and still keep their spine straight. You don't bow when others would break."

Before Ren could find anything resembling a comeback, the doors to the dining hall slammed open.

Talen strode in, boots echoing loudly against the stone. His usually collected expression was pale. His eyes locked on Ren. "The dead have been sighted near Greymoore village."

Ren straightened, shoving away her bowl of porridge. "How many?"

"Too many. We've already lost two scouting parties. If we don't move now, the whole village will fall before dusk."

"How many soldiers will be coming?"

Talen hesitated.

Ren narrowed her gaze. Through gritted teeth, she asked, "How many?"

His jaw clenched. "A handful. Most don't want to risk the garrison for a village full of humans. They say... the loss isn't worth it."

Ren felt the silence around her turn brittle. Her chair scraped loudly against the floor as she stood, fury simmering just beneath her skin. But she willed it away with the urgency of the matter. "Then we go with however many soldiers we've got. Come on."

Kaelin rose like a blade being unsheathed. "And I'll personally make sure every coward is reminded what House Vaelaran stands for."

"Father's in council now," Talen said. "He's arguing options with the council members, trying to measure loss against gain. He wants a plan." His jaw worked as if grinding down words he hadn't yet said. "But I don't think there's time to wait for plans. I'll ready the horses." Talen's nod was brisk. "I'll ready the horses," he repeated, voice threaded with something like resolve.

Ren nodded. "Let's go." As she followed Talen toward the exit, she caught Kaelin's gaze once more, and for a flicker of a second, it held something Ren hadn't expected.

Pride.

And maybe, just a sliver of faith.

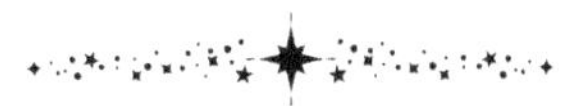

The dead had to be burned.

Ren and Talen learned that in the space of one frantic, blood-soaked hour.

Severing their limbs didn't stop them. Cut off a leg? The corpse dragged itself forward on a splintered bone. Slice through the neck? The head still snapped its rotten jaw as the body stumbled forward.

But fire silenced them for good.

The streets of Greymoore were slick with rain and mud. Most of the villagers had been evacuated, but not all had escaped the horde that swept in overnight, tearing through homes with an unstoppable hunger. Death clung to the air, and Ren's boots squelched through mud turned black with blood.

The creatures were clumsy, but they learned. One staggered toward her gripping a rusty shovel, attempting to parry Ashrend with a swing as clumsy as a child's.

But it wasn't fast enough.

Ashrend sliced cleanly through its spine, sending it crumpling to the ground.

In the center of the square, Talen and Ren found a woman heavy with child lying amid the wreckage, half her body torn apart, her legs chewed down to bone. One of the dead was crouched over her, gnawing at her ribs until Talen's sword drove it back into the dirt.

Ren knelt, pressing her hand against the woman's trembling one. The woman's lips were pale, cracked. Blood bubbled in her throat as she rasped, "Is my baby...?"

Ren's gaze fell over the ruin of the woman's lower body. Flesh mangled beyond repair, bones gleaming through shredded muscle.

There was no saving her or her baby.

Gauging the look on Ren's face, the woman let out a low, broken moan. "Not my baby," she wept, her hands gripping Ren's fingers with desperate strength. "Anything but my baby..."

Ren's vision blurred. She squeezed the woman's hand, murmuring something, she didn't know what. A promise. A lie. A prayer.

And then she sensed a shift in the air, a subtle hum of a familiar magic.

She turned and saw Talen standing nearby, his face set in quiet concentration. His hands glowed faintly with that crackling energy dark as midnight and threaded with faint embers of green.

The woman's trembling eased. Her grip loosened. Slowly, her breath steadied, her panicked eyes softening into something that resembled peace. The woman's smile waned, her breath a faint sigh.

And then she was gone.

Ren gently closed the woman's glazed eyes. Talen's steps were slow, measured as he came to kneel beside her. "I gave her something to hold onto," he murmured. "I wanted to show her what her life might have been. With her child. She deserved that much."

For a moment, Ren could only stare, the weight of his words settling heavily in her chest. "Why?" she asked hoarsely.

Talen's jaw tightened. His eyes, dark as midnight, flickered faintly with green embers, the last traces of the magic he'd woven. "Because sometimes mercy isn't just about ending suffering. It's about giving someone a moment of peace before they cross beyond the Veil."

Talen simply moved to gather the next body, his movements steady, his silence saying more than words ever could.

Talen had shown her what might have been. A life where they grew together, laughed together, grew old side by side. He'd given her that memory, that peace. Even if it was only an illusion.

Ren whispered a prayer for the woman's safe passage across the Veil, brushing the woman's hair gently back from her blood-streaked face.

"We're not leaving them like this," she announced, rising to her feet.

More soldiers trickled in, all of them silent, their expressions carved into grief-hardened restraint. Ren turned at the sound of boots. Elric approached from the far side of the wreckage, torch in hand. He gave Ren a brief, somber nod before bending to light another body. Not one of them spoke, yet every motion carried the reverence of duty, as though words themselves might dishonor the fallen.

When at last the bodies were ablaze, they stood before the pyre. Sparks rose into the dusk like fleeting souls, vanishing into the night.

Ren felt the shift before she saw it.

Her blood turned to ice. She recognized it instantly. *Magic.*

Talen's sword was already unsheathed. Ren drew Ashrend. Together they swept their eyes across the tree line.

A lone figure emerged from the trees.

Near Ren, Elric let out a curse.

"No," Talen breathed, his voice a snarl beneath his breath. His canines bared in silent warning.

"Is this even possible?" Elric wondered. "I've heard of humans coming to life, but..."

The figure drew closer, stepping into the light. Their fears solidified into a cold, ugly truth.

A fae.

Dead, but moving.

The fae corpse's skin was ashen, and its eyes glowed an unnatural green. Its jaw clenched, snapping as though tasting their fear. Cracks of power licked up its arms, with magic surging from its palms.

"Elemental," Talen growled. "Lightning. High-born, judging by the remnants of those robes."

Above, the clouds boiled into dark thunderheads, rumbling like a war drum.

Then the fae corpse attacked.

Lightning spurted from its fingertips, spearing the ground at their feet. Ren dove aside, rolling through grass. Talen met the fae head-on, his sword singing as they fought.

Thunder cracked overhead. The air screamed as a bolt struck too close, fire exploding. Smoke and light bled together.

Ren didn't have time to look because the dead were coming.

Her battle was her own. Four, no, five, now clawing free from the darkness like nightmares made into flesh.

Ashrend met bone and decay, the wet crunch of impact reverberating up Ren's arm. One dropped. Another took its place.

She swung.

Again.

And again.

But there were too many.

Talen was a storm of shadow and steel on the other side of the field. But Ren was drowning in bodies.

A hand tangled in her hair, yanking her sideways. Ashrend slipped from her grasp. She hit the ground hard, the wind tearing from her lungs. One of the corpses lunged for her throat. Its mouth opened wide, teeth black and jagged.

Ren twisted. Panic surged.

But it was too fast. Too close.

And then—

She was there again. In the fighter pit. The stench of sweat and blood. The roar of a drunk man demanding blood and gore. Her first fight.

She was fifteen – barely old enough to hold a sword, let alone wield it. And across from her stood a man easily five times her size. Confident she'd fall in the first ten seconds.

She had no magic. No armor.

Just fear and *rage*.

And one truth burned into her bones: *If she didn't fight, she didn't live.*

Ren had fought until her hands were slick with blood, until her ribs ached with every breath. Until his body dropped at her feet and the crowd screamed her name like a war chant.

Her legs had trembled. But they had held.

Back in the present, something in her snapped.

Ren gritted her teeth and screamed, not in fear, but *fury*.

The corpse lunged, and she dove for Ashrend, fingers curling around her blade's width before driving Ashrend through the corpse's jaw, burying it to the hilt. The corpse spasmed.

Another came. She slashed it down in a wide arc, severing a limb. Blood sprayed across her face.

She kept swinging.

Covered in gore. Surrounded by smoke and thunder and flame.

If Ren had learned anything in this life, it was to fight. Fight with teeth bared and fists bleeding. Fight even when the gods turned their backs.

She shoved the next creature back with a snarl, her lips drawn in a bloody grin. "Come on, then," she rasped. "Let's see who breaks first."

And then, a horn blast split the sky.

Shook the *world*.

Silhouettes of soldiers appeared at the clearing of trees across the field, arrows released in perfect arcs at a new horde of reanimated creatures that emerged from the left. They fell under a rain of steel.

And through the clearing smoke, Kaelin appeared astride a midnight black horse, her presence as chillingly beautiful as moonlight on frost.

Kaelin's lips curved into a dangerous smile that belied her steely tone. "It's astonishing what obedience you can buy with a well-placed reminder of oaths. Fae pride folds quickly under pressure. You can thank me later."

Ren kicked at a corpse's hand tugging at her ankle. "You talked them into it?"

"I convinced them," Kaelin corrected, dismounting her horse with effortless grace. "Which is nobler than dragging them by the ear. Though I considered that, too."

From across the field, Ren heard a female's voice call, "Ready. Archers – go!" Another rain of steel rained across, sending a few more undead to the ground. There was a male who then roared, "*Charge!*" and a few figures dashed from the archers, breaking from the formation, and Ren watched in awe as the fae used the elements – fire, ice, rumbling the very ground of the earth to destroy the last of the undead.

And Kaelin watched with a curl of her lips, pleased.

Ren, still reeling, finally found her voice. "A moment later, and we would have been toast."

Kaelin's eyes lingered on Ren. Ren thought she saw the fleeting hint of an unnamed emotion cross Kaelin's violet eyes. Concern? Worry? Ren didn't know, and before she could decipher just what that emotion might have been, it passed as quickly as it came.

Behind Kaelin, several more armored figures on horseback emerged through the trees, their crests glinting in the light.

Talen stumbled next to Ren. He had struck the fae corpse's head clean off its shoulders, but its body was wandering the field, arms outstretched, searching for him. "How many did you bring?"

"Enough to make the cowards who stayed behind feel ashamed when they hear what we did here," Kaelin answered.

Ren stared long enough for the world to narrow to nothing but the fae princess before her. It wasn't until her jaw went slack that she caught herself and snapped it shut.

Beneath the carnage of shattered corpses and the crackle of lingering lightning, Kaelin stood like some vision torn from myth, armor gleaming, starlit hair spilling wild over her shoulders.

Eyes lit with the kind of fire that could burn kingdoms.

The sight hit Ren so hard, her knees nearly betrayed her.

"You're full of surprises," Ren managed to say.

Kaelin's eyes gleamed as her gaze met Ren's. "You haven't seen anything yet."

40

Ren didn't remember pushing the doors to the throne room open. She didn't remember walking there at all. One moment, she was dragging her bruised body through smoke and ash. The next, she was standing in the throne room, transfixed by the dais.

Four thrones.

But it was the fourth, the farthest left, carved of obsidian and adorned with slivers of starlight, that fixed her in place.

Kaelin's throne.

Ren's legs felt suddenly too heavy, the ache of the day's battle catching up all at once. She should've gone to the infirmary. She should've found Talen. She should've done anything but this.

But her feet had carried her here anyway.

Suddenly, there was the whisper of silk and heels.

Ren turned to see Kaelin poised in the archway to the right of the thrones.

Kaelin's usually perfect hair was wind-tousled, a single braid unraveling down one shoulder. The fae princess moved fluidly, every line of her form accentuated by the midnight blue gown clinging to her. The fabric shimmered as though woven from shadow touched with frost, catching the light in fleeting glimmers that made her seem both untouchable and unreal. Her eyes found Ren's, and the world seemed to hush around them.

Kaelin's gaze swept over Ren, trailing down to the smudges of blood along Ren's temple, the tear in her sleeve, the dark bloom of bruises along her collarbone before her violet eyes slowly lifted to meet Ren's eyes again.

"You look like hell."

Ren straightened, forcing her spine stiff despite the exhaustion weighing on her limbs. "I've had worse days."

"Talen said you were overrun. That you barely made it out."

"We made it out, thanks to you," Ren retorted, voice clipped. "That's what matters."

Kaelin's lips pressed into a faint line, betraying her doubt. Her gaze lingered on Ren not with judgment, but with something else.

Something that made Ren's throat tighten.

"You didn't have to stay," Kaelin stated finally. "You could've run when the fight turned. My brother was nearly overwhelmed, and yet you stayed." Her voice fell to a whisper, laced with incredulity, as though she could scarcely believe them herself. "A human life burns faster, ends sooner than ours, and you despise us. So why risk your life for him?"

"Why would I leave him?"

"I've seen people leave others for less."

Ren's jaw tightened. "Well, I wouldn't leave a friend."

The word left her before Ren could stop it. *Friend.* It caught even her off guard, hanging in the air between them. But it was true. Talen, for all his titles and fae blood, had never looked at her the way others did. He didn't see her as lesser, or fragile, or disposable. Through his actions, she'd seen the kind of person he was.

Someone *good.*

Ren crossed her arms and shrugged. "And because nobody deserves to die alone. I'd have stayed with him, through whatever end awaited us."

Something shifted in Kaelin's face, not softening, not exactly, but a flicker of respect. Admiration, even, before it was shuttered away behind her usual cool mask. "You're hurt."

"Why do you care?"

Kaelin stepped forward until they stood only a breath apart beneath the empty watch of the thrones. "Because every time I think I hate you, you go and prove me wrong," Kaelin murmured.

"Funny. I keep thinking I should hate you, too."

The weight of the room suddenly occurred to her – the marble floors smeared with dirt from her boots. Ren forced a wry smile. "I'm just trying to catch my breath. Don't worry, I won't get mud or blood on the tapestries."

Kaelin's eyes flicked toward the throne behind her. "Strange, isn't it. Choosing *this* place to catch your breath?"

Ren bristled. "Maybe I just wanted some solitude."

Kaelin tilted her head. "Or maybe you sought me."

The words struck like a flare – too close and far too honest.

Ren turned away, pacing toward the far column to escape the heat crawling up her neck. "Don't flatter yourself."

"I wouldn't dream of it."

Kaelin moved again, slow as a stalking cat, every step a silent command for Ren to look at her. And gods help her, Ren did. She tried to keep her gaze fleeting, but it lingered on the graceful outlines of Kaelin's legs beneath her gown, the effortless authority in her posture, the gleam of challenge in those violet eyes.

And when Kaelin sank into her throne, crossing one long leg over the other, it was a predator settling into its vantage point.

Eyes never leaving its chosen quarry.

Kaelin leaned forward, resting her elbow on the armrest, her chin balanced lightly against her knuckles.

"Stay," Kaelin murmured. "Just for a moment."

For one reckless second, Ren considered turning and walking out the way she came. But something in Kaelin's gaze held her rooted to the spot.

Ren stepped forward.

Kaelin reclined back against her throne, chin lifting in subtle challenge as Ren ascended the steps.

Ren didn't break eye contact as she came to stand over the fae princess, close enough that the air seemed to hum. She leaned down, bracing one hand on the armrest beside Kaelin's thigh, the other settling on the back of the throne.

"You know, I was wondering. Why are *you* here? Don't tell me you just happened to stumble across me. Maybe *you* were looking for *me*."

Kaelin went utterly still. There was no sharp retort, no immediate bite.

Ren's lips lingered just at the shell of Kaelin's ear, close enough for Kaelin to feel the heat of her breath, before she straightened and stepped back, her smirk pure provocation.

"Despite all the trouble you've given me since stepping foot into this court, when I saw you riding that black beast of a horse today, I thought I might just kiss you."

Kaelin's eyes darkened at Ren's words.

Ren's smile faltered, her tone sobering. "Thank you. For saving us." She winced as she straightened. "As fun as this heart-to-heart is, I should probably limp my ass to the infirmary."

With a long, dramatic sigh, Kaelin rolled her eyes. "Yes, go," she urged quietly. "You're one breath away from collapsing, and I refuse to carry you." Yet her brow creased, the faintest sign of worry slipping through.

"What, you won't be valiant and carry me off? I'm *wounded*."

Kaelin's stare went flat enough to level kingdoms.

Ren only winked. "Relax, Princess. I'll try not to bleed on anything expensive."

Ren turned and sauntered toward the door. She didn't need to look back to know Kaelin's eyes were still on her.

And perhaps Ren's stride held a deliberate sway, a parting taunt she knew Kaelin wouldn't miss.

The door of Kaelin's bed chamber clicked shut behind her.

She exhaled, shakily. And then again, like it might calm the ache in her chest.

It didn't.

"Damn it," she muttered, pacing to the window. She threw it open, letting the cold wind slap her flushed face. The scent of frost and pine did nothing to extinguish the lingering scent of Ren against her cheek, warm and heavy.

Like spiced wine.

This wasn't supposed to happen.

Not this hollow yearning every time Ren walked away. Not this tether Kaelin couldn't seem to cut, no matter how many sharp words or mocking jabs she used to cover it. Not this awful, aching need.

Kaelin braced her hands on the windowsill, her breath fogging against the pane.

It skyrocketed the moment Ren refused to abandon Talen during the fight, when every sensible instinct should've told her to run, to save herself, to leave Talen behind if it meant surviving.

But Ren didn't.

She'd planted her feet beside him, despite all odds, defiant and stubborn and brave in a way Kaelin had rarely ever seen.

Kaelin couldn't shake the image of it. Ren standing between her brother and death, snarling like she'd carve the world apart before she let death take them.

Most people bowed to power.

Ren spat in its face and fought until her body gave out.

Kaelin admired that. Saints, she *hungered* for it.

Because beneath all her irritation, beneath the sharpness and the mockery and the cold façade, something inside her had cracked open. And every time Ren turned her back, every time she slipped out of reach, Kaelin felt that impossible, infuriating pull – something she didn't want, something she didn't ask for, something she could no longer deny.

Yes, she wanted more.

She wanted to trace every scar on Ren's skin, learn the history behind each one. She wanted to be let in, to see the whole of her.

With a guttural sound of frustration, Kaelin turned from the window and kicked over the nearest chair, the crash echoing off the marble. She stood amidst the silence that followed, chest heaving.

And then she sank onto the bed, hands trembling in her lap.

"I don't want to just look," she whispered into the dark. "I want... her."

But wanting her might cost everything. And she had never been good at wanting without taking.

She leaned back against the velvet pillows and stared at the ceiling for a long time, the image of Ren burning behind her eyelids.

In the throne room just minutes prior, seeing Ren standing before her, head lifted in defiance, Kaelin had wanted to reach out and pull Ren onto her lap right there. To feel the warmth of her pressed against her, to taste the heat of her breath, to claim her mouth in a kiss to make her understand – *you're mine*.

The desire had struck like lightning, hot and merciless.

And when Ren turned to leave, hips swaying with deliberate insolence, Kaelin had nearly sworn aloud. She'd watched Ren walk away with that infuriating swagger, as if she knew *exactly* what she was doing.

As if she enjoyed teasing Kaelin to the edge of her sanity.

It took every ounce of Kaelin's restraint not to rise from the throne, grab Ren by the wrist, and drag her back. She'd gripped the armrests so tightly the carved wood creaked.

Kaelin shut her eyes, breath shaking. This wasn't supposed to happen. Not to her. Not like this.

But the truth simmered beneath her ribs, undeniable and consuming: She wanted Ren.

And no amount of denial was going to smother that truth.

41

Hunger gnawed at the boy.

He stood at the edge of the still pond, legs trembling beneath the weight of nothing. His fishing pole lay forgotten on a rock beside him. He didn't remember placing it there. Didn't remember sitting. Only knew that he was waiting.

Always waiting.

The world tilted sideways, a haze of heat and dizziness pressing down on him. His stomach had long stopped growling. Now it only ached. When had he last eaten? He remembered a piece of bread. A kind woman. Yesterday, or maybe the day before. Time had become a blur. Days and nights smeared together.

The pond lay before him, lapping lazily against the banks. Once, long ago, in a life that smelled of pipe smoke and leather maps, his father had taken him here to fish. They used to haul in enough for dinner and to sell at the market.

The sun loomed overhead, hot and unforgiving, like a punishment for daring to still exist. To still live. His lips were split, dry as parchment, a smear of blood marking his chin where he'd picked the cracked skin too hard.

With a low, rasping exhale, he collapsed to the ground, the sand and grass soft beneath his skeletal fingers. His legs stretched before him as if they didn't belong to a boy anymore. Knees jutted at wrong angles. His ribs pressed against the fabric of his shirt like knives trying to break free.

He was dying.

Starvation didn't scream. It whispered. It stole the world inch by inch.

There was a soft rustle, the flap of wings.

He turned his head just enough to see dark eyes watching. A vulture stood a few feet away, its feathers ragged, its gaze merciless. It let out a rough *caw* and did not blink.

Another joined.

Then another.

He didn't have the strength to cry, not even for his father. He used to dream of following in his footsteps, tracing forgotten trails, mapping the world with a bold hand and a fierce smile.

But the plague had taken father, and now the vultures waited to take him.

The sun inched higher. More shadows circled above.

Waiting.

Watching.

The boy closed his eyes, feeling the heat of it all press against his skull. His thoughts were sluggish, heavy, curling at the edges.

Everything has to eat, he thought vaguely. Even death.

And then, a shadow fell over him.

He opened his eyes with effort, his vision swimming. A figure stood above him, backlit by light, cloaked in fabric blacker than night. Something glinted in their hand. A blade?

"Eat.".

The boy blinked, unmoving.

The stranger crouched beside him, pressing bread to his cracked lips.

The scent hit him first, a combination of yeast, sugar, survival. But he couldn't remember how to chew. His jaw felt locked, his tongue useless.

A canteen followed, tipped to his mouth. Warm water rushed in. He swallowed, then gagged from the shock of it, but still drank until the canteen was drawn away.

"Take your time."

The boy gasped as the stranger sat beside him in the sand. The scent that clung to him was wrong, metallic, burnt, sulfurous. Like the air before a storm.

Like something unholy.

"I have a job for you. A very special task. One that requires subtlety."

The boy turned his head slowly, eyelids heavy as stones. "I'm... clumsy," he croaked.

"No, boy. You're desperate, and desperation makes the best kind of blade."

The stranger stood then, brushing sand from the hem of his cloak. The boy let his eyes follow the motion. And that's when he saw hair, wild and silver, sticking up in all directions like lightning caught mid-strike.

"Do you accept?"

The boy only nodded.

42

Winter had crept in overnight, quiet as a thief and twice as unforgiving.

Ren had woken to find slender icicles curling against her windowpane, glistening when they caught the morning sun. By midday, much of the ice had melted into shining drops that slid from rooftops and branches, though the wind still carried a crisp bite.

Ren wondered how winter looked here in Pyraelia. Winters in the west or the southern reaches were fair and fleeting, a passing coolness rather than a season of deep frost. Here, though, she sensed the cold might settle in and linger.

The Iron Bridle was warm and loud, a welcome contrast to the bitter chill outside.

Ren sat across from Elira at their usual corner table, the rich smell of roasted meat and spiced ale wrapping around them like a familiar blanket. A half-eaten plate of lamb and thick-cut potatoes sat between them, and Ren nursed her tankard, letting the hum of conversation soften the sharp edges of her mind.

It had been a week since the battle at Greymoore Village – a blur of training, volunteering with the efforts in Greymoore, and sleepless nights. What struck Ren most wasn't the destruction, but the resilience that followed. The villagers, human through and through, possessed a toughness she couldn't help but admire. Men and women alike worked side by side, rebuilding homes with their own hands, refusing to bow to despair.

More than once, she'd stopped to watch them hammering, hauling, laughing through exhaustion and felt something tighten in her chest. Even Lucan had been spotted passing out water to the displaced folk one morning.

Ren had to look twice to be sure.

It had been a week, too, since that throne room encounter with Kaelin, and in all that time, Ren had seen little of Kaelin. The few glimpses she'd caught were fleeting – glimpsing the fae princess in council chambers, issuing orders with clipped precision, or striding through the courtyard flanked by guards. Always distant, always untouchable. Yet Ren caught herself searching for her anyway, as though her eyes couldn't help but seek her out.

"Feels like things are finally settling," Elira managed around a mouthful of bread.

Ren tipped her head in a half-nod, half-shrug. "Even the Witherblight seems to be keeping its distance." She hesitated. "And I've been actually working with Princess Kaelin."

Elira nearly choked on her ale. She coughed into her sleeve, eyes narrowing in exaggerated disbelief. "Well, I'll be damned. Miracles do exist."

Ren bristled, leaning forward in her chair. "It's not like that. She's not—" She broke off with a sigh. "She saved me and Talen. We were fixing to be food for the undead corpses, and then there she was with reinforcements. Not sure if we would have made it out alive without her."

Elira's brow lifted, genuine surprise flickering there. "Are we talking about the same person who's tormented you since you stepped foot here?"

Ren didn't answer right away. Her mind had already gone back to that moment – Kaelin astride a midnight-black horse, golden hair streaming behind her, violet eyes blazing. It was the kind of sight that branded itself into you.

"She's... not what I expected," Ren admitted at last.

Elira leaned back in her chair. "I'll give her this – she's the kind of terrifying that could lead an army straight to their deaths and have them convinced it was for their honor." She reached for her ale. "Makes you wonder what else she could convince people of."

Ren rolled her eyes as Elira nursed her ale, but the words stuck in her chest more than she wanted to admit. Ren pretended to focus on her food, but her thoughts were elsewhere.

Later tonight, she'd head to the library. She hadn't been since the battle, too busy attending to rebuilding efforts and training. The thought of seeing Kaelin there sent a faint, unwelcome twist through Ren's stomach, and it was not the usual churn of dread.

It was something dangerously close to eagerness.

Ren took another swig of her own ale, trying to smother the feeling. But it stayed.

Inside the library, the faint crackle of the hearth at the far end mixed with the soft, steady patter of rain and hail against the tall windows.

Ren slipped through the arched doorway at the back, still holding the warm paper bundle Veylan had shoved into her hands after an overly long conversation about his husband's "newest and fluffiest" biscuits. She hadn't planned to take them, but they were still warm to the touch, buttery steam curling up from the folds, so she couldn't resist. Veylan had winked as he passed them over, adding, "Perfect for the nip in the air. Nothing chases off the cold like these."

Near the third row of shelves, a familiar shape stood hunched, back turned to Ren, shoulders bobbing as he muttered under his breath. Sir Pindlewhip, his quill tucked carelessly behind one ear, floating before the spines of weathered tomes, sounded out a limerick that refused to resolve itself.

"There once was a fae from the coast..." he grumbled, rubbing his chin, *"...who claimed he could drink the most? No, no, blast it all – ghost? Boast?"*

Ren bit down a laugh and pressed closer to the shelves, careful not to let the soles of her boots squeak on the polished stone. She slid sideways past him, clutching the biscuit bundle to her chest, while Pindle-whip kept muttering strings of improbable rhymes to him-self—"roast, host, post, compost…"—oblivious to her presence.

Her boots barely whispered over the rug as she rounded the last shelf and immediately spotted Kaelin sitting in a deep-backed chair, one leg elegantly crossed over the other, a half-full glass of wine balanced on the table beside her. The dim lamplight caught on the pale gold of her hair, the soft waves tumbling over her shoulder as she bent over a heavy tome. Her gaze was locked on the page.

"Hey," Ren greeted.

Without glancing up, Kaelin replied flatly, "Hey."

Ren set her biscuits on the table, sliding into the seat across her. "Brought some food for thought. I managed to pass by Sir Pindle-whip before he saw me. Hopefully, we don't get another surprise from him tonight."

"I should hope not. I'd hate to endure another of his mangled limericks."

Ren grinned. "He tries."

"Hm." Kaelin's eyes flicked back to her book, her slender brows drawn tight in concentration. The pages caught the lamplight, the faint gold thread in her gown glinting each time she shifted.

Something about her posture felt off. The swagger was gone, her usual sly confidence replaced by a rigid, brittle stillness.

Ren leaned back, tearing off a bite of biscuit. "Penny for your thoughts?"

"I'm reading," Kaelin answered pointedly, the words clipped.

"Obviously. But I can tell something's gnawing at you." When Kaelin didn't answer, Ren tried again. "I'm a good listener. And I try not to judge too harshly."

That got Kaelin's eyes on her. She closed the book with a *snap*. "If I wanted to be annoyed, I'd go elsewhere."

Ren stilled, the heat in her chest replaced with an uncomfortable slap. Her gaze dropped to the biscuits.

Ren thought after the battlefield, after the moment in the throne room—

She forced her shoulders not to sag. "Right. Okay."

Kaelin reopened her book, her attention snapping back to the text as though Ren had ceased to exist.

Ren settled into her chair, tugging a tome from the nearby stack and flipping it open. She didn't see a single word. Her eyes skimmed the pages while her mind gnawed at the sting in her chest.

Why the hell did she get her hopes up?

Maybe she'd misread Kaelin from the start. Maybe the fae princess truly was exactly what she showed the world, and somehow Ren overlooked that.

Her chair scraped faintly as she shifted, the thought of standing and walking away tempting. But, no. She wasn't going to slink off like some dog with her tail between her legs.

Ren pressed her lips into a hard line, squared her shoulders, and stayed. If Kaelin wanted to sit there radiating frost, fine.

Ren could match her, minute for stubborn minute.

So they read in silence, the fire popping in the hearth, the rain whispering against the windows. Every so often, Ren's gaze drifted sideways, catching the faint movement of Kaelin's hand as she turned a page, or the rise and fall of her breath.

Details Ren hated herself for noticing.

The next morning, snow drifted in lazy spirals through the frigid air as Ren fell into step behind Elric.

A winter storm had blown through in the night, rattling shutters and whistling through the windowpanes. When Ren woke at dawn and peered from her window, she found the world remade beneath a thin, glittering sheet of snow. The rooftops wore white crowns, and the courtyards below lay hushed and still, as though holding their breath.

They moved single file, boots crunching over frost-hardened ground, the line of trainees winding beyond the skeletal treeline that bordered the training grounds. Ren's fingers ached around the steel shield in her grasp. It had to weigh thirty pounds, maybe more, and each step she took made it feel heavier. She gritted her teeth and forced her legs to match the long, unhurried strides of the fae ahead of her in the single file line.

Laughter drifted from the front – Lucan's voice carrying easily in the still air. His hair flashed like pale gold against the bleak gray sky.

A shiver worked its way down Ren's spine as she caught sight of Mount Solfira's jagged peaks, their white crowns stark against the horizon. Somewhere beneath the wind, she began to hear the soft, persistent trickle of water. The sound grew louder until the trees broke apart, revealing a wide, dark river. Its surface churned sluggishly, not yet frozen.

"Into the water," Ivan's voice cut through the hush of falling snow. "Shields in hand."

No one hesitated. They stepped forward in a crunching march. Pebbles shifted treacherously beneath Ren's boots, and she nearly lost her footing. The first lick of icy water against her ankle made her inhale sharply; it burned with cold, stabbing up her calves as she waded deeper.

She stopped beside Elric, meeting his eyes for a fleeting moment. His face was taut, mouth set in grim concentration. She returned her attention to Ivan.

"On the first day of frost," Ivan began, pacing with his hands clasped behind his back, "House Vaelaran conducts the Steel Hold. It is a trial of endurance and willpower. You feel the current beneath you?" His gaze swept over them. "It will try to pull you from your stance. Your own body will beg you to drop the shield. If your shield falls, you will start again, but this time with a stone lashed to your back. And you will hold until the river decides to take you under or until I give the order."

The current swirled around Ren's thighs. Her grip tightened on the shield's leather strap, and she forced her shoulders back. Whatever this trial was, she would not be the one dragged under.

But the river's cold was relentless. It sank its teeth into Ren's bones, chewing through muscle until her legs trembled under the water's pull. The shield's weight seemed to double with each passing breath.

"Remember that sometimes it is not the river you must fight, but the weight you bring into it."

Ren's breath steamed in ragged bursts, each exhale a desperate attempt to steady herself. She adjusted her footing, shifting against the slick stones beneath, but the current pressed and tugged in an attempt to sweep her away.

The others were silent, their own focus sharpening.

Ren's arms shook violently. She bit her lip until she tasted iron, trying to will the tremor away. But the burn was rising, creeping from her shoulders down her back, into her ribs, until it was everywhere.

Her grip faltered. She tried to hold, just for a moment longer—

The shield slipped from her fingers with a deafening *splash*.

Her horror was immediate. She'd failed.

Ivan's voice cracked like a whip. "Stone to your back, Harper. Now."

Someone splashed through the rough, strapping a rock into place on Ren's back, its weight pressing between her shoulder blades. Her chest heaved as she stepped back into position, the shield once again above her head. Every nerve screamed, but she gritted her teeth and planted her feet.

Lucan appeared to her right, shield held high, and voice low enough for only her to hear. "Square your feet. Lean into the current, not against it. And stop thinking about *here*."

Ren huffed out something like a laugh, more pain than amusement. "Right. And I'm supposed to forget I can't feel my toes."

"Think of somewhere else. Something else. Doesn't matter what – just not the pain."

She shifted as he said, feeling her weight root more firmly into the stones beneath.

Time blurred after that. The pain didn't fade, but it dulled at the edges, her mind flicking through half-formed memories – the hushed stillness of the library, Kaelin's violet eyes gleaming in the candle-light, how the fae princess's fingers tapped once or twice on the edge of the page whenever she found a passage particularly interesting, or how she scrunched her nose ever so slightly when she came across something she disagreed with, like she was silently arguing with the author.

Nights had blurred together like that, quiet hours spent in the glow of lantern light. And in pieces of Ren's training – when she got knocked flat on her ass or tasted blood after a strike to the teeth – Ren realized that some small part of her looked forward to the nights after, when she might find Kaelin waiting among the shelves, sharp-tongued and unpredictable, and yet... *there*.

A pang coiled in Ren's chest. Unease, yes, but not fear. If Kaelin thought her silence and frost could keep Ren at arm's length, she was sorely mistaken.

Ren might not have known what sin she'd committed to receive the fae princess's disdain, but she'd damn well figure it out.

By the time Ivan called the trial, Ren was shaking so badly she thought she'd collapse into the river. But instead of the smug jabs she'd expected, Elric clapped her on the back, some of the other fae even shooting her grins.

"Hard task for your first frost," one fae complimented with a grin. "You held longer than most."

Lucan gave her an approving nod, the faintest glint of respect in his pale eyes, before another voice from the group called out an invitation to join them for drinks.

Ren blinked, still dragging air into her lungs, each breath burning against the cold that had settled deep in her chest. Her muscles ached, yet she caught herself smiling.

And she met Lucan's eyes. She bowed her head in silent thanks, and he returned it.

43

"Again."

King Maelion's voice was smooth as he moved the first piece across the wooden board. Kaelin's eyes narrowed on her dwindling army of pieces.

"You're so intent on watching my hand," Maelion murmured, resting his chin on steepled fingers, "that you've forgotten to mind your own."

Kaelin's fingers hovered above a piece in hesitation. Her father's eyes followed the motion, dark and sharp as a hawk's. She shifted the piece forward, lifting her gaze to meet his.

"You always taught me to be three steps ahead," she said coolly.

"Five," Lyra corrected from her seat near the window, reclining against velvet cushions with a glass of red wine poised elegantly in her hand.

Maelion made his next move. A simple flick of his wrist, and suddenly Kaelin's strategy unraveled. She hadn't noticed one of her pieces cornered. By the time she realized, his pieces swept in to claim it, the trap snapping shut.

Maelion folded his hands together, studying her. His smile was not mocking but patient, proud. "You're perceptive."

"Which you get from your mother," Lyra added, swirling her wine.

Maelion ignored Lyra's comment, eyes never leaving Kaelin. "But your gaze is always outward – watching, anticipating. Don't neglect the steps you take yourself."

The fire cracked, filling the silence as his words settled. Outside, the wind pressed against the windowpanes, as though the storm longed to intrude.

"One more round?" Maelion asked.

Kaelin rose, her chair scraping softly against the stone floor. "I'll fetch another glass."

She crossed the chamber, her heels sinking into the thick carpet as she moved toward the small table near the hearth. A half-empty bottle of red wine awaited her, the glass catching the firelight like blood. Behind her, Maelion reset the board while Lyra hummed faintly, a tune Kaelin half-remembered from childhood.

She poured herself a glass, the crimson liquid rippling as she lifted it. But as she brought it to her lips, her thoughts drifted back to the library earlier that evening. *Ren.*

The memory struck with the sting of a blade. The look in Ren's eyes when Kaelin had snapped at her haunted her even now. Kaelin had told herself this morning that whatever spark lingered between them had to be smothered. That it was a weakness, a distraction. The kingdom demanded clarity, not clouded thoughts.

And yet –

Kaelin's grip on the wineglass tightened. Ren's face lingered in her mind, the faint parting of her lips, as if Kaelin had struck her with something sharper than words.

Kaelin hated herself for it. Hated how her chest clenched, hated the guilt gnawing beneath her ribs. But she also knew she would do it again if it meant keeping both Ren *and* Vaelaran safe from the consequences of her weakness.

Because in the courts of the fae, power was the board, and sentiment the first piece to fall.

Before going to the library, Ren stopped by her room.

Ren disregarded Mirella's comments about her dripping hair and soaked appearance. When Ren got too close, Mirella jolted back, muttering something about water never being good for her varnish. Ren had gone straight to the warm springs, sinking into the heat until her muscles loosened and her mind nearly drifted into sleep. The warmth of the water wrapped around her, soothing and steady, so different from the biting cold of the river that still lingered in her bones.

By the time Ren returned to her room and began pulling on her clothes, Mirella eyed her from the corner. "You're dressing like you're going into battle."

"Moody fae princesses *are* battles."

"Oh, admit it. You like sparring, whether it's with swords or words."

Ren tugged her cloak tighter, refusing to answer, though the corner of her mouth betrayed the faintest twitch. She left before Mirella could see.

The library had become Ren's second battlefield.

Not of blades and blood, but of patience, parchment, and the steady grind of searching for something that didn't want to be found.

Night after night, Ren came back. She would settle into the far table in the shadowed alcove, the one with the warped leg and the view of the window that overlooked the torch-lit courtyard. Stacks of tomes leaned precariously around her, their cracked spines muttering stories of long-dead kings, forgotten realms, and fragments of prophecies that never seemed whole.

Dragons. She kept returning to them, to the old ballads, the half-legends that spoke of fire-wrought creatures bound to the bones of the land.

Sometimes, between one candle burning down and the next, she'd catch a new thread.

One night, it had been a faded scrap of vellum, ink bled nearly to nothing, hidden in the margin of a crumbling history of the Western Wastes. She could barely make out the words: *"The flame reborn shall stand at the edge of ruin, and the world shall hold its breath."*

The phrase settled heavy in her gut, the way truths often did when they came too close.

Kaelin was there almost every night, too.

For several evenings in a row, they coexisted in an uneasy truce – if truce was even the word for it. Kaelin would drape herself in a corner chair with a glass of wine, and open some book bound in leather so fine it might have cost a soldier's year of wages.

She never spoke to Ren. Never even looked at her.

Ren tried to ignore it, burying herself in her own hunt for answers. But she always knew when Kaelin's attention shifted, even if only for a moment, like the faint change in the air before a storm. Ren caught herself glancing over far too often, tracking the way Kaelin's slender fingers turned each page as if coaxing it open, the way her golden hair caught the lamplight.

Tonight, Ren knew something was off the moment she walked in. Kaelin sat rigid at her table, back straight, but her gaze kept flicking to the far door, to the windows, as if expecting someone, or something.

Ren buried herself in a particularly dense record of border wars, eyes skimming past the neat calligraphy without retaining a single word. The tension in the room had built, a dense fog that refused to leave. Finally, Ren slammed the book shut and leaned back in her chair.

"All right," Ren snapped, her voice cutting the hush between them. "What's eating you?"

Kaelin didn't look up. "I'm reading."

"You're *brooding*. I know the difference."

A spark of annoyance followed by a hint of surprise crossed Kaelin's eyes, but she still didn't answer.

Ren leaned forward on her elbows, refusing to let it go. "I don't care if you throw every foul word you know at me or if I'm annoying you. What's wrong?"

Silence stretched. Ren was about to bite out something sharper when she saw the subtle shift in Kaelin's expression.

"It's the traitor," Kaelin answered finally, her voice low and taut. "The one who revealed Talen's location the day of the ogre attack."

"You think they're here at court?"

"I know they are. I've been looking for them. Especially during the balls."

"The balls?"

Kaelin's gaze locked on hers. "You'd be surprised what people let slip when the music is loud, the wine is strong, and they think no one's listening. The gowns and dancing are a distraction. The real work is in the conversations, the eavesdropping."

Ren considered that, remembering the way Kaelin had seemed to glide through those events like she owned every inch of the room. "So, it's all strategy."

"Always," Kaelin answered simply. "I have... suspicions. Sylven, for one."

"I'd gladly drag him into the ring and make him eat his arrogance, but whatever else he may be, his devotion to the crown seems certain," Ren said.

"He comes from one of the oldest families sworn to House Vaelaran," Kaelin agreed, though her tone was more measured. "Loyalty like that should be unshakable. And yet..." Kaelin let the words trail off, her expression unreadable.

"Does he want wealth?"

"I think you underestimate how far the fae will go for the throne. We've been smiting each other for it for centuries. Gold, glory, revenge – it's all the same currency."

"That's one hell of a thing to live with."

Kaelin didn't reply. Instead, she poured herself another glass of wine.

For a long moment, neither of them spoke. Ren leaned back, trying to make sense of the unease crawling under her skin. This was the most Kaelin had said to her in days, and yet... the princess still felt out of reach.

Ren wanted to say something to bridge that gulf. But the weight of the silence pressed her back into her chair. So she picked up her book again, the words blurring, and resigned herself to reading.

Out of the corner of her eye, she caught Kaelin studying her. Only for a second. And then the princess's attention was buried once more in the pages.

Ren was a distraction Kaelin did not need tonight.

The tome in Kaelin's hands was heavy with dust, its brittle pages whispering secrets of the Embersworn. She had only just uncovered a chapter detailing their darker histories when movement in the doorway caught her eye. *Ren.*

Kaelin's jaw tightened, a sharp dismissal already forming on her tongue. But before she could speak, Ren crossed the room with that steady, unhurried stride and sank into her usual chair as though it belonged to her alone.

Something inside Kaelin shifted.

Because Ren didn't speak. She didn't prod or poke, didn't fill the quiet with needless words the way every noble in Pyraelia seemed compelled to do. Most fae at court found silence unbearable and were desperate to smother it with idle chatter. But Ren let the silence breathe. And Kaelin found that silence tolerable. Even welcome.

Her gaze dropped back to the page.

The Embersworn are a secretive order, feared not for their numbers but for the abhorrent magics they practice. Chief among these is the art of soul binding, a dangerous discipline that seeks to manipulate or imprison the very essence of a living being.

One of their most direct methods is the Soul Trap spell. Blood is required as the tether, spilled by the caster. If the victim died before the spell's thread unraveled, the soul would be torn from its vessel and imprisoned in a crystalline gem known as a soul gem. The practice has been forbidden in every court of fae and man alike, yet the Embersworn pursue it with ruthless devotion.

Records speak of a woodland messenger, scarcely grown into his adulthood whose spirit was bound into a common gem, his essence diminished to little more than fuel. The Embersworn shattered that gem across their forges, using the trapped soul to enchant blades with unholy abilities and to brew potions that gnawed at both flesh and spirit.

Kaelin's thoughts strayed to the night Ren's parents were slaughtered. Ren spoke about how she saw crimson robes in the firelight, and heard the cadence of their voices raised in unison. She had always assumed they were chanting prayers.

But what if those words had been a spell?

A *Soul Trap* spell.

If those in crimson robes were members of the Embersworn and had performed a soul trap that night, then Ren's family's tragedy was deliberate.

Kaelin's eyes flicked up.

Ren sat across from her, posture loose, legs tucked carelessly beneath her. A picture of ease until Kaelin noticed the subtle furrow between Ren's brows, the way her lips pressed together in concentration as her gaze swept across the page before her. One stubborn strand of hair had fallen across her face. Kaelin's fingers twitched with the ridiculous urge to reach over and tuck it behind her ear.

She forced herself to look away. Just as she did, Ren's eyes lifted.

Silence stretched. Kaelin pretended to study the curling script in her tome. When she dared another glance, she caught Ren doing the same – looking away too quickly.

And so it went. Their gazes circling, brushing, darting away.

A game neither had agreed to play, but both kept returning to.

H ouse Vaelaran's balls were about far more than dancing, laughter, and expensive wine.

These were battlegrounds of silk and smiles, parliamentary spaces where words weighed as heavily as steel, where alliances could be forged in the span of a whispered exchange, and futures undone in the curl of a smirk.

As she drifted through the crowd, Ren kept her gaze steady, but her ears open. Snippets of conversation floated to her.

"If Lord Merrow keeps skimming the tariffs, the southern ports will bleed coin before winter ends."

"The queen grows too bold – she'll find herself cornered if she plays both sides."

"We should keep the queen close and flatter her pride. Princess Kaelin, though, sees too much."

The voices blurred together into a low hum, but the undercurrent was unmistakable: plotting, scheming, and maneuvering dressed up as polite chatter.

Talen fought the threats that prowled Vaelaran's borders with blades and armor. Kaelin hunted the threats woven into the court itself with the clink of crystal, and the measured weighing of every ally, every foe.

The first chords of music spilled into the air. Ren caught the scent of spiced wine, roasted venison, and freshly baked bread. She shifted where she stood, crossing and uncrossing her arms, the bodice of her dress digging in uncomfortably. Mirella swore the cut was flattering, but Ren adjusted the bodice again.

How was she meant to kick a fae's ass when she couldn't even bend far enough to tie a boot?

Ren had already had one too many glasses of Vaelaran red wine, the kind that left a slow heat curling in her chest. Still, she had to give House Vaelaran credit where it was due.

They knew their wine.

Red, white – every shade in between. Some sweet as summer berries, others dry and heavy that coated your throat with musk and smoke. She'd tried more than she should have tonight, the edges of the evening blurring.

The Vaelaran Solthaine was supposedly in honor of the royal lineage, a spectacle of duels, music, and dance meant to show both their refinement and their strength.

Ren's gaze drifted over the crowd. Talen was easy enough to spot, standing near the queen's dais with his head bent in conversation, but Kaelin had yet to make her entrance.

So, Ren let her eyes wander across the gathered nobles, remembering Kaelin's words from the night before about a traitor in their midst. She studied posture, glances, the way some fae leaned in to speak while others angled their bodies away in guarded silence.

Her gaze snagged on Sylven Draeth. He stood with two other fae warriors, one with a scar raking across his cheek like a claw mark. Sylven was deep in conversation until, as though sensing her stare, his eyes cut to hers. Ren tore her gaze away and took another sip to mask the heat prickling the back of her neck.

"Care for a dance?"

Ren turned to find a tall fae male standing before her, his smile an easy curve, green eyes. His dark hair brushed the tops of his pointed ears, and he carried himself with the effortless charm of one who never doubted his appeal.

She hesitated. But... why not?

"Sure," she answered, setting her glass on a nearby table.

He offered his arm, which she accepted. They moved across the floor. He was an easy partner, guiding her with a light touch and a faint smirk whenever she misstepped.

"You're not half bad," Ren admitted.

"High praise from someone who looked ready to refuse me outright," he teased.

They traded light remarks, his tone friendly enough until his hand at her waist drew her just a fraction closer. His breath warmed her ear as he leaned in. "You look far better in silk than steel, you know. Though, I wouldn't mind seeing you without either."

"Really? *That's* what you went with?" Ren deadpanned. "Congratulations, that might be the stupidest thing anyone has ever said to seduce me."

"Don't be shy," he coaxed, his hold tightening as he spun her. "I've been watching you for weeks now. I wasn't sure what to think of a human at first, but I'm starting to think you might be worth the curiosity."

"Here's a tasteful idea," Ren stilled in his grasp, narrowing her eyes. "Take your curiosity and shove it up your ass."

The male fae's grip slid from her waist to her lower back, pulling her flush against him despite her stiffening. "Fight me all you want. Resistance just makes the hunt sweeter."

She opened her mouth to respond when a hand landed firmly on the fae's shoulder.

"Is there a problem?" Lucan asked cooly.

"Oh, there's a problem," Ren cut in. "And if this bastard keeps flapping his lips, it's about to turn into a full-blown catastrophe."

The fae male let off a low whistle, eyeing Ren like she had sprouted 3 heads. "We were just dancing, is all."

"Looks to me like the dance is over," Lucan deadpanned.

The tension crackled for a moment, neither fae male backing down until Ren stepped away, breaking the hold.

"I'm leaving for *your* benefit," she said flatly. "I walk away, and you keep your dignity. I stay, and I beat your smug face into the floorboards. I figured you'd choose the latter."

Ren didn't wait for the fae male to argue. She weaved her way toward the edge of the ballroom. She just wanted fresh and far away from the suffocating heat of that moment. It wasn't until her back was turned did she allow her features to drop.

But as she rounded the marble archway leading toward the corridor, she nearly ran straight into Kaelin. Ren brushed past before Kaelin could open her mouth to say anything.

Cairis Draven.

Kaelin knew the name the way one knew the first bite of winter – cold, all too familiar, and very much unwelcome.

A striking specimen by any courtly measure, he had golden hair that caught the light like spun coin and eyes the color of spring leaves after rainfall. But his mouth curved in a perpetual roguish smirk, the kind that promised trouble and delivered it in spades. Amongst the nobles, he was a favorite for his easy laugh, his lightning-quick footwork on the dance floor, and, more notoriously, his even quicker hands. He moved through people the way a thief moved through shadows, slipping in close, taking what he wanted, and leaving only when he'd wrung the last drop of value from his quarry.

And Kaelin knew exactly how he treated those who had the misfortune of becoming his 'collections.' His family's business of debt collecting had taught him early to view people as transactions. Lovers were no different. He rarely let them go without extracting some price, whether in whispered threats, in coin, or in the bruises they left trying to get away.

Kaelin had just stepped onto the landing above the stairway when the sight below made her freeze. Ren, caught in the whirl of the dance floor, moving in time to the music with Cairis.

The sight struck her like a blade to the ribs – Ren in another's arms, even for a dance, even for politeness' sake. And worse, Cairis was leaning in too close, murmuring something against her ear that sent an unwanted flush to Ren's cheeks. Ren stiffened at his nearness, her discomfort plain, but still he pressed closer, his hand firm at her waist.

Kaelin saw red.

Her jaw clenched, every muscle in her body burning with the sharp edge of jealousy. It wasn't just the impropriety of it, nor Cairis's persistence; it was the thought of Ren being made to endure the closeness of someone else. Of *his* hands.

Then, Lucan swooped in. Kaelin caught the exchange from above, the way Lucan's presence cut cleanly into Cairis's smug persistence. Relief and gratitude flickered through her, but it did nothing to cool the fire boiling in her chest.

By then, Kaelin was already descending the stairs with deliberate grace, though her pulse thundered. She fought to keep her composure intact, even as her hands itched for her blade.

Even as the urge to storm across the floor and put Cairis flat on his back nearly overwhelmed her.

Kaelin nearly collided with Ren at the opening of the stairway, halting just short. Ren's cheeks were flushed, her eyes still glimmering with the edge of what had just transpired. The sight was enough to unravel Kaelin's control.

It took every shred of strength not to hunt down the bastard who had dared put that look in Ren's eyes.

Kaelin's hands curled into fists at her sides, nails biting into her palms. Kaelin forced herself to breathe, to straighten, to move forward. With each step back toward the gilded music and laughter of the ball, her composure knit itself around her like armor – thin, brittle, but just enough to hold until she decided how best to make Cairis Draven regret ever laying a hand on Ren.

The music swelled, a lilting tune threaded with the haunting cry of a high violin. Courtly pairs swept and spun across the marble floor.

Kaelin didn't wait for Cairis to come to her. She strode across the floor, the midnight silk of her gown trailing behind her. A dozen heads turned at her approach. House Vaelaran's princess heir did not often cross the dance floor with such clear intent.

Cairis saw her approaching and grinned, already holding out his hand. "Your Highness. I was beginning to think you'd avoid me all evening."

"Oh, I wouldn't dream of it," Kaelin purred, slipping her hand into his. "Dance with me."

He swept her into the next measure, clearly expecting flirtation, the kind of easy banter he traded with his partners.

But Kaelin wasn't smiling.

From the first step, she took the lead with calculated precision. Her movements were sharp, her steps perfectly timed, each turn executed with the kind of elegance only years of grueling training could produce. She steered him across the floor like a general maneuvering an enemy into a trap.

Cairis tried to adjust, tried to reclaim the lead, but each time he attempted to turn her, she spun out of his grasp and brought him back under her control. The crowd began to notice. Whispered murmurs swelled at the edges of the music.

"You're... forceful tonight," he remarked, his smirk faltering as she spun him in a move that should have been hers to follow, not lead.

"I like to keep my partners on their toes. You never know what they might do otherwise."

She swept him into a pivot so abrupt he stumbled enough for nearby dancers to glance over, eyebrows raised. Kaelin's hand at his back was unyielding, guiding him back into position as though nothing had happened.

"You have a reputation, Cairis," she murmured, her voice a silken thread woven through the music. "Fast hands. Faster exits. I wonder how many people in this room could recite your conquests."

His jaw tightened, though the smirk was still there. "Some call it charm."

"Some call it something else entirely."

The music rose, and Kaelin used the swell to spin him again, this time in a move that forced him to bow slightly in recovery. A ripple of laughter ran through a few watching nobles.

Cairis leaned in, trying to recover ground. "If I didn't know better, I'd think you were trying to humiliate me."

"If I wanted to humiliate you, Cairis, you'd already be on your knees."

For the rest of the dance, she kept him dancing just shy of awkwardness, pushing the tempo, controlling every turn, every sweep. Her barbs each landed with the surety of a dagger finding its mark.

By the time the final note rang out, a fine sheen of sweat had gathered at Cairis' brow from the effort of keeping his composure under her lead.

Kaelin ended the dance with a crisp turn that left her in perfect position, while Cairis found himself half a step out of place.

She leaned in just enough for only him to hear. "Unworthy of a partner on the floor. I can only imagine you're just as disappointing in bed." His jaw twitched, but Kaelin added, "And hear me well, Cairis Draven. If you so much as look at Ren Harper with ill intent again, I will cut the eyes from your skull and feed them to the hounds of Vaelaran. They like to savor their food." She straightened, the contempt in her gaze obvious. "Pressing yourself on someone who clearly did not want you is disgraceful. Test me again, and I'll see those titles of yours revoked."

She released his hand with icy grace, leaving him to bow stiffly. The heat of her words burned in his ears as he slipped back into the crowd. Kaelin watched him go, satisfaction curling at the corner of her mouth, not the giddy triumph of a win, but the satisfaction of someone who had just sent a message and knew it had been heard.

It had been two days since the Vaelaran Solthaine ball, and Ren's mind kept circling back to the fae male she'd learned was named Cairis.

She hated how easily he crept back into her thoughts. Hated that when she pictured him now, she wanted nothing more than to have knocked him flat on his ass in front of the entire hall.

Worse, she hated that Lucan had been the one to intervene. She could handle street brawls, being mugged in the streets, even the sting of steel at her ribs. But the intimacy of Cairis pressing in, trying to force something that wasn't his to take had felt different.

Violating.

Ren used Cairis' face to drive her training today, striking harder, faster, until sweat stung her eyes. Blow after blow, she imagined knocking the smirk from him. Her sparring partners muttered under their breaths, grumbling at the ferocity she unleashed.

Her boots dragged against the marble floor now. She stopped in front of her chamber door, shoulders sagging. Her body ached from hours of sparring, being thrown to the ground more times than she cared to count.

But the pain was a welcome distraction. Training meant purpose. It meant sharp focus. It meant remembering exactly *why* she was here.

Last night was a grim reminder that she'd let herself get too close to the fae. Laughter over wine with the princess, all those quiet moments in the library – it had almost convinced her that the line between human and fae could blur and that maybe she wasn't just a pawn on their board.

She should've known better.

Here, she was a tool to be deployed when it served them. And the moment she wasn't useful?

They'd toss her aside.

She stepped inside her room and –

Crunch.

Brow arching, she found a single folded letter beneath her boot, the parchment delicately pressed and sealed in dark wax. Her name had been scrawled in elegant, looping cursive.

Ren,

I trust you haven't managed to set anything on fire today.

The court is insufferably dull this time of day, and I find myself craving something more stimulating. Join me for afternoon tea in the greenhouse. I've had the staff prepare something simple. I thought it might suit your taste.

Try not to keep me waiting. I detest cold tea.

Regards,

Princess Kaelin Vaelan

P.S. Wear something that doesn't reek of sweat. The roses are delicate.

Ren stared at the letter like it might catch flame in her hands. Her stomach twisted, equal parts dread and reluctant intrigue. She set the note down on the small table beside her armchair and sank into it with a groan, yanking off her dirt-caked boots and letting them fall with a thud.

"Rough day?" Mirella asked.

Ren let her head tip back. "Surprisingly, no. Had a lovely time getting bruised and battered by fae twice my size and age." She lifted the letter, waving it like a white flag. "But now I've been summoned to afternoon tea by the princess."

"Princess Kaelin invited you personally?"

"Unfortunately. Would I survive the political fallout if I ignored it?"

"Likely not. If she's requested you directly, there's a reason."

Ren groaned. "That's exactly why I don't want to go. I spent all day in the training yard. The last thing I want is to spar with Kaelin over pastries, no matter how good they taste."

Mirella purred, "Perhaps she'll bring wine?"

Ren gave a dry laugh, already imagining Kaelin pouring her a glass with that infuriating smirk. "She's such a royal pain in my ass."

"And you, darling, reek. I'd recommend a bath before you insult the roses into wilting. They're delicate."

Ren shot the wardrobe a glare, though the edge of her mouth tugged upward. "Are enchanted wardrobes always this brutally honest?"

"I'm one of a kind, darling."

The greenhouse was bathed in golden light, the high glass panes casting soft shadows over vines that curled in delicate tendrils.

Blossoms in shades of blood-red and deep violet hung from the ceiling in perfumed clusters, their petals trembling in the gentle breeze wafting through the open archways.

Ren stepped through the doorway cautiously. The scent of jasmine and something sharper, maybe starroot, laced the air. Ahead, a table waited under a flowering arc of moonvine, two chairs tucked beneath its silver-inlaid frame. The teapot was already steaming.

And seated like she belonged to the garden itself was Kaelin. She wore a silk blouse in white with delicate embroidery at the cuffs. Her hair was half-bound with a pin shaped like a thorned rose. She tilted her head in greeting.

"I was beginning to think you'd decline," she remarked, lifting her teacup without breaking eye contact.

"I thought about it," Ren replied dryly, sliding into the seat across from her. "But curiosity won."

"Dangerous thing, that." Kaelin poured Ren a cup of tea. "Some people lose their heads over it."

"I'm not most people."

"No," Kaelin admitted softly, as if tasting the words. "You're not."

For a few moments, they sipped in silence. Birds flitted past the glass above them, and somewhere, a fountain murmured.

An assortment of pastries rested on a tiered stand beside it, flaky fruit tarts, miniature cakes glazed to a glossy perfection, sugared lavender biscuits arranged in a spiral.

The entire spread looked like something plucked from a dream.

Ren shifted in her seat, trying and failing not to wrinkle her nose as the garden's earthy and floral scent thickened around her. Before she could stop herself, a sneeze burst from her, muffled hastily into the crook of her elbow.

Across the table, Kaelin's brow lifted. "I did warn the gardeners about the valerian," Kaelin mused, gaze drifting over the blossoms behind Ren. "It bloomed early this year."

Ren narrowed her eyes, half-wondering if Kaelin had orchestrated this whole setting just to see how she'd squirm. "Just the air," she muttered, blinking against the prickle in her eyes.

Kaelin tilted her head, lips curving. "Let me know if you start swelling. I'd hate for you to miss dessert."

Ren met Kaelin's gaze across the table, studying the delicate arch of her brow, the way her teacup hovered just shy of her lips, as if she were more interested in watching than sipping.

Ren fought the urge to rub her eyes. The scent still clung, invisible fingers wrapping around her throat, and the mention of valerian made her wonder just how many of these blooms had been chosen specifically to get under her skin.

"Noted," Ren managed dryly, sniffling once. "Next time I'll bring an elixir or a plague mask."

"How charmingly dramatic."

Ren leaned forward, pretending not to notice the way Kaelin's gaze tracked her every movement. She plucked a small tart from the pastry tray, something with a glazed fruit center and a sugared crust too delicate for her calloused fingers. She took a bite. It was sweet, buttery, and infuriatingly good.

"Well?" Kaelin asked. "Did it pass your taste test?"

Ren licked a crumb from her thumb. "You get points for sugar and for not poisoning me."

Kaelin laughed. "The afternoon is still young."

The sound caught Ren off guard. Kaelin's eyes sparkled when she laughed, and the hard lines of her face softened. Ren found herself savoring the sound. It was unexpected, light, and far too rare.

"Tell me something about you," Kaelin set down her cup. "Something real. Not whatever polite nonsense people give me."

"What makes you think I know how to be polite?"

"You're doing a decent impression."

Ren hesitated, her fingers brushing the rim of her cup before she set it aside. The request was simple, yet it pressed against places she rarely let anyone see. For a heartbeat, a memory flickered – herself as a girl, perched on the edge of her narrow bed, carefully twining a stolen ribbon through her braids. The frayed satin was too bright, too fine for her, but in that moment, it made her feel softer, girlish, almost beautiful.

"I used to steal hair ribbons from the market. I rarely wore them, just kept them in a box under my bed like some idiot hoarding color. We could never afford things like that – not when every coin went to rum... whiskey... whatever bottle my parents could get their hands on."

Kaelin didn't laugh, and she didn't joke. She merely drank in the words for a moment. Then, she asked softly, "Did they at least feed you?"

Ren looked up, surprised by the gentleness in Kaelin's voice. She shrugged again, but this time it wasn't bravado – just a simple truth. "When they remembered."

Kaelin's brows knit, and her jaw tensed. After a moment, she murmured, "Surely, you deserved more than stolen ribbons stuffed in a box."

"Yeah, well. Stolen things were the only ones that ever felt mine."

Kaelin leaned forward slightly, her voice low. "I used to tell myself you were reckless. Which you are, but it was easier than admitting the truth – that what you've fought for, I've been handed." Her gaze softened. "I was wrong about you."

"Didn't think I'd live long enough to hear you say you were wrong."

"I seldom misjudge others. It's a skill I pride myself on. And yet with you, I missed the mark entirely."

"Careful," Ren leaned back, crossing her arms, and grappling for levity. "You sound like you're starting to actually like me."

"What if I am?"

Gone was the glimmer of jest in Kaelin's gaze; what remained was truth, stripped raw and startling.

Ren held her gaze, her heart drumming a war-song in her ears. "Should I be flattered?"

"You think everything's a joke when you're scared."

Ren turned her hand, studying her nails with exaggerated interest. "I'm not scared."

"You run from what's real the second it gets too close."

Ren stiffened, amber eyes meeting violet eyes. "Real? You wouldn't recognize it from behind all those practiced smiles of yours. Don't fool yourself into thinking you know me."

Kaelin inhaled as if steadying herself, then leaned in just enough that Ren felt pinned by her presence alone. "But I want to know you, and it terrifies you. Doesn't it?"

Ren set her fork down with a soft *clink*. "Since the moment I stepped foot here, you've made it your sport to cut me down every chance you get. And just when I think we might actually be able to stand in the same room without drawing blood, you turn cold, like I'm carrying the plague itself." Ren leaned back hard, letting the chair creak beneath her as she hooked her elbow over the back and pulled one knee to her chin, flaunting the posture she knew would scandalize any court-born noble. "All right. Enough dancing around. What are you *really* after?"

"I mocked you because you were nobody showing up on our doorstep. We knew nothing about your background, where you came from, or what *your* motive was. Now, my motive is clear." Her fingers tapped lightly against her knuckle, her jaw locking like she'd chosen her next move with ruthless certainty. "But I know exactly what I want now." A pause. "*You.*"

Ren's heart stuttered. "You-you're joking." But even she heard how thin the accusation sounded.

The silence that followed was charged, coiled like the moment before a lightning strike.

Goosebumps rose on Ren's arm as her chest rose and fell. She tried to look away, to douse the heat creeping up her neck. "I didn't ask for your attention," she finally managed to whisper. "And I'm not sure I want it, not if it's another game."

Kaelin's features flickered. "This isn't a game."

Still, Ren fought to keep her voice steady. "You're *fae*, and I'm human."

Kaelin reached for her anyway, one hand tentative but deliberate, fingers brushing Ren's as if to anchor her there.

Kaelin's expression softened, her fury ebbing. "You don't have to be anything but who you are, Flameborne or not, I don't care."

"You speak like you already know me," Ren whispered.

"I know some parts of you," Kaelin admitted, her thumb grazing the back of Ren's knuckles. "But that's not enough. I want to know *all* of you."

"If I let you in," Ren said quietly, "you might regret it."

Kaelin leaned closer, her eyes never leaving Ren. "Then let me regret you with my whole damn heart." Kaelin's eyes flicked down to Ren's lips and then back up, as if giving Ren the chance to pull away.

Ren didn't.

The air between them seemed to condense into something heavy and fragile and utterly combustible. Kaelin closed the space with aching slowness, her other hand rising to cup the side of Ren's jaw, fingers calloused and warm from the tea.

Her lips brushed Ren's in question.

Ren's breath hitched, her eyes fluttering shut as she leaned in, her mouth answering before her thoughts could catch up. The kiss was soft, like Kaelin was afraid Ren would vanish if she pressed too hard. It was careful and reverent and –

Gods.

Kaelin made a sound in the back of her throat, something low and full of wanting.

In one swift motion, Kaelin's heel caught the table leg and shoved it aside, wood skidding across the stone floor. Before Ren could react, Kaelin's hand closed around her wrist, tugging her forward, until she was caught against her.

Kaelin's hand slipped to the back of Ren's neck, the other at her waist, and she pulled Ren into her lap with a fluid motion that made Ren gasp against her lips. The kiss deepened, all breath and hunger now, Kaelin's mouth fierce and demanding as if she was making up for every cruel word, every biting insult she'd thrown since Ren's arrival.

Ren gripped Kaelin's shoulders to steady herself, knees bracketing the princess's thighs. "You're—" Ren began, breaking just enough to draw breath. "You're so damn infuriating."

Kaelin only smirked against Ren's mouth. "So are you. And if you think that's going to stop me..." Her thumb dragged softly along Ren's hip. "...you really don't know me yet."

46

Kaelin trailed her fingers up Ren's spine, achingly and deliciously slow. "I've wanted to kiss you since the first time I saw you kneeling before me."

Ren let out a breathless scoff, eyes narrowing despite the flush crawling up her neck. "Of course you did. Fae royalty sees one dirt-covered mortal on her knees and goes faint."

Kaelin's response was a wicked grin. "And what a lovely sight it was."

Ren growled low in her throat. "You're lucky I'm already on top of you."

Kaelin's smile slowly faded. "No," Kaelin added, voice gentler now, a truth uncoiling between them. "It wasn't then. Not really. It was the first day I saw you training."

Kaelin's hand came to rest against Ren's jaw, thumb brushing just beneath her cheekbone. "You were bruised, beaten. Surrounded by fae who wanted you broken. And still, you got back up." Kaelin's finger gently traced the outline of Ren's lips. "I couldn't look away. Not because you were strong, but because you were angry. Gritty. *Alive.* Like a fire they tried to stomp out that only burned hotter." She exhaled, a soft breath against Ren's skin. "That's when I knew."

Ren's mind reeled. All this time, she had thought Kaelin despised her and saw her as little more than a nuisance, a filthy human dragged into the splendor of the fae court. Ren remembered those first days of autumn, the cool air biting at her skin while Kaelin's eyes had seemed colder still, cutting her down with every glance.

Ren swallowed, voice unsteady as she whispered, "You're not what I expected."

"I'd hate to be predictable. It's achingly boring." Kaelin's hand lingered at Ren's jaw, the tip of her nail tracing the gentle curve of Ren's lower lip with a touch so careful it sent a shiver racing down Ren's spine. The gesture was almost reverent, as if Kaelin herself was caught between wanting to tease and needing to cherish.

Silence stretched between them at Kaelin's words, their mouths no more than a hair's breadth apart. Ren looked up into the violet storms of the princess's eyes, trying to understand a silent battle raging within her. Beside Kaelin, Ren felt dull. Kaelin's beauty was the kind that demanded notice, and she looked untouchable, carved from something finer than flesh and blood. And yet, her gaze lingered on Ren, the human who was all bruises and rough edges, who had never been anyone's vision. *Why in all the hells would she look at me like that?*

But all of that – every reason, every damn argument – crumbled when Kaelin's fingers found her chin.

Before Ren could rebuild her walls, Kaelin's lips were on hers again, an exploratory kiss that conquered and claimed every crevice of Ren's mouth.

Logic was gone. Survival instincts were gone. All that remained was the searing heat of Kaelin's mouth against hers and the way it made Ren feel like she'd stepped into dangerous territory with no map and no intention of finding her way out.

Kaelin's hand slid from Ren's jaw, tracing down the side of her neck, her fingers curling around her throat. The contact was warm, commanding, sending a shiver down Ren's spine. Kaelin drew her closer until there was no space left between them, their bodies aligned in a way that made Ren's breath hitch. The princess's intoxicating scent enveloped her, pulling her further into a fog of want and need.

Ren's hands slipped into Kaelin's hair, the silky strands gliding between her fingers as Ren's hands fisted there, seeking an anchor in the seemingly never-ending storm of lust that had formed between them.

"I'm not letting you go," Kaelin murmured, voice low enough to tangle in Ren's chest. Ren's pulse roared in her ears. Saints help her, she didn't *want* to be let go.

Suddenly, a thunderclap cracked through the sky like a whip, shattering the stillness of the garden.

Kaelin froze. Ren stilled too, her chest heaving as the air suddenly shifted, no longer charged with their shared passion, but with the promise of an impending storm. Another thunderclap sounded, punctuating the sudden shift, and both looked through the windows to see storm clouds blooming in the distance.

Kaelin's hands were still on her waist, but her expression had changed, distant eyes reflecting the stormlight.

Ren slid off her lap, heart pounding.

The moment had shattered. The spell broken by the gods themselves, it seemed. They stood in silence, the taste of what had just passed lingering between them.

What the hell was I doing?

Ren had just *kissed* Kaelin. As if this were some fairy tale instead of a world gnawed raw by rot and war. Ren raked a hand through her hair, jaw clenched. Her lips still tingled from the kiss, but her mind was already storming in another direction. She didn't know when the shift had started – weeks ago, maybe longer. The stolen glances. The arguments that had balanced somewhere between disdain and desire. That magnetic pull.

It hadn't come all at once. It had crept in like water through a cracked roof, slow and silent until it soaked her through. Now, even as she tried to steady herself, she felt wildly unraveled, especially between her legs, her body betraying her with a hunger she hadn't meant to acknowledge.

Damn it.

She couldn't afford this – whatever this was. She wasn't about to play heartstrings with a royal, let alone a fae one. She was here to fight, earn her coin, and get the hell away from here.

Not get tangled in feelings she couldn't name.

Ren turned to Kaelin, who hadn't spoken. Ren's mouth felt dry suddenly, as if she had swallowed a mouthful of sand. "Let's just agree to be civil. Neutral."

Kaelin said nothing, her crown of golden hair catching the flickering lamplight as she turned her face away from Ren. She remained seated, back straight despite the chaos still humming in the air.

"You don't need to test me anymore. I want nothing from you but enough coin to vanish into some quiet corner of the world. We both know this was a mistake and nothing more," Ren said.

Kaelin's fingers flexed, as though resisting the urge to reach for Ren. "A mistake?" she echoed softly. Her eyes softened with a heat that made Ren's breath falter. "I've been aching for that kiss. And when it finally happened..." A faint, helpless smile ghosted her lips. "It ruined me, Ren. Because it was better than every fantasy I've had of you. And I want more. *So* much more."

Ren's breath shuddered, her voice cracking despite her best efforts. "Kaelin, this will never work. You have an entire court of suitors who'd kill for a fraction of your attention. You don't need someone like me."

Kaelin captured Ren's gaze with quiet intensity. "I don't want anyone else. I only want you, Ren."

Ren turned her back, shoulders curling inward as if bracing for a blow. "Kaelin, stop. Just... stop." The words shook despite her best attempt to sound indifferent. "I don't want this life. I don't want to be tied to a crown, or a court, or *you*." Her breath hitched, barely noticeable, but enough to betray her. "There's nothing here worth chasing. It's better if you let me go." Her hands trembled at her sides, hidden from Kaelin's view. "This is for the best," she whispered.

Silence fell between them, thick enough Ren could hear the faint hitch of Kaelin's breath. When Kaelin finally spoke, it was barely above a whisper. "You don't want me?"

Ren kept her back turned. "I'm certain."

Another long, brittle beat of silence. Then Kaelin's voice returned emotionless. "Very well, then."

A beat passed.

Two.

Then Kaelin said, "As you wish."

But Ren's eyes betrayed her. They flicked back to Kaelin's lips, still flushed from their kiss, slightly swollen, the ghost of Ren's mouth lingering there. Ren cleared her throat sharply and stepped back, nearly stumbling in her haste. "Right. Neutral," she muttered.

Without waiting for a response, Ren turned on her heels and forced herself to walk away.

Because if she lingered even a moment longer, she feared that she'd break her own damn rules.

Sitting across from Kaelin, Esme sipped her tea with the serenity of a priestess.

Talen glared at the wooden board as if it had personally offended him. "This game is unfair," he muttered.

"Or perhaps," Kaelin said mildly, "strategy isn't your strength, dear brother."

They sat in one of the palace parlors reserved for the royal family alone, lit with a warm hearth of fire. On the low table next to the hearth waited an unopened bottle of Emberwreath Mulled Red, the signature winter wine of the Pyraelian foothills, its deep garnet color glinting through the glass.

Esme took another sip of her tea, her brows knitting as she swallowed. "Saints," she rasped hoarsely, touching her throat gingerly, "this feels worse every time I drink it."

Kaelin didn't look up from the board. "It's honey and chamomile, Esme. It's known to ease sore throats."

Esme glared into the cup. "Well, it's doing a spectacular job at it."

Kaelin finally glanced up. "Your throat hurts because you refused to wear a cloak outside yesterday." She returned her attention as Talen moved one of his pieces. "Drink your tea."

Esme lifted her chin with wounded dignity. "I refused because Sylven was in the gardens yesterday, and I wanted him to see a bit more of my skin." she waved her hand flippantly. "Tastefully, of course. Just enough to intrigue, not enough to be uncouth."

Talen reset one of his pieces. "Esme, there were *snow flurries* yesterday."

"And?"

Kaelin sighed through her nose, pinching the bridge of it. "You are going to drink that tea until your voice returns to something other than a parched crow."

"At this point, I think the tea is what's murdering me."

Talen hid a smirk behind his hand. "Then it seems you and Sylven have something in common. He tries to kill everyone's mood, too."

Esme gasped. "Talen!"

Kaelin didn't look up from the board as she slid another piece forward with cutting precision. Talen grimaced. "Speaking of Sylven," Kaelin said coolly. "He asked to court me."

Esme froze.

"And I declined," Kaelin added smoothly.

Esme set her cup down very slowly. "Oh."

A silence stretched, which was unusual for her. Then, in a much quieter voice, she murmured, "Perhaps he'll consider courting me."

Talen and Kaelin shared a glance.

Sylven had probably retreated to the gardens yesterday to kneel before the gods and salvage whatever scraps of pride he had left. Maelion carved Sylven's dignity into neat little pieces that morning, and Kaelin had savored every second of it.

After Maelion's reprimands, Sylven knelt, head bowed.

But not low enough.

"I did what I thought best for Pyraelia," he explained. "Why waste resources protecting human prisoners? I have been loyal to this court my entire life, as well as my ancestors. And yet you defend them over me?

"You mistake loyalty for entitlement," Maelion responded. "And you mistake cruelty for strength."

Sylven's jaw clenched. His fists tightened. He clearly did not understand, and worse, he did not *want* to.

Kaelin had seen it, then. Something hungry. Something *dangerous*.

Esme looked down at her tea, cheeks flushed pink. "He's very handsome."

Kaelin folded her hands neatly in her lap. "If it's prestige you're hunting for in a marriage, then Sylven may not be the glittering prize you imagine."

"Why not?"

"Because if he keeps defying the crown and behaving like an insolent fool, he'll lose what reputation he has left. Titles can be stripped. Favor can vanish. I'd recommend choosing your suitors with care. Some loyalties are unpredictable."

Talen let out a low whistle under his breath. "In other words, pick someone who's not moments away from royal ruin."

Esme stared into her tea again, suddenly very quiet.

Kaelin didn't feel even a flicker of satisfaction as she slid her winning piece into place. Talen cursed softly, shoving a hand through his hair in frustration.

Because her true victory had slipped from her grasp two days ago in the greenhouse..

Kaelin's mood curdled as she swept the game pieces aside. She rose with a sharp rustle of silk, crossing straight to the wine table.

Ren was brave. Ren was fearless. Ren was everything Kaelin admired in a fighter.

But Ren was a wretched liar.

Kaelin replayed it again and again, the moment Ren turned away, shoulders rigid, voice trembling at the edges. The refusal had sounded strong, Ren hadn't let Kaelin see her face.

And Kaelin knew why.

The truth lived in Ren's eyes.

In the way Ren had kissed her back, fervent, desperate, as if starving for something she had never allowed herself to want. Kaelin could still feel Ren's weight in her lap, the press of her palms, the heat of her breath. There had been nothing reluctant or uncertain about it. No hesitation.

So why had Ren pushed her away?

Kaelin poured herself a glass with a steady hand. Behind her, Esme had finally found her voice again, rambling about some trivial matter to Talen. Kaelin lifted the glass to her lips, eyes narrowing at the far wall.

Because whatever excuse Ren had given her, it wasn't the truth.

And Kaelin intended to know the truth, no matter how long it took.

Even later that evening, as Kaelin retired to her bed chamber, Kaelin could still taste Ren on her lips. They had come together, two storms crashing into one another. The way Ren had gasped into her mouth with something hungrier.

Kaelin braced her palms against the carved edge of her vanity, her reflection a blur in the gilded mirror. Her memory replayed over and over how Ren's lips were still flushed as she backed up, a mark of what she'd let happen.

Of what Kaelin hadn't finished.

"Damn it," she growled.

Her chambers were too quiet. Too still. She slumped onto her bed, feeling as if something had been ripped from her chest. Her fists tangled in the sheets in an effort to anchor herself, but all they did was remind her how empty her bed was.

Kaelin rolled onto her back. But even behind closed eyes, she could not escape the human who had unknowingly stolen her heart.

Kaelin wanted her. By the gods, she wanted her in ways that made her chest ache and her temper snap.

Her breath hitched. Heat coiled low in her stomach like a slow-burning ember. Her fingers dug into the velvet beneath her. They wandered under the silks of her dress, brushing against her flesh, feeling the heat and wetness of her aching desire.

As thunder boomed overhead and wind swept against the walls and the windows, Kaelin lost herself in thoughts of the red-haired human with freckles scattered like stars of constellations on her cheeks. Recalled how soft her lips were, how sweet her breath smelled against hers. How Kaelin felt fire in her core when their chests pressed against each other, every curve aligned perfectly.

Kaelin groaned into the stillness of the room, eyes fluttering shut as she succumbed to her fantasy.

Ren knelt before her, settling between Kaelin's parted legs. Her lips were parted, her hot breath ghosting over Kaelin's sensitive skin as she prepared to take a pert nipple into her mouth.

Ren's tongue darted out, swirling around the stiff peak before drawing it between her lips. Kaelin moaned, the phantom sensation sending sparks of pleasure shooting through her body. She could almost feel Ren's fingers splayed across her breast, holding her in place as she suckled and nibbled.

Kaelin's hand drifted down once again, ghosting over her own thigh, and she imagined that it was Ren who touched her instead. Those clever fingers would part her legs, trailing up to stroke Kaelin's most intimate places. Kaelin's hips bucked at the mental image, a needy whimper escaping her.

Ren continued her lavish attention on Kaelin's breasts, teasing and tormenting until Kaelin was writhing with want. Only then would Ren allow those talented fingers to delve deeper, to bring Kaelin to the brink of ecstasy and beyond.

Kaelin bit back a curse as she came undone and reached her peak. The force of her release left her breathless, limbs trembling with residual pleasure that seemed to radiate from her core out to the tips of her fingers and toes. Panting, she felt as though the stars exploded overhead.

But even in the haze of her post-orgasmic bliss, Kaelin knew one thing with absolute clarity: she was in deep trouble where Ren was concerned. Ren had gotten under her skin, tangled up her mind and body in ways she'd never experienced before.

Kaelin had always been in control, in every aspect of her life and relationships. But Ren made Kaelin feel things, need things, that challenged her iron-clad control. And if the fae didn't watch herself, she would lose that control entirely.

The thought should have terrified Kaelin. But sprawled there on the bed, still quivering from the force of her climax, all she could feel was anticipation.

47

Damn that royal pain in the ass.
Ren hated the way her body betrayed her. She tossed and turned even nights after the kiss.

Every time she shut her eyes, she felt Kaelin's lips against hers again. It set her blood simmering, made her cheeks burn until she wanted to bury her face in the pillow and never emerge.

But two days later, the sun still crawled through her window and life didn't give a damn about her sleepless night. Training waited. If Ulfric had them doing something brutal enough, maybe she could beat the princess out of her head.

"I take it the afternoon tea went well," Mirella purred from across the room.

Ren groaned into her pillow. She debated telling Mirella, or anyone, for that matter, what had actually happened. But the words in her head didn't make sense. Kaelin was a fae *princess*, heir to a kingdom older than Ren's bloodline.

Why would Kaelin look twice at someone like me?

And yet, the memory of the way Kaelin's gaze lingered haunted Ren. But even as warmth curled low in her chest, doubt slashed through it. Maybe Kaelin was interested now. Maybe the novelty of a human who wouldn't bend or bow had caught her attention. But one day, she'd get bored; the thrill would fade. Ren would just be a passing amusement, a short-lived affair in a fae princess's long, glittering life.

The thought hollowed Ren out. Ren could almost see the moment Kaelin's eyes would look right past her, as though she'd never mattered at all. Ren squeezed her eyes shut, unease rising at the thought. She could face blades and monsters alike, but not the slow unraveling of being cherished until the wonder faded.

"I don't want to talk about it," Ren mumbled into the pillow.

"It was impactful enough to keep you up all night for the past 2 nights."

Reluctantly, Ren dragged herself upright, swinging her legs over the side of the bed. Her bones ached like she'd been in a fight already. "The pastries were too damn good," she muttered, yanking on her clothes over her head. Her arm got caught in the sleeve, and she paused when she nearly burst the seam. *Damn it to high hells.* "And—"

"I can sense the lie coming, darling," Mirella sing-songed. "You may as well tell me the truth."

Ren fumbled with her belt, her hair falling into her face. Mirella didn't have eyes, yet Ren felt her *stare*. Ren began braiding her hair too tightly and winced when the strands tugged at her scalp.

"At this rate, you'll tear half your hair out," Mirella chided.

"She *kissed* me!" Ren blurted. Her voice ricocheted off the walls. She finally turned to Mirella, eyes wide, as if she'd just confessed to a heinous crime.

Mirella went utterly still.

"She—the princess—kissed *me*," Ren repeated, the words tasting foreign even as she spoke them. "One minute, she's got a blade to my throat. The next... she's showing me something close to respect. And then it's like she can't stand breathing the same air. And two days ago—" her voice spiked, breath catching "—she couldn't keep her hands *off* of me."

"Sounds like someone's fighting a losing battle with their feelings."

"This is stupid. Nothing would ever work out between us. And I don't think I could be someone's mistress."

"Oh, but the mistress can have all the fun without the crown's shackles."

Ren's face went hot again, heat crawling up her neck. "That means something to me. More than that. I've never even...you know."

There was a beat of silence.

"You're a *virgin*?" Mirella asked, her voice equal parts surprise and curiosity.

"Yes," Ren hissed, glancing at the door as if the walls themselves might go whispering. "I've had offers, stolen kisses, a hand on my thigh at a tavern or two, but never anything permanent. I moved too much. And now—" She swallowed hard. "She'd never seriously *want* someone like me."

"And why's that?" Mirella's voice softened, the teasing gone.

Ren didn't answer right away. She looked down at her calloused knuckles. Kaelin's hands were soft, adorned with rings and delicate. Ren could still feel those same fingers ghosting against her throat when they'd kissed, gentle but firm.

"I don't deserve it."

There it was. The thought she never said aloud.

It landed in the space between them, a stone dropped in deep water, ripples spreading through her chest until they reached the oldest wound she carried. She saw it all again – the night Eve betrayed them all.

She remembered the rough, cold hands pushing her down as the sack was thrown over her head, the world spinning as they hauled her away. She'd screamed until her throat burned raw, called out until her voice was nothing but a rasp.

In one last desperate breath, she screamed Eve's name.

But only silence answered.

They carried her for what felt like forever, her body jostled and bruised inside the bag, until they finally flung her. She landed on damp grass, the earth cold and slick with mud. It took everything in her to claw free, tearing through the coarse fabric until air struck her face again.

And above her, stars glittered over a world that had already forgotten her.

If not even Eve could stay... who would?

Nobody.

"Oh, darling," Mirella murmured, "you've been walking through storms so long you've forgotten the sun belongs to you, too."

Ren looked up at Mirella, her vision blurring with tears.

"You're not scraps to be chosen or discarded. Anyone lucky enough to stand close should count their blessings, not your worth."

Ren sniffed, brushing the tears away with the back of her hand. "It's far too early in the day for this," she joked, half to Mirella, half to herself.

"Come on, darling. Dry your tears – you've got egos to bruise, and the fae's egos are *very* delicate."

Ren walked the alley near the stables with her hands tucked into her coat, fingertips still chilled from the wind that came down off the northern hills. After training, she decided to go for an evening stroll.

From within the stalls, Ren heard hooves shuffling. She rounded the corner and nearly collided with a tall, wiry figure.

Talen.

"Ren! And here I was thinking my evening would be dull."

Talen leaned against a post with a half-emptied wine bottle dangling from his fingers. Beside him stood Kaelin, her hair braided back to bare the sharp line of her jaw. She wore riding leathers and pants, something Ren wasn't used to seeing her adorned in. Ren couldn't help but let her eyes look over Kaelin, lingering where the leather pants hugged her thighs.

Then, violet eyes slid up to clash with hers.

Ren's feet should have carried her past, but she stopped at the next stall where Kaelin's mare waited. Black as a shadow, the horse turned her pale eyes on Ren and snorted.

As if she wasn't impressed.

"Come rescue me. My dear sister is lecturing me about the merits of day drinking before a two-day ride," Talen called.

"I only said you snore like a dying boar when you drink," Kaelin said coolly.

Talen pushed off the post and lifted the bottle. "We're heading north tomorrow to our ancestral winter keep. Our family visited each year before our parents abandoned the tradition." He flashed her a grin, all fae mischief. "We keep the celebration alive regardless. One last send-off to winter. Only a few still make the pilgrimage. Fires, cards, frostbite. You should come."

Ren asked, "You're inviting me to catch frostbite?"

"I'm inviting you to watch me win at cards," Talen corrected, amiably blunt. "Are you by any chance feeling lucky?"

"No. Thanks for the invite, but I'll be staying. Safe travels," Ren answered automatically. The word jumped out before she caught it. By the veil, this was the last thing she needed right now.

Kaelin brushed a fingertip over her horse's muzzle. "The north is warmer when you've got the right company."

"And we have wine," Talen said, waggling the bottle.

"I have training here. I – "

"I can give you a purpose to be there," a voice cut in.

Zakhar moved like an ink spill, one moment part of the shadow beside the tack room, the next standing at Ren's shoulder. He beheld a grin that was pleased and almost eager, as if their journey had just saved him the trouble of a dozen wasted steps.

Ren's spine went wire-taut. "Do you make a habit of listening from corners?"

"I make a habit of knowing when people are about to make decisions that save me time," he retorted, unbothered. "Near the keep, there's a vale where the wind gets trapped. A particular herb blooms there once a year. It responds to the last full moon in the winter lunar cycle and stays potent for seven days, then wilts."

Talen lifted a hand. "And what would 'it' be, exactly?"

"Fasil," Zakhar said, as if they were fools for not knowing. "You'll recognize it by the silvered leaves and pale veins. It's the stabilizer the Verdant Elixir requires. I would collect it myself, but court obligations as you know," he gave a shrug.

Kaelin's eyes had found Ren again, watching from beneath her lashes with that flat, assessing calm that made Ren want to pace the length of the stable. "We'll be close enough to the vale," Kaelin said.

Zakhar's gaze flicked to Ren. "You asked to learn what ingredients move an elixir from folklore to function. Consider this an education and a favor I will not forget."

"I didn't ask you for an education," Ren insisted.

Zakhar's mouth tilted. "You rarely ask for anything. It's tedious."

A gelding banged a hoof against the stall boards as if punctuating the insult. Ren wouldn't give Zakhar the satisfaction of bristling. She hadn't put a name to the itch in her hands that she'd had since she'd first seen the Verdant Elixir simmer in the palace alchemarium. But the itch was there all the same – the urge to see if she might be able to do something about this illness.

Ren exhaled and looked up to meet Kaelin's mare. She watched Ren with an unnerving intelligence.

Five days. And a chance to be useful.

"Okay," Ren said at last. "I'll go. For the herb."

Talen whooped, then cleared his throat when Kaelin shot him a look. "For the herb," he echoed, nodding.

Zakhar inclined his head. "I'll send you a sketch of the plant and a charm to keep it from losing potency on the ride back. See that you don't wake it wrong; it wilts if handled harshly."

"Plants don't wake," Ren said, then paused. "Do they?"

"Everything wakes, if you touch it the right way," Zakhar said, and reached into the folds of his cloak. He produced a small, weathered box stitched with faintly glowing runes.

"I'm trusting you with this," he handed it over to Ren. The box felt incredibly light. "It'll hold the fasil safely enough, but be warned. I enchanted it long ago, when I was first learning the craft. Let's just say its personality is striking." A faint smirk ghosted across his face. "No matter how hard you press, it won't give its name. And it absolutely won't shut up. It's rather sentimental, though it'll never admit as much."

With that, Zakhar drifted backward, the shadows swallowing him once more.

Talen tipped the bottle toward Ren. "To bad choices that turn out to be good ones."

Ren ignored the bottle he extended, but some of the tightness in her chest eased. "What constitutes a bad choice in your opinion?"

"Agreeing to ride north with a handsome, intelligent fae prince who cheats at cards and a princess who won't admit she snores," Talen said.

Kaelin's brows arched, her chin lifting. "I do not snore."

"Keep telling yourself that. The rest of us will keep counting sheep," Talen started toward the stable door, humming off-key. "Dawn, then. Pack warm."

For a heartbeat, neither spoke. There was something different about seeing Kaelin wrapped in riding leathers instead of the finery of court—something raw, unguarded, that made Ren's core go molten with desire. She had to force her gaze to stay on Kaelin's face, not on the way the leathers clung to her form, accentuating her full breasts. Breasts that had brushed against hers as they had kissed on that fateful day in the greenhouse.

Gods to hell, Ren cursed, shaking her head in an attempt to clear her thoughts. Kaelin's violet eyes were still staring at her, her lips curving as if daring her closer.

She was impossible to look away from.

Kaelin arched a brow, the faintest grin ghosting across her lips. "You think staying away will keep me in line? You've clearly never tested my limits."

"Who says I'm avoiding you?"

Kaelin's gaze swept over Ren. "I can read emotion as easily as the weather," she said coolly. "Fear sharpens the eyes, tightens the throat, pulls the shoulders inward. Tries to make itself small. Lust, on the other hand..." Her lips curved. "Lust dilates the pupils, catches the breath, makes a person lean closer without realizing it." She angled her head, her gaze skimming over Ren with scrutiny. "So, when you lied in the greenhouse and said you didn't want me, which feeling do you think gave you away?"

Ren's jaw tightened. "Believe what you want. I wasn't feeling anything."

Kaelin's gaze dipped to Ren's chest, noting the rapid rise and fall, then traced slowly up the line of her throat to her jaw. "Your body gives you away long before your mouth does." Her gaze darkened. "You're building a wall between us. I can see every brick."

Ren threw up a hand. "We are not having this conversation." She shook her head, scoffing. "Chasing whatever we did would be a spectacularly bad idea. Aren't *I* supposed to be the impulsive one?"

Kaelin said nothing for a long moment. When she finally spoke, her voice was barely more than a breath. "I've seen people use others for power, for coin, for prestige. I know what it looks like when someone wants a person for all the wrong reasons." Her eyes found Ren's again.

"But I've never seen someone turn away the chance to have something good, and I cannot fathom why you'd deny yourself that."

Ren let out a sharp huff. "My life isn't up for your analysis. What I do or don't want is *my* business." She folded her arms. "We agreed to be civil. So let's be civil."

Kaelin smoothed a hand along the mare's cheek as if considering how honest to be. "Come north," she murmured simply. "It's different there. More pure."

"Dawn," Ren agreed.

"Dawn," Kaelin repeated.

Ren stood alone with the smell of hay and horse and the knowledge she'd just said yes to a trip that would tangle everything tighter. She let her palm rest against the stall door of Kaelin's mare before leaving for the courtyard.

Looking up, the moon looked too full, too bright. A warning of some change yet to come.

Like a coin pressed flat between impatient fingers, ready to be spent.

48

Ren slung her knapsack over one shoulder, the worn leather creaking against her earth green cloak. Beneath it, she wore plain leather armor over a brown tunic, just enough protection should trouble find them on the road.

"Maybe find boots that match your cloak!" Mirella called in a singsong voice that was annoyingly chipper and grated at Ren's already frayed nerves.

To high hells with matching colors, Ren thought as she opened the door to her room. She was immediately blasted with the last bitter cold of winter, and despite her thick cloak, a shiver racked down her spine. Ren couldn't wait till winter finally loosened its tight grip on the world. While she didn't hate winter or the cold, she did find it to be a nuisance the longer it stayed. Ren continued her journey down the hallway before finally stepping out of the building into the frigid morning air, heading toward the horse stables.

The nearer Ren drew to the stables, the louder the morning chorus became – a symphony of hoofbeats thudding against packed dirt, the low murmur of voices, the steady huff of horses snorting.

A splash of movement caught her eye. Lucan sat tall on a snow-white stallion whose mane had been braided with meticulous care, each plait tied with a strip of silver and blue ribbon. "Glad to see you joining us," he called. "This should be interesting now."

Ren smiled back. To Lucan's right, Kaelin swung gracefully into the saddle of her midnight-black mare. Lucan's expression shifted slightly when his gaze flicked to the horse. "Name's Whisper. Proud and temperamental, that one. She decides whether you'll ride her on *her* terms. She accepts Kaelin without question, but most of the stablehands keep their distance."

As if to punctuate the point, the mare's ears flicked back, head lowering as though she were approving.

"She is exceptional in both speed and agility," Kaelin stroked a hand down the mare's rippling mane. "Whisper can weave through the chaos of battle like water around rocks."

Talen led his own mount past them then, a brown gelding with warm, liquid eyes who trailed after him like an old friend. "And she refuses to be handled or mounted by anyone but Kaelin," he remarked dryly. "Which makes her useless to anyone else in an emergency."

Whisper's head snapped up at that, ears flicking forward before she stamped a hoof and tossed her head.

"She heard you," Kaelin murmured, eyes glinting wickedly as she smoothed a palm over the mare's neck.

"Ah, yes. My mistake," Talen grumbled. "She's just *selectively* cooperative."

Ren shifted her weight, gaze finally leaving Kaelin's as she scanned the line of horses that the other fae mounted. She counted—once, twice—and came to the same uneasy conclusion.

There weren't enough saddles.

Talen didn't miss the way her face fell. "Ah, looks like you'll have to ride with one of us."

Lucan's brow lifted, but he only gave a slight shrug. "Don't look so grim, I can make decent conversation."

Ren's gaze leapt back to Kaelin, who was still watching her with an expression that was all effortless calm except for the gleam in her eyes that made Ren's pulse stumble.

"Whisper doesn't usually share, but I think she'd make an exception for you," Kaelin purred.

Ren deadpanned, "Generous."

Kaelin's mouth curved. "*Practical.* You'd see more of the road from up here. And," she added with deliberate lightness, "I'll behave, unless you'd rather I didn't."

"Tempting. But no."

Kaelin's brows lifted the smallest fraction. "No?"

"I'll take my chances with Talen," Ren said, stepping toward the gelding.

Talen grinned as if he'd won a wager. "Wise choice. *My* horse doesn't bite."

Ren felt Kaelin's gaze on her back all the way to Talen's saddle. And, Saints help her, something in her responded. Her hips swayed a little too easily, her hand brushing a strand of hair over her shoulder as if by accident. The moment she caught herself, irritation flared hot beneath her skin. What in the hells was she doing? She was supposed to be ignoring Kaelin, not *inviting* her attention.

Still, she felt that gaze linger all the way to Talen's saddle.

From behind them, Lucan gave a low chuckle. "I'll wager by the end of this trip, you two will be tangled up in each other."

Talen shot him a glare. "That's not a fair bet. It's painfully obvious."

Lucan winked. "Then I suppose I'll just collect my winnings early."

Ren muttered, "One more wager out of either of you, and I'll drag you off your horses myself."

Ren swung easily onto the gelding's back, the worn leather of the saddle creaking beneath her weight. Her knees settled just behind Talen.

"Name's Cider," Talen said over his shoulder, patting the horse's muscled neck. "Loves hay and rolling in the mud right after a fresh bath. Bit of a menace if you ask the grooms. Luckily for you, Cider's got a smooth gait and an even smoother gallop." His eyes glinted with mischief as he turned forward.

With a soft click of his tongue, Talen guided the gelding forward, hooves drumming a steady rhythm against the frost-hardened earth. The rising sun poured over the land in a wash of molten gold, so bright Ren had to squint through her lashes. For a few minutes, the world was nothing but the glare of light and the thunder of hooves, her hands gripping Talen's broad shoulders as Cider carried them across the open plain.

As the minutes stretched into an hour, she glanced back over her shoulder. Pyraelia was already shrinking into the horizon, its gleaming spires softened by distance until it seemed more dream than stone. The cold air tasted sharper out here, clean and tinged with pine.

Out of the corner of her vision, she caught Kaelin astride Whisper. The princess rode with effortless precision, her spine straight, her gaze fixed ahead. Whisper's dark coat rippled beneath her. Kaelin's brows were drawn in deep thought.

Ren studied her a moment longer before looking away.

They rode through the morning and into the heatless glow of midday, the sky a pale winter blue overhead. When Talen finally drew Cider to a halt beside a babbling stream, the sound of water was almost startling after hours of nothing but hoofbeats. They dismounted, letting the horses lower their heads to drink.

Ren crouched at the bank, cupping icy water into her hands to splash over her face. The shock of it cleared the road's haze from her mind. Talen passed her a hunk of dark bread and a wedge of sharp cheese from his saddlebag, both of which tasted far better in the cold air than they had any right to.

By the time they set off again, the wind had a sharper bite. The land began to change, rolling hills flattening into open stretches of frost-silvered grass. Farther north, the horizon darkened with a fringe of evergreen forest.

They entered the woods as the sun dipped toward the treeline, shadows stretching long across the path. The air here was quieter, hushed beneath the weight of thick branches overhead. Pine needles muffled the sound of the horses' steps, and the scent of resin and damp earth hung heavy.

Talen slowed Cider, scanning the darkening undergrowth. "Here," he called to the others. "We'll make camp before night falls."

Ren glanced upward. The last shards of sunlight were bleeding out of the sky, replaced by the deepening indigo of approaching night.

Somewhere behind them, Kaelin's voice was low as she soothed Whisper to a halt. The mare stood proud and still, pale eyes catching what little light remained. Ren looked away quickly, focusing instead on Talen as he swung off Cider's back with practiced ease.

It was going to be a long night.

T he fire crackled against the night sky.

Cold ribbons of mist floated out from between the trees into the camp, as if the forest itself was exhaling a breath into the cold night air. Ren's body shook with the cold. She hadn't realized just how much colder it would be here compared to back at the palace. She was already starting to regret her decision to come and missed her warm bed dearly. In an attempt to further warm herself, Ren pulled the furs tighter around her shoulders, letting the heat of the flames soak into her bones. Beside her, Talen and Lucan debated some political point neither would remember come morning, their words slurring as the ale and rum loosened their tongues.

Lucan passed Ren a flask without ceremony. She took a swig, and the bourbon heat bloomed in her chest, its smoky edge speaking of House Tharowen's deep forges and richer earth. House Tharowen was renowned for producing the best bourbon and whiskey.

Across the fire, Kaelin lounged with a glass of wine that caught the firelight in shades of molten ruby. Of course she'd brought a glittering goblet all the way through the mountain passes, and of course it had survived without so much as a crack.

The road to this place had been carved from a cliff, curling through peaks that vanished into the clouds. Even Ren had felt the prickle of nerves when the path narrowed and the land dropped away into nothing but wind and distant river. One wrong step from Cider and they'd be over the edge.

Sparks leapt from the fire like tiny fleeing stars, and someone began coaxing a slow, mournful melody from a fiddle. Laughter softened, conversations thinned, and the air settled into the stillness waiting for a song to fill it.

"Princess Kaelin," Lucan called. "Sing one of the old ones."

Ren's gaze shifted. Kaelin sat on a low log, one knee bent, the fire painting her in warm amber and shadow. Her eyes found Ren's for a heartbeat before slipping away as the fiddle's notes lowered into quiet.

Kaelin's voice followed, low and unadorned, like it had been torn raw from somewhere deep inside her. It wasn't perfect. Kaelin didn't linger on every note with polished precision. Sometimes her voice rasped, sometimes it wavered just a fraction off key, but that imperfection made it all the more piercing. Among the fae, songs were vessels for memory, woven threads of legend and loss, the way their stories survived across centuries.

Beneath the boughs where the cold winds sigh,
I waited alone 'neath the silver sky.
Your shadow lingered, your voice was flame,
But the night came on, and it called your name.
When the ember fades, will you still know me?
When the frost takes root where the heart should be?
I will wait through the dark, through endless snow,
For the one I lost, and the love I know.
The river froze where we once would meet,
Its song now silent, its pulse grown weak.
Yet I hear your laughter through winter's breath,
And I'll walk that sound to the edge of death.
When the ember fades, will you still know me?
When the frost takes root where the heart should be?
I will wait through the dark, through endless snow,
For the one I lost, and the love I know.
Even if lifetimes must turn to stone,
Even if stars burn and leave me alone,
Your name is a vow carved deep in my bone,

And I'll follow it home.

The last note lingered before dissolving into the night. The air around the fire felt thicker somehow, as if everyone had been holding their breath without realizing it.

Talen's voice broke the quiet first, low enough that the fire nearly swallowed it. "*When the Ember Fades,*" he murmured. He leaned back on his palms, eyes on the flames. "My mother used to hum that before winter campaigns. It's older than most of the stones in the capital. Came from the time when dragons ruled and the skies over Vaelaran burned for weeks."

His gaze shifted past her, somewhere deep into the dark between the trees. "They say it's about Prince Aeyren Vaelaran, and the woman he loved, Serenya of the Silver Vale. She was a healer who could call warmth back into dying hearts. During the last siege, she was taken beyond the northern passes by enemy forces. Aeyren followed her into the storms, chasing the last glow of dragonfire on the horizon."

"Did he find her?"

"No. But every winter he returned to those mountains, hoping she'd wander home under the right moon."

The fiddle player plucked idly at a string, as if even he wanted the end of the story.

Lucan added, "Soldiers sing it before they march. Lovers sing it before they part. It's a way of telling someone that no matter what the cold takes from me, it won't take you. And so the song turned into a winter ritual as a reminder that love might survive even when all else felt lost."

Talen bumped his shoulder, eyebrows raised. "Look at you. Didn't peg you for a secret poet."

Then, the fiddler struck up something brighter, paired with a tavern song about a drunk man waltzing his wife into forgiveness under the moon.

He came home swaying, boots caked in ale,
Sang to the doorway, "I've conquered the vale!"
She crossed her arms, said, "You're late again, dear—"
But he spun her 'round, saying, "Dance with me here!"
Spin, spin, my bonny moonlight,
Hold me close 'til the morning's bright.
If we argue, we'll just spin faster,

In the arms of my one disaster.

By the first chorus, fae had sprung to their feet, stomping boots and swinging each other. Even Lucan and Kaelin joined, the princess's hair unbound and her skirts swirling free.

She scolded him twice, then tripped on his toe,
He laughed and he bowed, "It's part of the show!"
They waltzed 'round the yard, the chickens in fright,
While the moon tipped her hat to their quarrel that night.
Spin, spin, my bonny moonlight,
Hold me close 'til the morning's bright.
If we argue, we'll just spin faster,
In the arms of my one disaster.

"Come dance with me," Talen leaned over Ren, holding out his hand. Ren shook her head, but he only grinned wider. "Don't make me drag you."

Ren relented, her fingers warm in his as he pulled her into the light. The world tilted and spun, fire and faces blurring as they moved. She found herself laughing, and he laughed with her.

Then one fatal turn brought her tumbling into Kaelin's arms.

From the tavern to the fire's glow,
Through the frost and the drifting snow,
They say love's rough, but I'd never trade,
For a partner who dances through every mistake.
Spin, spin, my bonny moonlight,
Hold me close 'til the morning's bright.
If we argue, we'll just spin faster,
In the arms of my one disaster!

This dance was different from any dance they'd had before. There was no challenge, no duel of sharp eyes and sharper tongues. Kaelin's palm found the small of Ren's back, guiding her in a slow spin that had nothing to do with the reel still bounding around them. Her steps softened; the rest of the camp fell away until there was only the glow of the fire on Kaelin's cheeks and the silver scatter of moonlight in her hair.

Kaelin's movements were unhurried, her body close enough that Ren could feel the rhythm of her breath. There was something grounding in it, like they'd stepped into a quieter world that belonged to neither court nor camp.

When Kaelin's hand slid from her back to her fingers, Ren let it happen, letting herself be turned beneath the sweep of a deep twirl before Kaelin drew her close again.

Without the usual armor of words, without the bite of rivalry, the space between them felt impossibly small.

Kaelin's fingers tightened around hers, pulling her just that last breath closer. Ren didn't think about it; she simply met her halfway. Their lips brushed light, fleeting.

The fire roared in the pause that followed, and then –

"Finally!" someone whooped from the edge of the firelight. There was a ripple of cheers, clapping, and exaggerated whistles that broke across the camp.

Ren averted her eyes and felt heat rush to her cheeks, but Kaelin only smiled before spinning her once more, the two of them slipping back into their own rhythm as if they hadn't just handed the entire camp something to talk about until morning.

Ren didn't realize she was smiling until Kaelin said, "You should do that more often."

"Do what?"

Kaelin's answering smile was soft, almost wistful. "Smile. You have no idea what it does to me."

Warmth hummed in Ren's belly, spreading from her cheeks to between her legs, goosebumps rising along her arms. Laughter from Lucan and Talen came from her left, but the noise barely registered to her.

"What is it doing to you?" Ren murmured before she could stop herself. Inside, her head chastised her. *You're supposed to be civil. Nothing more. This is not being civil. This is being –*

Kaelin moved before Ren could draw breath, closing the space between them in a single, quiet step. Her hand found Ren's arm, swiftly drawing her close. Kaelin's lips brushed the edge of Ren's ear as she breathed, "It's undoing me piece by piece, until there's nothing left but the ache of wanting you."

The words settled between them like a fragile flame. Ren couldn't move; she couldn't breathe. Her thoughts splintered, her body suspended in that moment between wanting and knowing what she *shouldn't* want.

But Kaelin lingered only a heartbeat longer before easing back, her touch falling away like the ghost of warmth. She just reached for Ren's hand and guided her back into the slow rhythm of their dance, as though she hadn't just laid her heart bare and then quietly folded it away again.

Though Ren couldn't yet name what she felt, she felt grateful that Kaelin had bared her heart and yet asked for nothing in return.

And when the music swelled, they didn't quicken to match it. They stayed in their own rhythm, holding on just a little longer before the song carried them back into the rest of the world.

50

The water was so cold, it burned.

Ren poured water from the ladle into her coop and let it wash over her tongue, icy and clean. Mountain cap water, Talen had called it. Straight from the spring, born of ice melt. It was the best thing she'd ever tasted, and this morning, her body was desperate for it.

Her head still thudded from last night's drinking

Her gaze flicked to the other side of camp. Kaelin lingered beside Whisper, stroking the mare's sleek muzzle, her fingers moving in unhurried circles. She was quieter than usual this morning.

Truth be told, they were all quiet.

Something had shifted last night. Ren wasn't sure if it was the fiddle music, the heat of the fire, or simply the distance from the palace and all its watching eyes. But even through the haze of drink, she had felt as though she'd set something down, without knowing what it was.

The rhythmic pound of hooves broke through the stillness. Talen rode in at the head of a small group. Behind him, a male and female fae kept pace. Draped across Talen's front was the broad, tawny pelt of a kill.

Only then did Ren notice how small their party truly was, including Kaelin, Talen, and Lucan, there were just the two fae warriors and a healer trailing behind them. Yesterday had been so frantic she hadn't even realized.

"Nothing more refreshing than a morning hunt," Talen called. "Bagged an elk big enough to feed us for weeks. Means we don't have to live off dried meat, cheese, and bread the whole time up north."

Lucan, gnawing on a strip of jerky, gave a reluctant grunt. "Thank the gods."

Packing began in earnest after that. When Ren turned toward the horses, Talen rubbed the back of his neck, a crooked grin tugging at his mouth. "Sorry," he said, patting the elk pelt. "You've been replaced."

"A shame," Ren muttered, though the word tasted heavier than she meant.

"Don't look so disappointed," Kaelin drawled from her saddle, a smirk curling at her lips. "There is plenty of room up here."

Ren's gaze desperately flicked to Lucan, whose color was rapidly shifting toward seasick green.

Talen sighed. "Don't mind him. Poor fool can't hold his drink to save his life."

In response, Lucan groaned, clutching the reins.

Ren sighed and approached Whisper warily. The mare was taller than Cider by a hand, her presence as imposing as her rider's. The mare shifted her weight as Ren came near, watching her sidelong with an unnerving, intelligent pair of eyes.

Ren hesitated, the urge to murmur something—*anything*—rising unbidden. But she caught herself. Horses couldn't understand, and Whisper didn't strike her as the type to appreciate flattery, anyway.

Ren begrudgingly swung into the saddle behind Kaelin. Whisper shifted again, tail flicking hard against Ren's thigh, as if to make her displeasure known.

Ren grumbled, "You and your nightmare horse are made for each other."

Kaelin shot her a wicked smile. "Oh, I quite agree. She kicks, I plot, and together we're unstoppable. Hold on tight, Ren."

An hour later, the forest spilled away behind them, giving over to open, frost-tinged hills.

Whisper's gait was smooth, every step rolling into the next like flowing water. But it wasn't the mare Ren's mind kept circling back to.

It was the way Kaelin's hips moved with each stride, the faint sway that pressed her inevitably, into Ren's front. The way her braid swayed against Ren's shoulder. And *saints*, her scent – an alluring symphony of wild lavender and frost-kissed grapefruit. It wrapped around Ren, making it damn near impossible *not* to think about the fae princess.

"Comfortable back there?" Kaelin asked, her voice just loud enough to carry over the hoofbeats.

"Depends on your definition."

Kaelin shifted *deliberately*, Ren suspected. "You'll have to hold on when we hit the pass. The climb's steep, and the drop is dramatic. But the views of the mountains?" Her lips curved as she glanced over her shoulder, meeting Ren's gaze. "*Breathtaking*."

Ren's blood went cold. The color drained from her cheeks before she could mask it, her fingers tightening on the saddle.

Talen quickly caught the way Ren paled. "Not a fan of heights?"

Ren clenched her jaw, leaning forward as if bracing against the wind. "I'm a fan of solid ground."

Kaelin chuckled. "Don't worry. I won't let you fall."

Ren scoffed, heat creeping up her neck despite herself. "You say that now. But if I do, I'm dragging you with me."

"If it means your arms wrapped tight around me, I might not mind the fall."

Ren snorted, rolling her eyes. Without thinking, she retorted, "Saints, you'd flirt with a stone if it looked at you the right way."

Kaelin leaned back just enough for her words to curl hot against Ren's ear. "No, Ren, darling. Just you."

From behind, Talen and Lucan exchanged a knowing look. Lucan mouthed, *you owe me*, and Talen scowled, digging out a coin.

Ren's pulse stuttered, her sarcastic armor crumbling for a heartbeat as heat licked down her spine. Kaelin's laugh was low, pleased. And then she leaned back just enough for her shoulder to brush Ren's chest. "Are you enjoying yourself?"

Ren clenched her jaw, heat crawling up her neck. "Are you swiveling your hips on purpose?" she asked, each word ground out between her teeth.

A slow smile curved across Kaelin's mouth. She didn't look back, didn't need to. "Darling," she murmured, her voice low enough for only Ren to hear, "you should see what I can do in bed."

The words struck in Ren's chest, hot and dangerous. She forced her eyes to the road ahead, willing her pulse to steady though she was sure Kaelin could feel it in the space between them.

They rode in silence for a stretch, Talen and Lucan having already trotted ahead, locked in a heated debate over some absurd political point neither of them would ever concede.

Only when their voices faded did Kaelin finally speak. "So..." she began, drawing the word out, "about last night."

"What about it?"

"Our kiss."

"Don't know what you're talking about."

Kaelin laughed. "Oh, you know exactly what I'm talking about. The way your lips felt soft, warm... like you'd been waiting for it." She shifted her hips, her voice dropping to a near-whisper. "Makes me wonder where else I could put them."

Heat slammed into Ren's face, her breath catching. "Kaelin – "

"What?" The single word was all silk and provocation. "You didn't like it?"

"Saints, do you hear yourselves sometimes?"

Kaelin turned her head just enough to glance over her shoulder, a wicked smile curving her mouth. "You're adorable when you're flustered." Against her will, Ren's cheeks warmed even further to Kaelin's delight. "Mmm... and there it is. That gorgeous little flush you get."

Ren clenched her jaw, refusing to give her the satisfaction of a reply, but it didn't matter. She could feel Kaelin's quiet amusement radiating off of her, and saints help her, a treacherous part of her wanted more.

"You know," Kaelin murmured. "*I* liked it."

Without so much as a glance, Kaelin slid her hand behind her, capturing Ren's with a fierce, deliberate grip. Without giving Ren the chance to pull away, Kaelin pressed a swift, mischievous kiss to the pads of Ren's fingers before letting her hand fall back to Ren's side. Ren drew in two shuddering breaths, trying to wrestle her treacherous pulse back under control. "I liked it more than I should have." She glanced over her shoulder, her eyes catching Ren's gaze. "And as good as my lips felt..." Her voice dropped into something sinful. "...my fingers can do *much* more."

A soft whimper left Ren's lips before she could stop it, her core becoming pure molten heat. "Kaelin – "

"You don't believe me?"

"I think," Ren ground out, trying to compose herself and her thoughts, "that you like hearing yourself talk."

Kaelin's grin widened. "Only when I'm making you think about all the ways I could show you."

Ren willed the cold air to strip away the raging heat that had consumed her body, but it didn't work. She could still feel Kaelin's laughter in the subtle shift of her back, the scrape of her teeth against her fingertips as she had kissed her hand, and she could still hear that promise in her voice. Saints help her, a dangerous part of Ren wanted to know exactly what those fingers could do. How they would feel exploring every secret part of her body and allowing Kaelin to touch her where no one else has.

Ren's pulse thundered. She told herself it was the cold, the ride, but the truth lay in Kaelin's words, still warm and wicked in her mind.

Kaelin's grin curved. She faced forward again, braid brushing Ren's arm. "Someday," she murmured, barely audible over the hoofbeats, "I'll show you."

Whisper's head snapped up. The mare's ears pinned flat, muscles coiling under them.

Kaelin's posture shifted instantly, that playful warmth vanishing. Her eyes flicked to the ridgeline ahead, then to the rocky slope on their right. "We're not alone," she stated.

Talen's voice carried from ahead, clipped. "Eyes forward, all of you."

Lucan swore under his breath. "Really? *Now*? Of all the gods-damned times – come on." He reached for his sword, the humor in his tone replaced by grim readiness.

Before Ren could respond, six figures stepped into the path ahead, bows in hand. Behind them, more emerged from the rocks—six, maybe seven—closing off their path.

"Bandits," Kaelin confirmed, her hand already dropping to the hilt at her hip. She cast a single glance over her shoulder at Ren, and in it was both command and promise. "Hold on."

Kaelin clicked her tongue, and Whisper lunged forward as the first arrow hissed past Ren's ear.

Talen's shout split the air, Cider rearing as Lucan charged with his horse, blade flashing. The clash of steel erupted ahead, the narrow pass turning into a funnel of chaos and shouting.

Kaelin's hips moved with precision, her body anchored and lethal in the saddle as she drove Whisper straight into the thick of the fray.

Kaelin leaned forward in the saddle as Whisper barreled forward. She veered Whisper hard to the left, slipping between two lunging attackers before either could land a blow.

Ren's eyes darted between the shapes closing in. Every instinct screamed at Ren to jump off Whisper so she could join the fight. Up ahead, Talen and Lucan were boxed in with three bandits circling them like wolves. Arrows arced toward them from the ridge, and more shapes spilled from the trees.

This was no random attack. The narrow pass was a trap carved into the mountain where bandits waited on the ridges and in the trees for unsuspecting travelers.

Kaelin's voice cut through the chaos. "*Ren!*"

Heat bloomed in Ren's palms before she even thought to stop it. The familiar thrum of magic pulsed up her arms, ready and waiting.

Ren said, "Give me an opening."

Whisper surged forward, weaving through the melee with impossible grace. Ren braced herself, lifting one hand from the saddle, and sent a ball of flame scorching into a cluster of attackers. The fire blossomed midair, scattering them with shouts of alarm. The heat seared her face, the recoil singing in her bones. She hadn't meant to let *that* much out.

"Good," Kaelin called over her shoulder. "Again!"

They spun through the chaos, Kaelin guiding Whisper in precise arcs while Ren hurled bursts of fire from above. The air stank of smoke and scorched leather, the roar of the flames matching the thunder of the hooves.

A bandit on horseback broke from the ridge, arrow notched, aimed straight for them. Kaelin saw him a second before Ren did.

Many riders might have faltered, hesitated, or pulled back to dodge.

But not Kaelin.

She met danger head-on, as if the thought of yielding had never once crossed her mind. With one fluid motion, she slipped a hand to her hip and unsheathed a small, curved blade, its edge catching the glint of sunlight as if hungry for blood. The steel looked almost delicate in her grip, but Ren knew better.

"Hold steady," Kaelin ordered, urging Whisper into a full charge.

Ren's fire caught the arrow midflight, turning it into a streak of burning ash. Kaelin was on the archer a heartbeat later. She knocked his bow aside before cleaving into him with her sword and shoved him clean out of the saddle.

They kept moving, Kaelin's commands short and clipped, Ren's magic answering each one. They didn't speak beyond that, but something unspoken clicked into place. Every turn Kaelin made was exactly where Ren needed to be to land her next strike; every burst of flame cleared Kaelin's path before her blade answered.

By the time the last bandit broke and fled into the rocks, the air was thick with smoke. Kaelin didn't look back at Ren right away, but when she did, there was something fierce in her smile.

Kaelin slowed Whisper to a trot, the mare's sides heaving from the fight. The clang of steel and the shouts of their companions gone. The only sound was Whisper's hooves crunching over the frozen ground.

Ren glanced over her shoulder, scanning the trail behind.

"We were driven farther from the others than I realized," Kaelin said.

Somehow, in the chaos, they'd broken free of the ambush, but the rest of the group hadn't. Now it was just the two of them, alone in the pass, with smoke curling from the battlefield behind and nothing but the silent, snow-swept mountains ahead.

Kaelin turned Whisper toward a narrow slope winding deeper into the range. "Looks like it's just us now," she said, meeting Ren's gaze. "You're safe with me."

Ren snorted. "I can take care of myself. What about the others? Are they okay?"

Kaelin slowed, glancing back with a sly grin. "Oh, I imagine they're more than fine. It's the bandits I'd worry for."

Then they rode on, the horizon swallowing the last echoes of the fight.

The narrow pass opened into a sweep of forest, the jagged peaks behind them fading.

Kaelin slowed Whisper to a walk, her voice carrying easily over the steady rhythm of hooves. "Not far now," Kaelin said. "The keep's just ahead, and there's a river nearby. We can rinse up there."

Ren could have wept at the thought. They were a mess, spattered with blood, streaked with grime, cloaked in the stink of exertion. Kaelin, though, had been deep in the fight, her blade work brutal and close. Ren stared hard at her back.

Saints, we actually made a formidable team.

The air shifted as they moved beneath the forest canopy. The earthy scent of moss and pine wrapped around them, muting the world into something quieter, calmer. Whisper's tread was nearly soundless over the bed of fallen needles and moss, but soon Ren caught the falling trickle of running water. Relief loosened the tension in her shoulders.

They reached the riverbank. Ren swung down first, boots sinking into the damp earth, and stepped aside as Kaelin dismounted with her usual easy grace.

Kaelin lingered by Whisper's head, stroking the mare's nose before leaning in close, her voice dropping to a murmur. "*Veyra'thiel, shaen draveth.*"

The cadence of the words was unfamiliar to Ren, yet they rolled from Kaelin's tongue with the intimacy of a secret. "What's that mean?" Ren asked.

Kaelin walked toward the water's edge, fingers brushing the hilt of her sword as if out of habit. "Heart-bound one, you fought fiercely. In Vaelaran, *veyra'thiel* is a fated partner. A soulmate. *Shaen draveth* is praise for a warrior after battle."

To anyone overhearing, it would have sounded like nothing more than a rider's affection for her mount. But Ren heard the undercurrent in it, the way *veyra'thiel* settled in the air like a vow, an unbreakable thread binding Whisper and Kaelin.

Before she could decide what to do with that thought, Kaelin's fingers were at the buckles of her armor, the leather straps whispering loose. Then she was peeling away layers, shrugging free of her tunic.

Ren jerked her head toward the trees, heat blooming in her cheeks. *Does she have no modesty at all?*

"I'll be over here," Ren called, though her voice betrayed her with a faint waver that made her want to cringe.

"Nonsense," came Kaelin's swift reply. "Come join me."

Ren's steps faltered. The memory of the fight flared bright in her chest – the two of them splitting from the others, striking hard and fast, moving as though they'd been fighting side by side for years. The rush of it still thrummed in her blood.

Something about that same pulse returned now, but hotter. Closer. Kaelin's eyes found Ren's. "I haven't fought like that in a long time," she said, voice low, almost reverent. "With someone who matched me blow for blow. You fight like someone who's bled for every inch she's earned. You see the strike before it lands, move like instinct itself. I see that, Ren Harper. Let it be known. I see *you*. I recognize you not as a human, not as lesser, but as a warrior."

Kaelin's gaze lingered on Ren, tracing the lines of her face, the way the firelight played across the curve of her armor. "Let me see you," she said softly. There was no command in it, only quiet sincerity. "*You*."

Ren's breath caught. For a heartbeat, she thought Kaelin meant her body, but then she saw the truth in her eyes, the plea to be seen in return.

"I want you to look upon me, too."

Ren had never had someone look at her bare skin before. Not with intent, and certainly not in a way that felt this intimate. She had no doubt Kaelin had her fair share of lovers, all well-versed in basking beneath that kind of gaze. But as their gazes locked, she realized this wasn't about marveling at one another's beauty.

No, it was something deeper.

They were basking in the silent acknowledgment of what it felt like to fight and survive together and to want more of that.

For a moment, Ren just looked at her. *Really* looked.

When they'd first met, she'd seen a spoiled fae princess draped in silks and lace, the kind who sipped wine and looked down on the world from behind crystal goblets. But that image had shattered somewhere between the clang of steel and the echo of Kaelin's command during the battle.

Now, Ren saw someone entirely different. A warrior, breathtaking in motion. The kind of fae female who could cut you down or save your life with the same steady hand.

And for one disarming heartbeat, Ren thought she'd never seen anything so arresting.

It was then and there that Ren decided she'd very much like to see *all* of Kaelin.

52

The cold water bit against Kaelin's skin.

The shock stripped away the heat of battle, leaving only clarity.

Kaelin kept her eyes on Ren's back, noting the way her shoulders tensed, how she stilled like someone teetering on the edge of a cliff. Ren's shoulders finally eased, and she turned.

A flicker of anticipation stirred in Kaelin's chest.

Ren didn't meet Kaelin's gaze. Her fingers went to the buckles of her armor, working them loose, the leather straps whispering secrets as they fell away. Then came the layers beneath – fabric peeling from her skin, revealing curves and lean lines of muscle.

Kaelin brushed damp strands from her face, afraid to blink and miss something. Ren's body struck her silent for the stories it told. Faint scars tracked along Ren's ribs and the curve of her hip, pale silver against warm skin – marks that were remnants of wounds from fighting where one wrong move could end you.

It made Kaelin's chest ache in a way she hadn't expected.

Who did this to you? Kaelin had seen warriors marked by battle before, but never one whose scars made her want to kneel.

Ren stepped toward the river and eased into the water, as though bracing for both the cold. Kaelin watched as if she could memorize every inch before Ren disappeared beneath the surface.

And for the first time in longer than she could remember, Kaelin had no words.

The river clasped Ren like a living being.

She hissed in a breath, arms crossing instinctively over her chest as if that could keep the cold at bay.

Amber eyes met violet eyes. Kaelin stood half-submerged, water beading along her collarbones. Strands of her hair clung to her cheeks.

Kaelin drifted closer, the water parting around her. Her gaze lingered on the smear of dried blood along Ren's shoulder, the faint bruise darkening near Ren's collarbone.

"Turn," Kaelin murmured.

Ren hesitated only a breath before obeying, the river whispering around them as she turned her back. She felt Kaelin's presence before her touch came, then fingers, warm despite the cold water, brushed her shoulder. Kaelin's thumb swept through a streak of blood, then traced the curve of Ren's neck where the pulse still beat fast from battle.

Kaelin dipped her hand beneath the surface, lifting water to pour over Ren's back. The chill made Ren tense, but Kaelin's touch soothed the tremor as she worked in deliberate circles, wiping away the remnants of dirt and blood. Her movements were reverent, like cleansing a blade after war.

"I didn't know whether to protect you or to just stand back and witness you. It was a sight to behold," Kaelin whispered.

Ren wanted to answer, but the words tangled in her throat.

Kaelin reached for Ren's hair next, gently combing her fingers through the strands, separating them where they'd knotted. A shiver rippled through Ren before she could stop it, goosebumps rising along her arms.

Ren couldn't remember the last time someone had touched her hair like this.

Kaelin's fingers moved again, the motion rhythmic and steady, and the world seemed to narrow to that single feeling of the slide of fingers through Ren's hair, the river murmuring around them, the steady thrum of her own heart answering Kaelin's nearness.

Ren half-turned, but Kaelin only smiled faintly, continuing to thread her fingers through. The gesture was so unexpectedly tender that it hollowed something inside Ren's chest. Kaelin leaned in, admitting softly, "I've never trusted anyone to watch my back the way I trust you."

Kaelin bent her head, lips brushing lightly over the curve of Ren's shoulder.

A warrior's benediction.

Kaelin closed the remaining space until the water between them no longer existed. Kaelin's gaze never wavered, the violet of her eyes deepening with arousal.

"Ren… may I?" Kaelin asked quietly, her hand still hovering in the water. "I don't want to touch you if it isn't what you want. It matters to me."

Slowly, almost imperceptibly, Ren gave a nod.

Kaelin's hand slid through the water until her fingers curled at Ren's hip with a reverence that made Ren's chest ache, and then Kaelin drew Ren forward, closing that last sliver of space.

The warm press of Kaelin's skin met hers, bare from shoulder to thigh beneath the water, and Ren's heart clenched in something dangerously close to surrender. She smelled the faint trace of lavender and frosted-kissed grapefruit tangled in Kaelin's damp hair, felt the steady rise and fall of Kaelin's breath against her chest.

Kaelin tilted her head, and the world narrowed to her violet eyes, the single bead of water sliding down her temple.

Kaelin's mouth brushed Ren's, light and inquisitive.

The second press of Kaelin's lips was surer, deeper. Her tongue brushed gently against Ren's slightly parted lips in a silent request for *more*, as the hand at Ren's hip tightened. Ren's own fingers found their way to Kaelin's nape then, holding her there as if she might vanish.

Somewhere in the distance, thunder boomed.

If that was the sign from the gods to stop, Ren thought, *then let the gods be damned.*

They didn't break. Didn't breathe, except into each other, the taste of river and heat tangling between them. Kaelin's other hand skimmed Ren's spine. The kiss deepened until Ren wasn't sure if the ache in her chest was from lack of air or the startling truth that she didn't want this to end.

Finally, they parted just enough for Ren to gasp, her lips tingling from the press of Kaelin's searing mouth. Kaelin's lidded eyes held Ren's gaze with a soft hunger. Kaelin's fingers trailed lightly up Ren's back, then curved around to her side, brushing the underside of her breast. The touch was feather-soft, sending another shiver through Ren.

Ren arched into Kaelin's touch instinctively, her own hands sliding over Kaelin's wet skin, tracing the delicate points of her ears before dipping to her shoulders. Kaelin smiled against Ren's lips, a supple kiss landing there before moving to Ren's jaw, then down the column of her throat. Each kiss lingered, as if Kaelin meant to memorize all the different planes of Ren's skin through touch alone.

Emboldened, Kaelin's hand cupped Ren's breast fully, thumb circling the nipple in slow, lazy spirals. Ren drew in a breath, the sensation blooming into a quiet heat low in her belly. Ren automatically mirrored the touch, her palm gliding over one of Kaelin's lush, rounded breasts, the generous flesh spilling slightly over her fingers. Ren teased the hardened peak with gentle pinches that drew a soft moan from Kaelin. Their bodies pressed closer in the shallow current, legs tangling as the water lapped at their thighs.

Kaelin's kisses trailed lower, nipping lightly at Ren's collarbone before returning to capture Ren's mouth again. Kaelin's free hand slid down Ren's spine, pulling her closer until their breasts mashed together, as if drawn by an unbreakable magnetic pull. They couldn't bear even a moment's separation, palms gliding over hips, thighs, and the curve of asses, squeezing and caressing with urgent tenderness that spoke of their insatiable hunger for one another. Their bodies grinded instinctively as passion overtook them, each caress fueling the fire that made parting impossible.

Ren's free hand ventured downward, skimming Kaelin's hip. Kaelin caught it gently, guiding it back up. "Let me," Kaelin whispered, her voice a husky murmur against Ren's ear.

With that, Kaelin's hand slipped from Ren's breast, trailing over her ribs, her stomach, until it reached the soft mound between Ren's legs. The touch there was even gentler, fingers parting Ren's folds with care, stroking the entrance without urgency. Ren whimpered into the kiss, her hips shifting forward as Kaelin's middle finger circled her clit in feather-light loops, building a slow ache that made Ren's thighs tremble.

They kissed languidly, tongues brushing in supple dances, while Kaelin's finger dipped inside Ren, shallow at first, then deeper with each gentle thrust. Ren's walls clenched around the intrusion, the warmth of it contrasting with the cool water. Kaelin's other hand returned to Ren's nipple, pinching softly in time with her fingering, the dual sensations weaving a tender rhythm.

Ren's breaths came faster, ragged against Kaelin's lips, her body coiling tighter as Kaelin's finger curled inside her, pressing against a sensitive spot that drew any ounce of sanity from Ren. The touches remained soft, insistent but never rough, coaxing Ren toward the edge with patient yet steady strokes. Kaelin kissed her neck, her shoulder, murmuring encouragements in a lilting tone that nearly drove Ren over the edge.

"Ren," Kaelin breathed against Ren's flushed skin, her voice husky, lips grazing the pulse point at Ren's throat. "You unraveled me completely. I feel like I've lost every shred of sanity just from touching you like this. You are driving me mad with want." Her finger thrust deeper, curling again to stroke that inner spot, while her thumb resumed its light circles over Ren's clit.

Ren gasped, her hands clutching at Kaelin's shoulders, nails digging in just enough to leave faint marks on the fae's pale skin.

"I can't get enough," Kaelin confessed, her golden hair falling wet over her face as she lifted her head to capture Ren's gaze, eyes dark with passion. "You're making me ache everywhere, Ren; my mind's spinning, all I can think about is feeling you come undone around my fingers, hearing you moan my name." She nipped at Ren's lower lip, then soothed it with a slow lick, her finger plunging steadily now, the wet sounds of her movements mingling with their shared breaths.

Ren's hips bucked involuntarily, chasing the building pleasure, her walls clenching harder around Kaelin's invading digit as Kaelin added a second finger, stretching her gently, scissoring them to rub against her walls from different angles. Kaelin's mouth returned to Ren's breast, tongue flicking the nipple before sucking it in with soft pulls, the suction syncing with the curl of her fingers inside. The combined menstruations pushed Ren closer, heat blooming deep in her core.

Kaelin pulled back just enough to whisper fiercely, "Let go for me. I've gone insane for you, and I need to feel you shatter." Her words were a heated plea as she quickened the pace ever so slightly, fingers thrusting with insistent tenderness, thumb pressing firmer on the swollen clit. Ren's whimpers turned to cries, her back arching as her orgasm crested, waves of release pulsing through her, walls fluttering and squeezing Kaelin's fingers in rhythmic contractions. Ren rode out the climax, body shuddering in Kaelin's embrace.

Kaelin held her through it, slowing her strokes to soft caresses, withdrawing her fingers only when the tremors faded. She kissed Ren's forehead, her cheeks.

They stayed entwined, foreheads together, breaths syncing with the lapping of the water.

By the time Kaelin and Ren reached the keep, the rain came down in sheets.

The stars had long since vanished behind a sweep of black clouds that rolled over the mountains, swift as a roaring tide.

They both dismounted and Kaelin guided Whisper to a small, wooden stable to the right of the keep. Ren opened a gate opening into the narrow stall beside Cider who was already feasting on a bundle of hay. They worked in sync to unbuckle Whisper's saddle, and Kaelin lifted it onto the wall rack with practiced ease. Ren tossed fresh hay into Whisper's trough and brushed her fingers along the mare's nose. To her surprise, Whisper leaned into the touch.

When Ren glanced back only to find Kaelin watching her, a faint smile lingering on her face. Kaelin gave Whisper one last pat along the neck. "Don't worry," she murmured to the mare. "I like her, too."

Ren's cheeks flared hot, and she spun away before Kaelin could see it. "Let's go before I freeze my tits off," she muttered, stomping back into the rain.

The keep's great wooden door groaned under Kaelin's shove, swinging open with a *bang*. When Ren stepped across the threshold, warmth wrapped around her like a thick blanket.

The stone walls glowed in the golden light of a great hearth, where a spit turned slowly, roasting meat that sent a rich, mouthwatering scent curling through the air. Somewhere to the side, in a small arched alcove, another fire cradled a round loaf of bread.

Flickering candlelight painted soft halos across the room, glinting off brass goblets and the intricate carvings etched into the mantle. Heavy green curtains framed tall windows, their fabric embroidered with gold thread. A wreath of evergreen hung above the hearth, filling the air with a faint pine scent that mingled with roasted herbs and smoke.

A long table stood near the fire, cluttered with the remnants of a late meal – half-drained mugs, a bowl of glistening apples, a knife buried halfway through a wheel of cheese. Beside it, a small cauldron simmered lazily, releasing curls of fragrant steam that smelled faintly of spice and honey. A few discarded boots and a fur-lined cloak lay strewn near a richly upholstered chair.

The whole chamber breathed warmth and life, a lived-in sort of magic that softened the hard edges of stone.

Ren shrugged off her dripping furs, hanging them on an iron hook by the door.

A male fae lounged near the fire, cheeks flushed from drink, fingers coaxing a bright, lilting tune from his fiddle. Talen and Lucan sat at a small table in the corner, deep in conversation over a card game, mugs of amber ale within easy reach.

"Glad you two could make it," Talen greeted without looking up, his voice warm despite the distraction of his hand. "I take it the rest of those bandits were dealt with?"

"Of course, dear brother." Kaelin's reply was smooth and punctuated by the briefest brush of her fingers at the small of Ren's back. The touch sent a quick, traitorous jolt up Ren's spine. "Ren and I made quite the team today. A force to be reckoned with."

Ren laughed. "I'd say we make a dangerous pair. The world should probably be warned."

"I feel bad for the other guy," Lucan drawled, eyeing his cards. "But I'll wager it felt good to let loose."

Talen gave a low whistle, still grinning at his hand. "They chose the wrong group to mess with. Ren, come here. I'll teach you how to play."

Ren stepped toward the table. Out of the corner of her eye, she saw Kaelin already moving toward the sideboard, selecting a bottle of deep red wine. The table was littered with cards, some stacked neatly, others fanned in messy arcs. Lucan's scowl suggested he wasn't having much luck; Talen, by contrast, radiated the smug contentment of a man who was several hands ahead.

"We draw seven to start," Talen explained, sliding a few cards across the table toward her. "Your goal is simple: *three of one kind, four of another*. But don't get too comfortable; things can turn on you fast. Each turn, you draw one. You can either keep it or toss it. Your choice."

He demonstrated, drawing a card, then tucking it into his hand with an infuriatingly pleased smirk.

Lucan muttered into his ale, "Talen's known for cheating. Most folk call him the *weasel*."

"And Lucan is a sore loser who wears his tells like a parade banner," Talen said lightly.

Lucan shot him a glare.

Kaelin gravitated to Ren's side, her eyes alight with a hunger that spoke of anything but sustenance. Ren shivered at the memory of what had occurred in the river not too long ago —the feel of Kalein's soft lips on hers, the way Kaelin's hands had felt on her bare skin as they had explored her.

Kaelin reached up and toyed with a loose strand of Ren's hair. She twined it between her fingers, eyes fixed on the game unfolding across the table where Lucan and Talen played cards. Her movements were casual, unthinking, and yet every slow curl of her fingers through that strand made Ren's pulse stutter.

If Kaelin noticed, she gave no sign. She only hummed softly under her breath, as though the world beyond that lock of hair were far less interesting than the quiet space they shared.

Lucan snapped something at Talen, no doubt having to do with their game of cards, breaking the spell.

Ren looked back over at Kaelin, a glass of deep crimson wine balanced between elegant fingers. Kaelin extended it wordlessly, and Ren accepted with a murmur of thanks. Kaelin's gaze lingering a heartbeat longer than necessary before she tipped back her own glass to take a deep drink.

Talen and Lucan played with the ruthless energy of fae males convinced victory was a matter of honor. Talen dealt cards with a flick and a flourish, Lucan responding with narrowed eyes and the twitch of his jaw. In the end, luck favored Lucan. He slammed his hand down with a victorious grin, and Talen groaned like a man betrayed before stalking off for more ale.

Ren slipped into his empty seat as Lucan reshuffled the deck. She watched carefully, learning the rhythm of the game—the push and pull between risk and reward. It was disarmingly simple, but addictive in a way that reminded her of dice games played in the back alleys and taverns during her pit-fighting days. They sparred silently over the table, Lucan's knee bouncing under the wood, his fingers tapping in anticipation.

And just as he smiled in triumph, Kaelin's voice slipped in. "Think again."

Ren laid down her hand with a grin, revealing three matching cards and another four to seal the win.

Lucan groaned into his mug.

"Looks like you need practice," Talen called from across the room. "Losing to a beginner? Tragic."

"I was going easy on her," Lucan shot back.

Ren smirked. "Let's go again."

They did, again and again. Lucan's every twitch gave him away, from the way he drummed his fingers when he drew well to the tight set of his jaw when he didn't. Lady Luck seemed to favor Ren tonight, and she racked up victory after victory until Lucan threw up his hands, muttering about ale as he stomped toward the kitchen.

Talen took his seat. He was harder to read. They played until the roasted meat was carved and bread was torn into steaming hunks, the scents mingling with the faint bite of wine in Ren's glass. Outside, thunder rolled like a slow drumbeat against the keep's thick stone walls, rain hammering the shutters in bursts.

And then the time came to face Kaelin. Kaelin leaned back in her chair with effortless poise, one hand resting against her chin, the other idly turning a card between slender fingers. She was the toughest opponent Ren had ever faced because her face gave nothing away. Her features were carved into composure, her gaze lethal, lips curved just enough to suggest she was always half a step ahead.

Every glance across the table felt like a match being struck. The brush of Kaelin's fingers on her cards, the tilt of her mouth when Ren laid one down, the heat in her eyes when Ren dared to meet her gaze—each move built a current between them, taut and impossible to ignore.

Ren shifted in her seat. It shouldn't have felt so intimate, this game of chance and wit, but it did. Every hand was a dare. Every round, a quiet battle threaded with something unspoken.

And then, finally, Ren set down her last card.

A winning hand.

For the first time, Kaelin's mask cracked. Her lips peeled back just slightly, baring the faintest edge of teeth.

She did *not* like to lose.

Ren smirked despite herself, feeling the thrill of victory mingle with the sharper thrill of having bested Kaelin.

One by one, the group drifted away, some to their chambers, others to quiet corners with their drink.

Ren lingered until her limbs began to ache with exhaustion, the wine's flush softening into a heavy pull toward sleep. Talen had told her she could take one of the small rooms near the attic, and she had every intention of finding it and sleeping until sunrise.

She padded down the dim corridor, her boots whispering against worn rugs. The storm outside seemed louder here, the wind howling through unseen gaps in the stone. She was almost to the narrow staircase that led upward when—

"Going somewhere?"

Kaelin stepped from a doorway, blocking Ren's path with an easy confidence that only she could master. Her hair spilled loose over her shoulders, catching the torchlight like strands of molten gold.

Ren opened her mouth to answer, but Kaelin reached for her hand. "You don't want the attic," Kaelin said softly, her smile carrying both mischief and something darker beneath. "It's cold and very lonely."

Ren sucked in a breath as every nerve ending came to life. She'd let herself get drawn into the card game, had used it as a distraction from the relentless ache of need that had thrummed straight to her core ever since they left that river. But now, with Kaelin standing before her, it was becoming increasingly hard to ignore. Ren forced herself to breathe, that stubborn part of her unwilling to give Kaelin the satisfaction of knowing just how deeply she affected her. She buried the heat of desire simmering beneath her skin and schooled her features into a mask of cool indifference.

Ren arched an eyebrow. "And I suppose you have a better suggestion?"

Kaelin's thumb brushed slowly over her knuckles. "Always. It's one of my more dangerous talents."

Ren could have protested. She could have insisted on the attic, on her independence, on keeping whatever this was in the realm of teasing and tension.

But she didn't.

Kaelin tugged gently, leading her down the hall in the opposite direction and away from the narrow stairs, toward the heavier oak doors at the keep's heart. Ren's pulse betrayed her, with every step quickening the farther they went.

Ren had expected Kaelin's chambers to flaunt extravagance, but Ren was surprised when the oak door opened into something far more simple.

The space was vast, with high stone walls. The soft glow of the hearth fire cast a warm, flickering light across the rustic interior of the bedroom. A wide bed stood in the center, draped in plain wool, a fur thrown carelessly at the foot. The furniture was sparse but well-crafted – a writing desk, a sturdy wardrobe, and a low chest reinforced with iron bands.

Ren's gaze lingered on the details. A pressed flower lay between the open pages of a book left on the desk, its petals fragile but carefully preserved. A half-finished sketch, done in quick, precise strokes, revealed a mountain range Ren had glimpsed on the journey here. And tucked beside the bed, as if Kaelin hadn't meant for anyone to notice, perched a small carved horse, its edges smoothed by years of touch.

The austerity was real, but the softness whispered between the cracks, revealing pieces of someone who kept fragments of beauty close.

The room revealed so little of Kaelin and somehow everything.

Kaelin reclined against a mound of pillows, her long frame stretched out with feline ease. Ren's gaze wandered over Kaelin, as if studying her form might offer some glimpse into the intricate maze of her mind. Ren longed to be the one to unravel Kaelin's secrets, to understand her in the way no one else did. Those thoughts lingered in Ren's mind as her gaze drifted back to Kaelin's face, curious to see what expression she wore, what emotions might be reflected in her eyes.

Kaelin's eyes remained fixed on Ren.

It wasn't a simple glance. The weight of Kaelin's gaze slid over Ren, tracing from her boots still damp with mud and dirt to the faint line of Ren's jaw.

Kaelin was stripping her bare without lifting a hand.

Heat pooled low in Ren's stomach. She should move, say something, do something, but her body betrayed her, rooting her to the stone floor. She had survived blades, blood, and bandits without flinching, yet one look from Kaelin made her pulse roar like a war drum.

Kaelin's lips curved, as if she knew the effect she had on Ren. "You're staring."

Ren's jaw clenched. She tore her eyes away, but the damage was already done. She'd stepped into Kaelin's chambers expecting a place to sleep for the night.

Instead, she found herself standing at the edge of something far more dangerous.

And far more alluring.

Kaelin lifted one hand from where it rested against the pillows and curled a single finger, beckoning. Ren's body obeyed before her mind caught up. Each step forward felt weighted, her mouth dry, her pulse betraying her calm façade.

"Closer," Kaelin murmured. Her eyes never left Ren's as she tipped her chin. "And take off those clothes. I've no interest in sharing a bed with someone wrapped in dirty linen."

Ren's hands trembled as she worked the clasps, fumbling with the buckles of her armor and the sweat-damp linen beneath. The sound of her own uneven breathing filled the quiet. Her mind slipped back to the river, recalling the cool water lapping against her skin, the rush of adrenaline from the fight still coursing through her veins. When Kaelin's lips had met hers there, it had been wild and reckless, but there had been something almost anchoring in it, too.

But now, there was no water to bear Ren's weight. Every brush of Kaelin's eyes on her and every tremor in Ren's own hands felt more real.

It was no longer just the heat of battle carrying them; this was a choice.

Kaelin noticed Ren's trembling hands. She leaned forward from her nest of pillows. "What's wrong?"

Ren's fingers stilled. Her chest rose and fell once, twice, before she forced the words out, unexpected nervousness caught in her throat. "I've never done this before," she admitted, motioning to the bed and space between them. "With anyone."

Silence stretched.

Then Kaelin shuffled closer. She reached out, her fingers brushing against the inside of Ren's wrist. Her eyes held Ren's steadily. Ren didn't move. Her gaze drifted to the door, where she could still walk through, if she had any sense left. Go back to the room where she was meant to sleep and to pretend none of this mattered.

It shouldn't happen.

And yet, every part of Ren ached to stay.

Kaelin shuffled closer. Her fingers reached up and caught Ren's chin, tilting her face to look at her, *demanding* her attention.

Kaelin's thumb traced the line of Ren's jaw before her lips brushed hers. Then a subtle tug at Ren's waist guided her closer. Ren resisted for a heartbeat, caught between sense and longing, before surrendering to the pull.

Kaelin eased back, drawing Ren with her until Ren was braced above her, caught between Kaelin's legs. Heat bled through the narrow space between them, every inch that separated them charged. Kaelin's hand trailed from Ren's chin to an auburn strand that had fallen loose, brushing it behind her ear.

Kaelin leaned in, her lips brushing the shell of her ear. "Ren, darling, it would be my honor to be the first to have a taste of you. I want to give you something to make those stubborn toes of yours curl until you forget every scar, every chain, every damned thing that ever tried to break you."

Heat rolled through Ren like wildfire, fierce and consuming. Her hands twitched helplessly at her sides, aching to touch, to anchor.

When Kaelin's lips finally found hers, the kiss was no longer gentle; it was claiming.

"Ren, darling. You tremble so sweetly when you try to resist."

Ren's breath caught. Heat rose to her cheeks before she could stop it, a flush that betrayed every ounce of composure she clung to. Kaelin's gaze caught it instantly, and Ren had to look away, her eyes dropping to the hollow of Kaelin's throat just to steady herself.

That was all the permission Kaelin needed.

In a swift, effortless motion, Kaelin flipped them, reversing their positions before Ren could even draw breath. The world tilted, and then Kaelin was above Ren, Kaelin's lithe frame pressing flush against her own.

Kaelin's thumb trailed down the center of Ren's throat, feeling the frantic pulse beneath. "Don't look away," she whispered. "You're mine until I say otherwise."

Kaelin kissed Ren, each slow coax of her tongue weaving them into a rhythm all their own.

When Ren answered with equal hunger, Kaelin felt her chest flutter, her pulse falter, undone by the ache of it.

Gods, she had been eyeing Ren all evening, letting her gaze stray across the room when she was certain no one would notice, counting down the seconds until she could have this moment, until she could have *her*.

And now, with Ren warm and trembling in her arms, Kaelin felt like the luckiest damn fool in all of Lytharien.

Sanity slipped through Kaelin's fingers, but she didn't care. In Ren's kiss, in the press of her lips and the heat of her body, Kaelin found something worth the unraveling. If this was madness, she welcomed it like air, like the one thing she could no longer live without.

Kaelin only broke away to wander, her mouth brushing along Ren's jaw before trailing down the line of her throat. Each press of her lips was punctuated with a teasing flick of her tongue, a lingering taste. Then came the gentle scrape of teeth, a nip at the hollow of Ren's neck that made Ren shiver in the most delicious way.

All the while, Kaelin's hands moved with unhurried purpose, easing the rest of Ren's clothes away. Where her fingers left, her lips followed with fluttering kisses replacing touch, trailing reverence over newly bared skin.

Kaelin lingered, kissing and nipping as though she meant to memorize every fragile beat of Ren's pulse beneath her skin. Kaelin took her time worshipping Ren's body, tracing the swell of her breasts with feather-light touches before capturing one rosy nipple between her lips. She swirled her tongue around the bud, drawing a breathy groan from Ren's lips.

Kaelin smiled against Ren's skin, trailing open-mouthed kisses down her trembling stomach. She settled between Ren's thighs, breathing in the intoxicating scent of her arousal. Ren flushed deeply, but she didn't protest as Kaelin eased her legs further apart.

"Gorgeous, stunning," Kaelin murmured appreciatively, her fingers skimming over Ren's inner thighs. "I bet you taste divine." She leaned in and dragged her tongue along Ren's slick folds, groaning at the sweet, musky flavor that burst across her senses. Ren bucked against her mouth, crying out as Kaelin circled her clit with the tip of her tongue.

"Please," Ren whimpered, her fingers tangling in Kaelin's silken blonde hair.

Kaelin smiled wickedly against Ren's skin, not ceasing her ministrations. "More?" she purred, circling Ren's swollen clit with the tip of her tongue. "You want more of... *this*?" She sucked the sensitive bud into her mouth, flicking it rapidly with the flat of her tongue.

"Kaelin!" Ren panted, her hips rolling shamelessly against Kaelin's face as Kaelin devoured her. Kaelin hummed in approval, doubling her efforts as she lapped at Ren's dripping core.

Ren was so responsive, so incredibly tight and hot and wet. It made Kaelin ache to feel her fluttering around something thicker than a tongue, perhaps her fingers, but she forced herself to focus on driving Ren wild first. She wanted Ren to remember this night for the rest of her life – to remember how good it felt to be worshipped like a goddess.

Kaelin's tongue plunged deeper into Ren's pussy, lapping in firm, steady strokes, while her lips sealed around her swollen clit, sucking with rhythmic pulls. Ren's thighs quivered, clamping around Kaelin's head, her fingers tangling in Kaelin's blonde hair, pulling her closer as if she could never get enough.

"That's it, my love," Kaelin murmured against Ren's skin, her voice vibrating through the sensitive flesh. She pulled back just enough to speak, her breath hot on Ren's exposed core, eyes locking onto Ren's flushed face. "Cry out for me, Ren. I want every soul in this keep to hear you, to know you're mine. Scream my name so they understand who owns this perfect body, who worships it like the treasure it is."

Ren bit hard on her lower lip, a whimper escaping. At the tantalizing sight, Kaelin growled, wanting nothing more than to bite Ren's plump, lower lip. But Ren arched her back, pushing her pussy harder against Kaelin's mouth, Kaelin's encouragement making her bolder. *Good girl.* Kaelin eagerly dove back in, tongue flicking rapidly over her clit before delving inside again, lapping up the fresh gush of arousal that coated her chin. Her hands gripped Ren's ass, fingers digging into the soft cheeks to spread her wider, exposing every single inch for Kaelin's devoted attention.

"Kaelin!" Ren cried out, her voice echoing off the stone walls of the chamber, louder than before, the sound raw and unrestrained. Kaelin's praise had unlocked her, and now she let the moans pour free, each one building in volume as Kaelin's mouth worked relentlessly, sucking, licking, *thrusting.* Ren's breasts heaved with every gasp, nipples hard and aching, begging for touch, but Kaelin was focused lower, worshipping the core that clenched and dripped under her tongue.

Kaelin growled in satisfaction, possessiveness surging through her like fire. "Louder, Ren. You're mine to devour, mine to pleasure until you shatter." She sucked harder on Ren's clit, teeth grazing it lightly in a teasing nip, then soothed with broad, flat laps of her tongue. One hand slid up Ren's thigh, fingers joining, two slipping inside Ren's tight heat and curling to stroke the spot that made Ren's walls flutter wildly.

Ren's cries grew desperate, filling the room with her pleasure. "Kaelin! Oh gods, yes—*yours*, all yours!" Her hips bucked frantically, grinding against Kaelin's face and fingers, the dual penetration of Kaelin's tongue on her clit and Kaelin's digits pumping deep, pushing her toward the brink. Kaelin's free hand roamed upward, finally claiming a breast, pinching the nipple sharply before rolling it in firm circles, the pain-pleasure mix drawing an even louder scream from Ren's lips.

Kaelin didn't relent, fingers thrusting faster, tongue swirling without mercy, her own arousal throbbing between her legs at the sight and sounds of Ren unraveling. "Come for me now, Ren darling. Let me hear how I claim you, how your pussy weeps for *my* tongue." Ren's body tensed, thighs shaking violently as the orgasm crashed over her, her pussy clenching around Kaelin's fingers in powerful spasms. Ren came undone with a choked scream, her back arching off the bed as she shuddered through her release.

Kaelin drank down every trembling breath of Ren's release, her touch softening, coaxing, until Ren sagged back into the sheets, flushed and breathless. Gentle as a tide receding, Kaelin eased Ren down from the dizzying heights, her lips pressing feather-light kisses along Ren's trembling thighs and stomach as she crawled her way back up.

"Was that... was that okay?" Ren's voice was shy, almost small, her amber eyes luminous in the low firelight, shining with the glow of release and an edge of vulnerability.

Kaelin grinned against her lips, her gaze warm. She pressed another lingering kiss there before pulling back just enough to murmur, "It was more than okay, darling. You truly are exquisite."

Ren flushed crimson at the praise, biting her lip to hide her smile. Kaelin's breath caught. Saints, she was beautiful like this – cheeks rosy with arousal, eyes darting as though she could conceal the effect Kaelin had on her.

The sight made Kaelin's chest tighten, an ache she hadn't anticipated.

Kaelin brushed a stray curl from Ren's cheek. Her hand lingered, fingertips grazing the warmth of that flush, marveling at how vivid it looked against her skin. So warm and alive. So untouchably human.

And in that instant, Kaelin knew she'd raze the world itself before she'd ever let its cruelty touch Ren again.

All too soon, exhaustion tugged at Ren's limbs, her eyes growing heavier with each steady beat of Kaelin's heart beneath her cheek.

She let herself curl into the warmth of Kaelin's body, the silk of Kaelin's hair tickling her temple, her arm draped over Ren with a possessiveness that felt safe.

Outside, the storm lingered, rain pattering against the stone keep, thunder grumbling low and distant. But within Kaelin's embrace, the world felt still.

Ren's last thought before sleep claimed her was that she'd never felt so utterly undone yet so wholly at peace. And then she surrendered to slumber, lulled by the steady rhythm of Kaelin's breathing and the rain's soft hymn beyond the walls.

55

From this path to the top of the mountain, the stone keep looked small and fragile against the immensity of the mountain peaks.

Ren stopped to draw in the view and to catch her breath. The air was thinning with every step higher, her lungs burning with exertion. Ahead, Lucan's steady stride didn't falter, his broad shoulders cutting a path through the cold.

Then came a vicious gust barreling through the vale. It caught Ren full force, nearly knocking her off her feet. She cursed under her breath, fumbling for balance.

Lucan half-turned, one brow lifting in amusement. "The wind is stronger up here," he said over his shoulder.

Before Ren could snap back, a gruff, rasping, and entirely unwelcome voice barked, "And you two call yourselves soldiers? *Pathetic.* They're training a bunch of ninnies nowadays. When I was a young soldier, I went headfirst into challenges, not stumbling around like milk-fed kittens in a breeze."

Ren glared at the leather pouch in her hand. According to Zakhar, the thing had once belonged to an ancient Vaelaran drill sergeant whose stubbornness had apparently outlasted even his flesh. Now he lived on as a cantankerous wisp bound to a pouch, tasked with "encouraging" anyone who carried it. Unfortunately, "encouragement" translated to endless insults, unsolicited advice, and occasional attempts at marching cadence.

Lucan glanced back, lips twitching as though he were suppressing a laugh. Ren tightened her grip on the pouch and muttered, "If I throw you into a snowbank, will you finally shut up?"

The pouch sputtered indignantly. "You'll address me as *sir*, you insolent whelp. And I'll not be telling you my name. That is a privilege that must be earned."

"Fine. *Sir Pain-in-the-Ass*, then."

Lucan chuckled under his breath as Ren caught up to him. Soon enough, with the climb growing steeper and the air thinner, the game became a welcome distraction.

"If he won't give us his name," Lucan proposed with a sly grin, "let's guess. He looks like a... Percey."

Ren snorted. "Percey? Too noble. He's more of a Bert. Or maybe... Clive."

The pouch vibrated with indignation. "How *dare* you! I'd sooner leap into a beast's maw than answer to Clive!"

Ren smirked. "So not Clive, then. Maybe... Buttercup?"

Lucan nearly choked on a laugh, his shoulders shaking as he pressed forward up the icy slope. The pouch wailed in outrage, cursing them both and insisting he'd once commanded a hundred men in battle.

"James?" Lucan guessed.

"Andrew?" Ren prodded.

"Bah!" the pouch barked. "The youth these days toss names around like dice in a tavern. No respect, no gravity. In my day, a name carried honor, weight, dignity. Now it's all James and Andrew, as if titles were something to be plucked from a tree! A disgrace, that's what it is. No one respects authority, *no one respects –* "

But Ren and Lucan had both fallen quiet.

The rant dimmed into a faint drone at the edge of her awareness as the path crested suddenly, and before them the vale stretched wide, carved between the ribs of the mountain. The wind howled, tearing at their cloaks, and far, far below, the world spread out in dizzying swathes of white and gray.

Ren felt like she was standing on top of the world. The peaks pierced the clouds like blades, the land below a toy map – distant and unreal.

Ren's stomach dropped at the sheer height, and regret rushed in. Why had she agreed to this climb? Her knuckles whitened on the pouch's strap, every instinct screaming to back away from the edge.

Lucan glanced at her, brow raised. "You've gone pale."

Ren forced a laugh that sounded more like a choke. "Turns out," she said, voice tight, "I'm not much of a fan of looking down."

The pouch cackled. "Afraid of a little drop! When I was alive, I dangled from cliffs by my fingertips for *sport*!"

"Do you know of a spell to shut him up?" Ren asked Lucan.

"I wish I did."

The pouch fell silent for the first time since they'd started climbing. Ren almost sighed in relief until it muttered, voice darkened with irritation. "There it is again… a voice. Lovely, lilting, insufferable. Singing like a thrush in springtime. How it *irks* me."

"What voice?" Ren asked.

"Don't play coy, girl. I hear it plain as daylight. She hums in the back of my skull, soft as silk. I loathe it. Don't get me started on the bells."

Lucan and Ren exchanged glances but said nothing, and the pouch's grumbling dwindled to incoherent curses as the wind carried them down into the vale. The descent was trickier than the climb up. The path narrowed, the ground pitching into steep, uneven stone. Ren placed each step with care, boots crunching on frost, her breath shallow as the drop loomed to her left. Lucan walked ahead but slowed his pace.

After a while, Ren asked, "Why'd you come with me? You could've let someone else deal with Zakhar's errand."

"I've never been this far north. I thought I'd see it for myself. My family's lands are to the east of Vaelaran. Rolling hills, good pasture, vineyards as far as you can see. That's the world I grew up in. I've spent little time in the north."

Ren studied him as they walked, noting how his words carried both pride and distance, as though speaking of a place that belonged to him but no longer felt like his.

Behind them, the pouch muttered sourly, "Blasted singing woman, following me still."

Then, Lucan said quietly, "I also came because you never ask for help, and I thought maybe you'd like someone to stand with you. I've seen good soldiers break when they're left to carry everything alone. With all the vineyards and gentle hills back home, things are comfortable, safe. I was raised to believe duty was a thing you could manage from a chair at a table." He glanced back at Ren. "But out here, I'm learning it's different. It's walking beside people who don't expect you to. It's showing up." Then his lips tugged a little higher, amusement flickering in his eyes. "Besides, you're far too stubborn to ever ask for help. I thought I'd save us both the trouble."

Ren adjusted her grip on the pouch. "Remind me again why we didn't take the horses? Seems to me their footing might be better than mine right now."

"After the journey to even get here? This path would break them. Too steep, too narrow. They'd fight the incline every step, and by the time we reached the vale, they'd be spent or worse, injured." He turned forward again, voice carrying easily over the stillness. "Besides," he added dryly, "I'd rather not explain to Kaelin why her favorite mare tumbled off a cliff because you thought it might keep your boots steadier."

Ren scowled at his back, muttering, "Would've at least cushioned my fall."

The pouch broke the silence with a snort. "Soft as butter, the lot of you. I'll take honesty when it's earned, not dressed up in sentimental nonsense."

Ren shot it a glare, but her gaze lingered on Lucan's broad back as they pressed onward.

Lucan said, "My father used to sneer at the west, call it barren, useless. He said these lands weren't worth a damn because they didn't yield coin." He paused as the wind tore past them, flinging snow like shards of glass. Lucan tilted his head back, inhaling deeply, as if the cold itself carried something worth keeping. "But standing here...There's a beauty in it. A strength that doesn't bow to anyone's will. My father was wrong."

Ren studied him as he walked ahead, shoulders squared against the wind, and for the first time, she saw not just a soldier beside her but a male fae trying to unlearn the weight of his bloodline.

Behind them, the pouch huffed sourly. "Bah. Poetic drivel. Next, you'll be kissing the rocks and whispering to the trees."

They continued their descent for what felt like an eternity. The path narrowed, twisting along the mountainside, and more than once Ren's boots slid against the icy stone, forcing her to steady herself with a curse.

As her gaze swept the vast sweep of white, she realized not even trees dared to grow here. They had climbed above the treeline and into a realm claimed only by stone, snow, and sky.

"Should be almost there," Ren muttered, teeth chattering despite her effort to sound casual. Lucan didn't answer, just pressed forward, his steady tread crunching over the frost.

Then, without warning, the wind died.

The sudden stillness made Ren's breath sound too loud. For the first time since their trek, sunlight broke through the smothering gray above, spilling in golden shafts that danced over the snow. It was dazzling; shards of light struck the white crust until the mountains glimmered like a sea of diamonds.

Ren slowed, struck with the eerie awareness that she was standing in a place few mortals had ever reached. She should have felt wonder. Instead, a prickle crawled across her neck.

That's when she heard the faintest chiming of bells.

At first, she thought her ears were betraying her. But the sound grew clearer, closer, the delicate jingle carrying like a lullaby through the still air.

The pouch twitched against her side, then growled, "There it is again! That cursed woman's voice. Sweet as honey, *vile as rot*. Do you hear it, girl? Singing, always singing..."

Lucan had slowed to a stop. His broad back was stiff, his head tilted as though he too were listening. And then, so low she almost missed it, she swore she heard him murmur, "Mother?"

The word sliced through her like a blade.

Before Ren could speak, the snow beneath them trembled.

The bells were no longer distant. They were all around them.

And then all hell broke loose.

Snow leapt from the ground.

Wind returned all at once, lashing them with claws of powder. Ren's hood snapped back; ice-crystals pricked her lips and eyes. She threw an arm up, but the world vanished anyway, engulfed in a whirl of white.

"*Lucan!*" Her voice was devoured.

His hand found hers. It latched onto her glove with a grip that hurt. "Here!" he shouted. "*Don't let go.*"

Ren could only hear a booming howl. The storm pressed on her from every direction at once, collapsing space until up and down swapped. Air thinned. Her lungs took in cold and got nothing for it.

The bells danced closer, sweet and coaxing, and under them, humming.

A lullaby.

"Not that way!" Lucan hauled her left, then slammed her back against rock. The sudden solidity saved her; her knees buckled in relief. "The edge is – "

The wind stole the rest.

Something brushed her cheek, feather-soft, warm. A woman's caress, her mind supplied, desperately trying to make sense of the senseless. The caress lingered, tender as a mother waking a child.

The pouch snarled at Ren's hip, "*Do not listen. Do not listen.*"

Ren clenched her teeth until she tasted iron. *Move.* The command in her head was hers and not hers. She shoved off the wall, fingers welded to Lucan's. They staggered together. The gale became a body, a thing that wanted them elsewhere – off the path, over the drop, into the throat of the vale.

A shape flickered in the storm revealing a silhouette of a woman's outline, blurred by snow. It lifted a hand. "Lucan," it said in a voice like summer fields.

He lurched. Ren yanked him back hard. "It's not her!"

Lucan's jaw worked, eyes blazing and lost all at once, and she realized the thing's voice had been a memory.

"Left!" he barked, as if reminding himself how to live. He dragged her into a narrow crease in the rock where the wind skated over instead of through. It gave them a breath of almost-quiet. "Snow wisp," he rasped. "Funnel-storms in the vale. Lures with what you desire most."

Ren couldn't feel her face. Her eyelashes had frozen together; she pried them apart with gloved fingers and saw nothing but white. "How do we kill it?"

"Heat," the pouch snapped. "Burn the air from its throat. If the human can manage anything more than shivering."

"*Sir Buttercup,*" Ren hissed through chattering teeth, "is about to meet a snowbank." But her hands were shaking too hard to lift. The cold had gnawed its way under her skin and chewed at the joints. Her breath came short.

"Ren." Lucan squeezed her fingers. "Stay with me." He let go only long enough to press his palm to her cheek. "With *me*. We move on my count. If I stop, you keep moving."

"I won't l-l-leave you."

His thumb brushed a line of frost from her jaw, his mouth quirking. "You're stubborn enough to argue until the end, Harper. I'm counting on it." The wind howled. His eyes held hers. "But if I tell you to run, you *run*. Deal? I'd rather not face Kaelin's wrath if I return without you."

She nodded because she didn't trust her mouth.

The storm inhaled like a beast and came for them.

They ran.

They shoved against the storm, and it shoved back, and each step was a bargain struck between gravity and will. Bells flitted at the edges of hearing, sneaking closer, until there were a dozen memories calling, a chorus of almost-loves whispering this way. Ren bit her tongue hard enough to steady herself with pain.

A shadow loomed belonging to an outthrust of rock. Lucan shouldered her behind it. He jabbed a finger at his eyes, then at the white. *Watch.*

When the wisp showed itself, it was not a thing so much as a place where the storm failed to stick. It was a negative space, a ripple in the air shaped like a woman, hair streaming into snow. Bells hung from her throat in a collar of frost.

Lucan slid away from the rock and drew steel. The blade looked dull and wrong in this light, already rimed with white.

The wisp moved without moving. It unfolded sideways and was suddenly right of Lucan, bells ringing all around them, voice a breath in Ren's ear.

You're tired, little ember. Lay down.

Ren gritted her teeth and swung on instinct. Her fist met air. The impact spun her. She slid, boots losing purchase, until her heel found the edge of a cliff and skittered.

Lucan's hand clamped her forearm and wrenched her back so hard the world went black for a blink. They crashed together into the rock, and he grunted, blade scraping stone. "Stay with me!"

"Trying!" She didn't mean the shriek in it.

The wisp sang. Snow heaved. The world narrowed again to a pinpoint of heat under Ren's ribs that refused to simmer. It flared now as the storm pressed, as fear tried to make her smaller.

No.

She opened her mouth and let the heat climb her throat. It came raw, all scrape and spark, but it came.

"Now!" Lucan shouted, already moving. He went wide, drawing the wisp's drift with the arc of his steel, taunting it into following the gleam. The bells tracked him. They loved him.

They wanted his throat.

Ren planted her feet. For some reason, she remembered Kaelin's voice saying *I will keep you safe*, and Ren's own voice answering: *then burn it all.*

Her fire answered.

It wasn't the neat spill of a torch. It was blue-white at the center, hotter than sense, a sudden winging of light that flared from her palms and burned the snow to hiss. Heat rolled off her in a wave that tasted like iron and summer and the first breath after drowning.

The wisp shrieked. It burst toward Ren. Lucan intercepted, steel biting the place where its throat might be. The blade didn't cut, but the heat riding it did. He slashed through steam, and the air screamed.

"Again!" he yelled. "Ren, *again*!"

Her hands shook so hard she barely got them up. The flame guttered, almost went out under the hunger of the cold. But the pouch bellowed right in Ren's ear, fury and pride braided into one impossible sound: "*Stand, girl! Burn!*"

Light exploded, and the wisp's form tore along one edge, unraveling into blowing threads of frost that the wind snatched and flung away. It recoiled, rang its bells like teeth chattering, and lunged for Lucan's exposed side.

Ren moved without thinking. She slammed her palm to his back and poured heat into the edge of his blade. Steel ate fire, glowed dull-red, and when he met the wisp's rush, the sword sang. Lucan carved a hot arc through cold.

The wisp came apart in a cry that shook the mountain.

Silence collapsed. The wind fell out of the air. Snow fell straight down like a curtain dropping.

Ren staggered. The world righted by inches. The bells were gone.

Lucan leaned on his sword, chest heaving. A crust of frost rimmed the edges of his hair and chin. His cheeks were raw red; his hands shook so violently he almost dropped his blade. When he looked at her, his eyes were too bright. "You with me?"

She tried to say yes. It came out as a laugh that was half-sob. "You?"

He nodded once. Then his knees betrayed him, and he went down into the snow, catching himself on one palm. Ren fell with him because her legs decided they were done, and they knelt facing each other while the quiet gathered.

The pouch loosened against her hip, as if it also had to remember how to breathe. "Hnh," it grunted at last. "Acceptable."

Ren snorted and only then realized her hands burned. She stared at her palms—pinked, not blistered—steam curling faintly from her skin in the lingering cold. Under the heat, a tremor lived that wouldn't stop. She couldn't tell if it was fear or elation. Maybe both.

Lucan swallowed, jaw working. He blinked once, and then seemed to remember something beyond his body. "The herb," he said hoarsely. "We didn't come here to leave empty-handed."

The vale had a heart where the wisp tried throwing them over. From this far of a fall, they wouldn't have made it alive. Below was a basin cupped by black rock where the wind didn't quite reach. In it, clustered close to one another as though for warmth, grew a little patch of winter-green leaves veined with silver, each crowned by a pale blue flower. Frost hung on their edges without touching them, a halo that never melted.

Ren had never seen anything so stubborn to live.

Somehow, they managed to make the trek down. Lucan unwrapped his scarf, hands gone white, and used the wool to pluck the flowers so his skin wouldn't steal their heat. By the time he tucked the sprig into a leather case, his fingers had turned an alarming shade of purple.

Ren caught his wrist. "Hey, you're – "

"Fine," he seethed, teeth chattering.

She cupped his frozen hands in both of hers and pressed heat into them, not the burst she'd given the wisp but a steady warmth she could hold. He hissed in pain at first, then sagged, eyes closing. When he opened them again, they were wet and grateful and a little ashamed.

"Don't," she said, because she couldn't bear the look. "You showed up. That counts."

He huffed a laugh. "You burned the sky."

"Don't tell anyone how clumsy I was."

"Harper, I would *never* ruin your reputation."

She rolled her eyes. The pouch made a noise suspiciously like approval.

By the time they hauled themselves upright, the sunlight had gentled to a winter pale. The world above looked impossibly far. Ren glanced at the drop and the drop glanced back, and her stomach went light, but the panic didn't own her this time. She had a hand on Lucan's elbow. He had one on her shoulder. It made the mountain feel less like a mouth and more like a road.

They started up.

Wind rose again and combed the snow into new patterns that lay over the old. The bells did not return. Ren listened anyway, long after the storm had given them back the sound of their own steps.

At the lip of the vale, Lucan paused and lifted the leather case. Inside, the rare herb glowed with a life that wasn't light. His fingers were mottled and ugly, but they held steady.

"Zakhar better be grateful," Ren muttered.

The pouch sniffed. "He won't be. But I am."

Ren sputtered, "Are you—did you *just*—"

"Don't get sentimental," the pouch snapped. "And mind your footing. I've no intention of spending my afterlife tumbling down a cliff because you two decide to swoon. Truth is, I don't remember my name. But I will surely remember yours – *Ren Harper* and *Lucan Brightbane*."

Ren smiled despite the ache in every muscle. She set her boots carefully, felt Lucan's steady weight at her side, and took the next step, and the next, and the next, down out of the place where the sky burned and back toward the world that needed saving.

The doors burst open.

Ren stumbled inside, Lucan at her side. Heat from the hearth hit her, but it did little to thaw the ice in her bones.

Every eye in the hall turned, but none struck Ren harder than Kaelin's.

Kaelin stood near the hearth, her crystal goblet untouched in her hand. Her gaze swept once over Ren, then lingered on the fae male beside her. Talen sat across from Kaelin, a blade in his hand being shined.

Ren's stomach tightened. She'd been through storms and wraiths, but nothing braced her for the edge in Kaelin's eyes.

"Come, sit." A fae healer gestured to one of the chairs by the fire as his eyes caught the color and stiffness in Lucan's hands. "With a bit of warmth and my magic, this should be okay. I've seen it before. Frostbite settles fast in these parts."

Lucan nodded and lowered himself into the chair, grimacing as he cradled his hands close to his chest. Ren wasted no time pulling a fur blanket around her own shoulders. Her teeth chattered so hard they ached. Now that the adrenaline was ebbing, the cold seeped into her bones like water through cracks. Not even the hearth's blaze could root it out.

She swore, just for a heartbeat, she heard the faint tinkling of bells again in the distance.

"A snow wisp," Talen murmured.

Ren forced her stiff fingers to lift the leather pouch, the herbs inside still miraculously safe. "Got it." Her voice was hoarse, barely more than a rasp.

"You went without any of us," Kaelin's voice cut across the hall, sharp as a drawn blade. "Did you think we wouldn't notice? Or did you simply decide we were unnecessary?"

Ren's jaw clenched. "You were still sleeping."

A ripple of murmurs broke through the room at the audacity of Ren's retort. Kaelin's eyes narrowed to slits, but Ren only pulled the blanket tighter around herself and glared at the flames.

Kaelin *had* been sleeping. Ren could still see the image of Kaelin sprawled among the cushions, hair unbound, the sharp edges of her face softened in slumber. For once, Kaelin hadn't been frowning or plotting. Just... *peaceful*. Ren had hovered in the doorway, one hand tightening on the frame, debating whether to wake her. But the thought of disturbing that fragile calm had made her chest twist.

She'd turned away instead.

Kaelin crossed the floor and crouched before Ren. "Do you think I enjoyed waking to find you gone, without any word or a note?" Her voice dropped, low and seething. "I don't appreciate being kept in the dark."

Ren lifted her chin, glare matching Kaelin's fire for fire. "I'm not yours to keep."

Gasps pricked the edges of the room. The silence afterward was taut as a bowstring, broken only by the hiss of the logs in the hearth. Kaelin's jaw ticked, her hands flexing against her thighs like she needed release.

From behind them, Talen cleared his throat. "Perhaps this is better discussed in... more private quarters?"

Kaelin's jaw worked once, twice. Then, without a word, she surged forward. Ren barely had time to gasp before Kaelin seized her around the waist and, with shocking ease, hoisted her over one shoulder like she weighed nothing at all.

"Hey!" Ren yelped, blanket tumbling from her grip as she kicked hard, fists pounding against Kaelin's back. "Put me down, you *insufferable* – " Her boots thudded against Kaelin's hip, but Kaelin only adjusted her hold, spine straight and unyielding, stride unbroken. She turned toward the hallway to her bedchamber with the authority only she could possess.

Gasps and murmurs swelled from those watching. Some half-rose from their seats, uncertain whether to step forward.

Kaelin's head snapped toward them, her teeth flashing sharp in the firelight. "*Try*," she said, her voice a razor's edge. "And you'll find out *exactly* how merciless I can be."

The room froze. No one moved.

Ren seethed, wriggling furiously against the iron grip that pinned her. "You pain in the ass, put me down right now or so help me – "

Kaelin's only reply was the faintest growl rumbling in her throat as she swept Ren out of the room, the doors thundering shut behind them when they entered her bedchamber.

Nothing relieved Kaelin more than the sound of those footsteps beyond the front door of the keep.

For a fleeting heartbeat, relief bloomed; Ren had returned *safe*.

But with that relief came a swift tide of anger.

Last night, they had fallen asleep wrapped in one another's warmth. Kaelin woke up more than once in the night, half-afraid it was only a dream spun to mock her. Each time she stirred, she found Ren's peaceful face pressed into the pillow, lashes resting against her cheek, lips parted with the rhythm of deep sleep. It ached to see her like that. Kaelin had kissed her forehead, her cheek, even brushed her lips more than once, greedy with the tender luxury of it.

For the first time in years, Kaelin had felt utterly content.

But come morning, Kaelin woke to an empty bed.

The sheets were tossed aside, the fire burned low, and the ache in her chest turned jagged. She rifled through drawers, the writing desk, even the sill – anywhere a note might have been tucked, providing some explanation. Anything.

But there was nothing.

Kaelin threw a robe across her shoulders and swept into the main hall. Talen sat near the hearth, sipping tea while polishing one of his blades. He looked up at her approach, his expression maddeningly placid. "Good morning. Sounds like you two had an enjoyable night."

Kaelin's glare could have split stone. "Where is she?"

"Who? Oh, Ren? She went to the vale for the herbs. Whatever Zakhar called them." He tipped the teapot toward her as though offering peace. "Want a cup of tea?"

Kaelin's lips curled around a curse. She strode across the hall in a sweep of silk and fury, her gaze locked on the front doors that led out into the snow.

"Lucan is not familiar with this part of the realm. They're going in blind."

"It's just a hike. Shouldn't take them more than an hour. And they'll probably see some amazing sights."

That earned him her full attention. Kaelin whirled, her eyes blazing. Talen's casual smile faltered, the teacup stilling halfway to his lips.

"There are *snow wisps* in that vale, and none of us warned them."

The silence pressed hard between them, broken only by the pop of the hearth.

Talen cleared his throat, setting down the teacup with deliberate care. "Right," he muttered. "So... I take it this is one of those times where 'amazing sights' isn't the right thing to say."

Kaelin's fists clenched at her sides, nails biting into her palms. Every nerve screamed at her to bolt for the stables, to tear through the snow until she reached them.

Pacing the length of the firelit hall like a caged predator, robe sweeping behind her in angry arcs, she stared at the doors until her vision blurred. With each hour that dragged by, her thoughts turned darker. Ren stumbling in the drifts. Lucan's strength giving out. The pale shadow of a wisp following them.

Hunting them.

Her jaw ached from grinding her teeth.

She tried to sit, to steady her hands by pouring tea as Talen suggested. The cup rattled in its saucer, hot liquid sloshing onto her fingers. She didn't even feel the burn. Her mind kept circling back to that empty bed.

The memory of Ren's peaceful face, lashes still, lips parted, had been the softest thing Kaelin had ever known, and she had left it. Left *her*.

Without even a note.

Kaelin's stomach knotted. Anger masked fear, but it didn't smother it. The truth gnawed at her ribs. She wasn't angry because Ren had gone without her. She was angry because she might never come back.

"Stop pacing," Talen set aside his blade with an annoyed huff. "You're making *me* nervous." Kaelin turned her burning glare on him, and he immediately threw up his hands. "Never mind. Pace away. Saints save us all when she walks through that door. She's tougher than most soldiers I know. *I'm* not worried about her. But then again, I don't feel about her the way you do."

Talen's mouth curved in a small, knowing grin, mischief barely leashed behind it. "I'm not against it, so long as she treats you well and you're happy." He lifted his sword by the hilt, idly dragging a fingertip along the flat. "But, should I give her the protective-older-brother speech where I warn her that if she hurts you, I'll kick her ass?"

Kaelin snorted, one corner of her mouth twitching. "You? She's the one who very well may kick your ass."

Talen pretended to be wounded, then laughed. "Already tried that once. Beat her fair and square – she still has a lot to learn." His voice softened on the last word, the teasing falling away enough that care showed through.

For the first time that day, the tension in Kaelin's chest loosened. Talen had a knack for catching the frayed edges of fear and weaving them into something steadier, something that made everything seem a little less impossible.

And so, hours later, when Ren *did* walk through the door, Kaelin's fury boiled over.

Ren kicked and cursed the whole way to Kaelin's chambers, fists pounding at her back. "Put me down, damn you! I don't need a keeper. Who do you think you *are*?"

Kaelin ignored every word.

Kaelin tossed Ren onto the bed with more force than was necessary. Ren bounced against the mattress with a furious growl, eyes blazing even as her teeth chattered. Kaelin stoked the fire until it roared, the flames catching quick, orange light painting the walls. She stripped off her own clothes without ceremony, movements clipped and efficient.

Like a soldier preparing for battle.

All the while, Ren spat venom. "I don't need you hovering over me. I'm fine. You hear me? I'm *fine*." But her lips were pale blue, her hands trembling as she pulled the furs around herself. The lie was written all over her.

Kaelin crossed the room and slid into bed beside Ren. She gathered Ren close to her chest, pressing her icy body to her own warmth. Ren thrashed in protest, fists pressing against Kaelin's shoulders, muttering curses hot against her collarbone.

Kaelin didn't let go.

She tugged at the laces of Ren's soaked tunic and peeled the sodden cloth away. Ren gasped aloud, but Kaelin was relentless, stripping her layer by layer until the furs wrapped around bare skin and their bodies shared the same heat.

"Kaelin, what the hell do you think – " Ren's protest cut short when Kaelin's hand slipped between Ren's thighs, bringing her legs apart so Kaelin settled between them. Her other arm wound firm around Ren's waist, the other splaying against the small of Ren's back to hold her steady. Ren's curses faltered, lost in the tremor of her teeth and the way her body instinctively sought warmth despite her fury.

Kaelin exhaled into Ren's hair, a low murmur slipping free before she could stop it. "You'll hate me for this tomorrow. But tonight, you'll live."

Ren's body stayed rigid, her fists still curled against Kaelin's shoulders. "I don't need your help." Her voice broke on a shiver, the last word lost to the rattle of her teeth.

Kaelin only pulled Ren closer, pressing her icy skin to the furnace of her own body. Her hand found Ren's damp hair, fingers slipping gently through tangled strands, stroking slow and steady. The rhythm was grounding, as if Kaelin was telling her through touch alone: *you're here, you're safe.*

Ren muttered something unintelligible, too weary to shape the words into venom. Her fists slackened, then fell away. Her breathing stuttered, caught, and then began to match Kaelin's, each inhale and exhale syncing as though her body had finally surrendered where her pride could not.

Kaelin tilted her chin down, brushing her lips against the crown of Ren's head, light enough it could almost be mistaken for an accident. She lingered there, inhaling the faintest trace of worn leather and spice clinging to Ren's hair.

Ren's eyes fluttered shut. The fight drained from her like snow melting in spring, leaving only the raw ache of exhaustion. With a sigh, she shifted just enough to burrow closer, her forehead brushing Kaelin's collarbone. Kaelin's chest tightened. Her fingers continued their slow sweep through Ren's hair, over and over, until the stiffness bled out of her frame.

For the first time all day, Kaelin allowed herself to breathe.

"Knock knock," Ren called into Zakhar's cellar study, the wood groaning beneath her boots as she carefully descended the steep stairs. "I come bearing gifts."

Dusty scrolls were stacked along every table and chair, candlelight flickering across the dark stone walls. Glass clinked softly from deeper within and the further Ren descended, the more the air temperature dropped.

Amidst shelves crowded with vials, jars brimming with powders, and bookshelves stacked of bones Ren didn't want to know originated from, Ren caught sight of Zakhar's thicket of gray curls.

A grunt responded to her arrival.

Ren stepped off the bottom stair. She exhaled slowly, realizing how refreshed she felt since returning to Pyraelia this morning. During their time at the keep, there were no battles, no running, no training – just a week of stolen reprieve with Talen, Kaelin, and Lucan, drinking too much wine and spiced rum, swapping folk tales until their voices grew hoarse, and winning and losing handfuls of cards by the firelight with the fiddle music accompanying them.

But most of all, Ren spent every second with Kaelin. Even now, Ren's fingers brushed her bottom lip at the recollection of what had happened barely an hour ago.

Kaelin had caught Ren in the hallway, fingers curling around Ren's wrist before she could so much as breathe. With one tug, Ren was pulled into the narrow dark of a closet, the door clicking shut behind them. Kaelin's wicked and daring grin flashed in the dim light before her mouth descended on Ren's.

Kaelin kissed like she had waited too long and wasn't willing to wait a heartbeat more. Hunger and teeth, heat and want, Ren's back hit the wall as Kaelin pressed close. Ren remembered gasping, but Kaelin swallowed the sound, her lips dragging over Ren's with intoxicating insistence before closing around her lower lip and sucking until Ren's knees nearly buckled. Fingers tangled in hair, nails scraping against fabric, the air in that cramped space turned molten.

When they finally broke apart, both were breathless, their hair mussed, clothes wrinkled. Ren could barely catch her breath as Kaelin's grin turned feral in the darkness as she sank to her knees and brought Ren well over the edge. Ren would be amazed that no handmaidens heard their voices and fumbling from the hallway – no matter how Ren bit her lip and tried to rein in her moans, Kaelin *encouraged* her relentlessly not to hold back. They stumbled back into the hallway moments later, grinning like fools who had just tasted something too forbidden to resist and knew they'd do it again, no matter the cost.

Ren's steps slowed when she spotted Zakhar bowing over his cluttered bench, exhaustion etched deep into his posture. The sight struck her harder than she expected.

She'd been enjoying herself lately while people were still dying.

A pang of guilt twisted through her.

What right did she have to feel *happy* when the world was still falling apart at the seams?

She set down the box beside him. "That herb was a pain in the ass to get," she said dryly, flipping open the lid to reveal the worn leather pouch and the bundle of herbs within. "But we whooped a ice wisp's ass in the process. Guess that's another first I can tick off."

A gruff voice rasped from inside the box, rough as gravel and twice as unimpressed. "Damn right you did," the pouch barked. "Never seen a fight that cold turn so hot so fast. You and Brightbane gave it hell, though your form could use some work, human."

"Still mouthy, I see," Zakhar muttered, picking up the pouch with two fingers as if it might bite.

"Still *here*," it shot back, its drawstring twitching like a scowl. "And I don't take orders from hermits."

Ren huffed a laugh. "He's been like this since we found him. I think the frost rattled his stitching."

"Frost did nothing but toughen me up," the pouch declared proudly. "Takes more than a little frost to get *me* rattled."

Ren's gaze shifted to look over the scarred wooden table, where Zakhar had previously been hunched over, grinding a herb into powder. She looked over Zakhar's features, noting the dark circles beneath his eyes had deepened into what appeared like bruises, and his pale skin was marred by smudges of unknown ingredients.

"Do you sleep?" Ren asked.

Zakhar sat the box of the herb gently onto the table and went back to grinding the herb into a powder. "Here and there."

"When was the last time?"

Zakhar hesitated, grinding the pestle slower, as though calculating days blurred together. "Maybe the other day."

Ren sank onto a worn stool nearby. "You'll burn yourself out at this rate."

"Hand me the bottle in front of you.".

Ren passed him the empty glass, her brows drawing together as she studied him. "Are you even eating?" she pressed.

Finally, his eyes met hers, a flicker of frustration in their depths. "Stop fretting. I'm *fine*."

From the table, the pouch scoffed. "Stubborn as a mule and half as aware of the time. You probably haven't slept a full night since the last moon cycle, have you?"

Zakhar dismissed them both with a wave, returning to his work.

For a moment, the only sound was the rhythmic scrape of the pestle against the mortar, the gentle clink of glass. Then, Zakhar murmured, "The death toll's climbing faster than we can brew the elixir. We're losing whole villages overnight. If we stop, the Witherblight will take us all."

"If there's something I can do, show me. I can help."

Zakhar snorted, not looking up from the mortar. "Sensitive information. Can't teach you a thing without permission from the crown first."

"Nothing like a bit of palace bureaucracy to save the world."

Zakhar's voice dropped further, as though speaking aloud might awaken old shadows. "I've been going through the old records, the fragments of the pact that held fae and dragonkind from each other's throats. It wasn't just a truce for peace. It was a binding. And now…"

He glanced around as if the dark might be listening. His lips pressed into a thin line.

"I think someone's broken it."

The weight of his words pressed down on Ren. The flickering candlelight threw her shadow long against the wall, dancing amidst the shelves of bottled secrets.

"The dragons and the fae were not always enemies," Zakhar said. "In the beginning, they were flame and root, destruction and rebirth. It was balance, in a way. A dance older than kingdoms. The fae feared the dragons. How could they not? Some of them razed cities to ash just for gluttony. For the glint of gold and the shimmer of power. It's in their blood, that craving. Yet, a dragon's hoard isn't just coin and gemstone – it's anything they deem precious. It could be a relic, a name, a secret, even a memory, if it's cherished enough."

Zakhar paused, and a dry smirk tugged at his mouth. "But gods help the fool who tries to take it. There's something ancient that awakens when a dragon's treasure is threatened. Not rage, exactly…something deeper. Obsession dressed as wrath."

Ren said nothing, but a flicker struck beneath her ribs, like a spark catching in a hearth long thought cold. She thought of the ribbons she used to steal, although she never wore them, never dared, but tucked them away like tiny treasures, hidden beneath loose floorboards. She'd told herself it was vanity or foolish sentiment.

That she was just a girl craving color in a world gone gray.

But now, the memory felt different. It felt too specific – too *instinctual*.

"That madness, is it always violent?"

Zakhar's eyes flicked to her, the faintest crease forming between his brows. "Only when the treasure's been taken or threatened."

Suddenly, Ren wasn't crouched in the cellar with Zakhar.

She was seven years old, barefoot on a creaking floor. Her small fingers trembling as they reached for the bottle tucked behind the broken wall panel, amber liquid sloshing inside. Her mother had passed out in the next room, slumped on a chair. Ren had just wanted to pour it out. To make it stop.

She hadn't even touched it before her mother lunged.

The glass shattered against the floor. Hands grabbing her, shaking her so hard that her teeth rattled.

"You don't touch what's *mine*," her mother had hissed, eyes wide and wild. "You don't steal from me. *Ever.*"

Her parents hoarded bottle after bottle.

Ren recalled tripping through the hallways once on the way to her room, glass glistening on the floor like specks of starlight. She remembered nights where Eve would hold a flickering candle and pick out the shards of broken glass from Ren's feet, one by one. Eve's fingers were always so gentle when she cradled Ren's heel.

And still, Ren had kept the ribbons, hadn't she? She tucked them away, and they were never worn. Looking back, it was like a dragon building a nest she'd never let anyone see.

But no, the ribbons weren't an obsession or signs of madness. They were something else. A tether, maybe. Perhaps they were proof that beauty existed beyond peeling walls and broken bottles – that somewhere out there, young girls wore color in their hair and laughed without fear of glass shattering at their feet.

She'd stolen them not to possess, but to pretend, if only for a moment, that the world outside was real. That softness *still* existed.

A cough from Zakhar snapped Ren's attention back to him. He coughed into his dark sleeve before straining back up and clearing his throat.

"Yes, I think someone broke it. Only that can explain why the world is so unbalanced now. Indeed," he nodded to himself, as if having the conversation with himself.

He jumped a little when Ren spoke, as if forgetting she was there. "What happens when an ancient pact is broken?"

"Balance unravels, and something always crawls out of the void to take its place. I don't know who broke it, but whoever did it means they're willing to tear the world apart to see what rises from the ashes."

Her fingers clenched against the edge of the stool. "You think it's connected to the Witherblight," Ren whispered into the space between them.

"I think someone paid that price, and if that's true..." He let out a shaky breath. "Truth most often isn't a gift, Ren. It's a blade. And once it's drawn, it never goes back into the sheath."

The days bled together, a quiet rhythm forged in routine.

Ren threw herself into every task the palace demanded of her – mornings spent on the training grounds until her muscles trembled, and afternoons spent with Zakhar grinding herbs into fine powders or measuring ingredients for the next batches of Verdant Elixir. Getting Maelion's permission to help had been surprisingly easy.

Once, Ren had caught a pair of noble fae in the marble atrium, laughter echoing off the vaulted ceiling as they uncorked a fresh vial of Verdant Elixir. *Just to be safe*, one of them had drawled, tipping the bottle back like it was nothing more than cheap wine. The other joined him, their jeweled cuffs glinting as the shimmering green liquid slid down their throats, their laughter and sneers echoing down the marble halls as the liquid dwindled away.

Before she could stop herself, the words slipped out. "Why cure the sick when you can toast to your own health? I'm sure the corpses outside the walls would raise a glass if they still *had* hands."

The laughter cut off. The male fae turned, his pupils narrowing to slits. "Watch yourself, human," he'd hissed.

The female beside him laid a manicured hand on his arm, eyes flicking to Ren with unreadable calm. "Leave it," she murmured. "The princess wouldn't take kindly to her little pet being bruised."

The words hit like a slap. *Kaelin's little pet.* As if that was the only reason they'd decided not to teach her a lesson. Heat rose in Ren's throat – a concoction of anger, humiliation, pride, all twisted together. Ren met the fae female's gaze, jaw tight enough to ache. She could've dropped them both before either of them reached for their magic or a weapon, and the fact that they'd only backed off because of Kaelin made her want to remind them who the hell they were conversing with.

The male fae's smile sharpened, his pride stung. "Whatever. Watch yourself, human. You forget your place."

Ren tilted her head, eyes lit with challenge. "Oh, I'm well aware of it. I just don't think you'll like where you're standing when I decide to *remind* you."

Ren's daring tone was all it took. He moved, hand shooting out toward her throat.

Ren was faster.

Her fist drew back, magic coiling at her knuckles, ready to shatter his perfect nose and his ego along with it –

"Enough."

Every head turned.

Queen Lyra stood at the top of the staircase, her gown a dark cascade of shadow and silk, her crown catching the light like the edge of a blade.

The male fae froze mid-step, his hand falling quickly to his side. The female bowed her head.

Lyra's gaze cut to Ren last, cool and assessing, before sweeping the rest of the room into silence. "If my court is so bored that it must prey on its own allies, I'll be happy to find you a more permanent form of entertainment."

But Lyra's gaze lingered on the male's hand. The vial still glinted between his fingers, half-drained, the last drop of the Verdant Elixir trembling at the lip.

"Tell me," Lyra said at last, her tone deceptively soft, "why are you drinking another?"

The fae male froze.

Lyra descended a step, each click of her heel echoing through the chamber. "I recall watching you drink one just yesterday evening – after dinner, wasn't it? You're allotted *one* a week, not whenever you feel the slightest tickle in your throat."

The color drained from his face. "I—Your Majesty, I simply thought—"

"That perhaps your life was worth more than those who actually need it?" Lyra's eyes flashed. "Or did you pay one of the apothecaries to overlook the tally again?"

The silence that followed was thick enough to choke on.

The male's throat bobbed. His excuses faltered and died on his tongue.

"You'll get no more for 2 weeks. Perhaps that will teach you restraint, or honesty."

The female beside him straightened, her composure cracking just enough to show indignation beneath the polish. "With respect, Your Majesty, why ration us at all? They're shipping loads to the human settlements, wasting it on *humans*."

Lyra turned her head slowly, and the temperature in the room seemed to drop ten degrees. "Wasting?" she repeated softly. "Would you like to go down there and explain that to them? To the mothers watching their children rot from the Witherblight?"

The female fae's lips parted, but no sound came out.

"I didn't think so." She turned back to the pair, voice dropping low. "Get out of my sight before I decide the punishment for greed should be a little more creative."

The nobles bowed stiffly and swept out, the faint rustle of silk and shame trailing in their wake.

Ren stood motionless, pulse hammering, fury simmering just beneath her skin. For once, she didn't have to say a word; Lyra had done it for her. But the satisfaction didn't last. Because the queen's gaze lingered on her next, and Ren couldn't shake the feeling that beneath that calm, regal poise, Lyra was calculating exactly how far her temper could be pushed before she'd turn it on her too.

Ren could feel Lyra's gaze settle on her. The queen didn't say a word, didn't need to. That quiet, assessing look was enough to make Ren's pulse stutter. There was power behind those eyes, the kind that could unmake her with a thought.

"I should – " Ren began, her voice catching before she cleared it. "Zakhar. He'll be expecting me."

Lyra didn't stop her. She didn't even look away. But Ren didn't wait for permission. She dipped her head in something that might've been a bow and turned on her heel before anyone could notice the tremor in her hands.

Ren moved quickly, every step echoing the storm still pounding in her chest—the anger, the humiliation, the bitter reminder that no matter how hard she fought, the court would always see her as less.

Kaelin's little pet.

By the time she reached Zakhar's study, the noise in her head had quieted only enough to make room for the ache beneath it. Ren shut the door behind her and leaned against it, exhaling slowly.

And then she got to work.

After observing her numerous times to ensure she didn't ruin the meticulous mixtures, Zakhar finally trusted her hands. She even managed to convince him to nap here and there while she worked, the court mage muttering half-hearted protests before surrendering to the lure of rest.

Beyond the palace walls, little news came of the Witherblight itself, but each day a new messenger arrived bearing grim tidings of another town fallen, another village attacked by the undead. The palace had grown quieter, its halls thinner of soldiers, most deployed to aid the outer provinces. Ren and Talen accompanied a few of those deployments, though Talen now spent most of his time behind closed doors, entangled in meetings and councils that debated how to fight a war against an enemy that could not be reasoned with, nor truly slain, and, most troubling of all, how to target an enemy they still didn't even know.

Ren hadn't even thought about how many of the creatures she'd already cut down, or how many remained before she could collect her coin.

Back then, it was about coin.

Now, it was about keeping the dead back from the living.

When she wasn't working, Ren was with Kaelin. Ren scarcely slept in her own quarters anymore. She missed Mirella's endless gossip and found excuses to stop by her chamber during the day, even if only for a few fleeting minutes. Maybe it was the thought of Mirella alone in that room with nobody but the walls to talk to, or maybe it was that Ren grew fond of the enchanted dresser.

But nights belonged to Kaelin.

Ren loved the simple intimacy of it; she loved the warmth of Kaelin's body beside hers, the soft sound of her breathing when sleep finally claimed her. Ren loved waking to the sight of Kaelin's face in the early light, her features gentled by dreams, and stealing a kiss before either of them remembered duty or decorum. Sometimes, those mornings ended in laughter tangled in sheets and whispered protests about schedules and appearances. For a time, it felt like peace. Like something whole.

But peace was fleeting.

The air was thick with rot and smoke, the moans of the undead echoing through the crumbling streets of Briarstead, a modest village of farmers and herders half a day's ride from Pyraelia's gates.

Ren's chest heaved as she ducked behind a fallen beam, heart hammering in her ears. Talen was somewhere behind her shouting orders, but the chaos had swallowed his voice whole.

The creatures kept coming, a relentless wave of snapping jaws and clawed hands. Ashrend was a blur in Ren's hands, her grip shifting, striking, flipping the blade into a dual-edged dance of steel and death. She carved through them one after another, the edge biting into rotted flesh, splitting bone, and sending blackened fluid spraying across her arms and face.

Blood and gore slicked her fingers, streaked her leathers, but she didn't falter. Her heart thudded in her ears, each beat a drum urging her forward.

One corpse dropped at her feet.

Then another.

And another—

Until the ground before her was littered with the motionless bodies of the dead she'd cut down, their twisted forms still twitching in the dirt.

But they kept coming.

Her muscles screamed, her breaths ragged as more of them broke through the smoke. Their snarls were deafening now, filling the air with the stench of rot and hunger. The press of them forced her back step by step until her boots struck something solid—a wall, cutting off her retreat.

A clawed hand swiped for her face. Another tore at her side.

Something inside her cracked.

It started as a pulse deep in her chest, like the heart of a forge flaring to life. Her vision tunneled. The world shrank to heat and movement and the blood pounding in her skull.

It tore from her like a scream ripped from the soul. A white-hot blaze burst from her chest, sweeping outward in a roaring tidal wave of flame. Her magic erupted, unbridled and primal, pulsing with something far older than herself.

Flameborne…

The word hissed through her mind, low, guttural, almost serpentine.

Flameborne, the voice growled again. *Pathetic, so frail, so small, and yet…*

Ren didn't notice the way the flames licked higher and higher until the sky itself glowed orange.

The voice slithered through her skull, scathing. *You wield flame like a mortal. I will show you how the gods burn. Rise, Flameborne. Destroy.*

Burn.

Burn.

BURN.

Ren was no longer in her body. Not truly.

She was fire.

She was fury.

She was wrath reborn.

A torrent of magic surged through every inch of her, cracking her open from the inside out. Her feet barely touched the ground, her limbs carried by something else, something ancient. The roar of her flame drowned out everything.

Her heart. Her name.

The *world*.

And then, nothing.

Ren fell to her knees, smoke curling from her fingertips, flames dying into embers around her. The world came back in shudders and fragments. Her lungs ached. Her vision blurred.

Blackened stone stretched for miles around her. Ash fell like snow. She blinked, dazed.

All she knew was the silence and the terrifying emptiness that came after the fire. The thing inside her had stopped hungering.

For now.

"**G**reymoor will be forever thankful for Your Highness' kindness."

The messenger bowed low, his bald scalp catching the candlelight in the throne room.

"We grieve for those who have crossed the Veil," King Maelion replied.

Kaelin sat poised beside him, her gaze steady on the messenger. The lower fae's hands trembled as he straightened, his throat bobbing. She tilted her chin a fraction higher. There it was, that subtle pause. The *but*.

"However, more undead gather on the horizon," the messenger said carefully. "We've sent legions to hunt them, but few have returned. The dead travel in vast numbers." His voice cracked. "We would be eternally grateful for more soldiers to aid us."

From the corner of her eye, Kaelin saw her mother lift her wine goblet—ruby liquid gleaming as richly as blood. Queen Lyra drank slowly, while Kaelin's father's expression remained unreadable. *Always listen before you speak.* His lesson echoed in her mind. *Fools answer too quickly before thinking.*

Kaelin's lips twitched despite herself. She knew someone who would have blurted out her thoughts without a second thought.

Ren.

Maelion leaned forward. "We understand your plight. My finest soldiers have already been dispatched to neighboring villages; our numbers here in Pyraelia have dwindled."

The messenger's shoulders drew tight, bracing for a blow.

"That being said," Maelion continued, "we will send what soldiers we can spare. In the meantime, evacuate any remaining villagers and send them here. We will house them within the walls."

Silence rippled through the chamber. The messenger exhaled shakily, bowing once more until his head nearly brushed the floor.

Maelion's words were merciful, but she could see the exhaustion buried behind her father's eyes, the unspoken truth on everyone's tongue.

The undead were spreading faster than they could be stopped.

And even mercy was beginning to run thin.

Lyra's voice cut through the stillness. "How fares your daughter?" She tilted her head, a fond smile crossing her lips. "Mare. I recall she used to plait flowers into her hair each summer solstice."

The man's face went slack, the color draining from his already-pale cheeks. "She has crossed the Veil, Your Majesty. She and her mother were slain in the night. The undead came through the village while everyone slept. No warning, no chance to flee."

The words struck like an arrow. Kaelin remembered the bright-eyed and wild-haired youngling, racing through the gardens with armfuls of daisies and thistle blooms, insisting every other youngling's crown of flowers needed more color.

Kaelin's voice was soft but steady. "You have our deepest sympathies. May the gods guide them both safely beyond the Veil."

The messenger nodded numbly and bowed again.

No one spoke after that. The only sound was the faint clink of Lyra's goblet as she set it down, her gaze distant, and the echo of a father's grief that lingered long after the messenger was gone.

Kaelin sat still, her fingers curling around the arm of her chair. Even the candles seemed to burn quieter, their flames trembling as though afraid to disturb the quiet grief lingering in the air.

Then, footsteps.

Hurried, uneven – echoing down the marble corridor.

The double doors slammed open. A second messenger stumbled inside, his cloak torn and streaked with ash. He fell to one knee before the throne.

"Your Majesties—" he gasped, his voice hoarse, "Briarstead... Briarstead has fallen." The messenger swallowed hard, his words tumbling out in broken bursts. "All of the villagers were evacuated, thank the gods, but—"

Lyra rose so suddenly her goblet toppled, crimson wine bleeding across the marble. "My son," she demanded, her voice a whip. "Where is he?"

The messenger hesitated. His mouth opened, then closed again, as if the next words might cost him dearly. "Prince Talen is unharmed, Your Majesty," he managed. "But..." He glanced up before lowering his gaze again. "The human girl. Ren. She... she burned everything to the ground."

For a heartbeat, no one breathed.

Kaelin felt the blood drain from her face, her pulse thundering in her ears. *Burned everything to the ground?* The image seared through her mind—flames devouring fields, homes collapsing into embers, the sky painted in orange and ash.

Maelion's voice broke the silence. "Explain yourself."

But Kaelin barely heard him. Kaelin saw red. Her pulse roared in her ears, drowning out the echo of her father's voice, the distant drip of spilled wine spreading onto marble. The messenger's words repeated in her mind like the toll of a bell. *She burned everything to the ground.*

Kaelin rose. "What of Ren Harper?" she demanded. Her voice cracked through the silence, sharp enough to make the messenger flinch.

The soldier's head snapped up, startled. "She-she lives, Your Highness," he stammered. "Injured, but the healers have her in care. She – "

He didn't finish.

Kaelin was already moving.

She descended the dais in a rush, the echo of her heels striking the marble. She barely registered her mother's sharp inhale or her father's barked command. The only thing that mattered—the only words pulsing through her—was *she's alive.*

But Kaelin couldn't breathe until she saw her with her own eyes. Couldn't think until she knew for certain.

The air seemed to crackle around her as she strode for the doors. The guards scattered at her approach, startled by the look in her eyes. Kaelin didn't care about royal decorum or that half the court was staring.

The world could crumble around her, so long as Ren still drew breath.

The wound was surprisingly shallow, but gods, it hurt like hell.

Ren gritted her teeth as the nursemaid dabbed at the torn skin, the sting of the cleansing salve flaring hot at her side. She tried not to make a sound, but a hiss slipped between her clenched teeth anyway.

"Would you like more pain elixir?" the nursemaid asked, her eyes darting with concern.

Ren shook her head, a motion that betrayed the memory behind her silence, what seemed like an absolute living hell.

What she did.

Now she was strapped to a cot in the infirmary, the scent of herbs thick in the air.

The door creaked open behind them, and light footsteps approached. "How is she?"

The nursemaid froze and immediately straightened. Ren didn't need to turn to know who had entered.

"Healing, Your Highness," the nursemaid replied quickly. "But in considerable pain."

The nurse began preparing the dressing, and Ren's stomach turned. She could already feel the sting of the wrappings on raw skin, the clumsy tug of fabric.

Ren nearly opened her mouth to request the elixir after all when a voice, velvet-smooth and sharp as glass, cut in, "Then why haven't you given her the pain elixir?"

The nursemaid stilled mid-motion. "Apologies, Your Highness."

"Go get it. I'll do the wrapping myself."

With a bow so quick it nearly stumbled into panic, the nursemaid scurried from the room.

And then it was just the two of them.

Ren turned her head and found Kaelin easing forward, sleeves rolled to the elbow. Her curls were loose, strands of pale hair spilling down around the angles of her fae features, and faint shadows clung beneath her eyes. It was the look of someone who had lingered here night after night, who had watched too long and slept too little. Yet every gesture, every move Kaelin made was practiced and fluid as she knelt beside Ren's cot and reached for her bandages.

"How long have I been asleep?" Ren asked.

Kaelin answered, "Three days."

"You shouldn't be here. I'm sure you have other duties to attend to."

"Perhaps."

Ren frowned. "Why are you so pale?"

Kaelin's gaze flicked toward the chair tucked into the corner of the room—a chair that bore the unmistakable slump of long nights sat vigil. "Because I've spent the nights here," she answered curtly, already reaching for the bandages as though to cut off further questions.

Ren's throat tightened. She lowered her voice, words slipping out before she could hold them back. "But... why? Why stay for me?"

Kaelin's jaw tensed. Instead of answering, her fingers brushed Ren's skin as she took her wounded arm in her hands. Her touch was warm and practiced, but her movements were clipped, precise, as if she were holding something back.

Her hands trembled once, just once, before she stilled them with a quiet breath. "You were bleeding all over the place," Kaelin muttered.

Ren flinched as Kaelin cinched the bandage tighter than necessary. But Kaelin caught herself, hands gentling immediately, her fingers smoothing over the gauze with excruciating care. Her lips were pressed into a thin line, her eyes sharp with unspoken fury.

She snarled the next words, lips curled back and teeth bared in barely controlled rage. "There isn't a soul in this realm who's going to hurt you while I still draw breath. And if anyone thinks they can—"

She broke off, jaw clenching harder. A muscle ticked in her cheek.

"When I saw you in this bed... when I thought—" She stopped, swallowing hard. "It gutted me. I felt like my chest had been split in two. I realized something then." Her gaze flicked up, fierce and unflinching. "I don't want to *share* you, Ren. Not with anyone. I want you. Just you.

And I want you to be mine." She drew in a breath, her voice quieter now, but no less intense. "So say yes, and you'll be mine, and I'll be yours. No courtly games, no distractions. Just us."

A faint smirk tugged at the corner of Ren's lips, but her voice lowered, threaded with something quieter. "Just us."

Kaelin's fingers lingered for a fraction too long, smoothing the bandage, before she added—half a breath, half a laugh, "I don't think I'd survive losing you." Kaelin's gaze drifted to the crook of Ren's wrist, where the skin was thinnest. Most vulnerable.

Ren's lips curved faintly. "Give me some credit where it's due. I've stared down tougher opponents in the pits. The undead? They're stupid and move on instinct alone. I could run in a circle and they'd follow me like fools before I finished them off with either Ashrend or my fire." Her grin curled into a wicked smirk. "I can handle a few scratches."

Kaelin's mouth parted, torn between a scold and a laugh.

"I can hold my own," Ren added, a spark of that familiar fire returning to her eyes. "You should know by now. I don't break easily."

Without asking, without hesitating, Kaelin bent low and pressed her lips to Ren's wrist. A soft kiss, tender. Her breath lingered, fanning across Ren's skin like a promise.

Ren's pulse thundered in response.

Violet eyes flicked to Ren. Kaelin leaned in close enough that her breath was a whisper against Ren's skin. "I don't like seeing you like this, and I hate—" Her breath caught, her teeth clenched. "I hate that you think you have to face it alone."

Ren tilted her head. "Alone? Hardly. I've got a prince who knows his way around a sword, and a certain princess whose blade swings as sharp as her tongue."

Ren reached over, her fingers brushing against Kaelin's cheek before settling there. Her thumb traced a slow circle along Kaelin's skin, smudging away the faint worry line that had gathered between her brows.

Kaelin's breath caught. Her eyes fluttered closed, unbidden, as she leaned into Ren's touch.

Ren's voice dropped, quieter. "You don't have to worry."

But Kaelin only hummed, her lashes trembling, her fingers curling against the bedsheets as though the loss of that touch might undo her entirely.

Finally, Ren cleared her throat. "If that's your way of keeping me all to yourself, I've heard worse proposals. I guess that makes us... what? Sweethearts? Or is it courting when royalty's involved? Should I start practicing my curtsies and table manners?"

Kaelin rolled her eyes, but her smile was soft like Ren had just handed her the moon. "I wouldn't mind seeing you curtsying at my feet. Might be the highlight of my reign."

Ren snorted, but the sound was swallowed whole when Kaelin kissed her, fierce and unrelenting at first, as if she needed proof that Ren was alive, breathing, *hers*. Then it softened, lingering, like a vow spoken in silence.

The door creaked open. The young nurse froze in the doorway, eyes wide, a tray of herbal salves trembling in her hands. "I—uh—should I...?" she stammered, looking between them like she'd walked in on something sacred or scandalous.

Or both.

Kaelin didn't even turn but stated, "Leave."

The poor girl nearly dropped the tray.

Ren reached over, catching Kaelin's wrist with a warning glance. "Easy, you're scaring the shit out of the person who's keeping me alive."

Kaelin didn't look remorseful, exactly, but she relented.

Ren gave the nurse an apologetic glance. "Maybe come back in five. Or ten. Also, maybe knock louder next time."

The girl nodded timidly and all but fled.

When the door clicked shut, Ren sighed and remarked to Kaelin, "You're going to stop half the court's hearts at this rate."

Kaelin smirked. "Then they'll learn not to interrupt when I'm kissing you."

Ren turned her head and stared at the ceiling, its cracked stone dimly lit by the flickering wall sconce nearby. Her breath came slow, deliberate, as if her body were trying to ground itself in the aftermath of something seismic.

Just an hour ago, she'd kissed Kaelin. Again, and again. And she could have kept going if not for her wound.

The memory struck like lightning – Kaelin's mouth on hers, all fire and hunger. A cold sweat clung to the nape of her neck, but it warred with the low, curling heat blooming in her belly, a confusing, maddening ache of want and warning.

Gods, what the hell was happening to her?

When this all began—whatever this was—she'd vowed to keep Kaelin at arm's length. Kaelin had been an infuriating thorn, a symbol of everything Ren loathed about this realm: powerful, poised, untouchable. The kind of fae who would've laughed at a gutter rat like her once upon a time.

And now?

Somewhere along the way, the fae princess who once made Ren's blood boil now made her burn in another way entirely.

A soft knock shuddered against the chamber door, barely audible over the crackling hearth.

Ren groaned, ready to close her eyes and let sleep pull her under again. But the door creaked open, and heavy footsteps echoed across the stone floor.

Talen moved like a storm held at bay, his face shadowed in the dim firelight. He sat where Kaelin had earlier, the weight of him pressing into the chair as though the burden he carried was too great to bear. His expression was drawn, lips tight, brows furrowed in a way Ren hadn't seen before, as though he were trying to solve a puzzle.

"How are you?" he murmured, his voice low, careful.

"I've been better." She hesitated, then added with a wry smile, "One hell of a fight we had."

The words struck something in him. His frown deepened. "What do you remember of it?"

Ren shifted, propping herself up against the headboard. "Too many corpses. Then the fire." She flexed her fingers absently. "Blackness after that until I woke up here."

Her lips pressed together, the memory flickering like a half-forgotten dream. That low and guttural voice scorching into her mind – *burn, burn, burn*. She'd almost felt it inside her chest, urging her, coaxing her to lose control.

And she did.

Thinking back, Ren wasn't sure what had been real. The battlefield was chaos, the air thick with screams and smoke. Maybe it had been her imagination. Maybe her mind had simply conjured something monstrous to make sense of the fire that had come from her own hands.

"Why?" Ren finally asked the question she had been dreading. "What else happened?"

"*You* happened," Talen answered, the words falling from his lips like a curse. "Your fire... it incinerated all the corpses. But the entire village is gone, too. My soldiers barely had enough time to get out of your line of attack, otherwise they'd be incinerated as well."

Her mouth went dry. The walls seemed to tilt around her.

"Was anyone...?" she whispered.

He shook his head, the tension in his shoulders easing. "Everyone was either already dead or evacuated."

Relief surged through her, mixing with a sickening swirl of guilt. "Thank the gods," she breathed.

"Yes," Talen murmured, but his voice was hollow. "Thank the gods, indeed."

Silence stretched between them, thick and suffocating. The nursemaid entered quietly, pressing a cup of bitter-smelling remedy into Ren's hands. Ren drank, grimacing at the taste, but the numbing effect seeped into her limbs almost instantly, making her head feel light and distant.

Talen remained, his eyes roaming over her. "You're certain you don't remember anything?"

Ren shook her head, her thoughts already clouding. "Nothing. I lost control, maybe. But it won't happen again."

"And how exactly do you plan to ensure that?" he murmured, gaze flickering down her body and back to her face.

Unease rippled through her. His stare wasn't one of compassion.

It was an assessment.

"I'll figure it out. I'll ask Zakhar, or... or someone trained in elemental magic. Trust me, I'm not just going to sit around waiting for it to explode again."

He rose slowly, the chair scraping lightly against the stone as he stepped back. "Rest, Ren. You'll need it."

And then he left, the door closing with a quiet finality that sent a shiver through her, as though something vital had been sealed away.

Talen paused in the corridor, his hand hovering over the latch as if he might turn back.

But what was there to say? What comfort could he offer when all he saw behind his eyelids was fire—*her fire*—consuming everything?

The village had been ash before the sun rose. Not just the dead. The homes. The fields. The stone itself.

All gone.

And she had stood at the center of it, her hair wild with flames, her eyes molten gold, her conduit an inferno of uncontrolled power. Talen recalled wings made of molten flame unfurling from Ren's back.

No human should wield such magic. No mortal should be able to raze a village to nothing but embers and ash.

Who are you, Ren? he wondered, his pulse racing. *What are you?*

He knew the answer. Flameborne. He remembered her as a woman in chains, frightened and fierce. But the woman in that firestorm? That was something older. Something dangerous.

Something not human.

A flicker of unease shivered down his spine. His loyalty to the crown, to his people, warred with the pull she exerted over him—the pull of something wild and terrifyingly untamed. If she ever turned on them... gods, he didn't know if even he could stop her.

Talen forced himself to turn away, his steps echoing down the corridor, leaving behind not just a prisoner in a sickbed, but a question that might one day shatter the kingdom.

What is she capable of?

61

R en slipped past the threshold of Kaelin's chamber, the door gently clicking shut behind her.

The room was swathed in shadows, save for the golden flicker of firelight casting warmth against the walls.

Kaelin slept on her side, one arm tucked beneath the pillow, the other draped loosely across her waist. Her golden hair spilled over the bedding. The silken sheets clung to the dip of her waist, revealing the rise and fall of her breath, the soft slope of her shoulder, the faintest crease between her brows that hadn't quite faded with sleep.

They had spent so much time together in the last three days that it had felt as though Kaelin's shadow was stitched to her own. While Ren was confined to the infirmary, Kaelin came and went with an almost absurd devotion – bringing her tea in the mornings, wine at dusk, and strategy board games Ren quickly grew sick of losing. Books appeared in Ren's lap as the days stretched on, and when the hush fell over the infirmary at night, Kaelin read aloud stories by candlelight until Ren's eyes grew heavy.

It had been enough to make Ren realize that Kaelin was a doting lover. The moment she was free from the infirmary, Ren found herself here.

Ren shuffled closer. Her hand hovered near the bedpost, aching to reach forward and brush a lock of hair from Kaelin's face, just to feel her and to know this moment wasn't a dream. Her eyes traced Kaelin's parted lips, the gentle flush to her cheeks, the way the firelight kissed her collarbone like a lover's touch. But it was the faint shadow beneath Kaelin's eyes that caught Ren's attention, a discoloration born from too many late nights and endless days of duty.

Kaelin gave so much to her people, to her court, to Ren herself.

What did she ever receive in return?

If there was any justice, Ren would find a way to make the princess feel good for once. With a deep breath to steady her nerves, Ren sank onto the bed, sliding under the covers and positioning herself between Kaelin's thighs. Kaelin stirred slightly at the movement but did not wake.

Ren leaned in close, fingers gently easing away Kaelin's clothes, her breath warm against Kaelin's most intimate area. Ren inhaled deeply, savoring the scent of Kaelin's arousal. Slowly, teasingly, Ren ran her tongue along Kaelin's folds, tasting her essence – *Gods, she is divine,* Ren thought as she fought back a moan against the heat of Kaelin's core. She was all honey and grapefruit, sweeter than any Vaelaran wine Ren had ever tasted.

Kaelin let out a soft moan in her sleep, her hips twitching slightly. Emboldened, Ren delved deeper, her tongue circling Kaelin's sensitive nub. Kaelin's breathing grew heavier, her body already beginning to respond to Ren's ministrations.

Ren took her time, lavishing Kaelin with slow, deliberate licks and kisses. She wanted to drive Kaelin wild with desire. She fluttered her tongue over Kaelin's clit, alternating between light flicks and firm pressure. As Kaelin's moans grew louder, Ren slid two fingers inside her, curling them just so to stroke that sensitive spot. Kaelin's thighs trembled, her hands fisting in the sheets as she finally began to stir.

"Ren?" Kaelin murmured. "What are you doing?"

In response, Ren doubled her efforts, sucking Kaelin's clit between her lips and pumping her fingers faster. Kaelin arched off the bed, her body yielding to Ren's skilled touch.

"Don't stop," Kaelin pleaded, her voice breathy with need.

"I'm sorry, what was that?" Ren purred against Kailen's arousal, pausing her fingers that were buried deep inside the fae princess.

Ren could sense Kaelin's frustration, could picture her clenching her jaw in defiance, not used to obliging others. Ren nipped at Kailen's folds, hard enough to deliver a sharp jolt of pain, before slowly lapping the area with her tongue in a soothing stroke. She heard Kailen's sharp intake of breath from above.

"Please," was Kaelin's quiet plea, a tone of desperation so deep and alluring that Ren nearly came undone from the sound itself.

Ren obliged, redoubling her efforts.

Kaelin tensed, her inner muscles clenching around Ren's fingers as she climbed toward her peak. With a keening cry, Kaelin reached her climax, her body shaking with the force of her release. Ren continued to lap at her, helping her ride out the waves of pleasure until Kaelin collapsed back onto the bed.

"Come here, you," Kaelin murmured, a smile tinging her voice. Ren pulled herself from the covers and leaned into Kaelin. Kaelin trailed her fingers along Ren's spine. A slow smile spread across Kaelin's lips.

"Ren, darling, that was *quite* the surprise."

Ren stirred slightly, her body arching into Kaelin's touch. But before Ren could respond, Kaelin's magic coursed through the room.

Ren found herself suddenly immobile, and slowly dragged across the covers by some unseeable force. She was then brought up, on her knees and on all fours. Her limbs were splayed out, leaving her cunt entirely exposed to Kaelin's devouring gaze behind her.

"What's happening?" Ren asked, attempting to move. But it was no use.

She was utterly at the mercy of Kaelin's magic.

Kaelin chuckled, trailing her fingers down Ren's spine slowly to cup her ass before delivering a sharp *spank*. Ren jolted, a curse slipping out between her teeth. Kaelin's smirk lingered, but her eyes softened as she leaned closer. "Is this okay? Tell me if you'd rather move, and I'll stop."

The tenderness cut straight through Ren's defenses. Her cheeks burned crimson, and she gritted her teeth as though admitting it cost her something. "It's... it's okay," she muttered, eyes darting away. She could never confess aloud how intoxicating it was to be unraveled in Kaelin's hands – stripped of her defenses, laid bare in a way that set fire to her very skin.

Kaelin's lips curved, relief and hunger mingling in her expression. "Good," she whispered, brushing a kiss just below Ren's ear. "Then be a good girl and let me take care of you."

With that, Kaelin buried her face between Ren's thighs, her tongue delving deep into Ren's slick heat. Ren cried out, her body shuddering with pleasure despite her initial shock. Kaelin feasted on Ren like a starved individual, her tongue exploring every intimate fold and crevice. She licked and sucked, her fingers gripping Ren's hips to hold her steady when Ren began moving, desperate to grind against Kaelin's skillful tongue. Ren could only moan and gasp, drowning in the sensations that coursed through her.

But just as Ren thought she would reach her peak, Kaelin pulled away, leaving her aching and desperate. Ren cursed, trying to buck her hips to gain more friction.

"Not yet," Kaelin teased, blowing cool air over Ren's heated flesh. "I want to hear you say it." Her soft fingers ran over the curve of Ren's ass and delivered another firm *smack*. "Tell me who you belong to."

Ren panted, her mind fogged with desire. Then a part of her pride perhaps, made her grind her teeth and seethe, "Like *hell*."

Kaelin let out a soft laugh, followed swiftly by another firm spank. Ren bit hard on her lower lip, wanting to move forward, to get away, but Kaelin's magic prevented her from doing so. "Try again, darling."

Apparently Kaelin's magic didn't extend to her neck and head because Ren sent a smoldering glare at Kaelin over her shoulder.

Kaelin clicked her tongue, tilting her head. "Very naughty, Ren darling." She leaned over Ren, her fingers traveling from her hips up to her breasts, to her hardened nipples. Ren squeezed her eyes shut when Kaelin fondled her nipples just as her other finger slowly delved into Ren's heat.

"You were mine the moment I laid eyes on you. The moment I saw you *kneeling* before me."

"Oh, yeah?" Ren managed to retort, breathless. It took every ounce of her to get out, "That's funny. I wonder how long it will be before you're on your knees before *me*. I think I shall enjoy that view very much."

Kaelin leaned in close, her teeth grazing the shell of Ren's ear as she growled, "Saints, you have no idea what you do to me. I could devour you whole and still not be sated." Her nails skimmed Ren's thigh, a tremor of restraint in her touch. "On my knees? For you, Ren, I'd *crawl*."

Ren inhaled sharply as Kailen returned her attention to Ren's most sensitive area, lapping at her, while her fingers delved deep within her. Ren began to see stars. Kaelin responded with her tongue, lapping and nipping at her to the point where Ren forgot her very existence, her own name.

And then, Kaelin stopped.

Ren wanted to cry.

"I-I belong to you," Ren gasped out immediately, seeping with pure and primal need.

"Louder. I couldn't quite hear you." Lazily, Kaelin trailed a finger warningly over the curve of Ren's ass. Ren could hear the wicked smirk in her voice.

"Only you," Ren managed. "I'm yours."

Kaelin purred in approval, rewarding Ren with a long, slow lick. "Good girl," she praised.

With that, Kaelin pressed forward, her tongue circling Ren's clit with ruthless precision. She slid two fingers inside Ren, pumping them in time with the thrusts of her tongue.

Ren lost herself in the sensations, her body tensing as her climax built. "Please," she begged. "I need...I need..."

"I know what you need," Kaelin growled.

Ren gasped aloud, throwing her head back.

"Come for me," Kaelin growled, her fingers curling just so. "*Now.*"

At Kaelin's command, Ren fell apart, her body convulsing with the force of her orgasm. She screamed Kaelin's name, her pleasure echoing through the chamber.

Kaelin held Ren close, her magic finally releasing her, as she rode out the waves of ecstasy, her touch gentle and soothing. When Ren finally stilled, Kaelin crawled up her body to capture her lips in a searing kiss.

The next morning, Ren had barely finished her breakfast when Talen brushed past her with a clipped, solemn command, "Come. Let's see what you've learned."

He left no room for refusal.

She wiped her fingers on her trousers and slid off the bench, trailing behind him with cautious steps. He had said little since she'd left the infirmary, but she felt his presence regardless – felt his eyes on her whenever she entered a room.

Was it because she was entangled with his sister or because he suspected something else entirely, something darker?

Ren wasn't sure which was worse.

They reached the sparring pit, its packed dirt floor darkened by morning dew. The faint clang of steel rang from the armory, but otherwise the grounds were nearly empty. Only a female fae soldier jogged lazy laps along the perimeter, leaving Ren and Talen in a circle of open silence.

Without a word, Talen grabbed his blade from the rack and tossed hers across the distance. Ren caught it by reflex, the weight settling into her palms with grim familiarity. She pressed her lips thin, rolling her shoulders.

They circled each other.

Ren shifted her stance, grounding herself the way she remembered from the pits—weight on the balls of her feet, arms loose but ready, blade angled just enough to guard her center. Talen, for his part, moved smoothly, his blade held with casual elegance that betrayed just how easily he could cut her down.

The first clash came suddenly. Talen lunged, steel meeting steel with a bright ring that jolted her bones. Ren staggered but recovered, teeth bared in concentration. She swung back, clumsy but quick. He parried without effort, twisting his wrist so her blade glanced harmlessly aside.

"Still too slow," he muttered.

Ren came at him again. Blow after blow rang through the pit, her strikes fueled by stubbornness more than skill. Talen blocked each one, sometimes not even bothering to shift his stance. His eyes narrowed, not with pity or patience, but with scrutiny.

Sweat slicked her brow, dripping into her eyes as she swung again. This time, Talen struck back with force. His blade drove into hers, the vibration rattling her teeth. His movements grew sharper, his voice turning clipped.

"Balance," he barked as she stumbled.

"Guard higher."

"Again."

She obeyed, panting, every strike heavier than the last, though her arms screamed in protest. He pressed her harder, footwork tight, blade snapping in a rhythm that left her breathless.

And then—

It slipped.

It was just a flicker, a spark. The heat in her veins surged at the wrong moment, bursting out in a flare that danced along the edge of her blade before vanishing.

Talen froze. His boots ground against the dirt as he stepped back, his hand instinctively raising his blade not as a sparring partner, but as a fae warrior before a threat. "Watch yourself," he warned, his voice calm, *too* calm. The kind of calm that masked unease.

Ren lowered her blade. She wanted to say something—any-thing—but the words refused her.

Talen's gaze bored into her, hard as iron. His grip flexed once on the hilt of his blade, then slowly released. "You need to understand," he continued, quieter now, "I can't protect you if you're going to be reckless. Next time, there may be others watching." His eyes darkened. "And they may not be so forgiving."

The air between them thickened with silence, punctuated only by Ren's harsh breathing and the distant patter of the jogger's feet circling the pit.

Ren knew he was right, and yet she hated the reminder that no matter how hard she fought, no matter how much she survived, one wrong spark could cost her everything.

Ren exhaled, lowering her blade and steadying her trembling arms. "I'll train harder," she managed. "I swear it."

Talen gave no answer, only looked away, as though the ground itself offered more comfort than her promise.

"Why have you been watching me so suspiciously?"

His head snapped up, emerald eyes narrowing. For a moment, she thought he might snap at her. Instead, he turned slightly, as if to call the session done.

"No." Ren stepped forward, blocking his path, her sword tip sinking into the dirt. "Don't brush me off. Not when it's clear you've already decided I can't be trusted."

"Ren – "

"You were the first one here I trusted," she blurted. Her chest heaved as the words tumbled out, the kind she hadn't meant to give voice to. "And now I feel like I've lost that. Like I've lost you. And I hate that I made you doubt me."

For a long, heavy silence, Talen's face betrayed nothing. Then, at last, his features softened. His voice dropped low, resigned. "It's not doubt, Ren." He hesitated, eyes flicking away before returning to hers. "That day, when you burned through that village like it was paper—it wasn't just flame. Something else seemed to take hold of you. Something... unworldly." His mouth pressed into a thin line. "And if it takes you again, I don't know what can stop you. I don't know if anyone could."

Ren's stomach turned cold. He was *afraid* of her. The words hit harder than any strike he had landed that morning.

For a heartbeat, she wanted to flinch away, to swallow it down and let silence cover the wound. But something in her rebelled, burned hotter than shame.

She lifted her chin.

"You know me, Talen. You've watched me fight, watched me bleed beside you. I will do whatever it takes to control this, whatever it is. I won't let it hurt anyone. That's the last thing I want." Her hand tightened on the hilt of her sword until her knuckles whitened. "But I need you to believe me. If I lose your trust now, then what's left?"

Talen's gaze flicked over her face, searching for cracks in her conviction. The hard set of his mouth didn't soften, but something in his eyes shifted, conflicted. "Gods help me, Ren... I want to believe you. I really do. But there's so much we don't understand."

Ren held his gaze, refusing to let him see how much the words hurt.

Without another word, she turned her blade point-down and drove it into the packed earth between them. The steel rang with finality as she sank to one knee, her head bowed and voice steady. "I give you my word that I will master this power. I will not let it harm those I fight beside. On my life, I swear it."

When Ren lifted her gaze, Talen stood frozen, his eyes wide with something close to shock. In Vaelaran culture, an oath sealed in steel and earth was a vow that could not be taken back without dishonor. To betray it was to invite a fate worse than exile: one was expected to take up their own blade, cut themselves open, and bleed onto the earth as payment for their broken word.

Talen's jaw worked, a flicker of conflict crossing his face before he inclined his head. "I accept your oath."

Ren's heart pounded, but she held still, waiting for him to dismiss her, to turn away. Instead, he lingered a beat longer, studying her as if trying to see through her skin to whatever truth lay buried beneath.

Finally, he spoke again. "There's one last creature. More dangerous than the rest. I'm still gathering word of its whereabouts. When the time comes, we'll face it together. And then you'll receive your final payment."

And with that, he turned, striding from the pit, his cloak snapping in the breeze.

Ren stayed kneeling a moment longer, her sword still anchored in the dirt, before rising slowly. Her palm pressed against the hilt, her vow thrumming in her bones.

Whatever came next, she would be ready.

62

R en needed answers.

Two names had risen in her mind. Veylan or Zakhar.

The first option would mean hours of poring over brittle parchment while avoiding Sir Pindlewhip's prattling commentary, and Ren didn't have patience for that. She needed the truth *now*.

So, Zakhar it was.

Even asking after him had earned her wary looks. Fae spoke of him with a strange reverence;; they knew he brewed the elixirs for the Witherblight, they knew he wielded magic older than memory itself. But beyond that? Nothing.

Zakhar was *vital*; he was the one who had created the Verdant Elixir, the only known weapon against the plague that had ravaged the realm. Without him, the cure would die with its secret. So how was it that no one truly knew who he was?

No history.

No origin.

A fae noble had muttered that Zakhar slipped into the forest earlier, searching for *some odd mushroom he needed for one of his brews.*

That was enough for Ren to go searching for him. After grabbing lunch in the market, Ren sauntered past the outer gates with a careless smile thrown at the guard stationed there. He only sighed, the kind that said *I don't care what you do so long as it doesn't get me killed.*

The forest outside of Pyraelia's gates swallowed her whole, and for a startling moment, she was reminded of the journey she made when she first came to the gates, with Talen and Elira.

Thick foliage reached greedy fingers across her path, thorns snagging at her sleeves as if to warn her back. She shoved them aside with a muttered curse. The light grew dim beneath the canopy. Her boots sank into damp earth, and the air grew cool, carrying the faint trickle of running water.

That sound pulled her forward.

And then, Ren caught a glimpse of a dark silhouette hunched by the riverbank. The figure's long robes dragged like smoke against the mossy stonest. Even before he turned, she knew who it was.

Zakhar.

He didn't look at her immediately. His wild gray curls were more unruly than ever, sticking out at angles as though the wind itself was caught in them. When at last he turned his head, his eyes caught the dying light—dark pools rimmed faintly with silver, ancient and strange.

Ren froze at the sight. Even now, after everything, she couldn't decide if his gaze unsettled her or drew her in deeper.

"You wander far for someone so small," Zakhar murmured at last. "Do the palace halls bore you already, Flameborne?"

"I came because I have some questions I thought you may know the answers to."

Zakhar tilted his head as though considering her request, then turned back to the river, dipping his hand into its current. When he drew it out, water slipped through his fingers. "Answers," he mused. "The sweetest poison of them all."

Ren stepped closer. "Every time I lose control, I hear a voice. Right before it happens. Is that... normal for a Flameborne? Or is something wrong with me?"

"What you're hearing may not be a flaw or a failing. It could be... a presence. One bound to your magic. One that has waited a very long time."

"Whatever it is... can I control it?"

Zakhar rose then. "Truth is a door, and once you open it, you do not choose what comes through."

Ren's skin prickled. But she held his gaze. "Then open it for me."

They stared at each other for a few seconds. That was when Ren noticed the river.

The river should have run downhill, away from her, but as Ren studied the current, she realized it bent the other way. The current surged upstream, climbing stone and root as if it had forgotten the pull of the world.

Zakhar grinned like a child with a dangerous toy when he noticed Ren's gaze. "Isn't it beautiful?" he remarked, eyes flashing with a fever-bright light. "How something so certain can be undone in a moment." He watched the impossible current dance, delighted, as if the world bending wrong beneath his fingers was the only music he ever needed.

"*You* did that?"

"Of course," he replied, as if she'd asked if the sky was blue. "Rivers run down. People bow. But with the right pressure, the right spark, anything—" his gaze slid to her, sharp and unsettling, "—and *anyone* can change direction."

A shiver chased down her spine.

Through gritted teeth, Ren asked, "And what are you saying, exactly? Just get to it."

"I'm saying that nothing is fixed. Not rivers. Not crowns. Not even *you*."

The river still clawed uphill, water climbing roots and stone as if the world had been turned inside out.

"Have you ever known any Flameborne who heard voices?"

Zakhar chuckled softly, the sound both mirth and menace. "Ah, the past," he murmured, crouching low to trail a finger through the backward-flowing current.

"Stop beating around the bush and answer me," Ren paused. "Please."

Zakhar's gaze softened. "Do you see why the river runs uphill now? Even what seems unchangeable can be undone. What was once cruelty *can end*. What was once a servant... can surely *rise*." He shifted a sprig of dried herb between his fingers. "Most Flameborne carry the blood of dragons. That alone is dangerous. But only a rare few can house a dragon's soul. And those are very different things."

"Zakhar, are you implying that the voice I've been hearing isn't *mine*?"

Ren looked again at the water crawling against its nature, relentless, impossible. She didn't know if his display was meant to comfort her or to break her further.

"What am I supposed to do with that truth?" she whispered.

"Ah, that is the question only *you* can answer."

Ren slipped into her room after an evening at the tavern with Elira.

After finding out about the events yesterday when speaking with Zakhar, she needed an evening of going out into the town. She couldn't help but feel guilty for nights of indulging in drink and revelry with Elira, yet these nights kept her going.

Her stomach still felt pleasantly full, but her pride ached from yet another swift defeat at darts. Elira's precision was inhuman, every throw a perfect strike that left Ren muttering about unfair advantages and reflexes.

Ren was already half-grinning at the thought of telling Mirella about it, gossiping over a bottle of wine before sinking into the steaming hot springs. Through staying in Pyraelia, Ren admittedly found herself growing almost fond of these small indulgences like the warmth of good food in Pyraelia, the hum of laughter in the taverns, the simple comfort of being clean and unhurried for once.

She tugged at the ties of her outer tunic, already anticipating the heat of the baths—

Then froze mid-motion.

There, sitting neatly in the middle of her bed, was a wooden box. It was plain, unadorned.

"Someone left a gift for you," Mirella trilled from her corner, her voice lilting in a sing-song mockery. "Go on – open it."

Ren narrowed her eyes, staring at the box as though it might sprout claws and leap for her throat.

"Go on," Mirella pressed. "What are you waiting for?"

"Who left this?"

"You'll know as soon as you open it." Mischief glimmered in Mirella's tone, like a child waiting for their prank to unfold.

Ren crossed her arms, unmoving.

Mirella sighed dramatically. "Trust issues, Ren, honestly."

Ren shot her a glare that could have curdled milk. "I'm going to pretend I didn't hear that."

She picked up the box, half expecting it to be heavier. But it was feather-light. She tilted it slightly, waiting for a rattle, a shift.

Nothing.

Gingerly, Ren slid her fingers over the lid, lifting it open as though disarming a trap.

Inside lay ribbons.

Dozens of them. Satin, silk, cotton—some glossy, some matte. All folded with care, arranged neatly in a rainbow of color. Crimson. Indigo. Gold. Forest green. Every shade imaginable, waiting like treasures in the modest box.

Strapped to the lid was a slip of parchment, tucked securely beneath the band. Ren's chest squeezed as her eyes fell upon the familiar handwriting, the elegant cursive she had already memorized.

Ren's hand shook as she tugged the note free, unfolding it with a reverence she couldn't disguise.

I remember what you told me—the ribbons you stole as a girl because you wanted to have something that was yours. You shouldn't have had to steal to feel that way. If I'd been there, I would have given you all the ribbons you could have ever wanted.

So here they are, darling. Yours. Always yours.

—Kaelin

Ren she sank on the bed, the note trembling in her hand. She blinked hard against the heat rising in her eyes.

It was foolish how something so small could unravel her, how one slip of parchment and a box of ribbons could feel more valuable than any piece of jewelry.

A smile tugged at the corners of Ren's mouth. She touched the ribbons, the silks cool and smooth beneath her fingers.

Mirella's voice broke through the haze. "Well, well, well."

Ren jerked, shoving the note to her lap as though hiding a guilty secret. But Mirella was already swooping in, ever so insightful. "What's that, Ren? Is that... a smile? Gods above, I didn't think your face even knew how to do that."

Ren scowled, though the expression wavered, betrayed by the softness still curling her lips. "Shut up."

"Oh, this is rich." Mirella jiggled excitedly, her drawers drumming together in mock swoon. "Whoever gave you that box must be very, very special. Look at you—smiling like a maiden in love."

Ren's cheeks flared.

Mirella only cackled, her laughter bouncing around the chamber like bells. "Oh, I am never letting you live this down. Never."

Ren rolled her eyes, trying to school her face into its usual mask of steel. But even she couldn't smother the warmth blooming in her chest, the way her heart ached with something dangerously close to hope.

Because Kaelin had cared enough to remind Ren she didn't need to steal scraps of beauty anymore.

Not when someone wanted to give her the world.

Ren braided her hair that night, fingers weaving with deliberate precision as she threaded a violet ribbon through the plait.

The color reminded her of twilight skies she caught once or twice here in Pyraelia when strolling the gardens. Ren caught her reflection in the mirror and allowed herself a fleeting moment of admiration before exhaustion lulled her to her bed.

For once, she felt like sleeping in her own room. The quiet was comforting, a stillness she hadn't realized she'd missed. She slipped beneath the blankets, the faint hum of the palace beyond her walls fading into calm.

As Ren's eyes grew heavy, she heard Mirella sigh from the other side of the room. "Falling in love. Makes me wonder what that might feel like."

Ren smiled faintly into her pillow but didn't answer; sleep found her before she could.

But sleep did not keep her.

Her instincts snapped her awake at the unshakable awareness of another presence in her room.

Ren scanned the room. Mirella's figure sat in her corner, perfectly still, likely deep in her trance-like version of sleep.

But someone else was here.

Through the darkness, Ren's gaze fell on a shadow in her doorway. Ren willed herself to remain limp, feigning sleep, waiting to see if the intruder would withdraw.

They didn't.

Their steps were soft, deliberate, bringing them closer with each breath Ren drew. Her muscles tensed beneath the sheets, hands curling into fists, Ashrend's hilt waiting only inches away.

The figure stopped beside her bed.

Ren shot upright, steel flashing. Ashrend met another blade, already drawn. The crash of steel clanged through the silence as Ren locked eyes with her intruder.

The hood obscured their features, shadows swallowing their face, but Ren felt the heaviness of their stare.

"Wrong room, I take it," Ren hissed, teeth bared. Her sword pressed harder against theirs.

With a burst of strength, Ren twisted, hooking her legs around the figure's waist, driving upward to throw them off balance. For a moment, she almost succeeded.

But the figure moved faster.

Gloved fingers shot out, wrapping tight around Ren's throat, and Ren was slammed back against her mattress. Her breath vanished in a choke. The intruder's weight pinned her, the pressure on her windpipe fierce enough to blur the edges of her vision. For a terrifying heartbeat, she thought they would crush the life from her.

Then their grip loosened, enough to allow air to scrape back into her lungs.

Ren coughed. She lashed out with Ashrend, steel singing as she carved through the space between them. The hooded figure only leaned back, avoiding the strike with a casual grace.

Their blade pressed against her throat in turn, the cool bite of metal kissing her skin.

"Leave this palace," the stranger whispered, voice low, threaded with menace. "Tonight."

Ren's lips curled, her voice steady despite the blade. "You'll have to do better than threats. If you're going to kill me, at least try to make it interesting. Who are you?"

The hooded figure tilted their head. "Names are for the living, and if you're not careful, you won't need mine."

Ren narrowed her eyes. "You're not answering my question."

"That's because you never learned when not to ask one." The blade at her throat eased away just enough for them to step closer, close enough that she could feel the whisper of their breath against her ear. "You speak when you should listen. You rush when you should think. And that—" they paused, voice dipping lower, "—will be your downfall. You clearly are in no position to make demands."

Ren's jaw clenched. "Then I'll die trying. It must be easy to sound brave when no one knows your face."

Then Ren spat up at the figure.

The intruder went deathly still.

Then, the first punch cracked against Ren's cheekbone. The second came harder, snapping her head to the side. She wheezed, tasting blood, but swung her fist anyway, but it only met air.

Fuck.

A third blow caught her in the ribs, and the world tilted. Ren gasped, the sound torn from her lungs as she rolled off the bed, landing on the floor in a huff of limbs. Another strike from the intruder's boots, another—the hits came in rhythm, efficient, unrelenting.

"Get off me, you coward, you bastard—" Ren managed in fury as each assault came. But her breath caught when stars burst behind her eyes. The edges of the room blurred, the world narrowing to a pulse and the metallic tang of her own blood.

Through the haze, she caught the glint of the stranger's blade sheathing, the shimmer of a cloak shifting toward the door. The figure paused only once.

Then they were gone, leaving Ren slumped on the floor.

Her cheek throbbed, her ribs ached, and blood dripped from her split lip, but her mind was already racing. She'd pushed their buttons on purpose. If they'd truly meant to kill her, she'd be a corpse cooling on the stone by now. No, this was a warning.

Still, there'd been something in those blows, more than temper, more than pride. Each strike had landed with precision, with intent. This was a message, carved into her with bruises and blood. *Stay out of it. Leave while you can.*

Ren pressed a trembling hand to the floor, forcing herself upright. And though fear bristled along her nerves, she couldn't ignore what she'd seen in those last moments—the swagger in the intruder's stance, the cocky tilt of their head, the effortless confidence in every movement.

It was familiar. Maddeningly so. But she couldn't place it.

Whoever they were, they *knew* her.

And they wanted her gone.

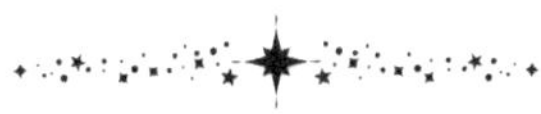

Ren had barely stumbled from her chambers before she found herself surrounded by guards, words tumbling out faster than sense. The palace erupted into motion—torches flaring, orders shouted, steel drawn—but despite her demands to hunt the intruder herself, she'd been dragged straight to the infirmary.

Now she sat on the edge of a narrow cot beneath the flicker of lanternlight, her head pounding in time with her heartbeat. The familiar female healer from the training yard loomed over her with her usual disapproval.

"Lucky they didn't break your ribs," she muttered, pressing a cloth of enchanted ice to her forehead.

Ren winced as the chill bit through her skin. "They're lucky I wasn't fully awake," she growled. "Coward, hiding behind a cloak, coming at me in the middle of the night. When I find them, I'll—"

Her hand shot up to rub at her temple, but the healer slapped it away with a sharp swat.

"Enough. You're in no shape to fight anyone. Talk all you want about how tough you are, but you're human." She leaned closer, voice dropping. "Which means you bleed and bruise and die easier. Whoever did this was fae."

The words cut through her anger. Ren's jaw tightened, her breathing slowed. "How can you tell?" she asked finally, her voice low.

The healer gestured toward her bruises. "Because it takes more than strength to do this kind of damage without finishing the job. They were precise, controlled. A mortal would've left you broken or dead. A fae knew exactly where to strike to make you hurt." She tapped a gloved finger near her temple, her tone turning grim. "An inch to the left, and you'd be gone. A dagger through the throat, and we'd be burning your body by dawn."

Ren swallowed hard, forcing down the tremor threatening her hands. The ice cloth dripped cold water down her neck.

The healer sighed. "Luckily for you, it's nothing you won't recover from. You'll have bruises, and that head of yours will stay swollen for a few days, but if you rest and keep it iced, you'll heal just fine."

Ren muttered something under her breath that sounded suspiciously like rest is for cowards, but the healer pretended not to hear it.

The healer finally straightened, giving her one last disapproving look. "Rest. No wandering tonight. And for the gods' sake, no heroics."

Ren managed a noncommittal grunt as she gathered his satchel and swept toward the door, muttering something about reckless mortals under her breath. The moment it clicked shut behind her, Ren swung her legs off the cot.

Her head throbbed in protest, but she ignored it. *Rest*, she thought bitterly, pressing the melting ice cloth to the table. *As if that's ever stopped anything.*

She moved quietly, testing her balance before slipping toward the door. If she was quick, she could get back to her room, grab Ashrend, and maybe—

The door opened before she could touch the knob.

Kaelin stepped through, the sweep of her cloak brushing the floor like a whisper. The princess's gaze found Ren immediately, taking in the split lip, the bruised cheek, and her defiant stance.

"Going somewhere?"

Ren froze mid-step, one hand still half raised in guilt. "Uh," she said dryly, "just stretching my legs."

Kaelin's brow arched. "You look like you're about to march into war."

"Maybe I am."

Kaelin's eyes narrowed the moment Ren took a step toward her. "Don't even think about it."

Ren bristled. "I'm fine."

"You can barely stand without swaying," Kaelin countered, her tone icy. "Go lie back down."

"Move, Kaelin."

When Kaelin didn't, Ren growled under her breath and shoved forward—

—only to find herself weightless a heartbeat later.

Kaelin moved in a blur, catching Ren by the wrist and tossing her over her shoulder as if she weighed nothing. The world spun, and Ren landed on the cot with a grunt, the breath knocked clean from her lungs.

"Gods damn it – "

Ren started to rise, fury burning through the pain, but Kaelin was already there, looming over her, one hand pressing against her shoulder to keep her down.

"Enough!" Kaelin hissed. The fire in her voice silenced even Ren. "You're being foolish. Impulsive. What exactly do you plan to do when you find them? Challenge them to another fight?" Her violet eyes flashed. "You already lost one, Ren. And if you don't stop and breathe long enough to plan your next move, you'll lose another."

Ren glared up at her, chest rising and falling in sharp, uneven breaths. Kaelin's grip eased but didn't fall away, her thumb unconsciously brushing against the fabric at Ren's collarbone.

Ren glared up at Kaelin, her lip split and her pride still bleeding. "If I find them again," she muttered, voice low and shaking with fury, "I'll make sure they don't walk away next time."

"And if they come back? What then, Ren? You'll throw yourself at them again until they finish what they started?"

Ren pushed herself up on her elbows, wincing. "I can handle – "

Kaelin cut her off, her voice cracking like thunder. "You nearly *died*!" The words hung between them, raw and trembling. Her breath came fast before she caught herself.

Silence settled, thick as smoke. The fury drained from Ren's chest, leaving something heavier behind.

Finally, Ren looked away. "There was something about them. The way they moved—their voice. It felt... familiar. Like I should've known them." Her hands curled into fists against the blanket. "Whoever they are, they know me."

Kaelin's eyes softened, the anger gone but the worry still etched deep. She sank onto the edge of the bed. "Then we'll find them," she said quietly. "Together. But not if you get yourself killed first."

Ren's mouth twitched into something that wasn't quite a smile. "You really don't like making things easy, do you?"

Kaelin's answering look was half exasperation, half something far gentler. "Not when it comes to you."

64

Three nights had passed since the intruder slipped into Ren's room.

Guards now lined nearly every corridor. She'd counted at least two stationed outside her chambers alone, another pair shadowing every turn she took through the halls.

Security had tightened ever since her visit to the throne room, when she'd stood before King Maelion and Lyra to recount every word the masked figure had said.

What struck Ren most wasn't the vigilance, but how safe it made her feel. Once, the sight of fae soldiers had set her nerves on edge. Now, their presence was oddly reassuring.

Still, no number of guards could help her tonight.

Ren's luck had run bone-dry.

For the third night in a row, Kaelin sat across from her, winning hand after hand as if the gods themselves tipped the game in her favor.

"You have to be three steps ahead," Kaelin slid a piece into place with the confidence of a queen toppling her opponent's king. "You can't just think about this next move. You have to know where it will take you."

Ren cracked her knuckle, the sound excruciatingly loud in the quiet room. Pain flared down her spine, a dull ache that reminded her she was still healing. Ren gritted her teeth, shoving her next piece forward.

Kaelin only clicked her tongue, a low, scolding sound that made Ren's eyes narrow. Kaelin advanced her counter, trapping Ren with one devastating sweep. "Whether it will lead you to victory..." Kaelin's eyes glittered. Her lips curved in a wicked grin as she leaned in, voice husky enough to stir the air between them. "...or your ruin."

Ren swallowed hard. It was yet again her ruin, indeed. "Again," Ren snapped, forcing the words through clenched teeth.

Kaelin reset the game with casual elegance, every movement controlled, deliberate. Even the way she tucked a strand of hair behind her pointed ear was distracting. Ren tore her gaze away before it lingered too long. But gods help her, her eyes betrayed her—dragging down to Kaelin's hands, slender, tracing the sharp lines of Kaelin's cheekbones, the long curve of her neck where her pulse flickered.

Heat flushed Ren's chest. She forced herself to focus on the board.

Still, a reckless part of her wanted to test the princess. To see if Kaelin's perceptiveness extended beyond battle and strategy – if she would catch Ren in the act.

So Ren slipped a piece beneath her thigh.

Kaelin's eyes snapped to the motion instantly.

Ren froze. *Shit.*

Kaelin rose slowly, predatory grace pouring off her in waves. "You're cheating? Against me?"

Ren tried for nonchalance, though her mouth betrayed the twitch of a grin. "Oh, come on. It's just a game."

"Pathetic," Kaelin spat, but the disdain in her tone only made Ren's pulse quicken. "You're supposed to be my opponent, yet you can't win without trickery?"

The amusement died from Ren's face. She shoved to her feet, meeting Kaelin eye-to-eye. "Maybe if you stopped toying with me and actually fought like you meant it, I'd stand a chance."

Kaelin's eyes darkened, molten and sharp. Her voice dropped to a hiss. "Careful. You're treading on thin ice."

Ren smirked, even as her heart pounded. "Or what? You'll fight me?" Her voice lowered, husky with challenge. "Please. I'd like to see you try."

Kaelin's anger flickered, then shifted – reforged into something hungrier, darker. Her lips curved into a slow, wolfish grin as she stepped forward, closing the space between them until Ren's back brushed the stone wall.

Her body radiated heat, and Ren's throat went dry.

"I'll do more than fight you, Ren, darling," Kaelin growled, every syllable thrumming through Ren's bones. She leaned close enough that Ren felt the whisper of her breath against her lips. "I'll break you down until the only word left in your pretty mouth is my name."

Ren shivered, part of her terrified, part of her aroused by the fae's words. "You wouldn't dare."

"Oh, I most certainly would," Kaelin replied, her hand snaking out to grip Ren's throat. "I want to make you beg for my touch, but your rebellion makes me want to fuck you senseless right here, until you're screaming my name and forgetting your own."

With that, Kaelin captured Ren's mouth in a bruising kiss, all teeth and tongue. Ren moaned into it, desire overwhelming her fear. Kaelin ravaged her mouth, marking her as her own.

When they broke apart, both panting, Kaelin's eyes were feral with lust. "Strip," she commanded. "Now."

Ren hurried to obey, practically tearing her clothes off in her haste. Kaelin did the same, revealing her toned, naked body. Ren glanced over her shoulder just in time to see Kaelin pull out a strap that wrapped around her waist, and when Ren saw what was jutting out in the front, her eyes widened. She had never seen such a thing before.

"On your hands and knees," Kaelin ordered, securing the harness around her hips. "Spread those legs wide for me. I'm going to pound your tight little pussy until you're begging for more."

"Where did you even get that?" Ren asked.

Kaelin's fingers wound their way in Ren's hair, grabbing a firm hold as she seethed into her ear, "I said, *get on your hands and knees*."

Ren scrambled to comply, arching her back and spreading her legs, revealing her already dripping arousal to Kaelin. She grabbed a nearby pillow to bury her head as she felt Kaelin's skillful fingers tease her folds, drawing out moisture.

"Someone's already dripping wet for me," Kaelin purred, pleased. Unconsciously, Ren went to pull her legs back together, but Kaelin clicked her tongue and tapped her ass as a gentle warning. "Ren, darling – I would stare at your swollen cunt all day if I could."

Ren couldn't stop the moan from leaving her lips as something hard and large kissed her opening, gently easing into her soaking folds. Her fingers clawed into the blanket, twisting the fabric in a grip so fierce the seams strained, knuckles blanching as if the cloth itself might tear beneath her hold.

"There you go," Kaelin purred as the thick strap-on slid deeper into Ren's slick pussy. "Take every fucking inch of me, Ren darling. I want to bury this cock so deep inside your tight hole that you feel me in your soul."

Ren gasped, her body stretching around the invading length, walls clenching instinctively as it filled her completely. Just as the tip pressed against her deepest spot, Kaelin started a steady rhythm – slow, deliberate thrusts that pulled back just enough to tease before driving in again.

"That's it, darling, relax and let your greedy little cunt get used to my size. Feel how it stretches you wide? You're dripping all over me already, aren't you? Tell me how much you love being stuffed full like this." Kaelin's hips rolled with control, giving Ren's swollen clit time to throb and adapt to the relentless pressure, her hands gripping Ren's thighs to hold her open.

"Y-Yes, please- – I need *ah*!"

Ren sat up, arching her back again and drawing her hips back for more. Kaelin snarled under her breath, pounding into Ren with all the force of her fae strength. Her hands gripped Ren's hips hard enough to leave bruises, pulling her back onto the thick strap-on, stretching her open. Ren could only moan in response, losing herself to the sensations crashing through her. Kaelin felt huge inside her, hitting depths she didn't know existed.

"That's it," Kaelin breathed, reaching around to circle Ren's clit. "Tell me who you belong to." Ren shuddered, the coil of pleasure in her belly winding tighter and tighter. Just as she thought she would come undone, Kaelin pulled out.

"No!" Ren cried out, disappointment and need warring within her. "Please, I need..."

"Shh," Kaelin soothed, trailing a finger down Ren's spine.

Kaelin flipped Ren over, spreading her legs wide and swiftly plunging back inside her wet folds. Ren arched off the ground, the new angle allowing Kaelin to hit that spot inside her that made stars explode behind her eyes.

Kaelin leaned down, her thrusts never faltering as she captured one of Ren's hard nipples in her mouth. She sucked hard, teeth grazing the sensitive peak, tugging it between her lips while her hips snapped forward in a deep, grinding rhythm. The strap-on plunged into Ren's soaked pussy with each roll, stretching her wide and hitting that sweet spot inside. Ren's hands flew to Kaelin's hair, tugging and twisting the soft curls as waves of pleasure crashed through her, her body arching up to meet every forceful drive. She buried her fingers deeper, clinging like it was her last grip on sanity amid the building storm.

"That's my good girl," Kaelin murmured against Ren's skin, her voice a rough growl laced with hunger as she released the nipple with a wet pop, only to lave it with her tongue before biting down just enough to sting. "Taking my cock like you were made for it. Fuck, I could pound this perfect pussy all day, every day." Her pace quickened slightly, hips circling to rub the base against Ren's throbbing clit with each thrust, drawing out those desperate whimpers. "You're so tight around me, squeezing like you never want me to stop. Keep gripping my hair, darling – show me how much you need this. I'll fuck you senseless if you beg pretty for it." Kaelin's free hand slid up Ren's side, pinning her wrist above her head to heighten the restraint, her mouth switching to the other nipple, sucking greedily as the tension coiled tighter in Ren's core.

"Come for me," Kaelin commanded. "Come on my cock, Ren darling."

At Kaelin's command, Ren shattered, her orgasm ripping through her. She screamed Kaelin's name over and over again as she convulsed.

Kaelin continued to thrust through Ren's climax, prolonging her pleasure until Ren thought she might pass out.

Finally, with one last deep stroke, Kaelin collapsed on top of Ren, both of them breathless.

Moments after they regained their breathing, Kaelin lazily stretched out on the bed. She unbuckled the harness around her hips and tossed it unceremoniously to the floor. Then, Kaelin crooked a finger at Ren, beckoning her closer.

Ren crawled toward her, her cheeks still flushed, and a slight tremble in her limbs.

"Come here and lick me clean," Kaelin purred, spreading her thighs wide in invitation as she lay back against the pillows. "Taste how wet you've made me."

Ren licked her lips, and obeyed, settling between Kaelin's legs. Ren leaned forward, her breath hot against Kaelin's slick folds. Kaelin tangled a hand in Ren's hair, guiding her where she wanted her.

With a tentative lick, Ren tasted Kaelin's essence. Kaelin moaned at the contact, her hips rolling forward, seeking more. Ren took the hint, her tongue delving deeper to lap at Kaelin's center.

"That's it," Kaelin praised, her voice breathy with pleasure. "Get your tongue nice and deep. I want to feel you everywhere."

Ren complied, sliding her tongue along Kaelin's slit and circling her clit. She suckled the sensitive nub, drawing gasps and moans from the fae. Kaelin ground against Ren's face, lost in the sensations. As Ren continued to feast on Kaelin, Kaelin's thighs trembled, her breath coming in short pants. She was so close, teetering on the edge of bliss.

"Don't stop," Kaelin gasped, her grip on Ren's hair tightening. Through gritted teeth, Kaelin uttered, "Right there – right there – "

Ren doubled her efforts, her tongue a blur of motion against Kaelin's clit. Kaelin's orgasm crashed over her like a tidal wave, her body arching off the bed as pleasure consumed her.

Kaelin collapsed back against the mattress, panting and sated. Ren looked up at her, her lips glistening with Kaelin's essence. Kaelin reached down, cupping Ren's chin and tilting her head up.

"You did well, darling," Kaelin murmured, her thumb gently trailing Ren's swollen lips. "I got you a gift."

Ren arched an eyebrow. "You're spoiling me."

With a wave of her hand, Kaelin summoned an item. She tossed it to Ren, a wicked grin on her face. "A little surprise I picked up at The Serpent's Kiss. Dangerous name, isn't it? Fitting, really. It's a shop tucked into the market's outer sectors. They sell all sorts of indulgences there: intoxicating wines, elixirs said to make your blood run hotter, and trinkets that claim to spark desire with a single touch." Her grin deepened, a sharp glint in her eyes. "Half the court pretends they'd never dare set foot inside, yet the place is always busy." She straightened, her voice turning firm. "I want you to pleasure yourself until you come undone. And I want to watch every second of it."

Ren's eyes widened, and she hesitated as she eyed the object. It was slick and small enough to fit in the palm of her hand. Yet when she held it, she felt warmth radiating from it.

"Go on," Kaelin purred, lazily suckling Ren's nipple until it hardened against the fae's lips. "Lay back and touch yourself."

Ren hesitated before lying back against Kaelin's shoulder to position herself. As soon as she held the object to her center, a low buzz filled the air. Startled, Ren instinctively pulled it away, but Kaelin brushed a strand of hair from Ren's forehead, her fingers cupping Ren's cheeks.

"It's harmless, Ren darling," she murmured. "Only intended to bring you pleasure."

Processing Kaelin's words, Ren pursed her lips and spread her legs apart, hesitantly pressing the object to her heat. Just as it made contact, the vibrating sensation tickled her clit, and immediately her body responded to its menstruations. With a moan, Ren pressed it firmer against her clit, her hips bucking up to meet the stimulation.

Kaelin settled back to watch, occasionally suckling on Ren's jutted nipples or nibbling playfully at her neck.

Combined with Kaelin's menstruations and the sensation between her legs, it didn't take long for Ren to cry out, her body quivering as ecstasy washed over her.

Later that evening, Ren let her gaze drift across the dining table, marveling at how strange it felt to be here again.

The last time she had dined with the royal family of House Vaelaran, Kaelin had seethed at her presence, her disdain visible. Ren remembered the way Kaelin's lips had curled in disgust, her body angled as far away from Ren as possible, as if the mere act of sitting beside her was offensive.

Now, it seemed Kaelin couldn't sit close enough.

Her shoulder brushed Ren's at every opportunity, her long fingers tracing casual patterns against Ren's wrist. She didn't even bother with subtlety. A crimson nail grazed Ren's elbow. A strand of Ren's hair caught between Kaelin's fingers, tugged gently as if testing how easily Ren could be undone. Ren tried not to stiffen at each touch, not to look like she was about to combust under the weight of it all.

But the royal family didn't seem to bat an eye.

Lyra seemed more interested in Ren's magic, leaning forward with keen curiosity to ask how Ren had first discovered it. Maelion wanted tales from the pits, his laughter booming across the hall when Ren admitted she'd once felled a man twice her size with little more than a broken chair leg.

After Ren finished telling that story and took another sip of her wine, Lyra asked, "What are your plans for after you complete your contract?"

From the corner of Ren's eye, she caught Kaelin's hand tightening against the table's edge.

Once, the answer would have been simple. That as soon as Ren finished her contract and collected her payment, she'd disappear into some quiet corner of the realm

But now, her gaze flicked to the fae at her side.

Kaelin.

Kaelin, who had once been Ren's bitterest thorn, whose sharp tongue and sharper pride had grated against every nerve Ren possessed. Yet what had begun as a rivalry had shifted, twisted, and bloomed into something she could no longer ignore.

Because when Ren thought of her future, she no longer saw an empty road leading away from everyone. She saw *Kaelin*.

The silence stretched, the table heavy with expectation. Ren parted her lips, but no words came.

It was Kaelin who broke the silence.

The princess's hand slipped into Ren's hair, twirling a loose strand around her red-tipped finger.

"Perhaps we might find a more permanent position for her here at court," Kaelin murmured. "It would be a waste to let someone with her skills vanish."

Across the table, Maelion set down his fork with deliberate care, his expression sobering. "Yes. There may yet be a more permanent place for her here in Pyraelia."

Once, Ren would have rejected the very notion of chains, no matter how gilded. But now, the thought of being bound here didn't feel like chains at all.

It felt like belonging.

The market was alive with color and noise and a tangle of smells.

There were spiced meats sizzling on skewers, leather oiled and polished, sweet honey cakes cooling on trays. Voices mingled in a dozen tongues, foreign dialects clashing like overlapping songs, each one vying for attention.

Ren marveled at how bustling it all was despite the season. Back in the north, winter meant shuttered doors and howling winds that gnawed at the bone. Here in Pyraelia, the winters were mild in comparison.

Through the hum of the crowd, a woman sat alone against a stone wall – a bard with hair streaked silver. Something in her gaze told Ren she had seen things too raw to ever unsee. She sang of the Witherblight, her melody threaded with decay, beauty, and despair, painting images of fields rotting mid-bloom and hearts blackened from within.

"Where children once played, laughter, only echoes answer now.
The Witherblight took their voices and left the earth to bow."

The contrast was jarring, life and death braided into every note. People skirted wide around her as though the melody itself might cling to their skin. They shunned her like a bad omen, as if ignoring her voice might keep the truth at bay.

Ren's gaze flicked for a bowl, a pouch, anywhere the woman might be collecting coin. But there was nothing. No offering plate, no scattered copper. The bard seemed less like a street performer and more like a death wraith made flesh, a siren risen among the living. Her eyes were hollow voids that had seen too much, her voice unraveling grief into the winter air. Ren felt a chill crawl up her spine as the truth struck her.

This was no song for coin, but a final act – a lament meant only to be lost into the world before silence claimed the bard, too.

Ren and Elira drifted between stalls like moths through lantern light, neither of them buying much but both pausing to watch the glassblowers shape fire into delicate forms, the fortune-dice throwers shouting over each other, the jewelers fanning out their wares where the sunlight caught every gleam of metal and stone.

They paused at a rack of dresses, browsing gossamer silks, the hems weighted with tiny coins that chimed together like distant bells when touched.

They made their way back into the market, and all too suddenly, the first fat raindrop splattered on Ren's cheek. Then came another. Within moments, the sky tore open in a torrent. Shouts rose across the market as vendors scrambled to cover their wares.

"Come on!" Elira grabbed Ren's wrist, her hand warm against Ren's cold skin, and together they darted through the downpour. They weaved between shuttering stalls, boots slipping on cobblestones now slick as glass.

At last, Elira shoved open the door to a tavern Ren couldn't catch the name of. Golden light and raucous laughter spilled out, chasing the shadows from the rain. They stumbled inside, dripping water, drawing a few glances but no real notice as the place was already filled with smoke, chatter, and music from a fiddle in the corner.

A fire snapped in the hearth, chasing the chill from Ren's bones.

"Two cups of whatever burns the fastest," Elira told the barkeep.

They'd barely taken a seat when someone dropped into the chair across from them.

"Well, well," Lucan drawled, raising a brow. "Looks like the storm decided my luck for me. Mind if join you ladies?"

Elira shrugged, clearly amused. "Suit yourself."

Lucan ordered a round for all three, and before long, the table was loud with conversation. Lucan had a way of filling the silence.

When the darts came out, Lucan challenged Elira, expecting to win. But Elira's aim was sharp, each dart sinking into the bull's-eye with steady confidence. Lucan whistled low.

"By the gods, woman. You'd give any marksman a run for his coin."

Elira bowed with a flourish, soaking in the applause of a few half-drunk patrons watching. "What can I say? I learned from the best."

Lucan nudged Ren playfully as she nursed her mug of ale. "First day of training and Ren passed out during her first round of sparring."

Ren whipped her head toward him. "Because your *friend* cheated and used magic during sparring!"

Lucan barked a laugh. "True. He nearly sent you flying off your feet."

Ren glared at him, but the corner of her mouth twitched.

Lucan lifted his mug. "Still. You overextended your stance."

Elira leaned her elbows on the table, swirling her drink with lazy amusement. "Overextending your stance leaves your heart-line wide open. A rookie mistake." she glanced at Ren. "I'm sure pit fights are different from fighting with steel."

Ren leaned back in her chair. "Finally, someone is speaking my language. In the pits, you don't talk about technique. You just hit first and hard enough that they don't get back up. Gods, I miss the simplicity."

Ren was so caught up talking with Elira that she didn't notice Lucan's expression had shifted. He set his mug down, eyes narrowing just a fraction. "That phrase. *Heart-line.* That's something we learn in training. Are you a fighter, Elira?"

The table went still.

"Elira is from House Tharowen," Ren drawled. "She's a kick-ass blacksmith."

But Lucan didn't look at Ren. His eyes stayed locked on Elira's.

And Elira had gone perfectly still. She also didn't look away.

Two warriors measuring each other in a room full of drunks.

Finally, Elira eased back in her chair. "Relax. You look like you're about to interrogate me for knowing a single fancy word." She lifted her mug and shrugged. "I hear that phrase every week. I spend my days surrounded by soldiers and their oversized egos. It's hard not to absorb their battlefield jargon."

Lucan thought for a moment and then demanded another round of drinks, on him. Elira offered a toast with her mug, to which Lucan clunk their glasses together. Music swelled, and someone began singing a bawdy song near the fire. The storm still howled outside, but within the tavern, the world felt brighter.

Ren leaned back in her chair. She turned her mug in her hands, watching the foam cling to the rim before taking a slow swallow. The ale slid down her throat, nothing remarkable in taste.

But Ren's gaze flicked sideways all the same.

Elira was no stranger to ale. Ren had seen her drink it often enough, so something about the ease in her voice and the quick glint in her eyes left Ren's instincts bristling.

65

Ren felt the familiar weight of Ashrend strapped to her thigh as she strode through the morning market of Pyraelia.

The crowd parted without a word. Maybe they felt the edge of her resolve in the air, or maybe it was the sword that kept them at bay. Either way, they kept their distance.

And why shouldn't they? She was on a mission.

Talen's words rang in her mind like a curse she couldn't outrun. "Our last creature to hunt." His tone had been flat, resigned. He had held up the coin purse then, leather heavy with gold. "And then we're done with our arrangement."

Done. As though everything they had fought together, bled together, had been nothing but a bargain struck and soon to expire.

Ren turned a corner, weaving past the chocolate district, where bakers were already setting out their stalls. Fresh bread lined the counters.

Her gaze snagged on the loaves of bread. That was how she'd ended up here in the first place, when she'd punched a fae soldier square in the nose for nearly sentencing a malnourished boy to death over a loaf of bread. A child who had looked at her with wide, hollow eyes and was on the brink of starvation.

"It's been an honor to fight alongside you," she had told Talen.

He'd given her that sharp, assessing look of his. "You did House Vaelaran a great service in aiding us in defeating the creatures."

She remembered waiting, holding her breath as if the silence between them might transform into something more. Into an offer. A tether. Something. But he'd only tucked away the coin purse and murmured, "Thank you, Ren."

The words had landed like an axe blow.

Talen hadn't offered her permanence. No place here in Pyraelia. No role to keep her anchored when all this was done. What about the threat of the undead? Maelion mentioned finding her more permanent work.

As Ren's gaze swept over the bustling market, seeing the patchwork of voices and faces, fae and humans mingling, art displayed in riotous color, spices thick in the air, she realized she wanted to stay. Saints help her, she liked the chaos, the beauty.

And, gods above, a certain fae princess who had carved herself into Ren's thoughts like a blade into stone.

She didn't want to leave.

Maybe when she collected her coin, she'd find a place to rent. Somewhere small, just enough to claim as her own until she figured out what came next. Maybe she could get a permanent role in the king's royal army to help defeat the undead.

Her thoughts tumbled away as the forge loomed ahead, alive with the roar of fire and the ring of hammer on steel. A fae male was bent over the anvil, sweat glistening on his brow as he shaped a glowing piece of gold. Sparks danced like fireflies, bursting in the dim morning haze.

Ren approached, her voice raised over the clamor. "Is Elira here?"

The male glanced at her, grunted, then went back to his work. "Her shift doesn't start until noon."

Ren's shoulders slumped, disappointment punching harder than she expected. She'd hoped to see Elira before leaving on this mission – maybe share a drink, even a word of farewell. Something to ease the gnawing tightness in her chest. But she couldn't wait hours.

She turned to go when the fae tossed aside his tool with a clang and wiped his meaty hands on his leather apron. "You a friend of hers?"

Ren didn't hesitate. "Yes."

He leaned against a wooden post, arms crossing over his broad chest. "She's a great blacksmith. One of the best I've seen in years."

"I know."

"Nearly turned her away when she showed up out of nowhere. But she spotted flaws in my workers' process right off and offered better. Took her in on the spot after that."

Pride warmed Ren's chest. "Her master must have been remarkable."

The fae frowned, shaking his head. "Wish I knew who they were. She didn't mention a master."

"She didn't show you her letter of recommendation when making her introduction?"

"No. She had no letter. Just her word."

That wasn't right. On their journey together, Elira had told her plainly she was bound for the capital with a letter of recommendation to present. That it was her reason for traveling.

"But with her," the fae said, oblivious to Ren's spiraling thoughts, "she's one I'd keep in my forge as long as she'll stay."

"I'll bet," Ren muttered.

The clang of the forge hammered through Ren's skull as she wandered away, the question gnawing like teeth at her ribs.

Why would Elira lie to her?

Ren wove back into the market's bustle, but her thoughts refused to quiet.

Maybe Elira had something else going on in her life, something she hadn't trusted Ren with yet. When they first met, they were little more than strangers thrown together by circumstance. Two women sharing a road, with the threat of death at their heels. In a world like this, trust wasn't given; it was earned slowly, painfully, and sometimes never at all.

Ren knew that better than most. She'd spent too long in pits where a smile could be a lie and a kind word was often just bait for betrayal. Even now, part of her whispered she was a fool to care, to even wonder.

But Elira didn't seem like the others. She carried her own shadows, yes, but she'd laughed when the nights were dark and hopeless. That had to mean something. Didn't it?

Ren exhaled hard, dragging a hand over her face. She could tear herself apart with suspicion, or she could wait and ask Elira herself.

Yes.

After this last mission, when the coin was in hand and the creatures behind them, she'd corner Elira over a few drinks. Look her in the eye, and if there were lies hiding behind that easy grin, she'd drag them into the light.

For now, though, Ren pushed the thoughts aside. The time for questions would come.

But first, there was a beast to slay.

66

"Does it ever bother you that all this is down here?"

Ren's voice slipped into the dark. The torchlight ahead wavered as Talen's steady stride led them deeper into the tunnel. Shadows clung to the walls, retreating only when the torch's glow licked their edges.

Lucan muttered something unintelligible, nearly tripping over his own boots when a rat skittered across their path. He let out a curse, jerking back and bumping straight into Ren. Some of these rats looked bigger than she'd ever seen, their eyes gleaming faintly red in the dark.

Still, they pressed on.

The palace might have been gilded and glorious above, but beneath its bones lay the true heart of House Vaelaran.

The tombs.

The corridor widened, opening into a vaulted chamber. Pillars of carved obsidian lined the hall. Sarcophagi rose in solemn rows, each lid etched with names worn by centuries.

Here lay the kings and queens of Vaelaran. The generals. The councilors. The warriors and loyalists who had carved their mark into legend. Statues stood sentinel between the graves: fae warriors with their swords lowered in eternal watch, queens with crowns carved to shimmer.

Ren had almost forgotten about the question she'd asked when Talen answered, "This is sacred history. Every step carries the weight of centuries. The saying goes that to walk among the tombs is to walk in the presence of every oath sworn, every crown borne. That the living carry their ancestors' victories and failures with them always."

"By the gods," Lucan hissed as he stumbled into a cobweb, swiping frantically at his hair.

Ren arched a brow. "Might be wise to tie that silky mane back. Pretty as it is, no spider down here cares."

Lucan shot her a glare but dragged his hair into a messy knot anyway.

Ren tilted her head, voice dry. "Why did you even want to come down here?"

Lucan grimaced, the torchlight catching his scowl. "I thought we were going to be out in the fresh air hunting beasts with real teeth, not trampling about in the dust of corpses and rotting crypts that should've stayed buried." His eyes darted to the looming sarcophagi around them, shoulders tightening as though the carved figures might step off their pedestals.

Talen had stopped several paces ahead, torchlight catching the hard line of his jaw. His voice had a controlled edge that silenced the space more effectively than any shout. "Enough." Talen turned slightly, emerald eyes glinting in the dim light. "These tombs hold my kin—kings, queens, warriors whose blood carved the realm you walk on. Show some respect."

For a beat, silence settled, even the scurrying of rats seeming to vanish.

Lucan swallowed and looked away, muttering something into his collar. Ren, though, held Talen's gaze for a heartbeat longer. She hadn't meant to mock him.

"Apologies. We'll tread lighter," she said.

Talen turned and pressed forward into the dark, torchlight carving the way through the stone corridors.

Ren tried to push past the humor, but something tugged at her blood. A purr, low and steady, humming beneath her skin. Her magic. It stretched awake like a restless beast, responding to something in the air. To something down *here*.

Talen must have noticed her tense because he spoke without looking back. "Zakhar told me once he wandered down here and felt it. Whatever it is. Said the stone remembers things most of us shouldn't."

Lucan scoffed. "He's bizarre. Half the time, I think he doesn't sleep. I don't think that helps his reputation."

"How long has he even been in court?" Ren asked.

Talen answered, "As long as I can remember. Since I was a boy."

"He's devoted, I'll give him that," Ren muttered. "Devoted enough to burn himself out if no one stops him."

"That's Zakhar for you."

Ren's lips pressed into a thin line. Another wave rippled through her, like a second heartbeat matching her own. The air grew heavier, almost damp with it.

Then—

Footsteps echoed behind them.

The torch sputtered violently, its flame struggling.

Talen drew his sword in one smooth motion. Ren unsheathed Ashrend, the steel singing softly. Lucan stiffened beside them, hand already twitching toward his dagger.

And then a figure bled out of the stone itself. Cloaked in fabric the color of withered lavender, a woman drifted barefoot across the cavern floor. Her hair was a tangled mess, her skin so pale it was nearly translucent. Her eyes seemed to hold a silvery light.

"Veyra," Talen whispered the name like a curse torn from him.

"Put your sword away, prince." Veyra rasped. "It remembers me better than you do."

Talen didn't lower his blade. "You're supposed to be dead."

Veyra chuckled. "Most interesting people are." Her gaze turned and locked onto Ren. Veyra seemed to strip her bare with that stare, peeling back flesh and bone until she reached marrow. Her nostrils flared. Her smile widened, predatory. "Oh," she whispered. "Oh, it's *you*."

"Me?"

"You reek of old flame. Of war-born magic and something older still." Veyra tilted her head, listening as though Ren's heartbeat was music. "You've woken it, haven't you?"

"I don't know what you're talking about."

"Liar," Veyra rasped, but there was no malice. Only certainty. "It's in your blood, girl."

"Who are you?"

Talen's voice cut through the air. "Veyra Morvain." His knuckles whitened on the hilt of his blade. "She was once a seer of this court, long before even my parents ruled, bound to the Vaelaran line by oath and blood. I only know of her from books. They say her visions carried both prosperity and ruin. She warned the crown of betrayal, that it would come from within these very halls."

Veyra hissed. "But kings do not like to hear of their undoing."

The torchlight caught in Talen's eyes. "They called her a heretic. They silenced her by entombing her alive beneath the palace, her name stripped from record as if she'd never existed." He paused. "I thought it was a myth."

Veyra's head tilted, the silvery void of her eyes catching faint torchlight. "They buried me, thinking stone and shadow would swallow me whole. But the stone remembers what the court tried to forget. The marrow of this place holds me, even when flesh rotted away. Neither living, nor dead, just the echo of what they feared most. And so, I linger. A spirit bound not by crown, but by prophecy."

"Then speak plainly," Talen snapped.

"I want nothing," Veyra murmured. "I only came to witness." Her head tilted again toward Ren. Veyra leaned close, whispering, "When you rise, kingdoms will fall."

The words pressed on Ren's chest like a weight she couldn't draw breath beneath. And then, as though she had never been there at all, Veyra dissolved into smoke.

Silence crashed down.

Lucan swallowed hard, his voice trembling when it finally broke the air. "If that's what court ghosts are like, I'll take my chances with ogres, thank you very much."

The silence between them stretched, pressing against Ren's ears until even her own heartbeat sounded too loud.

A low rumble stirred beneath their boots. At first, it was so faint she thought it was her imagination. But the sound deepened, swelling into a resonant growl that seemed to come not from one place, but from the very earth itself.

The ground shivered. Dust rained down from the cracked ceiling in thin streams, drifting lazily through the torchlight. The flames guttered.

"Perfect," Ren muttered. "Exactly what we needed. An ancient beast deciding now's the time to wake." She forced her gaze to Talen, her chin lifted even as unease gnawed at her ribs. "I'm assuming that thing is what we're here for?"

Talen nodded. His jaw was tight, his grip steady on his blade.

Ren drew in a deep breath. Unease coiled in her gut, wondering what the hell awaited them. But beneath it, something else stirred.

She was not the broken woman once dragged in chains. Not a pawn waiting for someone else to move her across the board.

The flame inside her flickered, restless.

The cavern shuddered again, louder. Lucan let out a curse. The sound surrounded them, pulsing through the rock, reverberating in their bones. Whatever it was, it definitely wasn't sleeping anymore.

It was waiting.

And so, they walked forward and into the heart of the dark, where the earth itself growled like a beast ready to tear its way free.

The narrow tunnel opened to a large cavern.

Coiled around a mountain of obsidian and smoldering rock, the beast's body stretched into shadow. Ren caught green scales gleaming, fractured by veins of molten gold that pulsed as if magma flowed through its flesh.

Ren had fought monsters. She had bled in pits. She had seen things that made grown men scream.

But nothing prepared her for this.

The sheer size of it defied reason. Each slow rise and fall of its chest sent gusts of heated air rolling toward her, carrying the scent of smoke, stone, and blood long since burned.

It opened its eyes.

Twin furnaces fixed on Ren. Every shield she had ever built crumbled beneath that stare.

Her heart thundered not only with terror but with a thread she hadn't known existed, drawn taut between her chest and the *dragon* before her.

As the dragon shifted, the cavern groaned around it. A growl rippled from its throat, shaking the walls until dust and pebbles rained from above. It was a language in a tongue older than mortal memory.

And impossibly, Ren understood.

Her name was *Fryphessyrth.*

The words curled through Ren's mind, not spoken aloud but sinking directly into her thoughts.

"You bear the blood of the Flameborne, Renaria."

Ren flinched. Hearing her *true* name now after all these years made Ren's blood sing and her skin crawl all at once.

"We have waited. The Pact frays, and the fire stirs anew."

"Is Ren communicating with it?" Lucan's whisper cracked, eyes darting between Ren and Fryphessyrth.

"I think so," Talen answered uneasily, flexing his fingers around the hilt of his sword.

Ren maintained Fryphessyrth's gaze. "I am no pawn. And I will not be your servant."

"Neither servant nor pawn," Fryphessyrth rumbled. *"Choose wisely, Flameborne. Your choice is our salvation or our doom."*

Ren straightened, refusing to yield beneath the weight of those eyes. "I don't know what I'm meant to be yet, but I'll decide that before anyone else does."

"You are not only flesh. You are a tethered flame. He stirs in you."

Heat surged through Ren's blood, a pulse not her own matching her heartbeat. Her vision flickered—flames, stone, skies torn with wings. She staggered, her breath ragged.

"What are they saying?" Lucan whispered again, desperate.

"Not sure, just stay ready in case we need to intervene," Talen snapped, eyes never leaving Fryphessyrth.

"You know of the Pact struck to preserve the balance of realms."

Ren's vision warped. The cavern fell away, leaving visions burned in firelight: dragons and fae queens and kings meeting in a world aflame. In the heart of it, a figure stood wreathed in living fire. Not fae. Not dragon.

Yet bowed to by both.

"One bloodline marked by dragonfire. Flamebearers. The fae feared what they could not control. They burned the line from the world."

"And now?"

Fryphessyrth's gaze was a storm of fire. *"Now, one rises again. The last spark. You."*

"Who broke the Pact?"

Shadows veiled Fryphessyrth's face. *"A creature cloaked in fae flesh. The Pact lies broken. The dragons will return. Some remember mercy, and others remember betrayal. Their vengeance will wake with them."*

"What am I meant to do, stand between them?"

Fryphessyrth lowered her massive head until the cavern boiled with her heat. *"Not stand between, but to judge."*

Fryphessyrth bent lower still, until her shadow swallowed Ren whole.

And bowed.

Not to a queen. Not to a warrior.

To her.

To Renaria Harper.

Daughter of flame.

68

Everything froze.

The dust in the air froze mid-fall. Fryphessyrth's movements halted, even Talen and Lucan were statues. Only their eyes remained wide, unblinking, suspended in the moment.

As if time itself had been caught in a snare.

Then, Ren sensed a new presence. Every hair on her body rose in alarm, sensing something was very, very wrong.

And then, movement.

The sound of boots against stone.

Ren's grip tightened on Ashrend as a figure stepped from behind Fryphessyrth's massive bulk.

Zakhar emerged, his cloak trailing behind him. His eyes snapped to hers, steady.

"You weren't supposed to find this place," he said at last. The words were quiet, almost mournful. "Not yet."

Ren's jaw clenched until it hurt. "Then I hope you're ready to talk. Not in riddles this time."

Zakhar leaned against Fryphessyrth's wing as though the ancient dragon were nothing more than a column carved for his ease. "Actually, you were always meant to find this place. Every path you've taken, every choice, I've tilted the board. You've been my key piece from the start, Flamebearer."

Through gritted teeth, Ren seethed, "You better keep talking."

"Oh, I've been talking, Renaria. Dropping hints. It isn't my fault you weren't quick enough to piece them together. Who first called you Flameborne? Who warned you the Witherblight was no natural sickness, but a weapon? Who whispered that your fire was something unnatural?"

Memory after memory sharpened like a blade, revealing Zakhar's offhand words, his unreadable stares, his sudden appearances in places he shouldn't have been. Always watching.

Always too knowing.

"Why?"

"Because I needed a champion." Zakhar stepped forward. "Do you remember the boy?" he asked quietly. "The malnourished one clutching a crust of bread – the one you nearly started a riot over when you struck that soldier?"

Ren bristled. "What about him?"

"I sent him to you as a test, Renaria. One you didn't even realize you were taking. A small tether between us. I could feel your presence drawing closer then. I had to be certain."

Ren's pulse hammered. "Certain of what?"

"That you were the one," Zakhar replied. "Bloodlines and magic alone are not enough. I needed to see if you'd risk yourself for someone powerless. That was the first test. Then, I needed to know if you could endure the fights with the creatures wreaking havoc in the realm – to determine if you were strong enough to carry what was left of him."

"Him?" Ren whispered.

Zakhar tilted his head, eyes glinting. "You've felt him. You've heard him. You know the answer to that question."

Ren nearly stumbled back a step. Her pulse roared in her ears.

Zakhar grinned upon seeing her realization. "One last hint then, before the game is done. You are not just Flameborne, Renaria. Vortharax lives in you. Shards of his soul are embedded in your flesh, his fire fused with your fire."

The name landed like a sword cleaving her chest open. Ren's heart stopped. Her knees nearly buckled, the world tilting around her.

Zakhar's voice coiled around her like a serpent, merciless. "That night when they came for you, the Embersworn sacrificed your family to call him back into this world. Only a Flameborne could hold a fragment of his soul without burning to ash. And so, they wove him into you with an ancient spell of soul binding. But a binding of that magnitude does not yield to mere offerings. It demands the greatest sacrifice – one's own kin. Blood of the same line, given willingly or not."

"No." The word was barely a breath. Her chest was tight, her stomach twisting violently. "No—that's not possible—"

Zakhar's smile was all teeth. "That is why your fire doesn't just burn; it devours everything in its path. It is hunger; it is conquest."

Ren thought of the whispers in the dark, the rumble in her veins when she unleashed her fire, that terrible voice that wasn't hers but called beneath her skin.

"That," Zakhar said softly, triumph in every syllable, "is *Vortharax* speaking directly to you."

Ren barely heard it. Her body felt foreign, her own blood a betrayal.

Not just Flameborne. Not just Renaria Harper.

A vessel.

A weapon.

A soul carrying shards of a god-breaking beast.

Zakhar's smirk deepened as he spread his hands. "You notice it now, don't you? The stillness. The silence." He clicked his tongue softly, mockingly. "That's me. The gift of a god who was never meant to sit still in this world. Time, bound in a thread, paused so you and I may speak without interruption. I dislike being interrupted. Makes me lose my train of thought."

"You're the one doing this."

He laughed. "Oh, don't you see by now? I've been doing everything. The monsters tearing through the realm? My hand. The corpses risen from their graves? My breath. One of my specialties: sweet necromancy. And one of my finer creations – the Witherblight." His eyes gleamed, bright with madness. He grinned wider, teeth catching the dim light. "You thought it only killed, didn't you? That it simply hollowed people out and left them to rot. But every death fed me. Every spark of magic it stripped from your people poured into me, building, ripening." His gaze burned like a forge. "The more they withered, the stronger I became."

He took a step closer, voice dropping to a hiss. "Magic is the soul's lifeline, and I have been drinking it dry. Chaos, death, decay – it is all the same language, and I am fluent in it. Chaos is the purest truth. And I have been peeling back the skin of this realm to remind them."

"Why?"

Zakhar stepped closer, shadows dragging behind him like chains. "Because when the world shatters, mortals and fae alike show their teeth. Strip away bread, strip away elixir, strip away the illusions of peace, and you will see the truth. They will eat each other alive to survive. They already have." His gaze sharpened. "Just as the fae have feasted on humans for centuries—not with knives and fire, but with hoarded elixirs, letting them rot while fae kingdoms thrive. Or using them as slaves until they wither and die."

The words hit, brutal in their honesty. Images flashed in Ren's mind—humans dying of Witherblight while fae lords sipped wine, their vaults brimming with cures.

"You see it, don't you?" Zakhar murmured, tilting his head, his voice slipping into a coaxing rhythm. "I only rip away the veil. I only give them what they already are. Chaos isn't the enemy; it is the only truth in this world."

Ren's fists trembled at her sides.

"Join me." Zakhar's voice dropped to a whisper, the madness behind his words vibrating like a string about to snap. "Together we could break this rotten world open and release the tide of chaos. We can tear down the false crowns, the prisons of tradition, the hoarded vaults. Let every secret, every hunger, every hidden truth spill into the realm."

Ren's chest heaved.

Zakhar leaned close, his words curling into her ear like smoke. "And Vortharax?" His smile turned razor-sharp. "Together, you and I could burn him out of you. Shatter him – *end* him. Chaos is the only fire hotter than conquest. You and I, flame and madness, could *unmake* the world as we know it."

The cavern seemed to groan, the weight of his offer pressing into her bones. Ren's breath hitched, fire licking under her skin, tangled with fear and fury. Her heart screamed to deny him, but some dark, dangerous thread coiled inside her at his words, a voice whispering that maybe—just maybe—burning it all down was the only way forward.

But was that her voice, or *his* voice?

Zakhar's eyes glittered, fever-bright. He paced a slow circle around her, his voice dropping to something low, coaxing, intimate. "You don't understand what you are. What you could be. The fae would make you a pawn of their court, a pet they leash and parade. The mortals would make you a savior, bleeding yourself dry for their scraps. But I—" he paused, his gaze burning into her, "I could make you a *queen*. Not their queen. *Mine*. The Queen of Chaos. The Queen of *my* Dominion. You would not kneel, Renaria, you would *command*. The world would tear itself open at your touch, and you would never be bound again."

"Why would you want me as your Queen?"

"Because strength is rare. Power is rarer still. But you—" his gaze raked over her, not in lust but in reverence, in hunger, "you have both. You survived where you should have died. You carry fire that should have consumed you whole. You are proof that chaos chooses well."

Ren steadied her breath, the question burning out before she could stop it. "Then why release Vortharax at all?"

The change was instant.

Zakhar's smile shattered. His lips peeled back into a snarl, his teeth bared. His voice rose, snapping with a violence that rattled the stone. "Because he is *mine* to destroy!"

The air itself shook.

Zakhar's fists clenched at his sides, his voice breaking into a growl. "He devoured kingdoms, bent gods, and still they bowed. He is the chain that binds every destiny, the shadow choking every flame. I will see him broken. I will see him gone. And if the world burns with him—so be it!" His chest heaved. His eyes were no longer calm, no longer calculated; they blazed with unmasked fury, fueled by centuries of hate and obsession.

Then, just as swiftly, he smoothed his expression again. His grin slid back into place. "But I cannot do it alone, Flamebearer. That is why I need you. Why you and I were always meant to stand together. Tell me, do you believe in destiny?"

He extended a hand, palm up, as if offering her not just an alliance, but dominion itself.

The torchlight caught the silver threads of his armor, casting sharp, fractured glimmers across his face, making his eyes blaze like twin shards of a broken star.

"Choose, Flamebearer," Zakhar said, voice low, soft enough to caress yet sharp enough to cut. "Walk back to your court, to their chains, their lies... or take my hand, and together we will unmake crowns, unmake gods, unmake *him*."

The cavern held its breath. Time itself was Zakhar's cage, bent around them like glass.

The weight of his words pressed down like the mountain above them, and still his hand remained.

"Tell me," Zakhar murmured, "what will it be?"

69

"**N**o."

Ren's voice rang like steel against stone. Ren raised her chin. "You've been hurt, that much is obvious. Whatever Vortharax did to you, it shattered your world. You wear your thirst for revenge like armor, dress it up in lies about chaos and truth, but underneath is a broken god clawing at his wounds." Her grip tightened on Ashrend, the blade whispering as she slid it free. "We won't tear each other down, not the way you want us to. I'll tear the throat out of anyone who threatens those I care about, but out of love, not hunger. That's what you'll never understand." Her eyes glinted like embers. "I know who you are. The *god of madness.*"

For a heartbeat, silence ruled the chamber.

Then Zakhar's lips split, and he laughed.

The sound wasn't human. It echoed too wide, too long, bouncing from wall to wall until the stone itself seemed to howl with him. He doubled over, shoulders shaking, laughter shredding into hoarseness, until he straightened with tears glistening at the corner of his eyes.

"Now you're catching on. Some call me that; I've been called worse. I am the itch beneath the skin, the voice in the dark when no one's left to listen. Families tearing at one another to survive? I've watched it for centuries. Mothers stealing from babes, fathers feeding from sons. Madness is the only truth this world has ever known."

Zakhar tapped his chin thoughtfully, as though sifting through the dust of old memories. "You think you're different? Your parents – ah, *yes*. I remember them. The stench of rum and cheap wine thick on their breath. They spent more coin drowning in their cups than feeding you or that precious sister of yours."

Zakhar's gaze gleamed.

"Tell me, Flameborne. Do you remember the way your belly ached so badly you thought it might devour itself? Those nights you shivered beneath threadbare blankets, praying you'd wake the next morning and not cross the Veil in your sleep from starvation?"

His tone dropped, almost tender. "And those times you reached for the bottle just to understand why they loved it more than you, and they beat you bloody for it. You cried, didn't you? But not for the pain. You cried because you *still* loved them. But they didn't love you, and they never would."

Zakhar clicked his tongue. "See, *I'm* not the monster here. Your parents, your world – they are already tearing themselves apart without my intervention. Fae, humans, ogres – none of that matters. I'm just the truth that crawls out from what's left, the voice inside everyone's head that they ignore. The real tragedy is that if anyone would simply embrace me – *embrace chaos* – it would all make sense. The pain, the hunger, the loss. There's freedom in surrender. The world only burns because it fights what it was always meant to become."

Ren's lip curled. "You really enjoy hearing yourself talk. But I'm done listening. To hell with your theories. You're just a bitter god hellbent on revenge. Tell me this, Zakhar – what did Vortharax do to you that was so bad?"

There was a flicker across his face. He scratched at the back of his head like a man clawing through memories too deep to bury, muttering something under his breath.

Ren's blood boiled. Or maybe it was the other thing inside her, the shard of Vortharax, thrumming at the presence of its old, familiar enemy. Whatever it was, the heat almost split her skin apart.

Zakhar's gaze turned grim. "One last chance, Flamebearer. Become my champion or drown in what's coming. Because tonight *will* tear your world upside down. Not just yours – the realm's. Nothing will be the same again."

Ren lifted a brow. "Is your memory failing? I already told you no. Why would repeating it make it any different this time?"

Zakhar clicked his tongue again, a sound of disappointment. "Very well. Then, let's see how you fare with some company."

Ren felt a cold draft slithering through the cavern, carrying the smell of decay. The torches sputtered, their flames shrinking as if smothered by unseen hands. The silence shattered with the groan of stone grinding against stone.

One by one, lids of sarcophagi shifted, runes cracking and flaring as though unwilling to release what lay beneath. Skeletal fingers, mottled with ancient flesh, clawed over the rims.

Silver, empty, merciless eyes blinked open in the dark.

Undead fae. Kings and queens of Vaelaran, councilors and generals long-dead, dragged from sacred rest. Their crowns of stone crumbled, their blades raised in brittle, rusted hands.

Zakhar spread his arms, shadows fanning out like wings. His voice slithered across the cavern, a final echo before he vanished into smoke. "Fight, Flamebearer. Let's see how long you and your *friends* last when the dead come to claim you." He shrugged. "I say it's never a bad time for a little," his eyes glanced at Talen, "family reunion. Don't you think?"

He lingered just a moment longer and sent Ren a wink. "That's the most beautiful thing about necromancy. The dead never stop piling up. Which means the dead are always an army at your command."

And then he was gone.

70

The honored dead of Vaelaran rose in silence, their steps heavy. Inevitable.

At Ren's side, Lucan's blade quivered in his hands, time resuming without Zakhar's magic, and Talen's jaw set grimly as the first of his ancestors stepped forward, all crowned in dust.

"What the hell happened?" Talen asked.

Ren said, "Long story. Zakhar froze time, so that's why you two missed everything. He's the god of madness, he betrayed all of us, and—" her voice cracked, "—I have Vorthorax living inside me. Somehow they're connected, and Zakhar wants revenge."

Lucan's voice cracked. "So, we're fighting a god and you're basically a dragon egg?"

Ren shot Lucan a look. "I'm not going to birth the bastard. Shards of his soul were bound to me by the Embersworn. That's why my parents were killed."

An undead lurched toward them, and Talen didn't hesitate. His blade cleaved through it in one brutal, practiced swing. "The bastard betrayed us all," Talen snarled, eyes blazing. "God of madness or not, he'll answer for this."

Ren's pulse roared in her ears. Her fire shuddered to life, licking up her arms as another corpse lunged. She carved through with a slash of flame, the body collapsing.

Talen cut down another undead, teeth bared. "Where did Zakhar go?"

Ren snorted. "Ran like a cowardly fuck with no spine."

Another corpse lunged forward.

And another.

"To your left!" Talen shouted. His sword sang as he split one through the chest, but even as the corpse fell, two more clawed from their sarcophagi, reaching with skeletal fingers.

Lucan cursed under his breath. He fought like a storm, his twin blades flashing as he cut down the risen nobles who pressed at them from all sides. "They remember how to fight!"

Then a roar shattered the cavern.

Fryphessyrth reared, her tail whipping through the horde with bone-crushing force. The ground shook with each strike, and when her teeth closed on a cluster of undead, the sound of breaking bone split the chamber. Fire burst from her maw, incinerating whole ranks in molten light.

For a heartbeat, Ren felt hope.

But then she saw charred bodies knitting back together, bones snapping into place, silver light dragging them upright again.

Even Fryphessyrth's fury wasn't enough.

"There's so many!" Ren shouted. Sweat slicked her skin as she cut another down.

Lucan's face twisted, pale beneath the grime. "We'll never hold them off. Not all of us."

Ren's blade met another corpse with a ringing crack. "Then we fight until we can't," she hissed. "We keep moving, keep breathing. Don't you dare give in now, Lucan. You're a better fighter than this, stronger than this. I've seen you take down twice as many with half the breath in your lungs, so *fight*!

Talen's blade cleaved through a corpse beside them. "She's right," he barked, voice hoarse. "Hold the line. If we fall here, there's no one left to hold!"

For a time, it worked – their rhythm returning in staccato bursts of motion and flame. Steel flashed. Fire roared. They fought shoulder to shoulder, the world narrowing to the next strike, the next breath, the next heartbeat that refused to stop.

But the dead didn't tire.

They didn't falter.

They just kept coming.

Minutes blurred together, each one heavier than the last. Ren's arms burned; her lungs clawed for air. Talen moved with mechanical precision, a soldier fighting on instinct alone. And Lucan's strength began to wane. His strikes grew sloppy. His stance wavered. For every creature they cut down, two more clawed their way from the darkness.

"I—" Lucan's voice broke as his sword deflected another blow. "We can't – there's too many—"

"Don't say it," Ren snarled, driving her blade through the skull of a corpse. Blood spattered her face. "Don't you dare say it."

But Lucan's eyes had already changed. The fight was leaving them, replaced by something hollow, something that knew this was a battle they couldn't win. His gaze darted to the cavern mouth, the narrow archway behind them that led to the stairs.

Then to Fryphessyrth.

"Listen to me," he hissed. "You're both too important for this realm to die here."

"We're not leaving you," Talen snapped, driving his blade through another undead. "We all go together."

"Always the prince, giving orders." Lucan's eyes softened as they flicked between them – his king, his comrade, his *friends*. "Sometimes soldiers don't come home. Sometimes they buy the way out for the ones who matter most."

"Lucan, no—" Ren's throat tore with the words. Tears trailed down her cheeks, blurring her vision as she kept swinging and swinging and swinging—

Lucan turned to Fryphessyrth, his voice breaking. "Block the exit when they've gone. Tail to stone. Don't let anything follow them out."

Fryphessyrth's eyes gleamed with something ancient and sorrowful, but she lowered her massive head in assent.

"Lucan—" Talen's voice cracked.

Lucan smiled then. A weary, broken one, but *real*. "It will be an honor to lay my life not just for my prince, but for my friends."

Fryphessyrth roared and, with a mighty sweep of her tail, slammed it against the cavern wall. Stone shuddered, cracks splintering like lightning across the surface. Dust poured from the ceiling.

"Go!" Lucan roared.

Ren lunged forward, reaching for him, but Talen's arm locked around her waist. He hissed in her ear, "He's giving us time. Don't throw it away."

Fryphessyrth's tail struck again, harder, rock exploding from the walls. The cavern screamed as it began to collapse, undead shrieking beneath the raining stone.

Ren fought, thrashing against Talen's grip, her nails scraping against his arms, his leather, his armor. "Let me go!" she screamed, voice tearing from her throat. "I'm not leaving him! I won't leave him behind, *damn you*!"

But Talen only tightened his hold, dragging her toward the archway as the ground buckled beneath their feet.

"Ren—" Talen's voice was a rasp, equal parts fury and grief. "If you go back, you both die!"

"To hell we will," Ren's voice took on a guttural hiss, animalistic. "I'll burn them all, Talen. *They'll all burn.*"

She kicked and fought against him.

But it was too late.

Fryphessyrth's bellow shook the cavern, shaking every bone in Ren's body. It was rage and farewell.

A beast's last defiance.

And then the world crumbled.

Stone crashed down, sealing Lucan, Fryphessyrth, and the dead behind a wall of ruin.

The roar of collapsing earth drowned everything until, through the chaos, Ren heard Lucan's voice. Faint at first. Then louder.

Steady.

"For crown, for kin, for every soul that stands, I will hold the line."

He shouted it over and over, a battle cry turned to prayer, each word forged from terror and defiance alike.

"For crown, for kin, for every soul that stands, *I will hold the line.*"

Again, as the world fell apart around him—
"If this is where I fall, let it be where they rise. *I will hold the line.*"
Until the sound broke, leaving only silence.

71

The ballroom glittered like the heart of a jewel.

Every surface glowed, every detail sharpened by candlelight and wine, until the hall felt less like stone and mortar and more like a dream of splendor spun into reality.

Kaelin had staged countless affairs of state, but this ball's splendor might very well have been her magnum opus. Even she could almost forget it was meant for politics and not a gallery. Kaelin glided through the throng of guests. Music surged and dipped from the string ensemble at the dais, dancers spun in whirlwinds of velvet and silk, jewels flashed at every throat and wrist. Scented oil, spiced and floral, mingled with the tang of their finest pastries and wine until even the air tasted decadent.

And yet, beneath the hum of voices and the clink of goblets, Kaelin felt the shiver in the stone, a tremor in the air.

The crystal chandeliers above trembled.

"Did you feel that shudder?" a fae noblewoman murmured over the rim of her goblet, cheeks flushed with wine.

Her betrothed leaned closer, his voice pitched low. "I felt it, too."

Kaelin's lips curved, smooth and practiced, as she waved a gloved hand gracefully. "Merely a draft, nothing more," she purred, before inclining her head in graceful dismissal. She glided from them, skirts whispering across marble.

Across the hall, her mother's laugh rang bright and brittle, gilded over with courtesy. But when their gazes locked across the sea of faces, confusion mirrored in both sets of eyes.

They had felt the shudder, too.

Beneath the scented oil and chatter, beneath the trill of violins, Kaelin's bones tinged with unease. Talen was nowhere in sight, nor Ren, nor Lucan. Kaelin's sharp gaze skimmed over the gilded crowd, noting the sea of smiling masks and flushed faces, couples sneaking into alcoves, courtiers toasting beneath painted ceilings.

Too many hands touching, too many eyes glittering with secrets and mischief.

Somewhere, the traitor lingered.

A steward materialized before Kaelin, a crystal goblet of rose wine balanced on his tray. Her favorite vintage. "A glass, Your Highness?"

Kaelin's hand didn't so much as twitch toward it. "No, carry on."

The steward swept to the next fae couple.

Kaelin stood still, every inch of her poise carved from marble, but her eyes raked the crowd with predatory patience. She would not be caught unaware. Not tonight.

And then, shadows thickened at the edge of the hall. When Zakhar stepped from the darkness, draped in his threadbare robes, the music did not falter. No one else seemed to see him; conversation carried on, laughter rang bright.

His wild, gray hair framed a face uncharacteristically grave. He dipped his head, his voice pitched only for her as he approached. "Your Highness. A private word, if you will."

Kaelin moved with him into a small alcove, away from prying ears. "Speak," she commanded.

Zakhar's fingers twitched once before he produced a folded scrap of parchment.

"Ren Harper is gone."

Kaelin unfolded the parchment with deliberate calm, her fingers steady though the weight of it pressed like lead in her palm. Ren's handwriting scrawled across the page.

Kaelin,

The exchange with Talen is complete. My obligations to the crown are fulfilled. There's nothing left to keep me here.

Don't send anyone after me.

—Ren

"Mm," Kaelin re-read the letter, word for word. "So, she left me a note."

Zakhar shifted, his expression uncharacteristically sober. "It's disappointing. I thought perhaps..." His fingers twitched as if plucking invisible strings. "I thought perhaps she'd chosen differently. It happens. People break, they run, they leave behind scraps of themselves, and letters are the weakest of all things, don't you think?"

He faltered when Kaelin folded the note neatly back in half and lifted her gaze to his. "Tell me, Zakhar," she said softly, "do you take me for a fool?"

Before Zakhar could answer, Kaelin seized him by the throat. She slammed him back against the stone arch, lifting him onto his toes. Zakhar sputtered, his hands clawing at her wrist, useless against the vice of her grip.

Kaelin snarled, "In what world do you imagine I'm that easy to deceive? To think I would believe Ren would slink away and leave me a flimsy letter?" She curled her fingers, squeezing, and Zakhar's face reddened. "If Ren Harper had something important to say, she would tell me herself. She has never returned my letters. Not once. So why," Kaelin's eyes flashed, the ice and fire of a storm, "would she start now? Unless someone *forged* this letter, stating it was from her." She tilted her head. "But that would be manipulative, and I cannot imagine why anyone would want to do that."

Zakhar choked out a hoarse laugh, half-mad in her grip. "I-I would never! Perhaps she started now...because... everything breaks... eventually."

Kaelin leaned in, her lips brushing the shell of his ear. "If Ren is in danger, and you knew or were somehow responsible for it..." Her nails bit into his skin, drawing a bead of blood. "Pray she's safe because if she isn't, I'll gut you slow enough to make eternity feel merciful."

Zakhar's laugh cracked out of him, raw and ragged, shaking in her grip. It wasn't a chuckle, wasn't even amusement—it was wild, bubbling, the sound of someone unraveling in her palm.

Kaelin's scowl deepened, her grip unyielding on his throat. "What," she hissed, voice low and dangerous, "is so *funny*?"

His head lolled back, teeth flashing in a manic grin even as her nails drew beads of crimson down his neck. His voice rasped between laughter, words jagged and trembling with glee. "You think you're so unbreakable, so superior, princess. But soon—oh, so soon—it will be *you* who breaks." His eyes gleamed. "And you won't even see it coming." He licked his lips. "I think I shall enjoy the sight very much. Yes, indeed."

Kaelin gave him one final, withering glare before shoving him hard to the floor, the sound of his laughter still echoing through the corridor like a curse.

CRASH.

The sharp shatter of glass split the air, followed by a scream that ripped through the hall.

Kaelin's head snapped toward the ballroom.

"Ah," Zakhar crooned. "Every good feast needs a little drama. Consider this the opening act." His eyes glittered. "Tell me, princess. Do you prefer your kingdoms whole, or in pieces?"

72

A wine glass shattered against the marble floor, shards scattering like fallen stars. Crimson liquid bled across the stone.

A female fae writhed among the glass, her body convulsing. Foam bubbled at her lips, frothing green as her eyes rolled back. The color of her veins darkened. Her escort knelt beside her, only to seize and cough himself, his skin blotching crimson. His fists slammed the floor once, twice, and then stilled.

"Poison!"

The shout was answered by the heavy thud of another body falling to the floor.

Then another.

Kaelin whirled to see the guards at the exit collapse one by one, their throats split open. Blood crept in rivers across the polished marble.

Gasps and screams fractured the harmony of music and laughter. Courtiers scrambled, skirts tearing, goblets clattering.

Sylven's lanky figure sauntered into the chaos. His silver hair caught the glow like a halo, though his eyes burned with something unholy.

"Marvelous, isn't it?" His voice was calm, almost admiring. "It's new. Scentless. Slips into your wine without so much as a ripple. It even tastes sweet in Vaelaran vintages."

"What is the meaning of this?" King Maelion thundered, pushing to his feet. But Kaelin saw the tremor in his hands. He had drunk deeply from his glass that night. So had her mother, who now sat wide-eyed and pale, clutching the stem of her goblet as if it could anchor her.

Sylven's smile curdled into something deadly. "The meaning is order. The order you've chipped away piece by piece, rotting centuries of tradition, all for the sake of... her." His chin tipped toward Kaelin. "And the mortal she plays with."

Several fae in soldiers' armor filed in behind him, blocking the exits. Kaelin recognized insignias of House Vaelaran on their breastplates, and betrayal gleamed like steel in their eyes.

"We could stand by no longer," Sylven continued, his voice rising over the panicked crowd. "You invite rot into the heart of this court, a human cur to sit at your table, and expect us to remain silent? No. Tonight, we cleanse House Vaelaran of weakness."

Before anyone could retort, movement stirred from the shadows near the musicians' platform.

A fae woman with dark hair.

Her braid had come loose in the commotion, strands of dark hair falling around a lean face hardened in resolve. The fae's lips curled into a rueful smile as her hand went to the dagger at her hip.

Her eyes swept the room before settling on the dais where King Maelion still stood. "I was sent to kill the prince during his return from exile," she said. "The ogre attack merely delayed the attempt. Tonight, it ends here." She raised her voice, addressing everyone listening. "Tonight, you will all die."

The hall erupted again in chaos, screams, sobs.

Sylven raised his voice. "There is no point in fighting."

The words stilled the crowd like a spell.

Sylven's gaze swept over them, calm and clinical, as if he were already presiding over their funerals. "The poison drains your magic first. You've felt it already, haven't you? That hollow tug at your core, the magic inside dimming. And when that's gone..." He let the silence stretch, a predator savoring the moment. "...you convulse. You choke. You die screaming. And before you ask – yes, it's painful." He paused as a woman began choking, grasping at one of the columns before losing her footing. "As you can see."

Gasps rippled through the chamber. A fae lord clutched at his chest; another noblewoman dropped to her knees, whispering frantic prayers.

"So, draw your blades if it gives you courage," Sylven went on. "But understand that you will not escape what is already in your veins. Better to save yourselves the indignity of thrashing on the floor like animals. Say your prayers. Prepare to cross the Veil." His face softened. "I never wished it would come to this. But to set Vaelaran back on its rightful path, we do what we must. Even if it means blood in these very halls."

The weight of his words pressed down on them all.

And what was once a glittering dream of splendor had curdled into a living nightmare.

73

"I trust you all enjoyed your frivolous drinking tonight," Sylven intoned. "You've grown quite used to your comforts thanks to this..." His gaze slid across the dais, to Queen Lyra, and finally to King Maelion, "family." The word dripped with mockery.

He turned, gesturing toward a line of grim-faced soldiers. "Those of you who did not drink will form a line here where you'll be executed."

Esme crumpled where she stood, sobs tearing through the hall like a dirge. Her father standing nearby caught her before she hit the floor, whispering frantic prayers into her hair.

Sylven only watched, detached, as if studying insects.

Kaelin's fingers curled into her palms. The air steadied in her chest as she commanded the magic to rise. It answered, fierce and ancient, a legacy of her lineage's unyielding will. She hadn't reached for it like this before, but there was no hesitation now, only purpose.

As Kaelin inhaled, she felt the panicked heartbeats of every fae in the room, fluttering like trapped birds desperately trying to escape their cages. The poison traveled through their veins, a sickly rot that clawed its way toward their hearts.

They were dying, one by one.

Her magic stretched outward, invisible threads tangling through the crowd until it snagged on a Esme. Kaelin's magic wrapped around her mind. Esme froze, then convulsed, choking on her own breath.

Kaelin gritted her teeth, nails biting into her palms. Esme gagged, vomiting the corrupted feast from her stomach. Kaelin urged into Esme's mind, *Get it out. Get it all out.*

Esme's bloodshot eyes locked on Kaelin's as she retched again, a silent plea breaking between them. Kaelin released her hold. Esme sagged in her father's arms, pale and shaking.

But still alive.

The poison, though, still slithered inside her, hungry for her heart.

Kaelin caught herself on the banquet table, the wood biting into her palms. She drew a shuddering breath and summoned her magic again, this time diving deeper and into the Esme's bloodstream.

The rhythm of her heart. The pulse of her veins. *Turn*, Kaelin's magic urged. *Turn the other way.*

And the blood shuddered, then reversed course, winding against the poison's current. Kaelin's knees wobbled. The room tilted, but she didn't stop.

A trickle of blood slid from Esme's nose, painting a red path down her throat, staining her dress.

More, Kaelin commanded. *Until it's pure.*

Esme groaned as blood spilled faster, dripping to the marble floor. Kaelin's own vision flickered. Her temples throbbed.

Then, it stopped. Esme's breathing steadied.

The rot was gone.

Kaelin sagged, every muscle trembling. A dull ache split through her skull, but Esme would live.

"Impressive."

Sylven's voice cut through the silence, having watched the entire exchange. Behind him, his soldiers had begun corralling courtiers into the execution line. Those who resisted were met with steel, a quick death that left crimson arcs across the floor.

Sylven's eyes met Kaelin's gaze. "The magic of your bloodline," he murmured, approaching her as though she were prey. "To command another's body, their very movements. Truly extraordinary."

He crouched near Esme. "But you were held back," he said softly. "You never honed it. Never turned it into a weapon." His head tilted, glancing at King Maelion and Queen Lyra. "If you had, perhaps you could've saved more."

"Enough of this," Maelion thundered, rising from his throne. Steel hissed as he drew his sword, the sound cutting through the chamber like a snarl. "You will not speak another word against her."

Sylven's lips curved. "Touched a nerve, have I?"

King Maelion leveled his blade at him, fury blazing in his eyes. "Try me, and see how long your tongue lasts. How dare you go against your sovereign."

"Your sovereign?" he echoed. "All your loyal guards lie in their own pool of blood. Every piece you thought you could move is gone. The board's been swept clean. It's game over."

Sylven took a single step closer, unhurried, as if pitying the king. "So tell me, how would you prefer to go out? Swinging that pretty blade in a useless fight, or walking away with what dignity you have left?"

Before Maelion could answer, two soldiers seized Queen Lyra by the arms, dragging her from the throne's dais. Her crown slipped, clattering across the marble as she struggled against their grip.

"Unhand her!" Maelion roared.

"Maelion!"

Sylven's attention slid back to Kaelin instead. The faintest smile curved his mouth as he stepped toward her, voice dropping to a low, venomous murmur. "Now... where were we?"

Before Kaelin could move, one of Sylven's soldiers seized Esme by the hair and slit her throat.

Kaelin flinched.

Sylven stepped over Esme's body without pause. "One life saved," he emphasized. "One. What a waste of such exquisite magic."

Kaelin lifted her chin, fury sparking beneath her exhaustion. Her magic flared—weak, fractured—but it answered. She seized Sylven's body in her grasp, forcing his limbs to lock.

His mouth curved into a serpent's smile. "Go on," he taunted. "Show me what you can do, now that you're nearly spent."

Kaelin's mind burned. Her magic screamed. But she thought of Ren—Ren, who never yielded, who stood bloodied and unbroken even when the world tried to crush her.

Panic knifed through her chest. Where in the hell was Ren? Was she safe or lying among the fallen? The thought nearly split her in two, but Kaelin forced it down, forced herself to breathe, to think. She needed a way out. A plan.

Yet as her gaze swept the hall, over the crumbling bodies of the loyal, the fae lined for execution, and Sylven's dark figure closing the distance, her thoughts stuttered into silence. There was no plan.

Only the tightening noose of inevitability and the bastard walking straight toward her.

I will not yield, Kaelin thought, forcing Sylven to his knees. Her muscles shook. The air trembled. *I will not falter. I will fight for my court, for my people, for my family.*

Sylven's knees bent an inch, then another, until black dots swarmed Kaelin's vision. Pain exploded behind her eyes.

Sylven laughed. A low, terrible sound.

And with an effortless twist, he broke her hold.

Kaelin stumbled, catching herself on the table's edge. She tried to summon her magic again, but it guttered like a dying flame.

Sylven closed the distance between them, his presence overwhelming, suffocating. He pinned her against a column, the cold marble biting her spine.

"I'll keep you," he murmured, brushing her cheek with mock tenderness. She slapped at his hand, but he caught her wrist, his grip iron. "You'll bear my heirs, children of royal blood and terrifying magic." He leaned in, voice dropping to a whisper. "And when you break, you'll thank me for it. Because I'm going to take good care of you."

Kaelin's head snapped up, fury blazing through the haze of exhaustion. "Go to hell," she hissed, voice low and shaking with restrained violence.

Sylven's smirk only deepened. "Oh, princess," he murmured, stepping closer, the shadows swallowing them both. His body pressed against hers. "We're already there."

Her breath came fast, chest heaving against his.

Kaelin bared her teeth. "Take your hands off me, *traitor*, unless you're eager to lose them." She twisted in his hold. Her magic flickered, slipping through her grasp like sand.

He caught her chin between his fingers, forcing her face up to his. His grip bruised, his thumb tracing the corner of her mouth as if testing the tremor in her breath. "No," he whispered. "You'll stay right here, with me. Where you belong."

Kaelin spat at him. "I'd sooner die than belong to you."

Sylven's eyes darkened, the faintest glint of amusement dancing there. "Die? No, my dear. You'll live. You'll live to see everything you love kneel or burn. And when the ashes settle, you'll stand beside me." He leaned closer, his lips brushing the shell of her ear. "You'll never want for anything again in this world. Not when you're at my side. You'll dine with kings, wield armies, bear heirs whose power will shake the heavens themselves."

Kaelin trembled from rage so raw it tasted like blood in her mouth. "Dream all you want," she said, forcing the words past the iron band of his grip. "I'll never bear your monsters." She drew a slow breath, every syllable a blade. "Ren was right. You're a coward. You always have been. You won't make it far." Her eyes seared into his. "I will be the one to drive a knife through your chest, Sylven. I will watch the life leak from your pathetic eyes. You'll beg for mercy with your last breath, and I'll grant you none."

Sylven moved faster than thought. His hand shot out, tangling in her hair, yanking hard enough to tear a gasp from her throat. Pain lanced down her spine as he forced her head back, forcing her gaze up to meet his. The world tilted as he dragged her down, her knees slamming into the marble with a dull crack that echoed through the hall.

"Coddled, like a spoiled princess," Sylven spat. "You will eat when I allow it, sleep when I allow it, and kneel when your *king* commands it. If obedience needs darkness, hunger, or iron, then that is what you will learn. And you will learn to be grateful for the hand that breaks you."

Kaelin's scalp burned beneath his grip, but she refused to look away.

He crouched, bringing his face close enough that she could see the faint flecks of silver in his irises, the cruel curve of his mouth. His fingers tightened in her hair until chunks of hair broke from her scalp, entangling in his fingers.

"I do enjoy it when you bare your teeth," he murmured. "That fire in you will make your submission all the sweeter."

But Kaelin held his gaze, unflinching, even on her knees.

Suddenly, a deafening bang split the air, shaking the very walls of the room. Sylven's smile faltered, just slightly, right before the doors burst open.

74

Ren stumbled through first, her tunic streaked with grime and blood, Ashrend clutched tightly in her hand. Behind her, Talen staggered, his sword dragging for a moment before he forced himself upright, the weight of battle carved across his face.

Sylven straightened, eyes darkening. "Seize them."

At once, half a dozen of his men surged forward. The circle closed tight around Ren and Talen, blades leveled.

"They live still," Sylven mused, striding toward them, his tone both admiring and venomous. "Impressive. But even stubborn flames must gutter out eventually. Tonight, you'll drink with the rest or join the line for execution. You'll die as your betters have. With dignity."

Ren's lip curled as she raised her blade, fire trembling at her fingertips despite the exhaustion that dragged at her bones. "Try me." And then her gaze slipped past Sylven, past the soldiers, past the fearful faces of courtiers huddled in corners.

To Elira.

Standing at Sylven's side, Elira's braid fell loose around her shoulders. Her hand rested on the hilt of her dagger, but she did not draw it. She didn't need to.

Her stance was declaration enough.

Ren's breath punched out of her chest.

Elira's eyes met hers. There was no denial there, no shame.

Sylven's smile widened as he followed Ren's stare. "Ah, you've noticed." His hand gestured lightly to Elira. "Our smith was never yours, human filth. She was mine from the beginning. A trained assassin whose initial mission was to kill *him*." He gestured to Talen.

The words landed like a blade driven between Ren's ribs.

"She betrayed us," Talen rasped, voice raw with disbelief.

Elira tilted her chin. "I was never yours to betray." She flung the braid of her hair over her shoulder, uncovering the sharp, graceful point of her ear.

Fae.

Ren's breath caught. The human girl she'd known had been nothing more than a glamour. Ren's eyes swept frantically across the chaos, her pulse hammering as nobles screamed and soldiers clashed steel. And then the storm momentarily calmed when she found Kaelin.

Alive.

Their gazes locked across the carnage.

Until Sylven slithered into the space, blocking Ren's view with icy precision. "Your presence here is an offense. Human filth does not gawk at my future queen. Remember your place."

It was too late. Ren had quickly taken in the sight of Kaelin's flushed cheeks, the wild strands of hair clinging to her face, and something inside her snapped.

The relief was gone, burned to ash by a cold, violent fury.

He'd *touched* her.

Ren's magic surged, roaring up from her chest like fire meeting oil. Every thought narrowed to a single truth that rang through her bones.

Sylven had laid hands on Kaelin. And he was going to die for it.

Ren bared her teeth. "Big mistake, bastard."

She lunged, fire detonating beneath her skin. Sylven twisted aside with inhuman grace, her fist slicing through the space where his jaw had been a heartbeat earlier. She struck again, but Sylven slipped past every blow like smoke.

Her magic surged hotter, spilling from her palms in a flash of blistering heat.

This time, she caught him – fire licked across his sleeve, cloth blackening, edges curling. Sylven hissed, staring at the scorched fabric as if it were the gravest insult he'd ever received.

His lips peeled back. "Enough."

Three soldiers closed in from behind. Ren whirled.

Too late.

A baton cracked across her ribs. Another caught her jaw, white light bursting behind her eyes. She snarled, flames flaring again, but a boot slammed into her stomach, knocking the breath out of her.

Blow after blow rained down – fists, knees, armored cuffs smashing into bone. Ren fought for each gasp, her vision tunneling, limbs refusing to answer as pain stacked and stacked until she was swaying on her feet.

A final strike to the temple nearly dropped her.

Hands fisted in her hair.

The world yanked downward.

Ren hit her knees hard enough to jar her skull. Her head was wrenched back by her hair, her gaze forced upward into Sylven's cold, gleaming eyes.

"You should have stayed down," he murmured, voice dripping with satisfaction.

Ren's gaze shifted, taking in the full horror of the hall. Near the dais, Lyra was on her knees before a soldier, a blade pressed to her throat. Nearby, King Maelion fought like a cornered beast, his sword flashing, cutting down two fae before another plunged a blade into his shoulder, driving him to his knees with a strangled cry.

Sylven stepped back towards Kaelin and lifted his hand with effortless grace. Shadows rippled outward, twisting and folding into a dark, shimmering portal that bled across the air like ink in water. He gave a sharp nod to a nearby soldier who seized Kaelin. Kaelin twisted, aiming a fierce punch at his face, teeth bared in a snarl. But the soldier dodged, driving his elbow up beneath her chin. He caught her around the waist, pinning her struggling form against his armor while dragging her toward the waiting void.

"Unhand her, bastard!" Talen roared, his teeth bared in something primal, more beast than prince.

Ren surged forward despite her vision blurring, snapping her head into the nose of the guard nearest her. Cartilage crunched beneath the blow, blood spurting hot across her cheek. Ashrend snagged into the next soldier's side, ripping uselessly across his armor. Another came at her, and she carved through him, her blade singing.

But they swarmed too many. Rough hands seized her from behind, another soldier's fist crashing into Ren's jaw so hard, stars burst across her vision. Her knees buckled, the taste of copper flooding her mouth. They forced her down again, pressing her against the cold stone until her muscles screamed.

"Ren!" Kaelin cried out.

Talen snapped curses, thrashing, but the numbers pressed them under.

Sylven's boots clicked against the floor as he stepped forward, his composure unshaken amidst the slaughter. He studied Ren on her knees, her lip split and bleeding.

"Perhaps we slit her throat here," he mused, voice almost thoughtful. His hand lifted, elegant as though conducting a symphony. "Let the Flamebearer bleed into the marble and watch the fire gutter out of her eyes."

Ren's head hung heavy, blood dripping from her split lip onto the marble. She forced her gaze up, forced the words through her clenched teeth as she met Elira's steady gaze, who remained by Sylven's side.

"Why?" Ren rasped.

Elira stepped closer. "Pray, you were so pathetic." Her eyes glittered with cruel amusement. "You wanted a friend so badly in this wretched little life that you welcomed me without even asking who I really was. No questions. No caution." She crouched just enough to sneer into Ren's bloodied face. "For someone who's been betrayed before, I expected better. And yet, there you were. Whispering your secrets during drunken escapades, telling me about the royal family, about Talen, about her." Elira's gaze slid to Kaelin, who still struggled against the soldier's grip. "Absolutely pathetic."

Ren's jaw tightened until her teeth ached, rage flooding her veins like wildfire.

Elira straightened as she moved toward Talen. Her dagger hovered, her free hand reaching for the goblet of poisoned wine. "Perhaps your prince will be the next to choke on his own blood."

Talen roared, surging to his feet, but two soldiers seized him before he could reach her. He fought viciously, knocking one back with his shoulder, but the other slammed an armored fist into his gut, driving the air from his lungs. His sword clattered from his grasp, skidding across the marble to rest a few feet away.

The soldiers forced him down, pinning his arms as he strained against their weight, teeth bared. Elira only smiled, lifting her blade and lowering it to Talen's neck. He fought wildly, sputtering out curses, but the fae soldiers held him still under the steel. Elira dragged the blunt edge along his skin, savoring his struggle. "Pity. The dagger's duller than I'd like. Your death may be inconveniently slow."

Ren lurched forward, vision swimming. "Wait—don't—don't hurt him." Her words spilled out in a frantic rush. "He's good, he's better than any of us. He doesn't deserve this. He saves people—he saved *me*. He doesn't deserve to die." She sobbed as she dragged herself forward, even as a soldier tightened his grip on her hair. Through gritted teeth, she seethed, "Kill me instead. Use me. Gods, just don't take *him*."

Talen jerked against the soldiers restraining him, but when he found Ren's gaze, something inside him went quiet. His eyes softened.

"When the Veil takes me," he said, "I'll meet you on the other side. You won't be alone."

Ren collapsed forward, a scream ripping out of her so violently she tasted blood.

"NO—NO—NO!"

Ren's voice cracked, failed, but she screamed anyway, clawing at the ground as Elira lifted her dagger.

"DON'T TAKE HIM—*TAKE ME!*"

And then Elira brought the dagger down.

75

Ren floated somewhere between it all, suspended in a place where nothing held shape. Not her breath. Not her thoughts. Not even her own body.

Zakhar's voice still clung to the inside of her skull.

Flameborne.

Dragon soul.

Test.

Manipulation.

My champion.

He had watched her. Guided her. Lied to her. Strung her along only to break her. And all along he'd known exactly how the story would end – knew exactly where to strike so she'd shatter completely.

And Elira's words that cut her from the inside.

Absolutely pathetic.

And Elira was right. Ren was pathetic. Pathetic that she couldn't save Lucan in the tombs and she couldn't even save Talen.

Ren's stomach twisted. The betrayal tasted metallic on her tongue.

Lucan's scream still rang somewhere in the back of her mind, startled, the sound of a life snuffed before it realized it was dying. A loyal friend. Someone who had laughed even when terrified, who had tried to fight the odds with trembling hands.

Gone.

And then Talen.

Talen with the bright green eyes.

Talen who called her *reckless* with that dimpled smile.

Talen who had stepped between her and death without thinking every time because he believed she deserved a life worth living.

Talen who had defended her the very day they met, when she should've been executed for stealing. He'd stood before a court ready to condemn her and convinced them to spare her, as though he saw something in her worth saving.

The realm needed a prince like him, one who actually saw its wounds and refused to look away, unwilling to accept that cruelty was the natural order. The realm needed his stubborn optimism, his unshakable belief that things could be better.

He could have changed everything.

And losing him felt like watching the future collapse.

"I'll meet you across the Veil."

The words struck her again with the same brutal force, like a blade sinking deeper each time she breathed. The way he'd said it, not afraid, not angry, but gentle.

Accepting.

She tried to inhale, but her lungs locked.

How could the world take someone like him?

How could this world decide he was the one to die?

Good people weren't meant to die like that.

But they always did.

Ren's mind recoiled, tearing backward into darkness. Anywhere away from the truth.

She folded in on herself, curling inward. The darkness welcomed her.

She sank.

And somewhere deep within her chest, the final thread of faith she'd held in humanity snapped.

Ren stumbled into the dark recess of her mind, though it did not feel like hers anymore. The ground beneath her dissolved into nothing, endless and depthless, until she no longer knew if she stood, or fell, or simply floated in nothing at all.

Was she still alive?

Or was this vast cavern of black death itself?

Her hands trembled as she reached for her body, only to find that even the outline of her form bled into the dark. No edges, no warmth. Just a void that pressed closer.

And that was when she felt him.

Vortharax.

The shadows peeled back, and the cavern trembled in his presence. He rose from the darkness like a mountain dragged into motion. His wings unfolded, blotting out everything else.

Compared to Fryphessyrth, this beast was apocalyptic. He was endless.

Vortharax's eyes seared into Ren's, ancient hatred seething in their depths. His voice was an earthquake rumbling through her bones.

"Why cling to them? They betrayed you. They all will eventually. Give me the reins. Let me take, let me burn – let me purge this world until nothing is left but ash and submission. And you will be free."

Ren shook her head, but the motion felt feeble. He dipped his enormous head, lowering it until his snout hovered inches from Ren. His breath stung her face, sharp with smoke and rot, like a pyre still burning the corpses it devoured.

His molten gold eyes locked onto hers, unblinking.

Ren's breath stalled. How in all the hells had something like this been living inside of her? How had her body held even the smallest piece of him?

"Speak it into fruition. Say yes, and I will end the game for you. No more betrayal. No more weakness. Only power. Only victory. Only fire."

Ren could see her reflection in the abyss of his eye. Ren's knees quivered, her legs trembling as though the ground itself wanted to cast her into his jaws.

No more betrayal.

The words sank deep because wasn't that all she had ever known?

Her chest tightened, breath catching as another memory layered over the first: Eve. Bright-eyed, daring, the one person Ren had once believed she could follow anywhere. Until Eve had betrayed her and the world had never looked the same.

Elira's betrayal bled into Eve's, the two faces overlapping until Ren could not tell them apart. Both of them laughing at her, both of them shaking their heads at her foolishness.

You thought we were yours.

You thought we'd stay.

How pathetic.

Ren swayed forward, pulled closer to the abyss of Vortharax's gaze, to the heat of his breath. Maybe he was right. Maybe trusting was the real weakness. Maybe the only way to stop being broken open again and again was to let him take it all.

Her fingers twitched, her body light, untethered. She felt like she was slipping out of herself, weightless, as though her spirit leaned toward him even as her body trembled where it stood.

No more betrayal. No more weakness. Only fire.

Her lips parted. She touched the scales below his eye, feeling his power pulse beneath – like the end of the world. Her heart thundered with the promise of release.

Closer.

Closer.

If she just whispered the word, it would all be over.

She opened her mouth—

Someone seized her from behind, wrenching her away. The world tilted, Vortharax's eyes vanished, and Ren was shoved backward into the abyss of her own mind.

Darkness swallowed her whole.

76

There was no air, no ground, no sound save for the steady rumble of Vortharax in the distance, somewhere in the abyss.

Vortharax saturated the void.

"*Let me burn it all down. No more betrayal. No more weakness. Only fire,*" he rumbled again, the words vibrating in Ren's marrow.

A sound split the void.

Light but steady footsteps.

Vortharax let out a low, guttural growl that rippled through the dark, carrying more annoyance than fear.

Ren whirled to the sound coming from behind and saw a figure emerging from the shadows, until the shape peeled free, coalescing into a woman.

Ren froze. Her throat tightened.

It couldn't be.

"Eve..." Ren whispered.

Her sister stood before her – older, sharper. The years had carved lines into her face, the kind that spoke not only of age but of battles fought and choices paid in blood. Her once-braided hair now spilled in wild, dark waves down her back, threaded with streaks of silver. Her frame was leaner, honed to something almost blade-like, as if life had pared her down to steel and sinew.

But it was her eyes that rooted Ren to the spot. Those same eyes she'd once trusted above all others now burned with a light she didn't recognize. A shadow lingered in them, an echo of someone Ren used to know, twisted into someone she could barely name.

"Ren."

Vortharax's growl rumbled deeper in the distance, as though irritated by Eve's intrusion.

Ren staggered, the sight before her cleaving through her like a blade. For a heartbeat, she couldn't breathe. She couldn't think. It was impossible that Eve stood there, flesh and bone and shadow, when Ren had buried her a thousand times in memory.

This couldn't be real.

"No," Ren hissed, the word scraped raw from somewhere deep, shaking her head so hard her vision blurred. "You don't get to say my name. Not after what you did."

Ashrend was heavier in her hand than it had ever felt, as though it too recognized the history between them.

Ren's body moved before her mind could catch up. The fury carried her forward, unspooling like fire through her veins. She lunged, sword flashing, teeth bared in something feral, something broken.

Eve didn't flinch. Didn't even blink. She slipped aside with practiced ease, the faintest turn of her body sending Ren's strike into empty air. Her hands rose in defense, in restraint.

Ren snarled, swinging again, desperate to sever the past from the present, but her strikes faltered. Every blow seemed slower, clumsier, as though the void itself reached for her, dulling her blade, dragging at her limbs.

"You still move like you're carrying every battle on your shoulders," Eve murmured, slipping past another swing. She didn't strike back. Didn't even draw a weapon. "Always pushing forward, afraid of what will happen if you stop."

"Shut up!" Ren spat. "You don't get to talk to me like you know me!"

Another slash, another miss.

Eve sighed as though they weren't locked in the hollow belly of the void with a dragon the size of a mountain looming over them. As if her little sister's fury were a child's tantrum.

"I came here to help you, Ren. We need to talk, and there's not much time."

Ren froze at that. Just for a heartbeat.

Vortharax's chuckle filled the silence. "*The one who already abandoned you once now comes crawling back with pretty words. Do you really think this time will be different?*" His voice slid into her bones, every syllable a poisoned hook. "*She'll leave again. They always do. And when she does, you'll remember what I told you: fire doesn't need loyalty. It only needs fuel.*"

Eve stepped closer, her eyes glinting. "I knew this day would come. The day you'd face him. The day Vortharax would try to take you. I couldn't leave you to face him alone."

Ren's jaw clenched, tears stinging her eyes, though she would have bitten her tongue bloody before letting them fall. "You already did."

For the first time, something flickered across Eve's face. "I can't undo the past. But I can help you remember who you are. You are not his pawn, Ren. You are not his vessel." Her hand lifted, tentative, palm open. "Don't let him strip away the last piece of you that's still yours."

Ren's heart thundered, torn between fury and longing, hate and the part of her that still ached for the sister she'd lost. Behind them, Vortharax stirred, tail lashing against the unseen ground.

"*Pathetic mortals,*" Vortharax snarled, his voice rattling their bones. "*You cling to blood as if it were a chain that binds you to meaning. But blood is nothing. Blood betrays. Blood rots. She will shatter, as you shattered,* kin-slayer."

Ren flinched at the word. Kin slayer.

Eve ignored him. Her gaze stayed fixed on Ren, unwavering. "Listen to me. The Pact is broken. The dragons will rise again, and they will remember the slaughter, the betrayal. They will not come with mercy. And he—" she flicked her chin toward Vortharax, "—will twist your pain into chains if you let him. But you are Flamebearer, Ren. That means you choose. Always."

"You think I can just... choose not to break? When you left me? When Elira betrayed me? When every step of this cursed life is just waiting for me to be stupid enough to trust again?" Ren's voice cracked on the last word.

Eve's expression softened. "I'm so sorry you had to endure all of that. No one should have." Eve stepped closer, and this time, Ren didn't raise her blade. "But you are stronger than us. Stronger than me, stronger than Elira." She leaned in, her voice soft but unshakable. "You are the spark that terrifies even him."

Vortharax snarled again, but Eve's lips curled in the faintest, defiant smile.

Ren's shoulders sagged, trembling under the weight of it all. Her hand ached where she clutched Ashrend.

She didn't know what she believed anymore.

"Ren..." Eve's voice was gentle, almost hesitant, as if afraid she no longer had the right to speak her name. "What happened back then... it was terrible."

Ren didn't look up. She wasn't sure she could.

Eve continued, voice thinning with something too raw to hide. "But you need to know one thing. I made you a promise, to always protect you. I held onto that, even when everything else was falling apart. Mom and Dad..." Eve swallowed hard. "They weren't strong enough. Or maybe they weren't good enough. When Dad shattered his leg and couldn't work anymore, everything spiraled. They were drowning – their money gone, options gone, hopes of working gone. And when the Embersworn came sniffing around in town, offering coin..." Her voice cracked. "They were going to *sell* you, Ren."

Ren's breath hitched, a small, broken sound.

"I couldn't let that happen," Eve whispered. "So I went to the Embersworn myself. I offered them more. I offered them *two people* instead of one."

Ren's head snapped up. "Eve – "

"Mom and Dad," Eve said simply. "They'd already chosen you as the sacrifice. I chose differently. I thought the flames might choose me. If Vorthorax had taken me instead, you would've been spared. You wouldn't have had to carry him. You wouldn't have had to live with this curse. But that's not what happened. The flames didn't want me. They wanted *you*. They crowned you the Flameborne the moment your blood sang to them. All I could do after that was make sure you survived what came next."

Ren stared at her sister, this woman she'd loved, resented, trusted, lost, and mourned, all knotted into a single unbearable truth.

Eve's eyes met hers. "I tried to save you, Ren. I swear I did. I would've given everything. But fate had already laid its hand on you. So I did the only thing I could. I rooted a small piece of my soul into yours, just enough that when this moment came, I could be here to tell you everything myself." Her features hardened in resolve. "You are the spark that makes the darkness retreat. Think back to the night the flames chose you. That was no accident, no twist of fate. They saw you for what you are. They answered to you. Fire does not kneel. It does not bow. It burns, it endures, and it is *you*."

The void trembled as if Eve's words themselves defied its hold. Vortharax's roar split the silence, a cataclysmic sound that shook the endless dark to its core. Still, Eve did not flinch.

Eve stepped closer, pulling Ren into her arms, her hands trembling as they cupped Ren's cheeks. Eve's eyes glistened with the weight of years stolen, of love unspoken.

Of all the moments they'd lost.

But even as Ren clung to her, the world around them began to dissolve, the darkness thinning. The air shimmered, the edges of Eve's form flickering. Panic clawed up Ren's throat.

"No," Ren sobbed, shaking her head. "Please don't leave me. Not again." Her fingers tightened around Eve's wrists, desperate to hold on. "I need you with me."

Eve smiled through the shimmer, her thumb brushing away a tear that wasn't supposed to fall here. "One day, I'll explain everything," she whispered. "I swear it. But for now..." Her voice cracked as the void trembled around them. "Your friends need you. It's time to go back."

The void rippled.

A broken whisper seeped through the cracks like water through stone.

R—Ren...?

Help... can't... please—

Ren's protest broke on her lips, swallowed by the blinding rush of light.

"I don't want to go back – I want to stay with you," Ren sobbed, shaking her head. "I want to be with *you*, Eve."

Then a second voice surged in, drowning everything else.

Ren, listen to me. Please. Come back. I need you. Ren, come back to me. Don't leave me.

Ren froze. Her breath caught in her throat. Recognition hit her like a blade to the chest.

Kaelin was calling her back. Commanding her back.

Begging her back.

"See?" Eve smiled softly. "It's time to go. But never forget," Eve pressed her forehead to Ren's, grounding them both in the light as Kaelin's voice echoed all around them. "I have always loved you. Fiercely. Beyond reason, beyond time."

Her lips brushed Ren's brow in a kiss as fragile as it was eternal. Her voice cracked, but the words carried like a vow. "And I always will. In this lifetime and the next, until every last star burns out."

And as the light and dark fractured, dragging Ren back into the present, Ren carried with her the echo of Eve's vow like a flame cupped against the wind, fragile yet unyielding.

Just before the blade dove into Talen's neck, Ren's eyes burned with an otherworldly light.

Kaelin watched as the soldiers restraining Ren recoiled, shouting. Ren's heat burned straight through their armor. They stumbled back, clutching blistered hands, horror twisting their faces.

Steam poured off Ren's skin in thick, curling waves, the air around her warping with heat. For a heartbeat, the entire hall froze as Ren's body began to shift.

To *become*.

And the marble beneath Ren's boots began to tremble and crack.

A thunderous *boom* slammed through the palace, rattling glass in its frames as thick smoke surged beyond the windows, turning daylight into ash-gray twilight.

Mount Solfira devoured the sky with fire and smoke. Kaelin tore her gaze from Ren and peered through the mosaic windows to see smoke spewing from the mountain's jagged crown – a black storm swallowing the heavens, blotting out the sun.

Sylven's men bolted for the exits. They fled while the true courtiers of Vaelaran remained behind to convulse and die as the poison still worked its way through the court.

Ren's body crumpled to the marble floor.

Kaelin was already there, her knees striking the floor. She caught Ren beneath the shoulders, trying to haul her up, only to hiss in pain. Ren's skin burned, searing Kaelin's fingers until she was forced to let go.

Steam curled where her touch had been.

"Gods," Kaelin rasped, staring at the faint steam curling where she'd touched Ren. To nobody in particular, she asked aloud, "Do you think..."

The question faltered—*Do you think she's dead?*—but Kaelin couldn't bring herself to say it.

Talen tore a jacket from a fallen chair, wrapped it around Ren, and lifted her carefully into his arms. The fabric smoked faintly against her skin.

"I don't know," Talen murmured, voice hoarse. "But we've got her."

Outside, Mount Solfira roared again.

A noblewoman clutched her throat before collapsing into seizures. Another fae clawed at his chest, coughing green foam.

Through the chaos, a fae mother stumbled toward Kaelin, a fae babe cradled tight against her breast. Her eyes were wild, rimmed red from tears, her lips stained with the wine that still glistened at the corners of her mouth.

She held out her infant with trembling arms. She sobbed, "Princess, who will care for her now? I drank the wine."

Before Kaelin could answer, another fae woman approached with silver-streaked hair and a face softened by time. She moved with surprising steadiness, unshaken amidst the ruin. Her voice was quiet but steady as she placed a gentle hand on the mother's arm.

"I was a nanny long ago. I did not drink the poison." Her gaze lifted toward the vaulted ceiling as if she could already see the mountain's wrath pressing down upon them. "But it is time to say your prayers. The fire from Solfira is coming, and it will bury us all."

The mother let out a broken wail, clutching her babe tighter, rocking as she turned desperate eyes to Kaelin, to Talen. "Please—please, tell me what to do! Save my baby!"

Talen's eyes met Kaelin's, and in that single look, Kaelin understood the horrifying truth.

There was no escaping this.

Talen bent toward the weeping mother, his voice gentle but carrying an authority that stilled her sobs. "Go and hold your baby close. Let her know your love, your warmth. That is what she will know before she crosses the Veil."

Talen's hand brushed over the child's curls, and the infant cooed up at him, unbothered by the screams and ruin around them. A fragile, perfect sound in the midst of despair.

Kaelin's gaze softened. "The Veil is not an end; it is a bridge. And when you cross it, she will still be in your arms. Nothing can sever that bond."

The mother clutched her babe tighter, but her shoulders no longer shook with panic. She rocked the infant gently.

A sharp tremor rolled beneath their feet, rattling the marble and sending a cascade of dust from the gilded ceiling above.

A hand seized Kaelin's arm. She turned, and her breath caught.

Lyra stood before her, skin pale as ash, eyes unfocused with pain. A violent cough wracked her chest, crimson staining her lips. Maelion's arm was already around her, holding her upright, though the tremor in his jaw betrayed the truth; he knew he could not shield her from what was coming.

Kaelin's heart fractured at the sight. Her mother's fingers dug into her sleeve.

"Mother—" Talen's voice broke as he heaved Ren's body. Ren's head lolled against his shoulder.

Kaelin's pulse roared as her hands pressed against Ren's face. The heat scorched her fingers, but Kaelin refused to move until she whispered, "Please. Come back to me."

No response. Only the faint flicker of breath, and Ren's skin growing hotter by the moment, as though fire itself had claimed her veins.

Lyra's cough deepened. Her arms pulled Kaelin and Talen into her trembling embrace. Kaelin felt the convulsions rip through her mother's body and held tighter, desperate to keep her standing, desperate to deny what was already written.

"My children..." Lyra rasped, her voice soft, strained. "I am so proud of you." Her eyes drifted toward the unconscious figure in Talen's arms, the girl who burned even in her sleep. "You just go and save yourselves. Take care of the Flamebearer."

A hand, roughened by years of war and rule, found Kaelin's trembling fingers, then Talen's. Maelion's voice was low, broken by the poison's slow grip, yet steady with conviction.

"What is destroyed can be rebuilt," he murmured, his gaze sweeping between them. "This is not the end of House Vaelaran. The halls may fall, the banners may burn, but our line lives on in you. The journey ahead will demand everything, but you are strong enough. Of that I am certain." His breath shuddered, but a faint smile ghosted across his lips. "If I could, I would walk beside you. If I could... I would have chosen both of you to reign. Together." He breathed a laugh. "Together, you would have been unstoppable."

Tears blurred Kaelin's vision, her grip tightening on her father's hand. Talen bowed his head, jaw clenched.

Maelion's eyes fell to Ren's still form in Talen's arms. "As rulers, never forget that your subjects deserve more than survival. They deserve a world where they may thrive." His breath hitched, and he swallowed, his eyes clouding with regret. "I have many sins," he admitted, voice breaking for the first time. "Deeds I wish I could take back. Choices that cost too much, wars that carved too deep." His hand squeezed theirs, weak but fierce. "But my hopes lie in you. Do what I could not. Pave the road I failed to walk. Create a kingdom where all—highborn and low, fae and human alike—can find peace." Maelion's eyes softened. "I am so proud," he whispered again, the words catching as the tremor beneath them deepened. "So very proud... of you both."

And then Lyra collapsed.

Maelion caught her, his arms cradling her frail form as the convulsions overtook her. He lowered them both to the marble floor and whispered, "You will not go alone, my love. I will be here until the end."

Kaelin could do nothing but watch in horror as her mother convulsed violently, her father's sobs silent and raw as he pressed his face to her hair.

Talen pulled Kaelin away, his voice hoarse. "We have to go, Kaelin."

Kaelin flinched, meeting his frantic gaze. For a moment, couldn't move until he shifted his hold on Ren, limp in his arms like a rag doll, her head lolling against his shoulder. That sight alone shattered Kaelin's paralysis. She forced her legs to move.

They stepped through the carnage, boots slipping on spilled wine and blood. Bodies littered the marble floor—nobles convulsing, foam at their lips, others clutching rosaries of bone or stone, whispering desperate prayers to gods who would not answer. Fingers clawed at Kaelin's gown, voices breaking as they begged for mercy, for salvation.

"Saints forgive us," someone sobbed, their body writhing in seizures. Another, eyes glazed and wild, pounded their fists against the floor, crying out for a god who had long since abandoned them. The air reeked of bile and fear.

At last, they stumbled into the hallway. Pillars loomed on either side, trembling with the tremors that deepened beneath their feet.

Kaelin's gaze was pulled inexorably to the windows. There, beyond the shattered glass, the sky was already gone—blotted out by rolling waves of ash. A storm of fire devoured the horizon, consuming the forest, swallowing the roads leading to Pyraelia.

Coming straight for them.

And then Kaelin turned her gaze and her breath hitched, the world narrowing to a tunnel of unbearable clarity. Along the palace wall, mounted like grotesque trophies, hung the heads.

Horse heads.

Whisper's sleek midnight mane, once brushed smooth beneath Kaelin's hands, now hung in a tangle, clotted with blood. Her ears, once flicking eagerly at Kaelin's voice, were slack. Those perceptive eyes that had carried Kaelin through battles and storms were glassy, staring at nothing.

Beside her was Cider. Talen's steadfast companion, the proud brown gelding who had never once faltered. His strong neck was hacked through, the wound cruel and jagged.

Kaelin's knees nearly buckled, grief surging through her like a physical blow. A sound tore from her throat as if her body could not decide whether to scream or collapse. Memories flooded her: Whisper's hooves pounding in rhythm beneath her, the warmth of her breath on cold mornings, the unspoken bond forged through trust alone.

Now reduced to *this*.

Kaelin's vision blurred, hot tears burning her eyes, and for a moment, she wanted to let the grief take her under. To sink into it, to weep until nothing was left. But the fire still roared on the horizon, and Ren's weight still hung in Talen's arms. Kaelin swallowed the sob.

"*Veyra'thiel*," she whispered to Whisper, the word breaking from her like a sob. *My soul.*

Talen grabbed her arm, dragging her toward the exit. His voice was frantic, wild. "Kaelin, we don't have horses. The mountain's erupting, the skies are ash. How in the gods' names are we supposed to escape?"

Kaelin turned her face toward the storm, toward the weight of Ren's burning body in Talen's arms, toward the ruin of her world collapsing stone by stone.

And for the first time, she did not have an answer.

Something shifted in Talen's expression. The hard edges of panic softened, resignation cutting deeper than fear. He shifted Ren's weight carefully against his chest, then stepped closer, placing himself between Kaelin and the looming blaze of Mount Solfira. His arm came around Kaelin, anchoring her against the trembling of the earth.

They stood together as sister and brother, clinging to the last fragile remnant of family as the world threatened to burn them away.

Kaelin closed her eyes, pressing her forehead against Talen's shoulder. Her lips moved in prayer, so soft the words barely carried: pleas to saints and gods, to anyone who might listen, for mercy, for deliverance, for strength when the end drew near.

The ground shook harder, ash choking the air, when a thunderous roar split the chaos.

Kaelin's head snapped up.

Cutting through the ash storm came a colossal shape, wings unfurled wide enough to eclipse the burning sky.

Talen murmured in awe, "The dragon from the tomb."

The dragon's scales gleamed, her eyes alight with fury as she dove.

On her back was Lucan, clinging for dear life. "Get up!" Lucan bellowed, his voice breaking through the storm. "Move! Now!"

Fryphessyrth slammed into the courtyard, tail whipping, and scattering soem of Sylven's men like broken dolls. The impact rattled the stone beneath Kaelin's boots.

Talen's grip on Kaelin's arm tightened. Together, they stumbled forward through the ash and ruin.

Lucan leaned down, hand outstretched, shouting above the roar of flame and thunder. "Climb, damn you!"

Talen passed Ren to Lucan, who swore aloud from her heat. Talen hauled himself up next, and Kaelin scrambled after, fingers burning against the dragon's hot scales as she heaved herself onto Fryphessyrth's back.

And then they were airborne.

The palace fell away beneath them, ash-smeared towers crumbling, fire eating through the banners of Vaelaran. The roar of the mountain chased them, a river of flame spilling down its slopes. Kaelin could only watch in bated silence as the ash and molten rock crash into the front gates of Pyraelia like hungry tidal waves, flattening all the buildings as it surged forward before swallowing the palace itself in a roar of fire and ruin.

Kaelin gathered Ren into her lap, clutching her against her chest. Her hands moved on instinct, brushing soot-streaked hair from Ren's face, stroking her brow in slow, trembling circles. Ren's skin still burned, searing against her palm, but Kaelin held on as if she could will her back into herself.

"Stay with me," Kaelin whispered, her voice breaking against the rushing wind. "Ren, listen to me. Please. Come back. I need you. Come back to me. Don't leave me."

The wind howled as the dragon dove below a cloud bank. Kaelin barely noticed. Her world had narrowed to the weight in her arms, to the steady rise and fall of a chest that still, mercifully, drew breath.

For endless, aching moments, Ren did not stir. Kaelin continued murmuring pleads into Ren's ear, hoping and praying she could somehow hear her.

And then, Ren's lashes fluttered.

Amber eyes cracked open, dazed but alive.

Kaelin's breath caught. Relief crashed through her so violently she sobbed. She bent low, pressing her forehead to Ren's, holding her as the dragon carried them higher into the skies.

The skies wept ash, the earth bled fire, yet as Ren's eyes focused on Kaelin, Kaelin clung to her and for one fragile heartbeat, hope itself drew a breath.

ACKNOWLEDGMENTS

I was incredibly lucky to have such an amazing team helping bring this story to life. Writing a book is never a solitary journey, and *Forged in Shadow and Flame* became what it is because of the people who walked beside me. I am deeply grateful to everyone who played a role in shaping this world and these characters.

To my husband – my greatest supporter, my sounding board, and my steadfast believer. Thank you for listening to every wild idea, for reading anything I placed in your hands, and for never once questioning the late-night bursts of inspiration that pulled us both away from sleep. Your unwavering love and encouragement carried me through every chapter of this journey. I truly couldn't have done this without you.

To my editor, Emma – thank you for helping shape this story into the strongest version of itself. Your dedication, insight, and care for Ren's journey transformed this book into something I am profoundly proud of. *Forged in Shadow and Flame* would not be what it is today without you.

To Obsi Art – thank you for creating the stunning book cover that now holds this world together. Your willingness to explore every tiny detail with me made this experience unforgettable. You captured the soul of this story with such talent and grace.

To Ismael – thank you for breathing life into the interior illustrations. Your artistry brought my characters and pivotal scenes into reality. Every piece of art holds a piece of this world's soul, and I am endlessly grateful.

To Melissa – thank you for crafting the beautiful map of Lytharien. Your talent in shaping this world visually helped ground the realm that was once only in my imagination. You truly gave readers a doorway into the magic of this land.

And to my dear friend Liz and my brother-in-law AJ – thank you both for your thoughtful, in-depth feedback and for being such crucial parts of the editing process. Your honesty, enthusiasm, and support helped refine this story into what it is now. I am so grateful to have had your voices guiding me.

Thank you all for helping *Forged in Shadow and Flame* become the story it was meant to be. This book carries pieces of each of you within its pages.

As Ren's story continues, I'm thrilled to say that a sequel is already on its way. If you'd like to follow my journey, see behind-the-scenes updates, and stay connected as this world expands, you can find me on Instagram and TikTok at **@sarahprimianobooks**.

COMING SOON

BOOK 2 OF THE FLAMEBORNE TRILOGY

BOUND IN NIGHT AND EMBER

The dragons have returned, and the world burns.

Kaelin's kingdom has fallen into ruin, its people hunted by the beasts now sweeping across the realm with vengeance. Their goal is simple: dominion over all.

And Ren is their greatest weapon.

Zakhar believes he's found the relic that can tear Vortharax free from Ren's body. Ren knows the truth, that unleashing Vortharax would end the world as they know it. When Ren crosses paths with a ruthless vampire princess, the balance of the world fractures.

New alliances spark. Old loyalties crumble. And every choice begins to carve the shape of a future balanced on blood and fire.

To save everything she loves, Ren must face the truth:

Some battles must be won with steel. Others with sacrifice.

And yet even in ruin, a single spark can ignite a revolution.

ABOUT THE AUTHOR

Sarah Primiano is a fantasy romance author who spends her days dreaming up fierce heroines and worlds brimming with magic. When she's not writing, she's reading books with a cup of coffee in the early morning, questing her way through video games, or being ambushed by her two overly dramatic dogs. She's a devoted mom, and she lives in Texas with her husband but daydreams regularly of mountain kingdoms and whimsical fantasy realms.